Dedication

To my boys.
You are my everything.

Something that could Last

Ashley Cade

Chapter One

Abby

I HATE BEING LATE. LOATHE IT, ACTUALLY. That's why I'm panicking, rushing around like a chicken with its head cut off and stumbling around my bedroom, hopping into my shorts one leg at a time. I nearly topple over but manage to catch myself on the bed frame before face-planting into the dresser. For once, I'm thankful for my tiny, cramped room. I throw on my New River Adventures t-shirt and comb through my hair, my nose crinkling at the pungent scent of wood smoke. I douse it with dry shampoo before pulling it over my left shoulder to braid, praying that does the trick. I can't go into work looking and smelling like I spent half the night in a field drinking moonshine around a bonfire with my friends.

I should have just stayed home. I never should have let Tiff talk me into going to that party. I knew better than to go. I knew *he* would be there. A little run-in with my cheating ex was enough to shatter my resolve to stay sober and join Tiff in inebriated oblivion. Once she broke out the shine, it was all over. It was peach flavored, of course. She knows it's my favorite.

Tiffany Ann Caseman doesn't play fair, and I kind of love her for it. For a few hours, I could let loose and forget all my troubles. Unfortunately, they all came crashing back this morning. Right on top of my skull.

When my alarm finally startled me awake after hitting snooze a few too many times, I sat bolt upright in my bed. Big mistake. I instantly covered my face with my hands, pressing their heels into my browbone, the pounding in my head a reminder of why I shouldn't go out drinking when I have to work the next day. I groaned when I peeled one eye open to check the time. Mistake number two. It felt like someone was taking a chisel to my frontal lobe. Against my better judgment, I kicked off my covers, jumped out of bed, and threw my clothes on before dashing into the kitchen to start the coffee pot. Now, five minutes later, I'm brushing my teeth while pouring the steaming brew into my cup.

"Shit!" I screech when scalding hot liquid splashes onto my hand. I clamp my mouth shut around my toothbrush, praying my little outburst didn't wake my grandmother. She wouldn't appreciate me cursing in her house.

I run cold water over my reddening skin before pouring enough cream and sugar in my travel mug to color my coffee lighter than the fur on a white-tailed deer. It's the only way I can choke it down. I'd much rather have a cappuccino, but I don't have time to stop by the coffee shop, so this will have to do.

I grab my keys and run out the door, already dreading this day. Saturdays are always insanely hectic for me. My day starts early and ends late. Both of my jobs can be physically demanding, and I know my feet will be aching by the end of the night.

Working at New River Adventures wouldn't be so bad if we could just take a turn on the zip line during downtime, but that is severely frowned upon. I won't be making that mistake again. I can't afford to lose this job. The only reason I even have it is because I used to babysit for the owners, Mr. and Mrs. Carlisle. They always thought I was *just wonderful* with their two children. To be honest, I dreaded watching them. They were spoiled, entitled brats who were too busy tormenting each other to pay much attention to me.

Thank the good Lord above for small mercies. I certainly don't miss those days, and I'm glad they're teenagers now.

Unfortunately, I desperately need the extra money this gig brings in. Waiting tables doesn't pay enough to cover my living expenses *and* save for fall semester. My scholarships and grants barely cover my tuition, but I pay for everything else out of pocket. I try to help my grandmother with the bills, too, since she's on a fixed income, all while stashing a little away each week for a new vehicle. I don't know how much longer my old Ford is gonna last, so I need to be prepared when it goes kaput. Since I can't work much while I'm in school, I have no choice but to work like a dog during summer break and save up.

Agonizing over all my financial woes reminds me that I really shouldn't have skipped my usual five-mile run this morning. I'm a mess; I'm sluggish and irritable. My head is so jumbled up with worries about money, school, and my tiresome employment. A long, grueling run would have cleared my head up just fine. That's my therapy. All my anxiety and troubles are forgotten when there's sweat dripping down my face and all I have to focus on is my breathing. Instead, I slept as late as possible and am breaking every speed limit between here and work to get there on time.

I swipe my time card at 8:59 and breathe a sigh of relief. I made it, narrowly avoiding the ensuing anxiety attack. I used to be chronically late for everything when I had to rely on my mother to get me places. It drove me crazy. Everybody stares at you when you walk into class ten minutes after the bell rings. I'll never forget the angry glare of my teammates after arriving twenty minutes late for the bus to regional finals.

I'm lost in my own thoughts, so I don't see Caleb approaching me until it's too late. I'm usually pretty good at avoiding him, ducking out of his sight before he notices me. Maybe if I don't make eye contact, he won't bother me. *Please don't talk to me. Please don't talk to me. Please don't ta-*

"Hey Abby, how's it goin'?"

Shit! He's such a creeper. He makes my skin crawl and the hairs on the back of my neck stand up. I don't know what it is, but I get an unmistakable, uneasy feeling around him, like he's capable of doing something awful. The way he's always brushing up against me, claiming it's accidental, and how he leers at me while I work makes me incredibly uncomfortable. I just wish we had different schedules. I want to ignore him, but the manners my grandmother instilled in me take over and dictate that I at least acknowledge him. It would be rude not to.

"Fine," I answer and try to rush past him. He looks as though he's considering grabbing my arm, but stops short when I glare at him with what I hope is a warning look. It must work. He pulls his hand back and straightens his spine, standing at his full height, smiling at me arrogantly before turning to head towards his station. Why can't he pester one of the other girls and leave me alone? Then again, I wouldn't wish his creepy fixation on anyone.

Customers start to trickle in, which is a nice distraction from the unsettling feeling left by my interaction with Caleb. People line up, we get them secured on a line, and let them go. Most of the time, people come in pairs or groups and want to go down together on our dual zip lines. With a steady flow of customers most of the morning, I don't have time to think about how tired I am. When things finally start to slow down, I steal away to the restroom for a much-needed break. After using the facilities, I splash a little cool water on my face and smooth down my flyaways with damp fingers.

As I'm walking back, I pull out my phone to make sure I didn't miss any calls from my grandmother. As independent as she is, she probably doesn't need me checking on her so much, but I worry about her being home alone. Since she started having trouble with her health, I try to make sure she can always reach me. With my focus entirely on the screen lit up in my hand, I pay no mind to the path I'm on, having walked it hundreds of times. I let out a tiny shriek when I trip over a downed branch spread across the walkway, my phone flying out of my hands as my body pitches forward. I reach out, grasping for anything to keep me upright and pinch my eyes shut, bracing for impact with the ground, but it never comes. Instead, my fingers brush against something warm and hard as two strong hands wrap around my arm and waist, my skin tingling at every point of contact. Once I steady myself, I look up into the face of my savior and nearly lose my footing again. As his icy blue eyes study me with concern, my whole face heats with embarrassment and I duck my head.

"Are you alright?" His voice slides over me like warm honey.

"Yeah, uh, sorry about that," I stammer. Why do I have to be so damn clumsy today? His hands remain on my body, steadying me. Wriggling myself out of his tantalizing grasp, I feel as though my skin is marked by the heat of his touch.

A sexy smile tugs at the corners of his mouth. "No problem."

Ah, that voice again. I need to get away from this guy before I embarrass myself any further. I excuse myself, pluck my phone from the dirt, and head back to my station. I chance one last glance over my shoulder and see him watching me. My cheeks burn with renewed embarrassment, knowing I must look like an idiot.

A few minutes later, I'm back to work, securing a boy who can't be more than twelve to the line. He's not making my job easy, squirming with nervous energy and excitement. Awareness prickles my skin and my hands still. Sensing that someone is watching me, I lift my gaze and my heart stutters in my chest.

This time, I'm able to take in every inch of his perfection. He has that all-American look with his dark, sandy blond hair, blue eyes, and mega-watt smile. With chiseled features and a strong jaw, he is a work of art. His fitted t-shirt strains against the sculpted muscles of his chest, arms, and shoulders. And he's tall. I like tall. His eyes rake over me from top to bottom, my toes curling when his gaze reaches them as though it's a caress instead of a look. My entire body warms, and I feel a blush creeping up my cheeks. I look away, hoping he doesn't notice my flushed skin.

I'm suddenly self-conscious of my make-up free face and dirty hair. Of course, today would be the day I see the hottest guy in the state of West Virginia, maybe even in the whole damn country.

My attention snaps back to my customer when the sound of retching invades my ears. Vomit splatters onto the toes of my shoes as the young boy empties the contents of his stomach at my feet. I freeze for a moment, trying to suppress my own urge to throw up. The sickly, sweet smell of maple syrup threatens my gag reflux. Poor kid must have eaten half a dozen pancakes. No wonder he blew chunks.

Once the boy's mom leads him away, I kick as much loose dirt over the pile as I can to cover it. It's not the first time this has happened, and it won't be the last. I pull my gaze back up, searching for the handsome stranger again. My eyes find his within seconds and he smiles. He's watching me with a sexy intensity that makes my stomach clench with anticipation. His body jerks, a frown erasing his sexy grin when another man brushes past him, bumping his shoulder. The tall, dark-haired guy mutters something to him and smirks before heading in my direction. They appear to know each other, and I wonder where these two insanely attractive men came from. Heaven? Olympus, maybe?

Once the newcomer is directly in front of me, I can appraise him fully. His black hair and stormy gray eyes are a stark contrast to the other man's lighter features. He's tall as well, but with a slightly leaner build. This guy is Tiff's type. Cocky, self-assured, and probably a player. He steps up to me, a look of relaxed confidence on his face.

"Go easy on me. It's my first time." He winks, an impish, lopsided grin gracing his lips.

I roll my eyes at his attempt at flirtation. "I bet that's what you tell all the girls."

He laughs, amused by my retort. "No, sweetheart. That's what they all tell me." Another wink. I just grin and shake my head. This guy is trouble. Trouble wrapped in a very good-looking package.

I check his harness one last time, making sure all the connections are secure and the straps are tightened. Before I can attach him to the cable, he turns to his friend, jutting out his pelvis and calling attention to his bulging man parts. Once he's done admiring his own package, he turns back around, allowing me to secure him to the line.

"I'm Luke, by the way."

"Abby," I offer my name.

"Nice to meet you, Abby." He gives me another one of his crooked, panty-dropping smiles. "My buddy and I are thinking about grabbing something to eat later. Any suggestions?"

"Rosie's Bar & Grille," I reply automatically, then mentally kick myself for it. I can't believe I just gave this wannabe Casanova the name of the restaurant where I wait tables. I'm so used to endorsing the place, it's just second nature to recommend it to customers.

"Is that where you'll be tonight?" He raises one eyebrow, shamelessly scanning my body.

Of course that's where I'll be. I freaking work there. But I keep that bit of information to myself. My eyes find his handsome blond friend again. He glares at Luke with irritation and I sense just a hint of jealousy. An involuntary smile tugs at the corners of my mouth.

"Yeah," I reply nonchalantly, certain he has no intention of showing up.

"Great, I'll see you there." His smile oozes confidence. I'm sure he's used to getting what he wants. Without another word he takes off, sailing through the air. Hoots and hollers echo through the open space.

His buddy doesn't appear to share his enthusiasm. After stepping into Caleb's line and waiting while his harness was secured, he stands at the edge, his grip tightening on the cable as he peers into the forest below. He squeezes his eyes shut and heaves a deep breath before staring into the abyss once more. Is he afraid of heights?

He throws one last look my way before refocusing his attention on what awaits, his features morphing from uncertainty to determination. He takes one last deep, cleansing breath and lets go. As he glides away out of my sight, I wonder if I'll ever see him again.

Chapter Two

Jacob

SHIELD MY EYES AGAINST THE BLINDING rays of the midday sun and breathe deep, filling my lungs with fresh mountain air. Yawning and stretching my stiff muscles, I take in my surroundings. Wet earth beneath my feet, lush green foliage, and a clear blue sky.

Freedom.

It's a relief to finally be here. I've spent the last five hours in a car with Luke, which is enough to test anyone's sanity. He may be my best friend, but he isn't someone you want to be in a confined space with for very long. Between his off-key singing, constant stories about all the hot chicks he's "smashed," and the repulsive stench of his never-ending flatulence, I'm considering leaving him here and letting him find his own way home. I would never actually do that, but a guy can dream.

I've been waiting months for this trip, desperate to get away from the constant pressure and expectations. It's just too much. I can't even think straight most of the time. The chaos is consuming me, like a tidal wave that won't recede. Eventually, it's going to drown me. Two whole weeks in the West Virginia hills with no family, no exams, and no microscope is exactly what I need. Nobody around to analyze my every move, telling me how to act and how to live my life. Maybe I can finally catch my breath away from my meddling mother and Dad's overzealous advisors.

That's why Luke and I are here, in this podunk West Virginia town. Here we can be anonymous. Nobody knows who I am, and nobody cares. After finals, we both needed a reprieve from the chaos. Of course, Luke's chaos is much different from mine. Finals week was tough for him since he likes to binge drink and go home with a different girl every night. Dude leads such a hard life. The asshole never studies. I don't know how he manages to maintain his stellar GPA. I, on the other hand, study to the point of delirium. Luke says that's my problem, that I need to *chill*. It's hard to *chill* when I've got so much riding on my education and my parents are up my ass about making the Dean's list.

"Hey, dick breath, what do you want to do first?" Luke asks, startling me from my thoughts. I glance at him over the hood of my car, a shit-eating grin plastered across his face. I mentally roll my eyes at his immaturity and ignore his insult.

"I don't know." I consider our options. "Whitewater rafting. Maybe zip-lining."

"Ambitious," he praises. "I like that. I'm glad your punk ass didn't say something lame like 'go for a hike,'" he adds mockingly.

"I bet you're relieved I didn't say hiking. Your lazy ass is so out of shape. You need to do fewer keg stands and more box jumps. I'm surprised you can even get a date." He's so damn vain, it's just too easy to taunt him about his looks.

"Hey, I don't hear the ladies complaining once I show them my *love* muscle. It gets plenty of exercise," he boasts with a smug look of satisfaction, his hands splayed on each side of his groin, outlining his package.

I can't help but laugh at his juvenile ass. Despite his crass sense of humor and penchant for uninhibited and indiscriminate sex, he's actually pretty charming. I can see why the girls like him. I'd never tell him that, though. His ego is barely tolerable as it is.

After some deliberation, we settle on zip-lining to kick things off. I already feel a spike of adrenaline coursing through my veins. I've never done this before and the thrill of doing something outside my comfort zone is exhilarating. I just hope I don't run into a tree or have my harness come loose or my cable snap. Luke assures me that these things never happen, but I've seen *1000 Ways to Die*.

I try to keep my nerves in check as we pay our way in and collect our tickets. Luke is rambling on about his latest conquest when I see her. Tan, sculpted legs jutting out of white denim shorts catch my eye as she scurries along. The crisp, bright material accentuates her beautifully bronzed skin. My eyes skim up the rest of her body, taking in her perfectly rounded backside and slender waist. My gaze lands on her chest, noting how deliciously the powder blue t-shirt clings to it. I stifle a groan at the sight of the cotton material stretched across her full, perky breasts. The pale hue further complements her complexion, which is undoubtedly natural. Not like the fake-baked sorority girls back home.

She's looking at her phone as we approach, our paths intersecting with hers. When we draw close, I open my mouth to speak, but my words are cut off when she stumbles just a few feet away from us. Instinctively, I reach out and grab her, my forearm wrapping around her waist and my free hand encircling her bicep. Her smooth, warm skin feels like heaven. A surge of electricity tingles the tips of my fingers and travels up my arms, landing in my groin. I fight the urge to pull away at the unexpected sensation.

My breath catches in my throat when she lifts her gaze to meet mine. There's fire behind those hypnotic, emerald eyes. They bore into me as if she can see into my soul, all of my secrets laid bare for her perusal, but I don't dare look away. Her gaze is soulful, haunting even. My eyes drop to her full, pouty lips when she speaks. She ducks her head when she apologizes and I wish she'd look at me again. Before I can ask her name, she bolts and I watch her retreating form as she hurries away.

"Fuck me! Did you see the ass on that one?" I swing my head around to glare at Luke. Of course, I saw it, I *am* a man, after all. But his big mouth and crude observation irk me. "What?" he asks, perplexed when he notices my irritation.

"You are the reason women think all men are pigs."

He laughs and claps me on the back. "Don't act like you weren't thinking the same thing."

I pretend to ignore him, not wanting to admit that he's right.

I'm still thinking about those killer curves and her petite, athletic frame when we reach the station we're looking for. My eyes wander, hoping to find her again. Before long, they land on the familiar blue shirt and I observe her for a moment, unnoticed. Her beaming smile lights up her whole face. It's infectious. I find myself grinning like an idiot as I watch her interact with her customers. I quickly school my features though, because if Luke notices, he will stop at nothing to embarrass me. When she finally looks my way, it's as if time stands still. I can't see anything but her. No sound registers in my ears. I no longer feel the light breeze on my skin or smell the earthy scent it carries. Everything else just fades away. We study each other from across the short distance, and I commit every detail, from her thick rope of dark hair to her tiny white sneakers, to memory. After a moment, she glances away shyly and tucks an errant strand of hair behind her ear.

My feet propel me forward, her gravitational pull drawing me in, but halt in my tracks when her customer doubles over, vomiting at her feet. She impressively keeps her composure, an almost imperceptible pursing of her lips the only sign of her discomfort. I'm frozen in place, hoping the smell doesn't reach me. That's when Luke makes his move, shouldering past me to get in her line.

"No way, fucker," he murmurs as he barrels past. "I'm zippin' down sugar tits' line."

I bristle at his vulgarity. My fists ball at my sides and I grate my teeth as a wave of unexpected anger rolls over me. I need to cool my growing temper. I don't even know this girl, but damn if she isn't the most beautiful woman

I've ever seen. I guess I can't really blame him for wanting to get close to her but the way he looks at her, like a lion watching a gazelle, ignites a firestorm of jealousy inside me. He's a horny little cocksucker who will try to get into her pants before he even learns her name.

I consider following him to her line but don't want to seem desperate, so I settle for the adjacent one. I fall in line behind a middle-aged man wearing khaki shorts that are three decades too short and a fanny pack. Who the hell wears those anymore? With a seriously receding hairline and an ill-fitting shirt stretched across his paunch, I see what I don't want to become. Mundane and mediocre. I want spontaneity. I want excitement. I want my existence to mean something.

"Holy shit, J. Look at my bulge in this thing!"

When I peer over at Luke, he's pointing to his crotch outlined by the straps of his gear. He is way too impressed with his own dick. *Jackass.* The green-eyed beauty behind him rolls her eyes, but a smile pulls up one side of her mouth, her amusement at his goofy ass a credit to her sense of humor.

Luke talks to her while she finishes buckling him into his harness and hooking him to the line. Once she's done, I expect him to take off, but he doesn't. They continue to converse for a few minutes, and I try not to envy how close he is to her. How he gets to hear her voice and make her smile. She seems to be enjoying herself, and that bothers me more than it should.

I tell myself I'm okay with her preferring Luke's company over mine, but that's a lie. I don't know what it is, but there's something special about this girl. It's not just her beauty and the fact that she has the sexiest little body I've ever seen. It's her shyness, her sweet smile. The way she throws her head back and laughs without reservation or insecurity.

Although his back is to me, he knows I'm watching the exchange between them. He reaches his hand behind his head and slides it down the back of his neck, pretending to scratch an itch. He balls up his fist and extends his middle finger, all without the girl seeing the obscene gesture. He's just taunting me now. Prick.

"Next." The guy working my line motions for me to step forward, his jaw tight and brows drawn together. He looks pissed, and all his simmering rage seems to be aimed at me. What the hell did I do to him? When I notice him continually glancing to my left at the girl I've been admiring, it all makes sense. Guess he's noticed my interest in her. This asshole has a major hard-on for her, judging by the way he's scowling at me. The furrow between his brows deepens when her eyes find me and she smiles. I can practically hear his teeth grinding together. His nostrils flare at my triumphant smirk. I'd better watch it since he's responsible for making sure all my safety gear is secure. He might let me plunge to my death if I keep pissing him off.

Luke takes off before Asshole finishes connecting my harness to the cable. I try to still my nerves, but my insides are in knots and I'm starting to regret this decision. I steal one last glance at her. Her gaze is focused on me, eyes full of concern, sensing my apprehension. It's not that I'm *afraid* of heights, I just don't *like* them.

Stop being a pussy and jump.

She's watching.

It's too late to back out now.

My stomach drops as I leap and hold on tight.

Chapter Three

Abby

I RUSH HOME FROM NEW RIVER ADVENTURES to freshen up for my shift at Rosie's. Can't serve food to people with dirt on my face and under my nails. I scrub myself clean and apply just enough makeup to accentuate my features. Some plum-colored eyeliner and black mascara to make my eyes pop, followed by a sweep of pale pink gloss over my lips do the trick. Letting my braid loose, I finger comb through the big, soft curls of my waist length hair and pull the sides back, securing them with a clip. I brush my teeth, throw on my freshly laundered uniform, and hit the door.

I pull into Tiff's driveway and double tap my horn, letting her know I'm here. A few minutes pass before she bolts out of her front door clutching her makeup bag, stopping only long enough to put on her shoes. She slides them on, one at a time, hopping from foot to foot. She lands in my passenger seat with a huff and slams her door shut. The contents of her makeup bag spill into her lap when she turns it over and begins shuffling through tubes and compacts. She doesn't share my disdain for tardiness and is never ready on time, so she ends up applying half her makeup in my truck.

"Hey girl, how's it goin'?" she asks absently, a mascara wand combing through her already black-coated lashes. Tiff swears that any less than two coats of mascara is a waste of time.

As always, she looks absolutely fabulous. Tiffany is the epitome of a siren. With champagne blonde hair laying in perfectly tousled waves down her back, dark blue eyes, and a killer body, it's no wonder guys go crazy over her. She's petite like me, but with slim hips and a more than ample bosom that's usually accentuated by a low-cut top and an overflowing bra. She is shameless and confident in her sexuality, and I envy her a little for it.

"Okay, I guess. I'm glad to be out of job number one for the day. Some poor kid threw up right in front of me this morning. Got my shoes this time."

"Again?" She stops fluffing her hair and scrunches her nose in disgust. "Didn't the same thing happen to you last week?"

I nod. It happens more often than you'd think. And it's always first-timers.

Our drive to Rosie's takes less than ten minutes. We step out of my old, beat-up Ford pickup in our matching black shorts and green t-shirts with "Rosie's Bar & Grille" printed across the front, the customary uniform for servers at the restaurant.

Grabbing our aprons, we head out to the dining room that's already buzzing with activity. I wave at Ros as we walk past the bar. She winks at us, her hands busy wiping down the bar. Aunt Roselyn, aka Rosie, owns the place with her husband Phil. She's my dad's sister, and she and Phil have looked out for me ever since he passed away. Ten is way too young for a girl to lose her father. After he died, Mom wasn't much of a parent to me and my little brother, Ethan. Ros stepped up and tried to help us. She even offered to let us live with her, but Mom wouldn't hear of it.

"I sure am glad to see you." The day shift server, Lindsay, presses her order pad in my hand and unties her apron. She lets out a puff of air to remove a rogue piece of hair from her face, but it falls right back into the same place. "Looks like you've got my section tonight," she informs me, exhaustion evident in the slump of her shoulders. "Oh, and your favorite customer was just seated at table six." She winks and I know exactly who she's talking about.

Great. Mr. Morrison was the junior high math teacher for as long as anyone can remember until he retired a couple of years ago. He was that teacher who everyone knew was a pervert, but completely harmless at the same time. He always asks to be seated in my section and tips me generously. I try not to worry that one day he'll want something in return.

"Thanks, Lindsay. You just made my night," I joke. Looks like I'll get at least *one* good tip. I usually do alright. Not as good as Tiff, but she flirts shamelessly with the male customers. They love the attention they get from her, especially the out-of-towners who don't know her and fall for her sweet, southern, girl-next-door charm.

I find my pen and make my way to table six to take Mr. Morrison's order. Once I get him settled in, I make the rounds to the rest of my tables, refilling drinks and handing out extra napkins. The dining area and bar fill up quickly. Rosie's is a pretty happenin' place on a Saturday night, and tonight is no exception. The first couple hours of my shift go by quickly with little variation from every other Saturday night. Lots of draft beers, baskets of onion rings, and hot wings. I'm dropping off a tray full of Bud Lights when I notice our hostess, Sarah, smiling wickedly at me as she heads back to her post by the front entrance.

"What are you up to now?" I ask skeptically as she approaches.

"O. M. G." she spells out. "Wait until you see the two hotties I just sat at table nine!" She sighs dramatically and fans herself, feigning dizziness.

"I should've known," I chuckle at her as I return my tray and head towards the booth designated table nine. It's kind of sweet how she gets all flustered around guys. She's young, barely eighteen, and still shy around the opposite sex.

I pull my pen and pad from my apron as I approach, my gaze focused on finding a blank sheet. "Hi, welcome to Rosie's," I begin automatically. "What can I get-" I inhale sharply and his eyes snap up to meet mine. *It's him!* In the elevated booth, he's as tall seated as I am standing. Up close, his piercing blue gaze nearly undoes me. *Get it together, Abby.* "...Um... get you to drink?" I manage to squeak out. I clear my throat and repeat my question, this time more composed. "What can I get you to drink?"

A slow smile spreads across his face. "Two Heinekens, please." My knees buckle at the sound of his voice. It's even sexier than I remember. Deep and warm, smooth like a Kentucky bourbon. My ability to form coherent thoughts melts right into the floor, along with my panties. My mouth opens to form a response when Luke takes the seat across from him. I was right earlier. They *are* friends.

"I damn near pissed myself waiting in line for the bathroom," he complains before his eyes spark with recognition. "Oh, hey... uh, Abby, right?"

"That's me." I smile nervously, trying to hide my cringe at the high-pitched sound of my voice.

"You'll have to excuse my friend. He has absolutely no manners." He shoots Luke a dirty look across the table.

"Fuck you, douche. I have manners coming out my ass," Luke retorts.

The gorgeous stranger huffs out a singular laugh and shakes his head, resigning himself to the fact that his best friend is a heathen. He gives me an apologetic smile. "I'm Jacob."

"Abby." I hope he can't hear the shakiness in my voice when I introduce myself.

"Nice to meet you, Abby." He offers me his hand and I press my palm into his. Heat spreads up my arm and into my chest, settling low in my belly. Just from a simple handshake. Imagine what those hands would feel like on the rest of my body.

"Hey, you never mentioned you worked here when you recommended this place." Luke's tone is playfully accusatory.

"You didn't ask," I answer with a shrug.

Jacob chuckles, a deep, throaty sound almost as alluring as his speaking voice. "So *that's* why you insisted on coming here."

"Yeah."

Jacob scowls at his unapologetic response, annoyance flashing in his eyes.

"So, two Heinekens? Can I get you anything else, or do you need a minute to look at the menu?" I interrupt, trying to ease the mounting tension growing between them. Luke came here hoping to run into me, and from the tight set of Jacob's jaw, I'm guessing he's none too pleased about that. I would never want to cause a rift between two friends, but Jacob's seemingly jealous reaction sends a little thrill down my spine. Even though I know it's a little silly, I kind of like it.

"We need a few minutes," Jacob replies, opening his menu.

"Okay, I'll be back with your drinks."

I put in their drink order and Ros hands me two open bottles. On my way back to their table, Tiff accosts me, pulling me in close by my elbow.

"Who are those two guys?" she asks, nodding towards their booth, her eyes dancing with intrigue. "Do you know them?"

"Not really," I answer, my eyes drifting toward them. "They went zip-lining earlier." She looks at me expectantly as if waiting for more information. I don't know what else she wants me to say.

She rolls her eyes and huffs. "Well, what are their names?"

I tell her, hoping she can't hear the quiver in my voice when I say Jacob's name. "Think you could introduce me to this Luke guy? He looks absolutely delectable." She eyes him lustfully from across the crowded restaurant, her bottom lip caught between her teeth.

"You are so bad," I exclaim.

"Yes, I am," she admits unabashedly, her head held high. She has no qualms about being a man-eater.

I head back to their table, a beer in each hand, praying I don't trip or say something stupid or have a booger hanging out of my nose. *Oh, no!* Just thinking that last part makes me a little panicky, so I retrace my steps back to the bar, lean over the lacquered wooden top, and check my reflection in the mirror lining the back wall. I inspect my nose and smile, making sure there's nothing stuck in my teeth, either. I hastily smooth my hands over my hair and reapply my lip gloss before returning to their table.

Chapter Four

Jacob

LUKE AND I HAVE HIKED FOR HOURS with nothing but protein bars and bottled water to keep us going. I'm ready for a beer and something to ingest that doesn't come in a wrapper. Luke suggests some place called Rosie's, and I'm so tired and hungry I don't even question his choice.

We shower and dress quickly, hunger our only motivation for moving our exhausted bodies. By the time we arrive at a little place off the highway with a parking lot jam-packed with cars, I'm ravenous and ready to throttle Luke. Thanks to his terrible navigation skills, we end up driving nearly fifteen minutes in the wrong direction before getting stuck behind a big green tractor.

"Are you sure about this place?" I ask. "It looks like we're going to be waiting a while, and I'm starving." My stomach lets out a loud gurgle, audibly confirming my hunger.

"Quit acting like a little bitch. It'll be fine," he says, brushing off my concern. "Besides, this is supposed to be one of the best restaurants in town."

"Alright, dickhead, but I don't want to hear you complaining because your out-of-shape ass can't stuff your fat face anytime soon." I can never pass up an opportunity to tease Luke about his physique. He's really not in bad shape, but he's so vain and arrogant, I get a kick out of cracking on him.

"Dude, you're such a dick. If your mom wasn't a grade "A" MILF, I wouldn't even hang out with you," he taunts. I don't take the bait, though. He's been doing this for years. It used to piss me off, but I finally realized my anger just added fuel to the fire, so I stopped giving him the satisfaction of reacting to his lewd comments about my mother.

We walk through the door of the small restaurant and bar and are confronted by the bustle of the popular eatery. The place is hopping and there's barely room to stand in the tiny waiting area. Luckily, the three groups ahead of us are seated quickly so we don't have to wait very long.

The hostess blushes and averts her eyes as we approach the podium when our name is called. "Hi, I'm Sarah. Welcome to Rosie's," she says with a nervous giggle. Oh, no. Luke loves this kind of reaction from girls. The shy, innocent ones are like an intriguing challenge for him as if there's a grand prize for bagging one of them. "Have y'all ever eaten with us before?" she asks, glancing over her shoulder as we follow her to our table. There's a twang in her voice that has grown more and more prevalent since we crossed the state line.

"Nope, first time here," Luke answers. "We're virgins."

Her step falters and she nearly trips, her eyes growing wide with his suggestive admission.

"O-okay," she stammers, a blush staining her fair cheeks. "Here's your table. Your server will be with you shortly." She hands us two menus and scurries off.

"I gotta take a leak. I'll be right back," Luke informs me as I slide into my seat. "Order me a beer," he throws over his shoulder as he heads to the restroom.

It's a few minutes before anyone makes it to our table since the place is so busy. I'm scanning my menu, so hungry I consider ordering one of everything, when someone finally approaches. My eyes are still glued to the laminated page in front of me when she begins to speak, but the little gasp that interrupts her sentence catches my attention and my head snaps up to meet her gaze.

Two emerald pools look back at me in surprise. Thick black lashes frame her almond-shaped eyes. Her long, dark hair hangs in waves that cascade down her back with the sides swept back, away from her beautiful face. I'm close enough this time to notice her high cheekbones and perfect little nose. Damn, she is exquisite. We simply stare at each other for a moment, neither one of us able to form words. I don't even know this girl's name, but I'm powerless to stop the images in my mind of her naked and moaning beneath me.

She repeats her question, shaking me from my lascivious thoughts. I order our drinks, but before she has time to respond, Luke plops down in the seat across from me, being his usual repulsive self. I want to punch his rude ass right in the mouth. Who says shit like that in front of a girl you just met?

My irritation grows when he greets her, addressing her by name. I know they talked earlier, but his familiarity with her is unnerving. I'm sure he started running his game on her back at the ziplines. An odd and unfamiliar spark of jealousy ignites my temper and I work to clamp down my irritation. As much as I don't want to see her end up as one of his many easily-forgotten conquests, I have no claim to her.

I try to excuse Luke for not having any manners as I glare at him. I don't want her to think we're just a couple of assholes. Well, she can think Luke's an asshole. He is.

We introduce ourselves, and I finally have a chance to talk to her, but Luke interrupts again. I get the distinct feeling he's doing this on purpose, trying to get under my skin. And it's working. The tension eases out of me a bit with Abby's smart-ass retorts to Luke's questions. A smart mouth *and* a killer body. Where did this angel come from?

Once Abby leaves to grab our drinks, I focus my attention back on my *friend.* "You're such a dick."

Luke looks up from his menu, surprise washing over his face. "What?"

"Are you *trying* to be a complete douche, or does it just come naturally?"

Luke doesn't miss a beat. "It's natural," he deadpans as he looks back at his menu.

I laugh at him and then curse under my breath. Damn it. I have a hard time staying mad at this asshole. When Abby returns and our orders are scribbled in her note pad, I jump on the opportunity to make conversation with her.

"So, where are you from?" I know it's lame, but I've got to start the conversation somewhere.

"Born and raised right here," she beams, her spine straightening with pride. "Where are y'all from?" There's just a hint of that twang in her voice, and it's the cutest damn thing I've ever heard.

"Arlington," Luke answers for us.

"Oh, what are you doing all the way out here?"

Running and hiding. Avoiding the press. "Just needed to get away. Wanted to try a few new things. White water rafting, rock climbing, ziplining." I smile knowingly at that last part and watch as a blush tints her cheeks, a coquettish grin tugging at the corners of her mouth. I continue before my mind can conjure all the things I'd like to do with that beautiful mouth. "We heard this was the best place to do it." I leave out the part about being the son of a United States Senator and having advisors and journalists up my ass all the time.

"Well, you heard right." She smiles this devastatingly beautiful smile and I sense the pride in her words. She loves this place and it shows. It's good to be proud of where you come from. Too many people are ashamed of their roots. "I'm gonna go put your order in so the cook can get started on it, but I'll be back to check on you soon."

"Thanks," I say before she turns toward the kitchen.

"Dude, you've got it bad," Luke taunts from across the table.

I pull my eyes from Abby's retreating figure to look at him in confusion.

"Don't give me that look, fucker. You know exactly what I'm talking about." "No, I don't," I answer with irritation. "So, enlighten me."

"I see the way you look at her. You can't wait to tap that."

"Does that tiny prick of yours dictate your every thought?"

He smirks, ignoring my insult. He reclines back in his seat and crosses his arms over his chest. "You're not denying it. Guess that means I'm right."

"Has it ever occurred to you that there is more to a woman than what's between her legs?" Luke's a great friend, but he is a base creature with no concept of how romantic relationships are supposed to work. Not that I'm a saint, but at least I don't view members of the opposite sex as a series of holes to bury my dick in like he does. Don't get me wrong, I'd like to explore every inch of Abby's amazing body, but there's more to her than a nice ass, plump lips, and killer legs.

"Of course." He feigns offense. "I find their mouths to be quite useful as well."

I'm really starting to hate his face every time he smirks at me like he is right now. I shake my head, hoping that nobody is listening to our conversation. I have a feeling most of the people in this little town would be appalled by what he just said.

Abby stops by our booth to let us know our order should be up soon. When she returns a few minutes later, she's balancing a tray with two hot plates on it with one hand and has two open green bottles in the other.

"Here's your cheeseburger and onion rings," she says, setting Luke's plate down in front of him. "And the country fried chicken platter for you." She places the steaming dish in front of me and the enticing aroma makes my mouth water. "Everything look alright?"

"Oh, yeah. It looks really good," Luke replies, his eyes scanning down her body. "And it smells delicious," he adds with a roguish grin. He turns his attention to his food without meeting my eye. I flatten my hands, palms pressed against the table on each side of my plate. The urge to slug him is like an itch I'm inevitably going to scratch.

"Great! Can I get y'all anything else?" she asks, oblivious to the fact that Luke is blatantly taunting me.

"Not right now. Just keep the beer coming," Luke answers with a mouth full of cheeseburger, devouring nearly half of it in one bite. He moans appreciatively, making Abby giggle.

"Sure thing."

"No more for me. I'll have a water." Somebody's got to get us home and Luke isn't showing any signs of slowing down. Not that he ever does.

"Oh, don't be such a pussy! We can call a cab," he chimes in, chomping on a handful of onion rings. He is disgusting. No wonder he doesn't go on many dates. The chicks he sleeps with would be repulsed if they saw how he eats.

"It's no big deal. We call cabs for patrons all the time," Abby says, looking back and forth between Luke and me.

"No, it's okay. I'm good. Thanks, though." I also want to keep a clear head around this girl. I have a feeling she's going to keep me on my toes.

"You're welcome."

She leaves us to finish our meal uninterrupted. When she comes back, she brings Luke another beer and me a water, and grabs our plates to clear them away. "Can I get you anything else? Dessert, maybe?"

Luke and I are both stuffed and turn down the offer, but I speak up before she has a chance to walk away. "This place looks like it's starting to clear out. Could I buy you a beer?"

She thinks on it for a few seconds before responding. "You could... but I wouldn't drink it."

I instantly feel my face fall, the sting of her rejection a devastating blow to my ego. Did I read the situation all wrong? I thought she felt the same electric attraction that I do. Guess the joke's on me. I'm feeling utterly deflated when a mischievous smile curls up her perfectly pouty lips.

"You see that lady over there? The redhead behind the bar?" She motions with a jerk of her head to the woman opening a bottle of beer and I nod. "That's my Aunt Roselyn. She owns this joint and she would drag me out of here by my ear if she caught me drinking on the job." She pauses for a moment, then adds, "Besides, I don't drink beer."

"What *do* you drink?" I suddenly have to know.

"Whiskey, usually. Or moonshine, if ya got any."

Wow, this petite country girl who drinks moonshine and can handle Luke's crude humor just knocked me on my ass.

Before I can respond, a busty blonde with a shirt that matches Abby's is standing next to our booth. I recognize her as the server who's been eying our table all night. She bumps Abby's shoulder with her own to get her attention.

"Who're your friends here?" she asks with a flirty smile.

"This is Jacob," Abby introduces, motioning to me with her hand. "And this is-"

"Luke," Luke interrupts excitedly, throwing his hand out to shake hers. Oh, boy. He sees something he likes. This girl better watch out.

"I'm Tiffany, but my friends call me Tiff." She accepts his proffered hand and they shake, both of them grinning deviously. The look on her face tells me she's used to players like Luke. I may be wrong. *He* might be the one who needs to watch out. There's something wild and uninhibited about Abby's friend.

"So, about that drink... Where can I buy you one when you won't get in trouble?" I return my focus to Abby, hoping I won't get shot down again.

"The Red Stallion," Tiff interjects. "They're open 'til two and there's no cover. Hell, half the time they don't have anyone at the door checking IDs. Good thing, considering how many times we've snuck in there."

Shit. How old are these girls? They look young, definitely younger than us, but not too young to be in a bar.

"Surely that won't be an issue. You ladies are old enough to party, right?" Luke asks casually. I'm glad because I'm sure I would have made an awkward mess out of asking them their age. The last thing I need right now is to get involved with some jailbait. The tabloids would go nuts. And so would my parents.

"Oh, yeah. We're both twenty-one," she assures us. "We just haven't been for very long." She shoots Abby a knowing, mischievous grin. "We've spent the last four years sneaking into places we shouldn't have been. Haven't gotten used to getting in the *right* way yet."

Without thinking, I let out a sigh of relief. Neither of the girls seem to notice, but Luke does. I can tell by the shit-eating grin on his face. We've had our share of fun with the ladies, but we both draw the line at underage girls.

"What time is your shift over?" Luke asks. He's awfully interested in spending more time with these two all of a sudden. I'm just glad his attention has shifted to someone besides Abby.

"Ten-thirty," Tiff replies, her lips pulling into a pout. I check my watch to see what time it is now. Only nine-fifteen. When I look up, Abby is watching me, her brows slightly furrowed. She relaxes her features and forces a smile when our eyes meet. *What was that all about?*

"Hey, we can stick around for a little bit and have a few more beers. Then we can all go to the Red Dragon."

Both girls laugh at Luke's error. "Red *Stallion*," Tiff corrects.

"Oh, so you think it's funny, do ya?" Luke teases and reaches over to grab her waist. She giggles and playfully swats his hand. Ah, fuck me! We've been in this town nine hours and he's already getting started. It's going to be a long two weeks.

"So, what do you say?" Luke asks, his gaze settling on Abby. "You in?"

All eyes turn to her, awaiting her response. She hesitates for a moment and then shrugs, her relaxed posture contradicting the apprehensive look on her face. "Sure. Why not?"

Chapter Five

Abby

HOLY CRAP, WHAT DID I JUST agree to? I don't go to bars with strange men I just met. Then again, most of the men I meet don't look like they just stepped off the cover of GQ. Or a movie set. This guy is from a whole other class. It's obvious, judging by the watch he's wearing, that he's used to the finer things in life. I'm almost positive it's a Cartier. I may be broke but I recognize designer when I see it. That thing probably cost more than my truck. I know he must have seen the look on my face when I saw it, even though I tried to conceal it. I'm not used to that kind of extravagance and it shows. This guy definitely has money. There's no doubt about that. Everything about him screams "wealth," and I must admit I'm a little intimidated by that.

He looks damn good, though, in his Armani jeans and light grey t-shirt. Those jeans hang deliciously on his hips when he stands up. His shirt sleeves cling to his muscled biceps, his arms flexing as he pushes up from the table. Somehow, he manages to make this simple motion look incredibly sexy.

His shirt is just loose enough on his torso that I can't quite make out the definition of his flat abs, but my imagination is running wild. I force myself to turn and walk back into the kitchen so he doesn't catch me ogling him like a horny school girl.

It's almost time for our shift to be over and, quite frankly, I'm surprised Jacob and Luke actually stayed. I figured they would get bored and duck out, but they kept their word and are sitting at the bar, sipping their beers. Tiff and I retrieve our purses and freshen up our hair and makeup in the bathroom before heading back out into the dining area.

As we approach the guys, Luke unabashedly stares at Tiff, eyeing her from head to toe. "So, are you ladies ready to have some fun?" he asks.

"Definitely," Tiff replies with a bashful, flirty smile. She really seems to enjoy his appreciative gaze. I'm sure these two will be hot and heavy before the night is over.

"Do you guys just wanna follow us there?" I ask before anyone suggests we all ride together. I may feel relatively safe around Jacob, but he and Luke are still strangers and I'm not about to get into a vehicle with them. I've seen too many episodes of *Criminal Minds* for that. There will be no Derek Morgan to save us if these guys end up being charismatic serial killers.

"Yeah, we can do that," Jacob replies. "We're parked out front. We'll meet you out there?"

"Okay, we'll pull around."

Tiff and I make our way out the back entrance to my truck. I wave goodbye to Aunt Ros as I pass by. Her hands are busy drying a glass, so she gives me a wink and a smile. It's getting late and there are only a few cars left in the parking lot. I know right away which one is Jacob's. The luxury SUV is parked on the farthest corner of the lot. Of course. A freaking Range Rover. Because I wasn't intimidated enough already.

Maybe this is a bad idea. We shouldn't be hanging out with guys like this. They probably have trust funds and Ivy League educations and spend their summers in The Hamptons. We're just two country girls trying to make a living in West Virginia's shitty economy. We are way out of our league here.

I let my apprehension get the best of me and stop the truck halfway across the parking lot.

"Uh, what are you doing?" Tiff looks at me worriedly.

"I'm not so sure about this," I reply.

"Why? What do you mean?"

"Look at them, Tiff." I jab my arm in their direction, palm facing the sky. "And look at us."

"And?" Her worried expression turns to irritation. "What about us?"

"A Range Rover? Really? And you saw how they're dressed. How are we supposed to compete with that? These guys obviously come from money. We don't exactly fit in with them." Maybe this is just something rich guys do. They find local girls to go slumming with when they go out of town and then forget about them when they go back to their Stepford Barbie girlfriends.

"It's not a competition, Abby. Besides, they don't seem to care about any of that, so why should we? We fit in just fine. It's not like we're hobos." Her lopsided grin puts me at ease. "They just want to have a good time and so do we. What's the big deal?"

For once, Tiff is being the rational one and I'm a little ashamed of myself. I've judged them unfairly because of my own insecurities about not being good enough. They deserve to be given the benefit of the doubt.

"You're right. We should just go out and have fun and not worry about the rest."

"That's the spirit," Tiff jokes and punches me in the arm playfully.

I pull up to the driver's side of Jacob's SUV and Tiff rolls her window down.

"The Red Stallion is just up the road," she says, pointing in the direction of the bar. "Just follow us."

We pull into the parking lot a few minutes later and the guys park next to us. My hands are shaking when I reach for the door handle and I'm overcome with nervous energy.

Before I have a chance to open my door, Tiff places her hand on my arm and I look up at her. "It's alright," she reassures me. "We're just having a few drinks with a couple of hot guys. No big deal. Just relax and have a good time. We've done crazier shit than this." She gives me a knowing grin. Once again, she's right, and I'd like to forget about some of those crazy things she's referring to.

I release the anxious breath I'm holding and nod my head. *Just relax. I can do this. It's no big deal. Just have fun.* I repeat this to myself as I step out of the car and walk over to meet Jacob. He's standing with his hands in his pockets, leaning up against his SUV with a subtle, show-stopping smile on his gorgeous face. My skin warms at the sight, despite the chill in the air. As I close the distance between us, my pulse quickens and I remind myself to breathe.

"Ready to go in?" he asks, placing his hand on the small of my back. The gentle contact sends a tingle up my spine.

"Hell yeah, we're ready!" Tiff answers enthusiastically for both of us.

Tiff and I lead the way to the door. Music from inside the bar drifts out into the night and I feel the bass thumping in my chest. Butch is working tonight, as usual, and lets us in without so much as a second glance. He never cards us. I'm not sure he ever cards anybody.

Once inside, we head for the bar. The floor beneath my feet vibrates with the heavy bass thumping through the sound system. Jacob turns to me, and though I can see his lips moving, I can't hear what he says over the din of too loud music blasting from the speakers.

"What?" I yell back.

He leans down, his mouth a mere inch from my ear, and I breathe in his intoxicating smell. I close my eyes and bask in his heady, masculine scent and the sound of his smooth, deep voice. Our bodies are so close, but not quite touching. Every cell in my body is on high alert, anticipation of physical contact consuming my senses.

"So, how about that shot of whiskey?" he asks with the sexy timbre that makes my stomach clench and my pulse accelerate.

"That sounds great." I'm going to need some liquid courage for this.

Jacob orders me a shot of Crown and I immediately down it in one gulp, earning a chuckle from him. I'm going to need another just to still my nerves.

"Maybe I should've gotten you a double."

I swallow nervously and straighten my shoulders. *Here goes nothing.* "Maybe you should have," I reply, attempting a seductive tone.

Jacob grins deviously at my sassy response and his eyes darken with desire. Heat floods my lower belly and between my thighs. He hasn't even touched me yet and already my body is responding to him. I have never felt this way about a guy before. I'm no virgin but desire this strong is uncharted territory for me.

Jacob turns to the bartender and orders me another shot, a double this time, and a beer for himself. I drain my glass in two big gulps, the smooth liquid going down easier than the cheap whiskey I usually drink. Jacob watches me over the brim of his bottle, his lips curling up on each side as he takes a swig. I reluctantly pull my eyes from his when I feel someone grab my arm.

"I wanna dance." Tiffany has a cup filled with amber liquid. She's drank most of it and I hear Luke ordering another from the bartender. I hope she doesn't get so drunk tonight that we have to carry her out. It wouldn't be the first time, and it certainly won't be the last. She drains the rest of her drink and discards her cup before Luke hands her a new one.

"Oh, come on, dancing queen. Let's hit the floor," I tell her. She squeals, bouncing on the balls of her feet before grabbing me by the hand and pulling me onto the dance floor. I'm already starting to feel the effects of the whiskey I consumed just a few moments ago. My mind and body relax a little as warmth from the liquor spreads through my veins. I begin to move to the music, letting the rhythm guide the sway of my hips and the motion of my arms. Tonight, the DJ is playing mostly pop and hip-hop, the best kind of music to dance to.

Tiff and I dance for a couple of songs as she sips her drink. At the end of the second song, I glance over my shoulder to find the guys leaned up against the bar watching us, a bottle of beer in each of their hands. Jacob's eyes burn into mine. He's watching me intently and I can tell he likes what he sees. His intense observation of my body moving to the music sends a shiver up my spine. I wonder what his hands would feel like grasping my hips, in my hair, all over me. I tear my gaze away from him and turn to Tiff when she yells my name.

"I need another drink. And so do you," she insists, pointing her finger into my chest. "Come on." Once again, she grabs my hand and leads me where she wants me to go.

"Need another drink, beautiful?" Luke asks her, his self-assured grin never leaving his face.

"Why, yes I do. Thanks, handsome." I'm just buzzed enough that this interaction makes me giggle. Tiff turns to glare at me, but her spirits are instantly lifted when Luke hands her another Long Island.

"Wow, that was fast," she exclaims.

"I went ahead and ordered it when you started back this way. You looked like you needed a refreshment." His cocky smirk is almost charming. Almost.

"Awwwww, you're so thoughtful," Tiff draws out, pressing herself up against his chest. Gag! She knows he's trying to run his game on her, and she's encouraging him. Luke may be a player, but he just met the coach.

"You want another shot of Crown?" Jacob's question is a welcome distraction from these two and their *very* public displays of affection.

"Yeah," I reply. "Oh, and just a single this time." I'll eventually have to drive Tiff and myself home, so I need to take it easy on the booze. Besides, I haven't eaten in over eight hours, and this top-shelf liquor is working fast. When he hands me my drink a few minutes later, I thank him and down the potent elixir in one gulp. He watches me with an intensity in those icy blue eyes that makes me feel naked and vulnerable. It's an unsettling feeling, but I kind of like it.

"I'm ready to dance again. Let's go." Tiff grabs my hand and leads me back to the dance floor. There are hot, writhing bodies everywhere, and we have to shoulder our way through the crowd to make it back to our spot.

We're three songs in this time when I feel hands on each side of my waist. I start to turn around to see which one of these assholes is grabbing me without invitation when he leans in and speaks into my ear.

"Abby," he breathes my name. This one word breaks my resolve to be a good girl and not get involved with this handsome stranger. I close my eyes and lean into him. I hear his quick intake of breath before his body molds to fit mine, the sculpted muscles of his chest and abdomen pressing against my back. He trails his fingers up my arm, leaving a searing path of heat in their wake. I can't suppress the shudder that moves through my body as a result. I am lost to his touch and all I can hope is that it never ends.

Chapter Six

Jacob

COULDN'T RESIST THE TEMPTATION ANY longer. I had to touch her, feel her. I needed to know what her body felt like pressed against mine. I watched her dance for a while, letting her seduce me with the sensual sway of her hips. When she looked at me over her shoulder with those smoldering green eyes, as if she was daring me to come to her, my resolve shattered. I observed from the sidelines until I simply couldn't take it anymore.

When we left Rosie's earlier this evening, I wasn't sure how this night would go. Abby's apprehension was palpable. I was afraid she'd bolt once she got in her truck. I'm pretty sure the thought crossed her mind, too, when she stopped her truck in the middle of the nearly empty parking lot. I was relieved when it continued in my direction.

On the way here, I had to listen to Luke describe, in graphic detail, all the ways he was going to *have* Abby's friend, Tiffany. Less than five minutes in a car with his drunk ass and I was ready to open the door and push him out of a moving vehicle. If I had to hear the phrase "hit it and quit it" one more time, I was going to throat punch him.

When we got to The Red Stallion, I still sensed a little uneasiness on Abby's part, but Tiff's excitement seemed to rub off on her. Once we were inside and Abby had a couple shots, she started to relax a little and her spirited personality began to reveal itself.

Now that I'm out here, dancing with her, all I can think about is getting her alone. It takes everything I have not to spin her around and kiss her in front of all these people, but I don't want to freak her out. I want to wrap my arms around her waist and pull her closer to me, so I do. The smell of her hair is intoxicating and I force myself to pull back to avoid burying my nose in it and sniffing her like a total creeper.

I move my hands from her hips to caress her smooth, tan arms, and she turns her head to peer up at me from the corner of her eye. I sweep her hair away from her beautiful face with the back of my hand. How can anyone be this perfect? Again, I contemplate kissing her, but I'm not sure if I should. She might slap me. But then again, it might just be worth it.

We continue to dance and I'm not sure how much time has passed, because all I can think about is her. Being near her, touching her. I am lost to her. When I'm finally able to focus on something else, I lift my gaze to see Luke and Tiffany grinding and shoving their tongues down each other's throats. Gross. Do neither of them have any shame? Of course not. They're both hammered right now. When Abby notices them, she turns to me with a disgusted look on her face.

"Eww," she says with her nose wrinkled and her face scrunched, which is positively adorable. "Let's go play pool," she suggests.

Yes, ma'am. Does she realize I would follow her anywhere?

"I need another drink after seeing that." She shakes her head as if trying to erase the memory of our friends dry humping on the dance floor from her mind. I order her another double shot of whiskey in the hopes that the image will soon be forgotten. She drinks it down and grabs my hand, leading me to the pool table. The unexpected contact takes me by surprise and I smile to myself like an idiot. Luckily there's nobody occupying the pool table, but whoever was here last left all the pool balls in the pockets. As she starts to gather them up, I decide to grab another beer, so I let her know I'll be right back.

The crowd surrounding the bar has grown thicker since our arrival earlier this evening. It takes a few tries for me to flag down the bartender, but once I flash him a couple extra bills, he abandons the bachelorette party he's been flirting with and shoves an open bottle at me. Drink in hand, I head back towards Abby. Tiff has joined her but Luke is nowhere to be found.

Halfway there, I notice some guy walk up behind Abby and start talking to her. His two buddies are flanking him like the most ridiculous wingmen to ever step foot in a bar. I'm immediately pissed off that some douche is hitting on her already. I haven't been away from her *that* long.

As I advance towards them, the hairs on the back of my neck stand up. Abby's posture and the look of irritation on her face are setting off major alarm bells. The way she's gripping the pool stick in her hand like she's about to hit someone with it concerns me. When I finally make it back to her, I realize what's fueling her anger.

"Come on, Abs. Just one dance. For old time's sake," the jackass in the plaid button down and baseball hat says, leaning into her. He reeks of tequila and desperation.

"Don't call me that," Abby spits out through gritted teeth.

I fight the urge to lay this cocksucker out right here and now. If he comes one inch closer to her, I'm going to lose my shit. She's visibly uncomfortable, bristling at his proximity. I need to keep my anger in check if I'm going to handle this civilly. Setting my beer down, I step up next to her, close enough to let him know she's not here alone.

"Hey, is everything okay?" I ask, placing a comforting hand on her back. Abby turns her body into mine slightly and I feel a little triumphant.

"Yeah, it's fine. Grant was just leaving," Tiff says, staring daggers at him.

"Who the fuck are you?" Grant demands, pointing at me.

This drunk redneck doesn't know who he's fucking with.

"That's none of your business, jerk off," Abby fires back before I have a chance to respond.

Grant lets out a humorless laugh. "Good luck with this one," he says to me, motioning with his thumb towards Abby. "Don't let her fool ya. She's a fucking prude. I wasted three months on her and couldn't even get a blow job."

His off-handed comment makes me see red. I won't tolerate him disrespecting her like that. I'm so mad, the edges of my vision start to blur and my arms tingle. I take a step towards him, but Abby's hand on my chest pulls me from my rage, smothering the flames of my ire.

"Just get me out of here," she implores, looking up at me with pleading eyes. "Please."

Tiff's voice draws my attention away from Abby. "There's an exit down that hallway that leads out back," she offers, pointing a few feet away from where we are. "I'll find Luke and meet you out there."

The sound of Grant's laughter, along with his douche bag friends' is enough to make me reconsider leaving. But Abby is upset and I need to get her out of here. I grab her by the hand and lead her down the hallway to the exit. I shove the door open and the cool night air hits me in the face, cooling not only my skin but my temper as well. I take a deep breath and release it before turning to face her. She's watching me intently, concern etched on her face. I almost lost my cool back there in front of her.

"Are you okay?" I ask.

"I'm fine. I just wanted out of there and away from him," she replies. "If I had stayed there any longer, I was going to break that pool cue over his head." She smiles weakly and lets out a small laugh. The tension drains from my body and I can't help but chuckle a little at her feisty temper.

Once we both stop laughing, something in the air shifts around us. We simply stare at each other, electric attraction crackling between us. That's when I take my chance. Closing the gap separating us in two short strides, I grab her by the sides of her face and crush my lips to hers. I back her up a few inches and press her against the brick exterior, ravishing her mouth. She kisses me back just as fervently and I press myself against her even harder, knowing she can feel how hard I am. She moans into my mouth, sending a pulse of need straight to my groin.

I need to get control of myself. We shouldn't be doing this here. She's a little drunk, and I don't want to take advantage of her. Besides, anyone could walk out and see us. I pull back and press my forehead to hers, both of us breathing rapidly.

"I've wanted to do that all night," I admit.

"What took you so long?" She grins, panting from our hastened kiss. Her cheeky response makes me want her even more. I lean in to kiss her again, but before our lips meet, the door next to us flies open, bouncing loudly against the exterior. I step back automatically when Luke and Tiffany burst through the exit.

"What the fuck, dude? Tiff said some dickhead was harassing Abby." Luke looks furious, his grey eyes darkening like the night sky.

"Everything's fine. We had to get out of there before she started a bar fight," I say teasingly, nodding towards Abby.

Luke's expression relaxes and he chuckles. "Damn, girl. That's gangsta." He offers up his closed hand for a fist bump. Abby indulges him, a sheepish grin curling her lips. "You wait until I leave to take a piss before starting shit with some asshole in a bar. Some friends you are," Luke teases.

"Grant is a world-class prick," Tiff slurs.

"I know. I can't believe I ever went out with him," Abby replies as she pulls her phone out of her pocket. She checks the time and looks back up at her friend. "We'd better get going. It's almost two and we have to be back at Rosie's at eleven. I can't skip my run again."

So that's how she keeps that insane body.

Tiffany sticks out her bottom lip and pouts. "It's not going to kill you to miss another run. Just run twice as far next time. I'm not ready to go yet." She turns to Luke and wraps her arms around his waist.

Abby rolls her eyes. "This place is closing soon anyway. I'm sure they're about to announce last call. We might as well head out."

"Fine," Tiff replies begrudgingly and mutters "party pooper" under her breath, earning her another eye roll.

When we try to get back through the door, we find that it's locked, so we make our way around the side of the building to the front. As we head towards the parking lot, I notice that Abby is swerving ever so slightly. She's not falling down drunk, but she's obviously tipsy. How am I supposed to let her drive home like that? Maybe she'll let me call her a cab. I'd offer to drive her, but that would be a little presumptuous at this point.

"Abby," I say as I reach for her. I grab a hold of her arm, steadying her. "I'm not sure you should be driving right now."

She looks up at me, biting the side of her full, bottom lip. All I can think about is how badly I want to be the one biting it. I suppress the urge to lean down and do just that.

"We'll be fine," she replies. "We'll go to Tiff's. Her house isn't far from here."

"Abby." My voice is pleading, worried, but what else can I say? She's a grown woman. I can't tell her what to do, but I can't let her drive, either. "Let me call you a cab."

"Why don't we just take them home?" Luke breaks in.

"Yeah," Tiff adds. "That's an awesome idea! It's like, two minutes up the road. It'll save us cab fare." She looks at Abby with a hopeful expression.

Jeez, why can't these two just keep their mouths shut? Abby is never going to go for that.

"How am I gonna get my truck back in the morning?" She's contemplating this proposal with apprehension.

"I'm sure Jack wouldn't mind dropping us off on his way to work."

Abby thinks on this for a moment before conceding. "Okay." I'm stunned that she agreed but relieved at the same time.

"You're riding in the back with me," Luke says excitedly to Tiffany as he picks her up. She wraps her legs around his waist, squealing with delight when he cups her ass and walks her to the Range Rover.

"Looks like I'm up front with you," Abby pronounces as our friends climb into the back of my SUV.

"If those two ruin the leather, I'm leaving them on the side of the road," I tell her, only half joking.

She laughs at my remark, a full-on belly laugh, and it's refreshing. I wait for her to grab a few things out of her truck before opening the passenger door. Luke and Tiff are already in the back seat, giggling and fondling each other. I take advantage of their preoccupation to share a private moment with Abby. Before she steps up into the front seat, I pull her to me and place a gentle kiss on her lips. When I back away, she's smiling at me, a sight I could get used to.

"I had a good time tonight," I tell her, brushing a stray wisp of hair from her face.

"Me too. Sorry I almost got you into a bar brawl," she replies sheepishly. "Sometimes my temper gets the best of me."

That's something I understand all too well. "I don't blame you. That Grant guy is a dick."

"That he is," she agrees.

We finally get into the car and take off, Abby directing me to Tiff's house. She was right. It's not far, but the winding roads and lack of street lights make this a dangerous route for even a sober driver. I'm even more relieved now that she agreed to let me take them home.

When we pull in to the driveway, Abby unfastens her seatbelt and reaches for the door. Before she opens it, she turns to me and says, "Thanks for the ride. I guess I'll see you around." She looks over her shoulder to the back seat. "Come on, Tiff. We're here."

She's brave. I would *not* have looked back there, considering the sounds they've been making.

"Already?" Tiff whines, the pout evident in her voice.

"Yep. Let's go."

"Bye, babe. I gotta go."

Tiff is talking to Luke now and I think I just threw up a little in my mouth. Abby makes a gagging gesture then rolls her eyes. My laughter fills the vehicle, drowning out the disgusting sound of lips smacking in my back seat.

"I'll call you tomorrow," Luke promises. *Yeah, right.* I've heard that lie about a million times.

Tiff jumps out of the car and Abby opens her door to get out.

"Hey," I say to get her attention. "I'll see you later." I mean it when I tell her this. I have every intention of seeing her again.

"Bye, Jacob." I watch her until she's safely in the house and Luke crawls into the front seat.

"What a night," he exclaims, raking his fingers through his dark hair.

"I take it you enjoyed yourself."

"Oh, yeah," he responds. "By the way, I'm pretty sure Tiffany's last name should be Dyson," he says, raising his eyebrows suggestively.

Son of a bitch.

Chapter Seven

Abby

THE RHYTHMIC SOUND OF MY FEET thumping against the pavement calms my jittery nerves. My legs burn and my lungs scream for oxygen. I've replayed the events of last night over in my head at least a dozen times. I can't believe I let Jacob kiss me after only knowing him for a few hours, but oh, what a kiss it was.

My lips tingle at the memory. I've never been kissed like that before in my life. His eyes drilled into me with a feral need before his mouth consumed mine. I was aroused the moment our lips met, his own arousal evident when he pressed it against my belly. My body responded to his immediately, moisture pooling between my thighs. I almost asked him to take me right then and there. I'd had too much to drink, and it had been far too long since I'd been that turned on. Scratch that. I've *never* been that turned on.

Even with the unbridled lust I felt for Jacob, I can't believe I let him drive us to Tiff's house. I barely even know him, yet I already felt so comfortable with him, like I could trust him with my life. He was so concerned about us getting home safely, and when Grant was harassing me, he came to my rescue, wedging himself between me and my drunk ex. I really wanted to deck him when he called me "Abs." I hate that nickname. That's what *she* used to call me. Before she ran off to God-knows-where with her drug dealer boyfriend.

I've only heard from her twice since, and the last time was nearly two years ago. Both times, she called to ask for money. At first, I was dumb enough to give it to her. I believed her when she said she'd pay me back. Of course, that never materialized. I'm sure she used the money to buy supplies to cook meth with Mickey instead of using it for food and gas as she said. The next time she called, I refused to give her anything else. She'd already swindled three hundred dollars from me. Fool me once, shame on you. Fool me twice, shame on me. That's when she reverted back to her old self. She cussed me up one side and down the other, calling me every name in the book. She must have really been fiending, her belligerence a sign of how badly she needed a hit. But I'd had enough of her abuse. I told her to get help and hung up the phone.

That's the last time I talked to my mother. I have no idea where she is. She could be dead, for all I know, but I hope not. Even with all the horrible things she has done and said to me, she's still my mother. I want her to get better, to be the person she was before Dad died. I don't have any illusions about her fate, though. She'll never be that person again. She's broken beyond repair, just like our relationship.

All the tension I worked so hard to get rid of has gradually built back up, just thinking of her. The muscles in my neck and back tighten with pent-up frustration, so I push myself harder, running faster than I usually do. Running until my lungs feel like they're about to burst and my legs won't take me any further is the only way I've found to deal with the anger, hurt, and disappointment. I collapse on the side of the road breathless, tears welling in my eyes. *Oh, hell no. I will not cry over her again!*

I manage to suppress the sobs but I can't control the dry heaves. Running on an empty stomach after consuming countless shots of whiskey last night was a bad idea. I need to get up and pull myself together before somebody drives by and sees me like this.

I finally get my breathing regulated and swallow down the bile clogging my throat. Regaining my composure, I stand back up and stretch my muscles. Unscrewing the lid on my bottle of water, I hesitantly take a sip. I don't want to put anything in my stomach right now, but I need to rehydrate. Sweat drips from my brow, perspiration soaking my tank top. Tentatively, I take another drink of cool water. It goes down easily, so I gulp half the bottle before taking off back towards Tiff's. I keep my pace steady this time, not wanting to risk another spell like I just had. Once I've established a rhythm and my breathing evens out, I relax a little. This is the reason I run. Everything fades away when I'm in my zone. It's just me, nature, and the air I'm breathing. There's a certain peace that comes with running, something that chases the demons away. Perhaps it's the endorphins, the runner's high. I don't know what it is, but I love it.

Since I ran further than usual trying to clear my head and make up for skipping yesterday, I'm pressed for time when I finally make it back. Tiff tosses me a spare uniform when I step out of her bathroom, steam from my shower billowing out through the open door. She takes her time, carefully applying her makeup as I hurry to get ready. She's still seated in front of her mirror, cosmetics scattered across her vanity when I head outside to meet Jack. Tiff's car is out of commission so her stepdad has agreed to drop us off at my truck on his way into town. Several minutes go by as Jack and I wait for Tiff to emerge from the house. If she doesn't come out now, we'll never get there on time. I consider going back inside and dragging her out of the house, but she finally walks out the front door.

MY HAIR IS still a little damp from the shower when we arrive at Rosie's. I gather it to one side and braid it loosely to keep it out of my face. We clock in right at eleven, not a minute to spare. Of course, there never is with Tiff. One of these days, she's going to make us late for work.

My BFF is hungover and grumbling incoherently as we set to work, placing napkin-wrapped silverware on all the tables and ensuring the salt and pepper shakers and condiment bottles are full. We also check to make sure the room is clean and ready to receive customers. Kayla and Mary Beth are the other two servers working today, so they arrive at eleven-thirty when it's time to open the doors.

It's past noon before we get our first customers, but people soon begin filling up the tables and booths, all of them in their Sunday best. By one o'clock, there's not an empty seat in the place and there are people packed into our small waiting area. I'm glad we're busy. It keeps my mind occupied, and I desperately need that today.

I'm gathering empty glasses off a recently vacated table when I sense someone behind me, a familiar surge of electric heat coursing through my veins when he touches my waist.

"Abby." I melt into his touch, nearly dropping the glasses in my hands at the sound of my name on his lips. His sexy rasp and the heat of his hand on my body has my legs wobbling and my nipples standing at attention. When I turn to look at him, his intense blue gaze pierces straight into me, a look of thinly veiled lust on his handsome face.

"Jacob," I reply breathlessly. "What are you doing here?" It comes out harsher than I intend, but I didn't expect to see him again so soon. A look of confusion passes over his face, and I immediately try to recover. "I mean... I just..." I stumble over my words. "I didn't expect to see you here. You caught me off guard, is all." At this, a grin pulls up the sides of his mouth.

"I told you I'd see you later," he says, stepping closer to me. He leans over me a little and I catch the scent of his body wash. He smells clean and fresh and a little woodsy, a delicious combination.

My stomach clenches as he flashes his perfect white smile at me. "You see, I realized I didn't get your number last night, and I don't think I can go another day without it."

I can't think clearly enough to even respond to him right now. I want to yell out the digits of my phone number, but I suddenly can't remember what they are. He takes my twitter-pated state as reluctance, and his smile fades as he starts to back away from me. "That is, unless you don't want me to call you," he begins, more of a question than a statement. "Or you're already seeing somebody?" He awaits my response, looking hopeful that I'll deny it. When I remain silent, he lifts a hand up to scratch the back of his neck nervously, peeking at me from under his lashes. When I fail to respond and just stare up at him like an enamored mortal gazing upon Adonis for the first time, he continues, defeated, "Okay, um, I'm gonna go back to my table and let you get back to work." He turns to walk away, but I reach out and grab his arm.

"No!" I say a little too loudly. He raises both brows in inquiry. "No, I *do* want you to call me. I *really* want you to call me." Uh oh, now I sound desperate, but I was afraid he would walk away and I'd never have another chance. He must not notice the desperation in my voice because his face lights up.

"Damn," he says, scrubbing his hand over the day-old stubble covering his jaw. "You had me sweating there for a minute. I thought I'd done something wrong and you were just too nice to tell me to get lost."

"There was nothing wrong with anything you did last night," I assure him, blushing a little at my candor.

"So, does that mean I'll get to see you again?" I'm rewarded with another sly smile as he steps closer to me.

"Yes." My breathy reply is barely louder than a whisper. He reaches for me and removes a pen and order pad from the front pocket of my apron. The light pressure of his fingertips on my stomach has my head reeling and my abdominal muscles tightening. He flips to an empty page and scribbles something on it before handing it back to me. When I open it up, his name and phone number are written diagonally across the ticket.

Jacob Daniels. Even his name sounds perfect.

"Just text me your name, and then I'll have your number."

"Okay," is all I can say in reply.

"See you later." He flashes me his signature Hollywood smile and walks off towards his table.

I look around to make sure nobody is watching, and pull out my phone. I punch in the number Jacob just gave me and follow his instructions, typing out a short message:

Abby Harris

I press send before I lose my nerve. I look over at Jacob as he pulls his phone from his pants pocket. He slides his finger across the screen and his face lights up, a grin curving up the corners of his mouth. I turn back to my waitressing duties, trying to suppress my own elated smile.

"What the hell are you so happy about?" I lift my gaze to see a pissy Tiff glaring at me through bloodshot eyes. Framed by perfectly winged eyeliner and impeccably applied eyeshadow, but bloodshot, nonetheless.

"Oh, nothing. Just glad to be here," I deflect. She's an unbearable grouch when she has a hangover. It would be unwise to share my joy with her right now.

"You're full of shit," she says matter-of-factly. She starts to walk past me but stops short when her gaze lands on something behind me. "Luke is here." She turns and faces me, fluffing her hair. She's always fluffing her damn hair. "How do I look?"

I hesitate for a moment. She doesn't look *terrible*. That's not possible, but it's obvious she had a late night. "Hungover," I answer reluctantly, preparing for her wrath. She just gives me a vexed look and pushes past me. I watch as she goes from Surly, Hungover Tiff to Fierce and Flirty Tiff in an instant. She begins her seductive, hip-swiveling walk towards Luke. Poor guy. He has no idea what he's gotten himself into.

Kayla is at Jacob and Luke's table refilling their drinks when Tiff saunters over. The moment Luke sees her, a huge grin stretches across his face. He stands up when she reaches their table and places a chaste kiss on her cheek like a true gentleman. *Ha!* I don't know who he's trying to fool. I return to my tables and finish collecting my tips.

Nearly an hour has passed when Kayla approaches and hands me a folded-up receipt. "Hey Abby, the guy that just left table three asked me to give this to you," she offers. I've been so busy, I didn't notice him leaving.

"Thanks," I mutter, perplexed, turning the paper over in my hand.

"Are you seeing him? He's not from around here, is he?" she asks.

"No, he isn't," I respond. I don't answer her other question because I don't know how. *Am* I seeing him?

"Because he is *hot!*" she swoons. "Like, ridiculously hot," she adds enthusiastically.

"Yeah. He is," I agree absentmindedly, fiddling with the receipt. Before I can say anything else, Kayla turns and walks back to her section, chestnut curls bouncing from her ponytail. I unfold the paper, wondering why he'd have her give it to me. In neat, but masculine script, the words "check your phone" are scribbled in black ink.

I hadn't even felt it vibrate. He must've grown impatient waiting for my response. I slip into the kitchen, excitement bubbling in my stomach when I open Jacob's text.

Dinner tomorrow 7:00, Wolf's Den Lodge?

My smile fades. Wolf's Den Lodge? I can't go there with him. It's the ritziest place in town. I've never even set foot inside the building. The Carlisles used to go there about once or twice a month, enlisting me to babysit for the evening. They would come home laughing and carrying on about what a good time they had. With all their rich friends, I'm sure. On those nights, Sydney Carlisle wore semi-formal dresses and exquisite jewelry. I don't even own anything remotely appropriate for dinner there. Of all the places to take me to, he had to pick that one. Is he trying to impress me, intimidate me by throwing his money around? If so, he needs to know I'm not that kind of girl.

I start to feel the panic creeping in, so I shove my phone back in my pocket. I have to find Tiffany later, tell her about Jacob's invitation and see what she thinks of it, but right now I need to focus on my customers.

It's not long before the crowd at Rosie's starts to thin out and I go in search of Tiff. When I find her, I take her by the arm and tell her, "We're going on break." I drag her toward the back door, ignoring her irritated protests.

Once outside, I take a deep breath and try to release some of the anxiety that's been festering inside me since reading Jacob's message. It's not working. My breathing is starting to become more erratic.

"What's wrong?" Tiff asks with a worried look on her face.

"Jacob asked me to dinner," I say between breaths.

Tiff lets out a relieved laugh. "Shit. Is that all?" She shakes her head, brushing off my anxiety. "Get it together, Abby. It's just dinner. You should be happy."

"He wants to take me to Wolf's Den Lodge."

"Oh." Her eyes widen with surprise. "That's a pretty serious place for a first date. Maybe he's trying to impress you?" she offers hopefully.

"I don't *need* to be impressed!" I contend. "He doesn't have to take me to a fancy restaurant. I'll just be uncomfortable there." I'm pacing by this point, launching into an addled tirade. "I don't have anything to wear to a place like that. I don't know which fork to use when. What do I order? What if I can't pronounce anything on the menu? It could be in French or Italian or some other fancy language!" I start to hyperventilate. "I'm freaking out here, Tiff!"

"I can tell." She rolls her eyes and snickers. Stepping in front of me, she firmly but gently grabs me by the shoulders, forcing my eyes to meet hers. "It's going to be fine. Just calm down." She's attempting to talk me off the ledge. "We'll find you something to wear. As for the silverware, just work your way in from the outside. And when it comes time to order, just go old school and let him order for you. Guys love that macho, alpha shit."

"Okay." I'm starting to feel better now, less panicked.

Tiff looks at me questioningly. "You good now?"

"Yeah," I answer. "I'm okay."

"Good. Let's grab a quick bite before our break is over."

"Okay, just give me a minute to text Jacob my answer." I pull out my phone and shoot him a one-word response:

Yes

I place my phone back into my pocket and head inside. As soon as I make it through the door, my phone buzzes with his quick reply.

I'm looking forward to it.

I walk back into Rosie's with a smile on my face. I already can't wait to see him again, even if I am nervous about where he's taking me. I'm just going to have to take a risk. And probably raid Tiff's closet.

Abby

IT'S AFTER SEVEN-THIRTY BY THE TIME we leave Rosie's, and I'm dog tired. Too much booze and not enough sleep is a bad combination, and it's starting to catch up with me. I decide to take a nice, long bath and go to bed early tonight. But first, I have to see if Tiff has a dress I can borrow for my date with Jacob tomorrow.

"I've got a couple of dresses in mind for you to wear to dinner," Tiff prompts as we pull up to her house. "You wanna come in and try 'em on?"

"Sure." I hope she has something long enough to actually cover my ass. Tiff's wardrobe tends to be a little on the, ahem, short side. "Nothing too revealing, though." She shoots me an exacerbated look but doesn't reply.

Once inside her bedroom, Tiff goes straight to her closet and starts pulling out hangers with dresses. Some of them are way too skimpy and I veto them immediately. Some of them aren't quite dressy enough. I weed through those quickly. That leaves only three options for me to try on.

"I did a little recon on our boys," Tiff informs me as I step into the first dress.

"What did you do?" I ask skeptically. Tiff practically lives on social media, and her cyber-stalking skills are impressive. And maybe a little terrifying.

She walks over to me and I turn so she can zip me up. The short, navy blue dress has a sweetheart neckline and ruching at the waist, with silver beads and navy sequins adorning the right side of the bust and the left side of the bodice in a cut-out pattern. The dress is beautiful, but it's not really my color and doesn't fit quite right.

"Nothing," she replies innocently. "Just creeping on their Facebook profiles. Jacob's is private, so I really couldn't see anything without sending him a friend request," she informs me, handing over the next dress. "Luke's consists mainly of tagged pictures of him at parties."

As she rambles on about Facebook and how neither of them has Instagram, I pull the one shoulder, magenta colored Grecian dress over my head. It, too, is beautiful with its wide, intricate silver belt. But it's much too flashy for my taste, so I take it off.

Finally, an impatient Tiff hands me the last dress. "Are you even listening to me?" she huffs.

"Yes, I heard you. Luke's the only one on Twitter and Jacob still hasn't accepted your friend request. It's like he's living in the Dark Ages." She scowls at my sarcasm.

"He's not the only one, ya know." Here we go again. Tiff acts like anyone in their twenties without social media is an agoraphobic social misfit destined to die alone and be eaten by their thirty cats.

"I don't have time for all that." I dismiss her with a wave and pull the dress over my hips, poking my arms through the sleeves. "Besides, what would I do with it? 'Going to work again. Hope nobody pukes on me today. Hashtag donteatbeforeziplining,'" I mock snottily. I just don't see any point in all the asinine status updates flooding everyone's feed.

Tiff secures the two fabric covered buttons at the base of my neck as she continues her lecture. "That's not all social med- Whoa!" Her mouth drops open and her eyes go wide when I turn to face her fully.

My gaze lands on the mirror and I gasp at my reflection. A satisfied grin pulls up the sides of Tiff's mouth when she peers over my shoulder into the mirror. The little black dress is perfect. It's strapless, with a three-quarter length sleeve lace overlay that lands at mid-thigh, just the right length. The dress is nearly backless with a large cut-out that reveals nearly every inch of tanned skin on my back. It's fitted, hugging my curves in all the right places.

"Oh. My. God. That is perfect," Tiff gushes to my reflection.

"I love it." I slide my hands down my hips, smoothing the fabric and appreciating how well it flatters them. Turning my body from side to side, I check myself out from every angle, our social media debate long forgotten. I'm not the most confident girl when it comes to my body, but in this dress, I feel unstoppable.

Tiffany's phone dings, alerting her to a new text. I simply stare at myself in the mirror while she retrieves her phone. I can't believe how perfect this dress is. I feel beautiful and incredibly sexy. It's amazing what the right dress can do for a girl. Perhaps this dinner won't be so bad, after all.

"Um, Abby?" Tiff interrupts my reverie, apprehension clouding her features as her eyes lift from the screen lit up in her hand. "Luke just asked me if I wanted to go to Wolf's Den Lodge tomorrow night. You know, as a double date with you and Jacob."

Oddly enough, I'm relieved to hear this. Having Tiff with me would alleviate so much anxiety. Then doubt begins to creep into my thoughts, rolling in like a fog and filling all the gaps in my consciousness with uncertainty. Why would Jacob ask Luke to go with us? I kind of got the impression he wanted to have dinner alone with me.

"Did Jacob mention anything to you about this?" she asks.

"Um," I hesitate. "No, he didn't say any-"

A faint ringing registers in my ears, cutting off my words. I follow the muffled sound, dropping to my hands and knees on Tiff's bedroom floor. I dig through piles of clothes looking for my shorts, pulling my cell from the back pocket when I finally find them. Jacob's name flashes across the screen and my pulse accelerates.

"Abby," he greets when I answer. His deep voice, just as sensual over the phone as it is in person, reverberates throughout my body, settling deep and low inside my belly.

"Jacob." I try to keep my voice steady, despite the fluttery feeling in my chest.

"Hey, I uh," he begins nervously. "There's a bit of a problem with our date."

"Hmm?"

"Well, Luke kind of hijacked it. And normally I'd just leave his ass behind, but he's already asked Tiffany to go." He seems nervous like he expects me to be upset.

"Yeah, I know. I'm with her right now."

The line is silent for a minute before Jacob responds. He seems to be deliberating on what to say next. "I'm sorry. I didn't know he was going to do that. I would have never told him about our plans if I did." He exhales slowly and I sense his irritation. "So... are you okay with that? Luke and Tiffany going with us?"

I chew on the corner of my lip, deciding how to respond. If I say yes, will he think I'm not interested in anything more than friendship? If I say no, will he think I'm a total bitch? Honestly, I want Tiff there. I will be so much more relaxed if she is with me.

"Sure. It'll be fun." I keep my response light and optimistic. He releases a quiet sigh of relief as if he's been holding his breath, awaiting my response. "Okay, then. I guess we'll pick you guys up around six-thirty." With that, we say our goodbyes and hang up.

"Well?" Tiff asks.

"You," I say pointing to her, "are coming with."

Tiff squeals with delight. "Now *I* have to find something to wear." She starts rummaging through her clothes. There are dresses on the bed, the dresser, the floor, and a few still hanging in the closet. She tries a few on. "Meh," she grimaces at the first one, tossing it aside. I guess that's a no. She doesn't even put on the next two she grabs, just holds them up to her body and checks her reflection. "No. And no," she groans, tossing them back onto the bed one by one. Two more dresses she tries on and discards just the same.

Finally, she picks up the navy blue one I tried on earlier and pulls it over her hips. I zip her up and she faces me. "How do I look?" she asks.

"Fabulous!" I tell her, and it's the truth. The navy hue brings out her deep blue eyes and complements her blonde hair. She turns and checks herself out in the mirror, admiring her gorgeous reflection.

"You're right. I *do* look pretty amazing." *Well, isn't she modest?*

She regards herself in the mirror a few minutes longer, turning and playing with different hairstyles. "Ooh, now we have to find shoes." She runs back into her walk-in closet, rummaging through her sizeable shoe collection. After a minute or two I hear, "Ah-ha!" and she bursts out of the closet excitedly, a pair of heels in each hand. She hands me a pair of black, peep-toe pumps with red soles. Louboutin knockoffs, I'm sure. "Try 'em on," she orders as she slides her own white pumps onto her feet.

She does this effortlessly, maintaining her balance like a flamingo. I have to sit on the edge of the bed to put mine on. It's rare that I get to wear heels. I only have a few pairs, and none of them are this nice. I once had a pair of Dolce & Gabbana boots Sydney Carlisle gave me. They were hand-me-downs and a half size too big, but I wore the hell out of 'em all the same. I envy Tiff's shoe collection. She has dozens of shoes in a myriad of colors and styles. Then again, she's not working her way through college and can spend her money on whatever she wants. Luckily for me, we wear the same size and she's willing to let me borrow them.

"Look at you," she praises when I stand up. "You look incredible!"

"Thanks! You look pretty damn good yourself."

She winks at me and turns back to the full-length cheval mirror, admiring her profile in the fitted navy dress. The white pumps are a perfect addition to her ensemble.

Tiff and I are attempting to find the perfect jewelry to complement our outfits when my phone rings once again. It's my grandmother's ringtone, so I hurry to pick it up.

"Hi, enisi," I answer, always using the Cherokee word for "grandmother" to address her. She doesn't talk much about her family or the time before she met my grandfather, but the Cherokee language is something she still cherishes from her childhood.

"Abigail, where are you? You haven't been home since yesterday morning." Her worried voice pulls at my heartstrings.

"I'm at Tiff's. I'll be home soon."

"Okay, sweetie. I love you."

"Love you, too."

"Was that your grandma?" Tiff asks when I hang up.

"Yeah, I think she misses me. I better get home."

"Please tell me you called her this morning to let her know where you were since you didn't go home last night."

"Of course. I called her first thing when I got up. She would've had the whole town out looking for me if I hadn't." My grandmother is fiercely protective of my brother and me. She tries to let me have my independence, but out of respect, I always try to let her know where I am. She's been so good to me, it's the least I can do. I think she feels responsible for my mother's actions and has been trying to make up for her shortcomings since Mom left.

"So, are you coming straight here from work tomorrow to get ready for our big date with the boys?" Tiff asks, unbuttoning my dress so I can hang it back up.

"I probably should, since I'll only have a little over an hour to get ready. I'll definitely need a shower. And probably some help with my hair," I add hopefully. She seems to be the only one who can do anything with this mane.

"Of course. Don't forget your makeup bag. And wear sexy underwear," she tells me with a wink.

I just laugh at her. "Goodbye, Tiff." I head towards home with a smile on my face and excitement blooming in my chest.

Chapter Nine

Jacob

STILL CAN'T BELIEVE THAT LITTLE FUCKER weaseled his way into my date with Abby. All I wanted was a chance to spend some time alone with her and get to know her, but Luke had to butt his nose into my business and sabotage my plans. I would've just told him to fuck off if he hadn't already asked Tiffany to go. I don't want to be the asshole that lets her down after she gets her hopes up. You never want to piss off the best friend of the girl you're interested in. They can kill your chances quicker than anything. At least Abby didn't seem upset. I expected her to get pissed off. Most girls would have. I guess she isn't like most girls.

An unsettling thought creeps into the back of my mind.

What if she's happy Luke and Tiffany are going with us so that she doesn't have to be alone with me?

Maybe she isn't interested in anything beyond friendship. That can't be the case, though, judging by her body's reaction to mine. I can tell my presence affects her. Her breathing becomes more rapid and her pupils dilate, her body instinctively leaning into mine. When we kissed the other night, I could feel her tremble against my chest. And the way she moaned. Had I not already been hard, I would have been from that soft sound reverberating in the back of her throat. But then again, she drank quite a bit that night. I'm sure that if she'd been sober, she never would have let me press her against that building the way I did. Besides, the short time we've spent together has included our friends as a buffer. If they hadn't instantly hit it off, we might not even be seeing each other.

I need to quit worrying about this. I'm over-analyzing everything, and guys don't do that. We just go with the flow. *Right.*

It's after eight o'clock and Luke is still in bed. If we're going to do the mountain biking tour and fit in some rock climbing, we need to get going. I walk into his room to wake his lazy ass up. Of course, he's naked and has kicked the covers off so his junk is all out in the open. And it's morning. Gross.

"Wake up, shithead," I tell him as I shove his shoulder. I'm still pissed at him and not in the mood for his fuckery today. He groans and rolls over in the queen-size bed. At least his package is out of sight now. "Dude, get up. We gotta go."

He grunts out an incoherent response but doesn't budge. I know what will get him out of bed.

"Luke, there are two naked girls in the hot tub at the cabin next door."

He sits straight up and cranes his neck to see out the window. Our neighbors are barely visible through the dense patch of trees and the distance that separates us from the other cabins.

"What?" he asks, rubbing sleep from one eye. "Naked?"

"Yeah, they said that if you get up now and get dressed, you can have a threesome with them."

"Fuck you," he grumbles and throws a pillow at my head. I duck and it hits the wall behind me.

"Get your ass up. We leave in five."

Luke takes his time getting ready. By the time he finally strolls into the kitchen, it's been a good fifteen minutes. He pours himself a cup of coffee and grabs a banana. I knew if I didn't have coffee made, I wouldn't get him out of here before noon. I grab myself a vitamin water and set a frying pan on the stove.

"Eggs?" I ask as he slides into a seat at the kitchen island. He nods as he takes a sip from his mug.

I turn on the burner and grab the carton from the fridge. This gourmet kitchen is kind of ridiculous, but Luke insisted on the luxury accommodations for the four of us. Our friends, Greg and Vince were supposed to come with us but backed out at the last minute, opting instead to spend a month with their ailing grandmother in Florence. Not that I can blame them. Sick grandma or not, I would've chosen to revisit Italy too.

The cabin itself is a little ostentatious if you ask me. It's thirty-five hundred square feet with travertine tile, granite countertops, and high-end appliances. The master bedroom boasts a king-size bed, a sitting area, a flat-screen TV, and an en suite bath with a walk-in shower and infinity tub. It's even nicer than my parent's bathroom back home. It's a little showy, but that doesn't keep me from imagining Abby in that tub, wet and waiting for me to join her. I picture her with her thick, dark hair piled on top of her head, her neck and shoulders bare. Her beautifully tan skin glistening under the soft glow of dimmed lights. Soaping her breasts and watching her nipples pull into tight peaks.

Fuck, now I'm hard. I just need to focus on making these eggs and stop thinking about her.

Naked and in my bathtub.

Dammit! My hard-on is never going to go away.

"J, are you alright over there, man?" Luke asks.

"Yeah, I'm fine. Just trying to find the whisk." I attempt to make an excuse for being so damn flustered.

"It's sitting on the counter by your left hand." From behind me, comes the distinct and subtle snort of a suppressed chuckle. He may not know what's got me so worked up, but my discomfort amuses him nonetheless.

Okay, got the whisk.

I imagine Abby's emerald eyes burning with desire.

Focus, asshole! Crack open the egg. Put it in the bowl. Whisk. Spray the pan. Pour. Salt and pepper.

I think I'm good now. No embarrassing woodies at breakfast.

OUR MOUNTAIN BIKING tour group is small, only three other people besides Luke and me. I'm hoping that makes our little excursion go faster. Then we can get on to what I'm really looking forward to: rock climbing. I'm nervous but excited at the same time. Even though I've always been a little uneasy when it comes to heights, I'm a bit of an adrenaline junkie, and the thought of climbing up the side of a cliff is exhilarating.

The mountain biking tour begins easily enough, descending trails that run down the mountain along the river. Luke rides next to me in the back of the group.

"So, what's the deal with you and Abby? You've really got a thing for her, don't you?" Luke prods.

Oh, boy. Here we go. "What do you mean?" I reply evasively, eyes forward and focusing on the terrain ahead.

"Dude, I thought you were going to rip my head off my shoulders when I asked Tiff to go to dinner with us."

I let out an exasperated sigh. "I just thought it'd be better to be alone with her. You know, so I can actually get to know her," I explain. "It's no big deal. She's fine with it being a group thing."

"Are *you?*" It's strange for Luke to be serious. It's even more strange for him to consider someone else's feelings.

"Yeah, man. It's cool." I brush it off, not wanting to make a big deal out of it.

"Awesome, because when we get back from dinner, I'm getting Tiff in that hot tub!" Aaand he's back.

We peddle along with our group, making stops in the abandoned town of Thurmond, among other places. The scenery is beautiful. Everything is green and lush, signaling summer's impending arrival. The sound of the flowing river creates a calming melody.

The sun is high in the sky when we finish the tour, and Luke and I are drenched in sweat. I take off my shirt and wipe my forehead with it before chugging a bottle of water. I toss Luke a protein bar and tear one open for myself.

"You ready for rock climbing?" I ask him between bites.

"Why not? You haven't managed to kill me yet," Luke answers sarcastically. He's still a little winded from our race. I beat him by a good twenty yards. "I'm gonna need that hot tub for more than just seducing Tiff tonight. I may not even be able to move by the time we get back."

"Quit your whining, you pansy ass."

He gives me the finger as he gulps down his bottle of water. I head back to the car and pull a clean shirt out of the back seat for myself and hand one to Luke. After we change, we head over to New River Adventures for rock climbing. It takes everything I have not to gravitate towards the zip lining area instead to see Abby.

"I know what you're thinking, dickhead. Don't do it. It'll make you look desperate," Luke cautions.

"I'm not going to do anything," I assure Luke, shooting him an irritated glare. "And I'm certainly not desperate."

"Good to hear you still have possession of your own balls. Now let's go climb this mountain. I'll race you to the top." I laugh at Luke's exaggerations and follow him to the rock-climbing station.

Two hours later, we're once again drenched in sweat and chugging water. Today has been one hell of a workout. My tight muscles feel amazing. All the stress just melts out of my body when I'm pushing it to its limits. There's no better feeling in the world. Well, except for the feel of Abby's body beneath my hands. I'm hoping I'll get to experience that again tonight.

When we arrive back at the cabin, we still have a couple hours before we need to pick up the girls. I shower and begin to straighten things up in case Abby and Tiff actually agree to come back here. I wash and dry the few dishes in the sink and sweep the main living area. Luke is passed out on the couch. That thing will probably need to be doused with Febreze now since he didn't bother to take a shower or change clothes before laying on it.

I head for my bedroom and make the bed. I don't know why. I doubt Abby will even step foot in here, but just in case, I don't want to look like a slob. I finish up and check my phone. Five text messages and two missed calls from my mother. That woman is persistent. I shoot her back a text letting her know I left my phone at the cabin and what all we did today. She immediately texts me back with a dozen more questions. I tell her I'll call her tomorrow, and that seems to placate her for the time being.

I wake Luke up so he can get ready for dinner and head into my room to get dressed. I'm starting to get nervous, my hands fumbling with the buttons on my shirt. I can't wait to see Abby, but I'm afraid she won't like where I'm taking her. If she's working two jobs, I'm guessing she doesn't have much money. It makes no difference to me. She's a beautiful, intriguing young woman. I don't want to come off as a pretentious womanizer by taking her to the most expensive restaurant in town. I just want to take her somewhere nice, somewhere no one has ever taken her before, and show her a good time. Hopefully, she'll see that.

Chapter Ten

Abby

AS SOON AS THE CLOCK STRIKES FIVE, I practically run to my truck. I need to hurry and get to Tiff's so I can get ready for dinner with Jacob. I'm nervous, excited, and scared all at the same time. I call my grandmother on the way to let her know I'll be getting in late tonight. I don't want her staying up and worrying about me.

When I get there, Tiff is almost ready for the evening ahead. She's adding the finishing touches to her blonde locks when I walk in. She looks gorgeous, as usual. Her eyelids are painted with a glittery silver shadow accented with navy blue in the crease, and black winged liner. Her hair cascades over her shoulders in big, perfect curls.

"You look amazing, Tiff," I tell her as I set my bag on her bed.

"Thanks, sis. Now get your ass in the shower." She swats my behind and laughs as I scurry to the bathroom.

"Okay, okay. I'm going!" I hop in the shower and try to hurry through my routine. I make sure to shave carefully and wash away all the dirt and grime from work. Even though I'm short on time, I can't help but think of Jacob as I lather my body with sweet smelling soap. I try to imagine how it would feel to have his big, strong hands all over me, soaping and caressing my skin. I don't usually fantasize about men in the shower, or anywhere really, but Jacob is different. I imagine his icy blue eyes staring into mine while he presses his hard body against me and…

BANG, BANG, BANG. Tiff pounding on the bathroom door startles me out of my fantasy.

"Girl, you better hurry or you're never gonna be ready on time."

What a buzz kill.

"Almost done!" I holler back as I rinse the last of the conditioner from my hair. I step out of the shower and dry off, toweling through and combing my hair before applying anti-frizz serum to my unruly tresses. I have no idea what Tiff plans to do with them, so I leave it as is. I throw on a pair of shorts and a tank top before stepping back into Tiff's room.

"Sit," she orders, pointing to the chair in front of her vanity where she's already set out my makeup bag.

I comply and plop down onto the pink cushion, facing the mirror. Tiff starts drying my hair as I apply moisturizer and foundation to my face. I choose a subtle smoky eye look for the evening, selecting shades of grey and brown. I finish it off with smudged charcoal eyeliner and black mascara.

In the meantime, Tiff finishes drying my hair and teases it at the crown, then she parts it on the side and sweeps it away from my face. I watch in the mirror as she works to transform my hair into a low, elegant chignon that rests on the back of my head. She crisscrosses and folds and pins my hair, concentrating as intently as an artist would on a masterpiece. Once she's done, she gives my hair one final spray and steps back to admire her work.

"Not bad," she boasts, smiling. "It's very Grace Kelly meets Kate Middleton." She hands me a large, hand-held mirror and I turn in my seat to check out the back.

"Wow, Tiff. That looks amazing." I am in awe of her raw talent. I look so chic and sophisticated. "You really need to go to beauty school."

"I've been thinking about applying," she admits. "Wouldn't start 'til the fall, though. That gives me time to save some money for tuition." She shrugs apathetically, but I can tell this means more to her than she's letting on. Tiff has never cared much for school, but I don't think she wants to wait tables the rest of her life, either.

Since Tiff is done pulling and tugging on my hair, I take this opportunity to finish my makeup. I apply nude lipstick and gloss and sweep a little raspberry-colored blush on my cheeks. It's six twenty-four, almost time for Jacob and Luke to pick us up, so we hurry to get dressed. I help Tiff zip up her dress before slipping into my own, then it hits me. My dress is backless.

"Um...Tiff?" I begin warily. "How am I supposed to wear a bra with this dress?"

"You don't," she replies flatly as she pokes a dangly silver earring through her lobe.

I scowl at her response and she chuckles. "Don't give me that look," she chides. "I have these adhesive cup things you can wear if you insist," she says, waving her hand dismissively like it's ridiculous for me to want to wear a bra. She walks over to her dresser and digs in her top drawer. "Here," she offers, pulling out what looks like the front half of a bra, minus the straps. "I think it's more trouble than it's worth, but you're welcome to it." She gives me the "bra" and I slip off my tank top and put it on. It fits okay, so I'm not sure how Tiff fits her ample... assets into it. No wonder she doesn't think it's worth wearing. It's not ideal, but it'll have to do.

I finish dressing and Tiff hands me some jewelry. The silver bracelet with rhinestones and chandelier earrings are a nice addition to the beautiful, lacy black dress. I put on the shoes Tiff picked out for me last night and look at myself in the mirror one last time. I barely recognize my own reflection. I feel beautiful. I *look* beautiful. I stand up a little straighter, feeling more confident than I ever have before. Maybe now I can be on Jacob's level.

Tiff hands me a small, silver clutch to put my lip gloss and cell phone in. "So you won't have to carry your purse," she explains. That's probably for the best. I don't think my raggedy brown crossbody would really go with this outfit.

It's six thirty-seven and I'm starting to get nervous. The guys are late and we haven't heard from them. I sit on the edge of Tiff's bed, absentmindedly tapping my foot. I check my phone every couple of minutes, worried I'll miss his call. I jump when it finally buzzes in my hand, alerting me to a new text message:

Running late, be there soon

I'm overcome with a sense of relief. A part of me thought that maybe he'd changed his mind and didn't want to see me again. I'm glad that's not the case. Five minutes have passed since the text from Jacob when we hear the doorbell ring. We grab our clutches and head for the front door.

"I'll get it!" Tiff shouts as we hurry down the hallway. "See you later, Mom," she yells to her mother when we reach the front door.

"Bye, sweetie. Be careful," her mom calls back from the kitchen.

Tiff swings the door open to reveal the guys standing on her front porch, but all I see is Jacob. He's leaning against a support column in light khaki pants and a blue and white striped button-down with his shirtsleeves rolled up, a dark blue blazer thrown over his shoulder. I'm not usually into the preppy look, but he can definitely pull it off. A slow, sexy smile curls up the sides of his mouth as his eyes rake up my body.

"Wow." He appraises me with his piercing blue gaze. "You are stunning."

I feel my cheeks flush and my stomach flutter at his compliment. "Thanks. You look rather dashing, yourself," I reply flirtatiously. I could get used to this new-found confidence. His smile grows even wider and he reaches for me. I accept his outstretched hand and let him lead me to his car.

"Oh, shoot." Tiff's voice breaks through the hypnotic hold Jacob has over me. "I forgot something. I'll be right back." She rushes back into the house for a moment and returns with a small cinched bag. I give her a questioning look, curious as to what's in the bag, but she just shoots me a wink and climbs in the back seat. *What is that girl up to?* I wonder.

We make it to Wolf's Den Lodge just after seven o'clock. The building itself is larger than I anticipated, the wood and stone façade fitting in perfectly with the surrounding landscape. Jacob leads me to the heavy wooden doors as a man in a tux opens one side for us.

"Good evening," he greets.

I am awestruck at the splendor of this gorgeous building. "Good evening," I reply, trying to keep my voice from shaking as we pass through the doors and into the foyer. My recently obtained confidence evaporates as I take in my surroundings. I'm so nervous that I'm going to do something wrong and embarrass myself, or even worse, embarrass Jacob. I'm not used to this kind of extravagance. These people are different. They think different, act different, and look different than I do. How do I blend in? I feel like I'm Cinderella and it's nearing midnight. They're all gonna know I'm a fraud and don't belong here. Panic begins to rise to the surface and my hands start to shake.

Jacob senses my mounting anxiety and squeezes my fingers, prompting me to look up at him. "Are you okay?" he asks, concern lacing his features. The look in his eyes dissolves my anxiety and I relax.

"I'm fine," I assure him, a soft smile playing on my lips. He gives the maître d' his name and we're ushered to our table, Tiff and Luke close behind.

The interior of the restaurant is beautifully decorated with subtle rustic accents and warm earth tones. Exposed wood beams support the high ceiling and a large stone fireplace dominates the far side of the room. Simple round, wooden chandeliers create a soft glow, illuminating the space with golden flickers of light. The dark, wide planked floors are made of reclaimed wood with varying grains and depths of color. Tables are covered in soft, cream-colored linens, and chairs made of sturdy wood finished with a walnut stain add to the warmth and ambiance of the room.

We are shown to our table and Jacob pulls my chair out like the gentleman he is. To my surprise, he settles into the seat across from me, leaving the chair next to me vacant. Luke pulls the empty chair out for Tiff and she slides into it, her eyes flicking towards Jacob briefly and then back to me, questioning our seating arrangement. I discreetly shrug my shoulders and scoot my chair in, wondering the same thing. I glance across the small square table and my eyes land immediately on Jacob's handsome face. Maybe sitting across from and not next to him isn't so bad, after all. I have the best view in the house.

I peer at him over the flickering candlelight, my stomach in knots, as the waiter recites the specials for the evening. I'm too nervous to really pay attention to what he's saying. Tiff, sensing my trepidation, reaches over and squeezes my wrist under the table. When I look up at her she smiles and mouths, "Relax." I nod my head and return her smile weakly.

"Would you like to start with a glass of one of our locally made wines?" the waiter asks.

"I'd like a glass of Moscato, please," Tiff answers.

"Excellent choice. And for you, Miss?" he asks, looking at me expectantly.

Since I rarely ever drink wine, I have no idea what to order. So I don't risk appearing unsophisticated, I simply say, "I'll have the same, please."

The waiter turns his attention to Jacob and Luke. "And for the gentlemen?"

"What do you have on tap?" Luke asks.

"We have over a dozen handcrafted, locally brewed selections," the waiter replies proudly. "They are listed on the back of the wine menu." He reaches for the tall, thin menu standing up in the center of our table and hands it to Luke. The guys place their orders and the waiter scurries off to retrieve our drinks.

"This place is unreal," Tiff gushes as she picks up her menu.

"Yeah, I'm glad we found it," Jacob replies. "I was looking for somewhere unforgettable to take you," he says directly to me.

"Thank you. I can't believe I've never been here before. It's beautiful."

"The pleasure's all mine." He smiles at me, but can't hide the fire in his eyes at the mention of pleasure. I squirm in my seat, his words and his voice licking up my spine and causing goosebumps to prickle my arms. I avert my gaze to study my menu, needing a distraction from Jacob's effortless sensuality. I'll never make it through dinner if I don't squelch the fire building inside me.

The waiter returns with our drinks and a loaf of dark brown bread on a wooden board. Tentatively, I take a sip of my wine. The sweet crispness hits my tongue and I'm surprised at how delicious it tastes. I want to down the whole glass, but then that would defeat the purpose of trying to appear refined. I don't want Jacob to think I'm just some hillbilly who can only guzzle her alcohol like a pledge at a frat party. Don't get me wrong, I've chugged my share of rot-gut from a mason jar, but he doesn't need to know that, and he certainly doesn't need to see it.

Jacob and Luke are enmeshed in their own conversation so I take this opportunity to lean over and whisper to Tiff. "Where are the prices? I don't know what any of this costs."

She bows her head towards me as I bring my glass to my lips to take another drink. "That's what super fancy restaurants do when everything is uber expensive," she explains. "I've heard that nothing on this menu costs less than fifty bucks," she whispers back, and I nearly spit my Moscato all over the table.

I choke on my drink and begin to cough, drawing the attention of our dates. Tiff pats me on the back, suppressing a smile at my unseemly reaction. Diners at nearby tables glance over at us, wondering what all the commotion is about.

"Are you okay?" Jacob asks, his face etched with worry.

"I'm fine," I squeeze out between coughs. "Just got choked." I take another drink of wine to clear my throat and hopefully numb the pain of embarrassment. I just want to crawl under the table and die.

"Here, take a drink of water." He pushes my glass of ice water towards me and I do as he's instructed. "Better?" His sincerity is palpable and warms my body. Or maybe that's the alcohol.

"Yes, thank you."

"Do you know what you're going to order?" he asks once I recover.

"Not yet. I'm not really sure what I want." I'm freaking out a little over the prices. At least the menu isn't in French and I can actually pronounce the names. "What are you having?" I deflect to take the attention off myself.

"I think I'm going to go with the filet mignon and lobster tail combo. I hear their steaks are excellent. I hope so because I'm starving."

"Me, too," Luke chimes in. "I'm pretty sure I burned, like, ten thousand calories today."

Tiff titters next to me. "Babe, I don't think that's even possible." She is playing her part tonight, and she's playing it well.

Luke smiles at her feigned naiveté. "Well, maybe not that many, but close," he jokes. He's fallen right into her trap and doesn't even know it yet.

I drain the rest of my wine, skimming the menu for the simplest thing they have, knowing that Jacob will insist on paying. I don't want to seem like I'm taking advantage of him so I peruse the salad selections, hoping that fifty-dollar minimum Tiff mentioned doesn't apply to them, too. Surely a bowl of lettuce can't be *that* expensive. My teeth dig into my lip as my eyes scan over each option trying to form the most economical strategy.

"Abby," Jacob says, leaning towards me as if to tell me a secret. I gaze up at him, releasing my lip from between my teeth and lean in to hear him better. "Order whatever you want." He gives me a knowing look and smiles at me softly, not with pity, but with affection.

It's a good thing because I can't stand pity. After my dad died and my mom spiraled into addiction, I had to endure people's sympathy and hear how sorry they felt for me, followed by their self-righteous comments behind my back. "What a shame," and "Bless her heart." If I never hear those two sentences until the day I take my last breath, it won't be long enough. I look away, unable to meet his gaze. Not for the first time, I'm ashamed of my poverty and embarrassed that he can sense what my disquiet is about.

"Seriously, I just want you to have a good time and not worry about a thing," he declares. "Let me spoil you," he adds with another of his crooked grins.

I can't help but smile back at him. Nobody has ever spoiled me. At least not since my father passed away. "And if you try to order a dainty little salad," he admonishes, closing his menu and relaxing back in his chair, "I'll just have to order for you." His challenging tone is softened by his mischievous grin.

"Okay," I acquiesce. *Damn, why is that such a turn-on?*

"Would you like another glass of wine?"

I nod my head. "Please." I need something to cool my libido after experiencing Jacob's take charge attitude.

He waves over our waiter. "More Moscato for the ladies."

"Certainly, sir. Another for you?"

"No, thank you."

"I'll have another," Luke requests.

"Right away, sir." The waiter returns shortly with another round of drinks and to take our order. I'm still unsure about what I want, so I ask to go last. When it's my turn, I glance over at Jacob and he gives me an encouraging smile.

"I'll have the sea scallops with grilled asparagus and roasted red potatoes." I close my menu and pass it to the waiter. He assures us of our *excellent choices* before walking away.

"Scallops sound good. I should have ordered some with my dinner," Jacob adds.

"I may be so inclined to part with a few of mine in exchange for a sample of your filet," I offer, doing my best to sound classy.

"Deal," he agrees before popping a slice of buttered bread into his mouth.

"So, Abby, what's your story?" Luke surprises us all with his inquiry. He glances at Jacob, gauging his reaction before continuing. Jacob observes him skeptically, unsure where his line of questioning is going. "There's got to be more to you than just waitressing and working at a zip line outfitter. Do you go to college?"

A scowl mars Jacob's flawless features. It seems as though Luke is encroaching on his territory. *Men.* I mentally roll my eyes at their ridiculous behavior, yet I'm intrigued by his reaction.

"Yes, I go to college. Biology major. I'll graduate next summer." I hesitate, not knowing how to proceed. There isn't much more to tell, at least not that I'm willing to divulge just yet. "I have a younger brother, Ethan. He's in a band and is an amazing singer," I add with exuberance, my voice etched with pride. Ethan and I have always been close. Sometimes we were all each other had.

"What about your parents?" Luke probes. Before I can answer, a loud thump sounds from under the table and Luke winces in pain. I turn to see Tiff staring daggers at him for asking such a direct and unknowingly insensitive question.

"Um," I begin uncomfortably, fidgeting in my chair. "My father died when I was ten. Coal mining accident," I add. "And my mom...uh...I haven't seen her in a few years."

"Oh," Luke exhales, glancing from me to Tiff, curiosity alight in his eyes. She shakes her head subtly, warning him to drop the subject.

I continue, trying to mask the sudden feeling of melancholy filling my chest. "I live with my grandmother now. She has some health problems, so I try to take care of her. She won't hardly let me, though. She's very stubborn," I add with a smile. The circumstances that lead to me living with her are some of my most painful memories, but I'm thankful for the bond we share because of them. "I don't know if that's a Cherokee trait or if it's just her personality, but I've never met anyone more tenacious."

"Your grandmother is Cherokee?" Jacob asks. He leans back in his seat and studies me over his glass.

"Full blooded," I confirm with pride.

"So *that's* what you are!" Luke exclaims, slapping the table in realization. "I've been trying to figure it out." His remark earns him another kick under the table. This time he grunts and leans down, no doubt rubbing the spot where Tiff has nailed him again with her pointy shoes.

"Luke," Jacob warns, his voice deep and stern.

I place my hand over my mouth to suppress a giggle. They must be worried about him offending me. I'm not offended, though. I'm proud of my heritage. I don't need to hide who I am.

"Yes, my mother is half Cherokee," I confirm. "And half Italian," I add.

"Damn, I bet she's hot," Luke exclaims. This time, Tiff just drops her head to the table with a loud thud. She must really be embarrassed now.

"Yes, she is quite beautiful." At least she was the last time I saw her. I don't want to think about what the drugs have done to my once ravishing mother.

"What about your father?"

"Irish, mostly."

"Is that where you get your green eyes?" Luke inquires. The muscles in Jacob's jaw tense and he shifts his gaze to Luke, his eyes narrowing in annoyance. He tries to hide his jealousy, but it's there, simmering just beneath the surface.

I shrug. "Must be." Our waiter comes out with our meal before we have a chance to further our discussion, and I'm relieved. I was worried someone would ask more questions about my mom, questions I'm not prepared to answer.

"Bon appetit," our waiter announces once our plates are settled in front of us. The aroma wafting from each dish is mouthwatering. We all thank him before he leaves.

I dig into my scallops first and savor their taste. They've been cooked in butter and garlic, two of my favorite ingredients. An involuntary moan escapes my lips. "This tastes so good," I proclaim.

Jacob's eyes darken and he watches me with a look of hunger, but not for food, I suspect. He shakes himself from his thoughts and skewers a piece of his steak before handing me his fork. "Here, try this." I take his offering and bite into the juiciest, most tender piece of steak I've ever eaten.

"That's incredible," I affirm, savoring the filet. "Here, try the scallops." I push a couple onto his plate for him to sample.

"Those are delicious," he praises after trying them. "That's what I'm getting next time." My pulse quickens and my heart flutters at the thought of a next time. "We'll have to come during the day so we can eat out on the deck that overlooks the river. I hear the view is spectacular." The prospect makes me giddy with excitement.

We enjoy the rest of dinner in relative silence after that, only making small talk here and there. I'm working on my third glass of wine when they clear our plates and bring the dessert menu. I'm not sure I can eat another bite, but I agree to share a slice of turtle cheesecake with Jacob. Unfortunately, we're subjected to watching Tiff and Luke feed each other crème brulee. Yuck.

Once our desserts are finished and we decline ordering anything else, the waiter brings our checks. Once again, I'm overcome with anxiety because I know Jacob's portion alone must be well over one hundred dollars. But he hands over his card without a second glance and signs the receipt when the waiter returns.

Jacob, unaware of my inner turmoil regarding our bill, grabs my hand and pulls me close, speaking into my ear. "Come with me. I want to show you something." He hands Luke his keys and asks him to get the car before leading me out onto the deck. There are a few other people outside, mostly men smoking cigars and drinking brown liquid from snifters at the small outdoor bar. We walk over to the far side, away from everyone else.

"Look," Jacob instructs, pointing out in front of us. The pink and orange hues of the fading sun sinking over the horizon dance across the surface of the New River, the deep blue of the night sky snuffing out the last rays of light. Soon, it will be illuminated by a million distant stars. It is absolutely breathtaking.

"It's beautiful." I admire the view as I lean against the railing.

Jacob wraps his arms around my waist from behind. "Not nearly as beautiful as you," he whispers in my ear, his hot breath causing goosebumps to rise on my arms. "I want to bring you back and show you this place in the daylight. Would you like to come here again? With me?"

"Of course. I'd love to," I answer without even thinking. I feel him smile against my neck. He places a kiss on my shoulder and turns me around to face him.

"We better get going. I'm afraid to leave those two unattended with my car." "You should be." He laughs at my quick response and grabs my hand, guiding me back to the entrance.

We make it out the front door just as the valet is handing the keys back to Luke. He tosses them to Jacob and slides into the back seat. Jacob opens the door for me and I climb in. As we take off out of the parking lot, Tiff leans forward and asks, "Where to now?"

"I was thinking maybe you guys could come back to our cabin and hang out with us for a bit," Luke answers. "We have a hot tub," he adds to make the offer more enticing.

Before I can open my mouth to object, Tiff chimes in. "That sounds like a great idea! Doesn't that sound like fun, Abby?"

Gee, thanks for putting me on the spot, bestie. "Well, uh..." I hesitate. "It sounds like fun, but, umm..." I try to think of a good reason not to go. It's not that I'm opposed to being in a hot tub with Jacob, but I feel like things are moving a little too fast, and I don't wanna give him the wrong idea. Call me old fashioned, but I'm not the kind of girl who puts out on the first date. Going home with him might lead him to believe otherwise.

I can feel Luke and Tiff staring at me, anticipating my lame excuse. I stammer for a minute, grasping for an answer. Suddenly, I remember one very important detail, one that will save me from seeming like a complete buzzkill. "We don't have bathing suits." Now if she suggests us going in our underwear, or skinny dipping, for that matter, I'll strangle her.

"Well, actually..." she begins nervously. Uh, oh. This can't be good. "I brought a couple bikinis with us," she reveals, holding up her cinched bag.

Of course she did.

"Wait a minute," I retort incredulously, turning in my seat to face her, my eyes narrowing with suspicion. "Did you *plan* this? How did you know we would need those?" The smug look on Luke's face and Tiff's impish grin give them away. Those two have been plotting this since before we left Tiff's house. I glance at Jacob, wondering if he had anything to do with it, but the tight set of his jaw reveals his irritation with their antics.

"Abby," Jacob begins, but can't seem to find the right words. "It's okay if you don't want to. I get it." I relax back in my seat, assured that he isn't trying to pressure me into anything.

"No, it's okay." I've always been good at reading people, and something in my gut tells me I'm safe with him. "We can go." Tiff's ear-piercing squeal of excitement fills the car and Jacob winces.

"Yay, we're getting in the hot tub!" Tiff declares, doing a little triumphant dance.

"Hey J, how 'bout some tunes, man?" Luke asks from behind me. Jacob reaches down to switch on his satellite radio.

"What do you like to listen to?"

I just shrug my shoulders. "Pretty much anything," I reply. I'm too nervous to care right now, flustered by the thought of soaking in a hot tub next to Jacob's deliciously enticing body. He starts to flip through the stations, stopping on a current pop hits channel. After a few minutes of listening to whatever garbage they're calling music these days, he starts pushing the buttons of his presets. When he clicks on the preset for a nineties station, the familiar opening chord of one of my favorite songs emanates from the speakers. "Oh, leave it here!" I exclaim.

He laughs lightheartedly at my enthusiasm. "Okay." I reach down to crank the volume up, all my anxiety floating away as I prepare to sing along. I know Tiff will join me in the second verse because we've done this a thousand times.

My irritation with my friend quickly forgotten, I turn to her and she leans up on the console between Jacob and me. Together we belt out the opening line. She giggles as I begin imitating Warren G, busting out the first verse to "Regulate" without hesitation. Jacob glances over at me with an expression I can't quite pinpoint. Impressed? Amused? I'm not sure if it's the wine or something else, but I feel completely at ease rapping in front of him.

At the end of my verse, Tiff joins in with Nate Dogg's rhymes. She does her best to imitate his deep voice, causing Jacob to chuckle. His laughter is like a drug, intoxicating and addicting.

I join back in with Warren's next lines, expecting Tiff to follow me up again. Jacob beats her to the punch, surprising us both as his voice fills the space between us. He nails every line and every word of Nate's second verse, and now I'm the one who's impressed. I did not expect this guy who looks like a Tommy Hilfiger ad to be so familiar with nineties gangster rap. I guess you really *can't* judge a book by its cover.

Once he finishes his verse, I pick up with the next one and we go back and forth through the rest of the song. When I look back, neither Tiff nor Luke appear amused. Tiff may even be pouting since Jacob stole her thunder. I don't care. I'm having too much fun and from what I can tell, so is Jacob.

When the song is over, I lower the volume on the radio and turn in my seat to face him. "I can't believe you know that song!"

"I do," he confirms with a wide grin. "It's one of my favorites. And you killed it, by the way," he flatters me.

I'm surprised to be having this much fun with him. Everything feels so relaxed and natural. I've never been able to let loose so easily and be myself around a guy before. It's refreshing.

"How did you get into this kind of music, if you don't mind me asking?"

"It's what my parents used to listen to. It was popular when I was little, and they were very young. They let me listen to stuff they probably shouldn't have. I grew up with these guys. Warren G, Dre, Snoop, Biggie, Tupac. It just stuck with me," I explain. "How do *you* know the song so well?"

His grin fades at my inquiry and I immediately regret asking the question. "Don't laugh," he implores grimly, and I nod. Why would I laugh? "Promise?"

"Of course."

"I had to take a music class my sophomore year of college," he begins. "One of my assignments was to write a paper on a genre of music and how it has influenced American culture. Most people chose pop, jazz, or rock 'n roll. I chose hip hop with a concentration on gangster rap. Needless to say, my professor didn't like my choice, but my paper was well written and well researched. That's how I discovered "Regulate," through my research," he explains.

"I presented a lot of ideas he obviously hadn't thought of before. Sometimes Ivy League professors can be such pretentious twats," he adds with a sly smile. I want to laugh at his use of that word, but I balk at the mention of an Ivy League education. He just confirmed what I already suspected.

"Luckily, he gave me an 'A.'" He shrugs, but I can tell he's proud of that. "Before that, I hadn't listened to much rap from that era, or anything before then, really. My parents were really strict," he explains. "My experience with hip hop began with Kanye and 'Lil Wayne when I was sneaking and listening to it with Luke after school."

"Aw, that's so sad," I tease, eliciting a laugh from him.

"Okay, smart-ass." He reaches over and squeezes my thigh just above the knee. I jerk and try to fight the giggles bubbling up in my throat. I'm extremely ticklish and a little tipsy, and he just hit gold.

"Hey, no fair!" I protest between gasps of laughter. "You're driving so I can't fight back."

"Exactly." He grins mischievously before releasing my leg and grabbing my hand, interlacing our fingers. This simple act sends a jolt of electricity up my arm. He doesn't release my hand until we arrive at his cabin.

Chapter Eleven

Abby

"Home sweet home," Luke announces and jumps out of the car. My eyes follow him, widening in surprise as he steps onto an expansive front porch, a tiny gasp parting my lips. I press my back deeper into the passenger seat, shrinking away from the sight in front of me. When Jacob and Luke mentioned they were staying in a cabin, this is not what I envisioned. This is more like a rustic mansion with its cedar columns and ornate trusses. Jacob opens my door and leads me onto the porch, my eyes taking in every detail of the luxury cabin's exterior. I run my fingers over the back of an Adirondack chair as Jacob slides his key into the lock and opens the heavy, solid wood front door.

"Wow, this place is insane," Tiff whispers in amazement. She's right. This place *is* insane, and I'm insane for agreeing to come here. That relaxed, easy feeling from earlier dissipates. I want to turn tail and run but Jacob grabs my hand and leads me into the foyer before I have the chance to bolt.

"Would you lovely ladies like to see the grand tour?" Luke asks in the most gentlemanly manner he can conjure. He bows and holds his hand out to Tiff.

"We'd love to," she replies, slipping her hand into his.

Jacob and Luke show us the living room and kitchen first. I've never seen such a beautifully decorated cabin before. Granite counter tops sit atop dark wood cabinets. There's a double oven and a ceramic cooktop, and all the appliances are stainless steel. The entire kitchen is immaculate. I'd almost be afraid to cook in here. I'm quite surprised that these two guys have been able to keep the place so clean.

We move on to the living room, which is just as tidy as the kitchen. The hardwood floors are pristine and a fresh clean scent permeates the air. When you rent out a place like this, it must come with maid service.

The family room is our next stop. A large flat screen TV rests atop a stone fireplace with a leather sectional facing it. A pool table occupies the opposite side of the room with a set of double doors leading out to the balcony just beyond.

"That's where the hot tub is."

I make the mistake of turning towards the sound of Luke's voice, whirling around just as he grabs Tiff by the ass, grinding his groin into her and shoving his tongue down her throat. Eww.

Jacob mutters something under his breath and leads me down the hall. He must be just as repulsed by their PDA as I am. "This is the main bathroom," he tells me, opening the door to yet another pristine room. "There are three bedrooms upstairs, plus another bathroom. Down the hall," he asserts, pointing towards a closed door, "is the master bedroom. That's where I'm at."

"Can I see it?" The question takes us both by surprise, but it's too late to take it back now. I hope Jacob doesn't get the wrong idea. I'm just curious to see the rest of the cabin. Yeah, we'll go with that.

He recovers his cool demeanor quickly. "Sure," he replies, and I follow him down the hall. He opens the door and ushers me through it before hitting the light switch. If the exterior of the cabin made me gasp, then the master bedroom takes my breath away. The room looks utterly cozy and inviting with its rich hardwood floors and warm, neutral tones. A huge four poster bed rests beneath a vaulted ceiling, an ornately decorated rug protecting the hardwood from its heavy posts. There's a coffee table and set of chairs facing a wall mounted flat screen TV. Another set of double doors leads out to a private balcony.

Somehow, without even thinking about it, I've gravitated toward the bed. I run my hands over the soft material of the grey and cream comforter, noticing that the bed is neatly made and the entire room is spotless. Impressive.

I'm still admiring the bedroom and its stylish, modern décor when Jacob strides to the far side of the room and flips another switch.

"Check this out," he directs, stepping through another door.

"Wow," I breathe before I can stop myself. "This bathroom is amazing! It looks like something out of a magazine." I glance around the room, taking it all in. The double sinks, massive shower, and the coolest bathtub I've ever seen. "I'd never leave this room if I were you." Jacob chuckles and turns to lead me back to the bedroom. I fight the urge to crawl in the tub and turn on the water.

"Do you want to grab a drink? Or are you ready to get in the hot tub?" Jacob asks when we step back into the hallway.

No, I want to take a bubble bath and I want you to join me. "A drink would be nice." It might help me relax a little. I'm a ball of nervous excitement right now.

We make our way to the kitchen where Jacob pulls a bottle of wine from the small fridge nestled under the island. "A glass of wine?" He asks, holding up the bottle

"Sure." I'm kind of surprised he keeps any here. He and Luke don't seem like the type to sit around and sip wine. Maybe he wanted to be prepared in case I agreed to come home with him. Or... maybe I'm not the first girl he's brought back here. He hasn't been in town long enough to have hooked up with anybody else yet, right? I push that thought out of my mind, hoping it's not a possibility. I need to take Tiff's advice and just relax and have fun.

Jacob pours me a glass of wine, red this time, and hands it to me before grabbing a beer for himself. I take a tentative sip as he pops the top off his bottle. It's not quite as good as the Moscato from the restaurant, but it's pretty tasty.

"So," Jacob begins, leaning against the counter across from me. "Tell me more about yourself." He takes a long drag of his beer and sets it down before placing both hands on the countertop behind him.

"What do you wanna know?" I ask as I lean back against the kitchen island.

He smiles at me and my insides turn to Jell-O. His smile is so sexy, so alluring. "Everything," he replies.

I wrack my brain for something to tell him that doesn't involve my family. I don't want him to ask about my mother. That's a wall I built very high and for good reason. "Well, let's see," I begin. *I need to keep this light. Don't want to scare him away.* "My birthday is April seventeenth. I love white chocolate. My favorite color is lavender." I pause, trying to think of something else to avoid talking about anything too deep. "And I'm a runner."

"A runner?"

"Yeah. I mean, I used to run cross country and track back in high school. Now, I just run to stay in shape. Plus, I find that it's a great stress reliever."

His eyebrows furrow slightly and I wonder what I said to cause that look, but it passes quickly. "I know what you mean about the stress relief," he admits. "I don't mind running, but I prefer weight lifting, CrossFit, stuff like that."

No kidding. I bet he's ripped underneath that shirt. Suddenly, all I can think about is ripping his shirt off, buttons flying in all directions, and revealing his sculpted torso. I finally snap out of it and realize I'm staring at his chest like a hungry lioness stalking her next meal. I pull my eyes up to meet his and see them burning with desire. He knows I was just mentally undressing him. I look away and sip my wine, face flushed with embarrassment.

I peer back up at him and meet his gaze. "So, what about you?" I ask. "I've told you about me. Now I wanna know something about you." I'm trying to shift the focus away from me, but I really *do* want to know more about him.

He pushes off the counter and steps towards me, nearly closing the gap between us. "I'm twenty-three and an engineering major. I played basketball in high school." He moves in closer and places his hands on the island counter behind me, effectively caging me in. "And my favorite color," he pauses and leans in close, his lips just a whisper from mine, "is green," he finishes, staring deeply into my eyes. I reach up and brush my mouth against his, surprising us both. I back away, but don't get very far. In a split second, I'm pulled against his chest with one of his hands pressed into my lower back and the other cupping the back of my neck as he crushes his lips to mine.

I pull him even closer as he slides his tongue into my willing mouth. I nip lightly at his lower lip and his appreciative groan makes my lower belly clench. I squeeze my thighs together to quell the throbbing need burning inside me. He releases my neck and wraps both arms around me. I run my hands up his hard biceps, resting them on his shoulders as he continues to kiss me until I'm breathless.

His hands slide down to cup my bottom, squeezing as he lifts me in the air before placing me on the island countertop. I gasp as cold granite hits the backs of my thighs, but the discomfort is quickly forgotten when his mouth covers mine and he moves to stand between my legs. He leans down to trail hot kisses down my shoulder as he tugs on the lacy sleeve of my dress. It slides down my arm, exposing more of my skin for his exploration. He kisses his way up my neck, cupping my other cheek, and I tilt my head back to give him easier access to my heated flesh. He works his way back to my mouth and devours it in a searing kiss.

Jacob's hands are all over me and I'm so turned on I can barely think. He consumes my every thought and everything else fades away. A small moan escapes my lips when he cups my breast and brushes his thumb over the tender bud. A ripple of pleasure shoots through my center and I arch my back, spreading my legs further apart, letting him in. He grabs my hips and slides me closer, pressing his erection against my throbbing core. I nearly whimper when he pulls back and breaks contact. But he grabs my hand and places it on his hardened length, groaning into my mouth when I squeeze.

I let go and push my fingers into his hair, guiding his lips to my neck. He obliges and leans down to suck and nibble my over-sensitized skin. His right hand caresses my leg and he pushes my dress farther up my thighs. I nearly come undone when he brushes the edge of my panties, hooking two of his fingers just inside the seam. I know he must be able to tell how wet I am just from that brief contact. I want more. I want him to touch me again, to move my panties aside and use those long fingers to bring me to the brink before sending me over the edge.

Jacob completely overwhelms my senses, making me forget that we're not alone in this house. When I hear someone clear their throat behind me, I jump and try to pull away from him. He removes his lips from my skin and his hand from between my legs but doesn't release me. He looks down at me with a reassuring grin, coaxing me to relax. I don't think he wants me to be embarrassed by our little display, but I can't help it. We've been caught, and I'm mortified. We are just as bad as Tiff and Luke. I can tell by the tight set of his jaw that he isn't happy about being interrupted, but he's not embarrassed like I am, nor is he ashamed of what happened.

I crane my neck around to see Luke and Tiff behind me. Tiff's brows are furrowed with a look of concern, but Luke's knowing smirk causes my cheeks to redden and heat rises into my face. He knows exactly what we were doing. How long did they stand there and watch before making their presence known?

"Um, we were just heading out to the hot tub. Thought we'd check and see if y'all wanted to join us," Tiff says cautiously.

For the first time since turning to look at them, I notice Tiff is wearing a black bikini and Luke has on navy blue board shorts with large white hibiscus flowers on them. They are both holding towels and Tiff has her cinched bag in hand as well.

I turn back to Jacob and he peers down at me with those panty-dropping blue eyes. "What do ya say? Wanna get in the hot tub?"

"Sure," I agree, even though what we really need is a cold shower.

He gives me a sultry smile. "Okay," he responds, wrapping his arms around me. "We'll be out in a minute," he informs our friends.

"I'll just set your bathing suit on the table here," Tiff answers.

I relax when I hear their retreating footsteps. At the sound of the balcony doors opening and closing, I release the breath I didn't realize I was holding.

"Sorry about that," Jacob offers, pressing his forehead against mine. His eyes are shut tightly and he looks as though he's struggling with something. "I just couldn't help myself. You look so beautiful and I had to taste your lips again. It's all I've been able to think about." At this, he pulls back and opens his eyes to look down at me, and my heart hammers against my chest. If he keeps talking to me like that, we may never make it to the hot tub. He bends down and brushes his lips gently against mine. "You ready?"

I nod my head in response. He grabs my waist and lifts me off the counter, placing me on shaky legs. Picking up the bag Tiff left behind, he leads me down the hall to the main bathroom.

"I would offer to let you change in my room, but I'd never be able to leave you alone in there, knowing you're naked and near my bed." Jacob kisses me sweetly and turns to walk towards his bedroom, but stops and looks back at me. "And make sure you lock that door. I don't need any more temptation."

My knees start to buckle and I hold on to the door frame to keep from melting into the floor. The look in his eyes tells me it's taking every bit of self-control he has not to throw me over his shoulder, take me to his bed, and ravage me right now. *What an enticing thought.*

Before I have a chance to chase him down the hallway and beg him to take me, I slip into the bathroom and shut the door. I pull the mint-colored bikini out of Tiff's bag and inspect it. *Where the hell is the rest of it?* There's barely any material here. Well, this is just fantastic. Tiff knows I'm more modest in my swimwear choices than she is, yet she packed me the skimpiest damn bathing suit she could find. What kind of friend does that?

The kind that wants me to get laid, apparently.

It's too late to back out now, so I sigh in defeat and slip my dress and undergarments off. I put on the bikini and turn to face the mirror. Whoa. I don't know how Tiff ever wears this. The triangle top barely covers *my* boobs enough to be considered decent. There's no way she can wear this in public without causing a scene.

The one hundred eighty-seven bobby pins that secure my hair into an updo are giving me a headache. I remove them and to my surprise, there are only fifteen. I shake my hair out and let it fall over my shoulders as I massage my scalp. Praying that Tiff thought to pack a hair tie, I dig into the bag, searching until my fingers find the familiar elastic band. Jackpot!

I take one last look in the mirror, making sure nothing is out of place, and open the door. I step out and start to pull my hair up into a ponytail just as Jacob is passing by. His eyes widen when he notices me and I could almost swear he lets out a low growl. I barely have time to drink him in – his sexy bare chest, washboard abs, and muscular, broad shoulders – before he presses me against the wall and captures my mouth in a steamy, urgent kiss. He picks me up and I instinctively wrap my legs around his waist. He seems to have a thing for picking me up and I like it. My fingers dig into the hard muscles of his shoulders as he devours my mouth. I don't want him to stop this time, but he pulls away, breathing heavily before placing me back on my feet. His body is still pressed against mine and I feel his arousal against my stomach. He seems torn, as though he's considering what his next move should be.

"Come on," he announces, grabbing my hand and leading me down the hallway. "We better get out there before they come looking for us again."

He's right. If we stay in here much longer Luke and Tiff will know why, and I'm in no hurry to get caught in a compromising position. Again. So, I mask my disappointment as best I can and follow him outside.

Chapter Twelve

Jacob

CAN'T BELIEVE HOW UNBEARABLY PERFECT Abby looks in that bikini. My hands and groin ache with the need to touch her. I'm trying to be a gentleman, but the testosterone coursing through my veins makes me think like a caveman. She already looked good enough to devour in that sexy black dress. It was an appropriate length for dinner at the Lodge, but still short enough to show off her shapely, tan legs. And that cut-out in the back... I had to stifle a groan when my fingers brushed the skin of her bare, sculpted back.

I wanted more. I wanted to touch her everywhere, to have my hands cover every alluring inch of her body. That's the only reason I didn't sit next to her at dinner. I knew I couldn't resist the temptation to touch her, to slide my hand up her thigh and under that dress. I needed to keep my distance, to keep her just out of my reach.

Once we got to the cabin, all I could think about was peeling that dress off her irresistible, receptive body. And I almost did. If Luke and Tiffany hadn't interrupted us, I may have taken her right there on that kitchen island. It's probably a good thing they walked in when they did. Abby deserves better than a quick fuck on a cold, hard countertop. She should be savored, worshipped. She deserves someone who will take his time pleasuring her, meeting her every desire. I hope I get the chance to do so, but for now, I need to slow things down with her.

I'll be damned if I didn't come dangerously close to losing all my self-control when she stepped out of that bathroom. I was done, completely gone when I saw her smooth, flat stomach, perfect, full breasts, and curvy hips. She's a wet dream come true, as Luke would say. He's a damn pig, but it's the truth in this case. I barely had time to take in the ink sprawled across her left rib cage before practically tackling her. Poor girl must think I'm an animal.

"Hey, hey, there they are," Luke announces when we step outside. "Didn't think you two would *ever* make it out here." He winks at Abby and smiles knowingly at me. My grip tightens on her hand and I focus all my attention on relaxing so I don't crush her fingers. I look down to see her cheeks flush at his suggestive remark. He is such a douche.

"Come on, guys. Get in. This hot tub is amazing," Tiff invites, giggling like a school girl. She's oblivious to the fact that her date is checking out her best friend, his eyes scanning her over from head to toe. Or more likely, chest to thighs.

His gaze lands on my face and he smirks. My teeth grind together, my jaws clenched so tight they could snap. I know I have no right to feel possessive over her, but I know my friend. Nothing has ever stopped him from putting the moves on a woman I'm seeing. This time is different, though. I know we just met a few days ago, but she has totally rocked my world, consuming my thoughts every waking moment.

Abby walks over to the hot tub and checks the temperature before easing down into it across from Luke and Tiff. I catch another glimpse of her tattoo, but can't quite make it out. I'm curious to see what she deems worthy of gracing her perfect, flawless skin for life. I climb in and sit next to her, putting my arm around her waist and pulling her into my side. I want her as close to me as possible. Her body feels incredible nestled into mine. I could stay like this for hours.

It's a cool night for this time of year and the warmth feels good on my aching muscles. I'm already sore from our excursion earlier today. "Yo, J, you look like you need a beer," Luke declares and tosses me a cold one. He's got a cooler full of them next to the hot tub. Shocker.

"Thanks, man," I reply. I ignore the niggling thought in the back of my mind that Luke drinks too damn much and pop the top off of my beer. I probably shouldn't have more than one or two myself since I'll need to take Abby home later. I want more than anything for her to spend the night with me, but that's not going to happen. Judging by her shy, demure countenance, she's not the type to hop into bed with someone she just met, and I think she's been pushed far enough tonight. Asking her to stay will probably send her running for the hills. Besides, if I get her in my bed, I'm going to seduce her, and I'm not sure she's ready for that.

My thoughts completely consumed with images of Abby writhing with pleasure in my bed, I don't realize anybody is speaking to me until I hear Luke's gruff voice bark out my name. My eyes snap to his face and his ornery grin tells me he knows exactly where my head was just at.

"Dude, Tiff was trying to ask you something, but you were a million miles away."

"Oh, uh, sorry," I stammer, trying to hide my befuddlement. "What was the question?"

Tiff presses her lips together to shield her amusement. "I have several, actually." My unease builds as her Cheshire Cat smile grows. I'm not sure I'm going to like where this is headed. I have nothing to hide, but there is much I don't wish to divulge just yet. "You seem awfully enamored with my friend, but we don't really know anything about you. You're somewhat of a mystery to us, Jacob Daniels."

"What do you want to know?"

"What you do for a living, what your family is like, have you ever been arrested… stuff like that." An impish grin tugs at the corner of her mouth.

"You know, the basics." I wince a little at her last question. Technically, I've never been arrested. *Detained* is not under arrest. Either way, I'll pass on that one. And I'm a little apprehensive when it comes to telling Abby about my family. I guess I'll settle on school.

"I'm still a student right now. I'll start the last year of my master's program in the fall."

"What are you studying?"

"Engineering."

"Engineering? Impressive," Tiff replies, giving Abby a hopeful look. "I've heard engineering programs are really tough."

"It's definitely a challenge. You have to be dedicated, but it'll be worth it."

"What will you do once you graduate?" Abby asks.

"I have no idea," I reply honestly before taking another drink from my bottle. "I'll probably end up working for an engineering firm for a few years to get some experience. Then I can pursue something I actually care about." I leave it at that, not wanting to sound like a PSA from UNICEF.

"What *do* you care about?" Tiff presses, her eyes flicking to Abby briefly.

"Jacob here thinks he's going to save the world with clean water," Luke goads me. He doesn't see the point in actually *participating* in humanitarian efforts, just donating money to others who are willing to do the "dirty work."

Abby and Tiff look at me inquisitively, confusion etched on their faces.

"There are a lot of people in this world who don't have access to clean drinking water or proper sanitation," I explain. "A few organizations are making great strides to change that, and I want to be part of it."

"That's very noble. I doubt many people think much about that."

Abby thinks I'm noble. I'll be damned if that doesn't make me want to slay dragons and become her knight in shining armor.

I nod my head. "Most of us just take those things for granted because we've always had them. We have no idea what it's like to live without it, but people die every day because they don't have enough food or clean water to drink." Hell, I'd never thought of it either, until I visited Africa with my dad when I was sixteen and saw it for myself. It sparked my curiosity, and that curiosity grew into a passion I knew I had to pursue.

"That's awful," Tiff agrees.

"Tell them about that internship you're up for," Luke prods. Jerk. H knows I don't like telling people about it.

"They don't want to hear about that," I declare, waving him off. The fewer people who know about it the better. My chances of being chosen are slim. "Besides, I don't even know if I got it yet. I'm up against two other grad students from my program alone."

"I'd like to hear about it." How can I say no to Abby when she's looking up at me like I'm the hero in her own personal fairy tale?

I study her sweet face and soft smile a moment before continuing. "There's this non-profit in D.C. that's working to get clean drinking water to remote areas of Africa, the Middle East, and Asia, and they allow engineering students to participate in a six-week internship every summer. They get to help develop irrigation and sanitation systems, build wells, and repair and improve any existing infrastructure. Every year, the organization recruits a handful of interns to take overseas. It's extremely competitive because an internship like this one looks good on job applications, but that's not why I'm doing it. Well, trying to do it. There's no guarantee I'll be chosen."

"I'm sure your dad could pull a few strings. Didn't your parents donate a shit ton of money to them last year? Besides, a United States Senator with friends in high places can probably make just about anything happen," Luke smirks. I want to wipe that stupid look off his face with my fist, but I grit my teeth instead.

"Senator?"

Abby's confused look makes my chest constrict with guilt. I haven't told her yet who I am, or who my father is. I'm not exactly ready for that conversation, but Luke can't keep his trap shut. Before I have a chance to explain, he opens that big mouth of his again.

"Didn't Jacob tell you? His old man is Arthur Daniels." She glances between us perplexed, the significance of the name lost on her. "You know," Luke prompts. "The senator from Virginia." That's it. I'm going to fucking kill him. My father's name and face have been all over the media lately due to his

᠌dership responsibilities and popularity among his constituents. ᠌ ᠌ way she doesn't know who he is.

᠌y's eyes widen with recognition and shock, and she starts to fidget in ᠌ms. "Oh. I didn't know that."

Great. She already seems uncomfortable with our socioeconomic ᠌fferences. I can't imagine how learning that my father is a politician makes her feel. Money and power don't attract girls like her.

I guess it's time to come clean now. "That's why we're here, actually. I needed to get away. My father has gotten a lot of media attention lately, and sometimes that attention extends to the rest of his family. I just needed a break from it all." I want to kiss the worried frown from her pretty face. "I'm sorry I didn't tell you." It's not like I wasn't going to. I was definitely going to tell her. I think.

"It's okay," she concedes, her posture relaxing again. "I'm sure you don't want to be defined by who your parents are. Nobody does." She smiles up at me, but there's pain behind her eyes. "I couldn't imagine living in the public eye. Do reporters bother you often?"

"Not all the time. They focus mainly on my dad. I did have a reporter approach me on campus one day between classes." The memory of that day still pisses me off. The guy was spouting off some bullshit about my dad being a corporate puppet and taking bribes. "I let him know I didn't appreciate him coming at me like that, and the whole incident ended up online." I don't tell her about breaking his camera and nearly breaking his fucking jaw. Hence, being detained. Luke grabbed me before I could land the first punch. Thank God. I would have ended up in jail, and my dad would have gotten even more negative publicity.

"My parents went ape shit. I don't know if they were more upset that a reporter tracked me down at school, or that I made the senator look bad." Okay, that's enough. I've said too much already. She doesn't need to know any more about my messed-up family life.

Abby looks at me sympathetically and I can't help but smile at her. This girl has probably been through more shit than I can even imagine, yet she can still find it in her heart to have compassion for the spoiled rich kid who has never wanted for anything... except for maybe a normal life and family.

"Do you have any siblings?" Abby asks.

"Yes, I have a brother, Logan. He's fifteen." I hesitate, debating whether I should tell her the rest. I guess it's best to be completely open and honest with her. It just hurts so damn bad to talk about it. "I had a sister. Her name was Peyton. She died when she was seven. Leukemia." I take a deep breath and let it out before continuing. The hardest part is thinking about the life she never got the chance to live. "She would have graduated high school this year." Another reason I needed to get out of there. The memories of her, in that house, I just couldn't take it anymore. It's not as bad when I'm away at school. Her dainty laughter and cotton candy smell don't haunt me there.

I stare down at the water bubbling around me, trying to suppress the emotions causing my chest to ache. I've never really gotten over Peyton's death. She was my little sister and I was her big brother. I was supposed to protect her from everything, but nothing I did stopped the cancer from consuming her frail body and claiming her life.

"I'm so sorry," Abby conveys, placing her hand on my chest, comforting me. I reach down to cup her hand with mine and pull her closer to me, nuzzling her head under my chin. She smells sweet, like vanilla and amber. It feels better just having her close, feeling her skin against mine. She brushes her fingers lightly across the tattoo covering my left pec. "Is that what the P stands for? Peyton?"

"Yes," I reply simply. The tattoo is a black, Celtic "P" with a circular border. Between the inner and outer circles is an intricate Celtic knot design. "I got it the day I turned eighteen. My parents were furious. They were even more pissed off when I told them I wasn't going to law school."

"Man, I wish I could have seen the look on Art and Evelyn's faces when you broke *that* news to them," Luke adds with a laugh, trying to lighten the mood.

"It wasn't pretty," I confirm. That was a really bad time in the Daniels household, but they eventually got over it.

"So, what about you?" I ask Abby. I don't want to reveal any more about my family, so I intentionally shift the focus onto her. "I saw that you have some ink, too."

She hesitates, uncertainty marring her features. After a moment, she stands up and raises her arm, revealing the tattoo sprawled over her rib cage. The dream catcher covering a large portion of her side has turquoise feathers and brown beads dangling from the bottom. Black, cursive script runs beside it in three lines. It's a beautiful work of art.

"Don't let yesterday use up too much of today," I read aloud.

"A Cherokee proverb. It's one of my grandmother's favorite sayings." Smart lady.

"Sounds like good advice," Luke admits before taking another swig of beer.

Abby sinks back down beside me and slides her hand into mine. "So, what are your plans after graduation?" I ask. "How will you use that biology degree?"

"My goal is to become a naturalist. Ultimately, I want to work for the national park service."

This girl just keeps getting more and more interesting. I can't envision this sweet, sensual woman dressed as a park ranger in drab khakis and a hunter green polo, teaching sixth graders about plants and bugs. Although, if anybody can make that outfit sexy, it's her.

"Having the opportunity to work outside surrounded by nature every day would be a dream come true."

"What are you, like, some tree-hugging hippie or something?"

"Luke!" Tiff screeches, nailing him in the ribs with her elbow. He lets out a grunt and grasps his side.

"Damn it, woman! What was that for?" He laughs, rubbing his side dramatically. Tiff rolls her eyes and crosses her arms over her chest.

Abby just snickers and shakes her head. Even though she's being a good sport and not letting Luke's idiotic remarks bother her, I still want to drown his ass. I still might if he manages to upset her.

"No," Abby replies, still laughing. "I am not a 'tree-hugging hippie,' as you put it, but I understand there must be balance. I just enjoy and appreciate what this earth has to offer. The beauty of it, the solitude. It's peaceful, and that's something I need when my chaotic life gets out of hand. My grandmother always taught me that life's most difficult questions can be answered if you just take the time to listen to what nature tells you."

"So... your grandmother is a tree-hugging hippie, then?" Tiffany gasps at Luke's impudence and splashes him, hoping he'll get the hint and keep his mouth shut.

Abby and I look at each other and when our eyes meet, we know we're thinking the same thing. I give her a wink and we shove our hands forward in the water, splashing Luke. Howls of laughter echo into the night as a soaking wet Luke shakes water from his black hair. A mischievous grin spreads across his face as fat droplets of water fall from his chin.

"Oh, it's on now," he threatens playfully. We begin splashing around in the hot tub, water spilling out over the sides. By the time we're done, the four of us are dripping wet, the girls' makeup running down their faces in black rivulets. I rub both of my thumbs under Abby's eyes, trying to remove some of the inky smudges, but my efforts are futile.

"I must look pretty ridiculous with my raccoon eyes and wet hair," Abby titters as I brush the damp tendrils from her smiling face.

"I think you look beautiful," I remark sincerely. Nothing could make her any less in my eyes. Before she has a chance to argue, I lean down and place a swift kiss on her lips. "Come on," I instruct, standing up. "Let's get you dried off." She reaches up to take my hand, and I help her out of the hot tub.

I hand her a towel before grabbing one for myself and wrapping it around my waist. She dries off quickly and encircles her tiny torso with the towel, tucking it under her arms. I take her back inside and lead her to my bedroom. It's all I can do not to throw her on my bed and peel that wet bikini off her. She follows me to the bathroom, where I find her a washcloth and some soap so she can wash her face. She does look kind of ridiculous, but in an adorable way. She catches my grin and lets out a small chuckle.

"I know," she answers. "I look like a mess right now."

My beautiful mess.

"Do you want some clothes to put on?" Surely, she won't want to put that dress back on. It can't possibly be comfortable.

"That would be great. Thank you."

I retrieve a t-shirt and a pair of boxers for her and leave her alone to change. I slip out of my board shorts and grab a pair of jogging pants to throw on. I'm trying not to think of Abby on the other side of that door, naked, wet hair clinging to her full, round breasts. I'm trying but failing, and now I have to find a way to hide my hard-on. I don't know why I bother. She's already felt it. She knows what she does to me. I don't want to scare her off, though, so I do my best to calm myself down.

Abby steps out of the bathroom looking sexier than anyone has a right to look in my underwear. Her eyes find mine across the room and I feel the heat of her gaze. She takes in my shirtless, barefoot appearance and a sly grin pulls up the sides of her mouth. Before I can make my move, she takes off running and leaps onto my bed, bouncing as she lands in the middle. In this moment, I see her free spirit shining through. There is something wild and untamable in her. I want to find it and explore it. Will she let it out just for me?

I hop up on the bed next to her and pull her into my arms. She rests her head on my chest and draws lazy circles over my tattoo with her fingers. She's quiet for a long time and were she not still caressing my skin, I would think she had fallen asleep. But then she speaks.

"Will you tell me about her?" She doesn't have to say her name. I know who she's talking about.

I inhale a deep breath before I begin. "She could light up a room like nobody I know. Her big, wide smile was infectious. She was sweet and playful. She never complained. Not even when the chemo made her sick and took all her hair. She wore these ridiculously colored wigs that my mom found for her." I smile to myself at the memory. "Purple, blue, pink, yellow. She loved them."

It was the only outrageous request she made the whole time she was sick. My mother hated them, but they made Peyton happy so she just smiled and told her how pretty she looked. It hurts thinking about how much I miss her and how helpless I felt, watching the beautiful, vibrant girl I knew and loved waste away.

"Hey," Abby whispers, running her soft fingers over my jaw. I don't realize until she does this that my whole body has tensed up and my eyes are squeezed shut with my brow furrowed. I open them and attempt to unravel some of the tension in my muscles. "I'm sorry." The sadness in her eyes is like a dagger through the heart.

"It's okay," I assure her. "I just have a hard time talking about her. But it's nice to be able to share all the happy memories I have of her with someone." My family never talks about Peyton. Other than the few family photos she's in and a locked door to a pink and purple bedroom, it's as if she never existed.

My mother barely survived her death. Peyton was her little girl, her angel. She hasn't been the same since. Poor Logan was barely four and our mother neglected him, nearly grieving herself to death. My father wasn't much help, either. He dealt with his grief in his own way, by burying himself in his work. He was a broken man, but he couldn't allow us, or the nation, to see that.

Finally, after months of seclusion in our house, Mom emerged a changed woman. She dried her eyes and, as far as I know, has never shed another tear. She threw herself into her role as a senator's wife. She knew what everybody expected of her and she gave it to them. With one exception: her remaining children. After a while, though, she realized she still had two boys who needed her. It was like a switch was flipped, and she became the fierce mama bear she is today.

Abby cups my face with her delicate hand and brings her lips to mine. The kiss is soft and gentle. It feels good to have her comforting me, and I realize I've never opened up to anyone this much. I feel safe with her. I know she won't tell my secrets or try to use them against me. I have to be careful with the girls back home and at school. Growing up in politics is like growing up in a shark tank. The charlatans won't hesitate to use your pain against you or sell your secrets to the highest bidder.

I deepen our kiss, wanting to feel even closer to her. She responds by opening her mouth and sliding her tongue along my top lip. I groan in appreciation and grab her hips, pulling her on top of me. My fingers trail up her thighs, dipping under the hem of my boxers. She straddles me with one knee on each side of my hips and I dig my fingers into her flesh, pressing my growing erection into her. She moans and rocks her hips against me. My hands move to her hair, holding her mouth to mine. I don't want this to end, but if I don't pull away, this is going to go farther than it should.

I want to pleasure her. I want to be able to give and not take. But I am a man, and I don't know if I'm strong enough to resist the temptation. I want her. There's no denying that, but this is about more than just sex. I *like* her. I want to *know* her. And I certainly don't want to rush this.

I break the connection between our lips and pull away, both of us panting. My arousal throbs against her, trying to find release.

"Abby." My voice is gruff and thick with need.

"Jacob, I..." she starts, but there's hesitation to her words. She wants more, but she's scared. Her heart is guarded and I don't know why. "I should probably be getting home soon."

I sit up, her still straddling me, and pull her body against mine. "Okay," I tell her. "I'll take you home." I give her a lingering kiss before releasing her, and she slides off the bed. I throw on a shirt and lead her out of my room.

We go in search of Tiffany so I can take them both home, but she and Luke are nowhere to be found. They've probably gone up to his room and won't be coming back down any time soon. Abby lets out a defeated sigh when she realizes where Tiff is. She pulls out her phone and calls her. I go to retrieve my shoes and keys and give her some privacy to talk to her friend.

When I return, she's ending her call, annoyance flashing in her eyes. "She says she's staying here," she tells me. "She refuses to leave."

Luke probably refuses to let her go.

I chuckle silently at her chagrin. She can be so easygoing at times, but so serious at others. Hmm, maybe if Tiff stays, Abby will stay too. "If you don't want to leave her here, you're more than welcome to stay."

She looks up at me, biting her lip in contemplation. She's quiet for a moment, mentally weighing her options. "I can't," she answers finally. "I told my grandmother I would be home tonight. She'll be expecting me," she finishes mournfully, giving me a weak smile. I smile back, trying to mask my disappointment and nod my head in understanding. "Let me just grab my things."

When she walks back out of the bathroom, my howl of laughter causes her to scowl at me. She looks adorably ridiculous wearing my boxers and t-shirt with four-inch heels.

"Don't laugh," she tells me, but she can't keep from grinning. "I don't have any other shoes to wear."

"Take those off," I instruct, pointing to her feet, "and come here." She obeys reluctantly and walks towards me, squealing when I scoop her up and cradle her in my arms. I walk to the front door and pull it open, careful not to drop her.

"What are you doing?" she asks as a pleased smile spreads across her face.

"I don't want you looking like a crazy person walking to my car." She rolls her eyes at me, but her smile grows.

I set her down gently in the passenger seat and slide in beside her, turning the radio down low, just loud enough to make out the song that's playing. It's still on the nineties station from earlier and Boyz II Men's "I'll Make Love to You" plays softly over the speakers. On second thought, maybe I should crank the sound up. I reach over and grab her hand. Noticing her fingers are a bit cold, I bring them to my mouth and breathe warm air onto them. She sucks in a sharp breath and her eyes flare with desire. I turn my attention back to the road and kiss the back of her hand.

"Do you have any plans for tomorrow?" I ask her.

"No. I actually have a day off," she replies.

"Would you like to spend the day with me?"

"What did you have in mind?" She tries to appear indifferent, but her lips curve into an intrigued smile.

"I was thinking about hitting a few trails. Do you do much hiking?"

"As a matter of fact, I do."

"Know any good trails?" I have a feeling I already know the answer.

"I might know of a few." She's beaming. This is her element. I knew she'd be up for anything outdoors.

"So, is that a yes?"

"Definitely." Her grin widens and it's contagious. I love seeing her happy.

We drive the rest of the way in comfortable silence, hands clasped together, my thumb rubbing gentle circles over her knuckles. When I pull into Tiff's driveway, I park behind Abby's truck and shut off the engine, turning towards her in my seat.

"I had a really good time tonight," she confesses. "Thank you for dinner. It was perfect."

"You're welcome," I tell her. "What time should I pick you up in the morning?"

"Nine?"

"I'll be there." I lean over the console and kiss her gently. Hopping out and jogging around the front of the car, I reach her door as it opens. "Would you like me to carry you again, Madame?" I ask in feigned chivalry when her stiletto-clad feet hit the gravel.

She giggles and replies, "No, thank you, kind sir. I believe I can manage." I laugh because we are the two biggest nerds right now and I don't even care. I help her out of my car, high heels and all, and grab her belongings. When we reach the driver's side door of her truck, I plant another kiss on her soft lips.

"I'll see you in the morning," I tell her as I pull myself away from her welcoming mouth. I'd love to deepen our kiss, but I don't want Tiffany's parents to catch us making out in their driveway. "Goodnight, Abby."

"Goodnight, Jacob."

Chapter Thirteen

Abby

THE NEXT MORNING, I WAKE UP TO birds chirping and sunlight flooding my bedroom. I shield my eyes from the blazing rays and roll over, snuggling deeper into my bed. I wish Jacob was here to snuggle into instead. The events of last night come crashing back into my brain. His lips on mine, his hands in my hair, his hard body pressed against me. The fire in his eyes when he saw me in that itsy-bitsy bikini. I should really thank Tiff for packing it.

But then he dropped a bomb on me. His dad is a U. S. senator, a rich and powerful man. Would he approve of what his son and I are doing? I seriously doubt it, but I have a feeling Jacob's not too concerned about his parents' approval. He's defied them before by getting a tattoo and refusing to go to law school. That's proof that he doesn't allow them to run his life, right?

Jacob and I are so different. We come from different worlds. I can't fall for him. He's only here for a short time, and falling for him could be devastating. Because eventually, he *will* leave. I'll still be here and he'll be in Arlington with his powerful family, living his life of privilege, attending fundraisers and campaign events and whatever else the rich and powerful do.

Oh, who am I kidding? I'm already falling. I've been falling since the moment I laid eyes on him. And I know he feels something, too. He bared his soul to me last night. He shared things with me I'm sure he hasn't shared with anyone. It broke my heart to hear him talk about his sister. He was forced to sit by helplessly and watch her succumb to a horrible illness that no one, especially a child, should have to suffer. I can't imagine losing my baby brother. He means the world to me. Both of our parents are gone, albeit in different ways, but they're both lost to us just the same. I would never survive if something happened to him.

Jacob surprised me last night. His career goals and outlook are not what I expected. I assumed he would be more concerned with money and choose a career that would lead him in that direction. Even before knowing who his father was, I could tell he came from a wealthy family. The Range Rover, the designer clothes and watch. But he doesn't seem to care much about any of it, and I love that about him. His big heart and selfless spirit make him even more attractive. I smile, thinking of his generosity and determination. I can just imagine him half a world away, helping those in need. He may be instrumental in saving thousands of lives one day. Who could resist falling for that?

My phone beeps with an incoming text, pulling me from my thoughts. I throw the covers off my legs and walk over to my dresser to unplug it from the charger. It's eight-thirty and I have a message from Jacob. It simply says:

Apple or cranberry?

My still groggy mind can't quite comprehend what he's asking me.

Hmm, apple I guess. Why you wanna know?

I add a winky face emoji to convey my playful disposition and hit send. A few seconds later, my phone dings again.

You'll see

I like surprises, and it sounds like this one involves food. I hope so because I'm starving and in desperate need of caffeine.

I brush my teeth and hop in the shower, needing to make myself presentable before Jacob gets here. I look like one of the "before" models in a shampoo ad with half my hair plastered to my head and the other half a frizzy rat's nest. There's no way to tame this mane without washing it. I lather up my body and my hair using the soap and shampoo my grandmother and I made. It's all natural and smells so good, and it leaves my skin and long, wavy tresses soft as silk. I don't mind using the store-bought stuff that Tiff keeps in her shower every once in a while, but there's nothing like our homemade products.

Once out of the shower, I wrap my hair in a towel and throw on a sports bra and tank top. I don't anticipate getting into any difficult terrain, so I slip into a pair of black, capri-length yoga pants and deposit my sneakers and backpack by the door. I let my hair down and squeeze out the excess water with my towel, shaping the curls as I go. The doorbell rings and my heart flutters in my chest, knowing it's Jacob on the other side of the door. Before I have a chance to reach it, Cero rumbles past me and paws at the frame.

"Cero, down," I command. He whines and walks in anxious circles. The last thing I need is for him to maul Jacob when he walks in. "Cero," I admonish a stern warning. He whimpers one last time and sits. Stubborn dog. I ease the door open and Jacob's flawless smile greets me on the other side.

"Hi," I greet him, sounding like a nervous teenager talking to her crush for the first time.

"Hi," he answers, and his smile grows. I drink him in, making note of his fitted t-shirt and khaki cargo shorts. He has a day's worth of stubble growing thickly on his gorgeous face. Good. I like a man with a little facial hair. His eyes rake over me with equal intensity, from my wet, wavy hair to my curve-hugging pants. "I brought breakfast."

I'm so smitten with him that I don't notice what's in his hands at first. He reaches out and hands me two brown paper bags but holds on to the cardboard drink holder.

"Thanks. Come on in." He passes over the threshold into the house, and Cero begins to whine again.

Jacob's eyes widen when he takes in Cero's large body and wolf-like features. With his size, he has a commanding and intimidating presence. He's a big baby with people he knows and likes, but he doesn't much care for strangers.

I flinch when Jacob kneels and reaches out to pet him.

"Careful, he's not fond of..."

My warning is silenced when Cero licks Jacob's hand and then nudges it with his head, begging to be petted. His rapidly wagging tail thumps against the hardwood floor.

"He's beautiful," Jacob marvels in awe. "What kind of dog is this?"

"He's a wolf hybrid."

"I've never seen anything like him."

"Yeah, he's pretty special." I've had Cero almost five years now. He's been my protector and loyal friend since the day I found him nearly frozen to death in the woods. It was the dead of winter, snow on the ground, temperature in the single digits, and he was just a pup. I'd heard his cries while waiting on the school bus that morning and went to investigate. My grandmother was furious that I had skipped school, but she was proud when I managed to nurse him back to health. He's more than a pet to me. He's family. And the fact that he seems to like Jacob tells me everything I need to know. I trust Cero's instincts. They haven't let me down yet.

"I brought coffee and muffins, and there's a French vanilla cappuccino in here for you." He raises the drink holder enticingly and looks down at me.

"How did you know that's what I like?" I take it from him and wrap my hands around the warm cup. The first sip of sugary, caffeinated heaven hits my tongue and I let out a soft "mmmm".

"You know, your friend isn't much of a morning person." A coltish smile pulls up the sides of his lips.

Well, that answers my question.

We both chuckle. "Yeah, I've noticed," I reply, leading him towards the kitchen. I can only imagine the string of expletives she hurled at him for waking her up. We settle our breakfast items on the small kitchen table and I grab a couple of napkins.

"I got two apple cinnamon muffins with raisins and two cranberry and orange with almonds."

"That sounds delicious." My mouth is watering just thinking about it.

"You need protein. You cannot live on muffins alone." The sound of my grandmother's voice startles me and I pull my gaze away from the divine smelling breakfast. I walk over to where she stands next to the refrigerator and hug her close, kissing her cheek.

"Who is your friend, Abigail?" she asks. She's the only person who ever uses my full name.

"This is Jacob," I tell her, leading her to the table. Jacob stands and holds his hand out to her.

"It's nice to meet you," Jacob asserts, smiling down at her. She's short like me, so he towers over her. Her long, straight, salt and pepper hair is pulled over her shoulder into a braid, much like I wear mine. Her deep brown eyes assess him as she holds onto his hand, searching his face. Her perceptive gaze lands on his eyes and she studies him a moment. She has always been a good judge of character. Her approval of Jacob would mean a great deal to me.

"It's nice to meet you, too," she finally replies. "Please, have a seat. I will make the two of you some eggs and bacon. Are you hiking today?" she asks, nodding towards my backpack and shoes. She knows me so well.

"Yes."

"Well then, you'll need your strength." She grabs the carton of eggs and the bacon from the fridge and places two pans on the stove. I go over to help her prepare our breakfast.

"Is there anything I can do to help?" I turn to see Jacob standing behind us, eager to assist.

"No, no, you sit down. You are our guest," my grandmother replies, eyes twinkling. Even *she* is not immune to his charm.

"Would you like some coffee?" Jacob asks her. "I brought extra."

"Yes, thank you," she replies with a smile. My grandmother looks over and winks at me as Jacob retrieves the coffee from the table. He brings back a cup of premium roast, aromatic steam rising when she removes the lid. She stirs a teaspoon of sugar into the warm, brown liquid and takes a sip. "Ah, that is delicious."

When the food is done, we take our places around the small table. Jacob is startled when my grandmother grabs his hand and then mine. He glances at me with a question in his eyes, but when I reach for his free hand, he slips it into mine, his warmth absorbing into my skin. He pauses for a moment when she begins to say Grace but follows suit when I bow my head.

As my eyes close, I wonder about Jacob's family. I have a feeling they do things a little differently than we do. I imagine they have big, impersonal dinners at a grand mahogany dining table so large that one must raise his voice to be heard at the other end. Nothing but fine china and crystal gracing their lips. Servants bringing trays of gourmet food from the kitchen. Monogrammed table linens and napkins I wouldn't dare wipe my mouth on for fear of soiling them.

Jacob's fingers close around mine, his thumb stroking the back of my hand and pulling me from my thoughts. I steal a glance at him as my grandmother continues her prayer. His eyes are closed and his head is bowed. He seems so at ease sitting at my table, listening to my grandmother's words of thanks. I realize that I've made so many assumptions about him since we met, and they've all been wrong.

"Jacob," my grandmother begins after we've said our Amens, "how long have you known my Abigail?"

Oh, no. Here comes the inquisition. I start to fidget in my seat until she pins me with her knowing stare.

Jacob swallows down his bite of muffin and clears his throat. "Only since Saturday, ma'am."

"Well, she must like you very much to be taking you hiking." Her eyes drift to me, and anybody else would read her look as impassive. But

I know her. I can read all the slight nuances in her facial expressions. She's questioning me and warning me with a single look. I give her a tiny nod, and she returns her attention to Jacob.

"I hope so," he replies, smiling at me. My stomach flutters as if a thousand butterflies are taking flight inside of it.

"It would appear that Cero is quite fond of you as well." She lifts one eyebrow and trains her gaze on my Cero laying at Jacob's feet, his head resting on his paws. He tries his best to project innocence with his big, puppy-dog eyes. "Although I'm not sure whether that is because he genuinely likes you, or if it's because you've been sneaking him bacon."

Jacob's face falls and he smiles apologetically. "I'm sorry. He just looked so pitiful. And I'm a total sucker." My heart melts a little when he says this. I'm an animal lover, and I know all about being a sucker. And my manipulative dog likes to exploit those weaknesses in people. *Brat.*

She chuckles and I know what she's up to. "Don't listen to her," I tell him. "She's just teasing you." Nobody gives that dog more table scraps than she does. My grandmother just likes to give people a hard time, especially any guy I bring home. The few who have made it that far always fell prey to her antics.

My grandmother laughs. "Abigail, you're ruining all my fun."

Jacob's laughter echoes through our tiny kitchen. "That's a relief. I thought I was in big trouble," he confesses, grinning from ear to ear.

Once we finish our breakfast, I gather our dishes and take them to the sink, turning on the water and squirting in a little dish soap. "Here, I'll help you with those," Jacob volunteers, approaching from behind. He steps up next to me, surprising me with his offer. Before I can respond, my grandmother steps in between us.

"I'll take care of these. You two go have fun." I begin to protest, but she cuts me off. "Go," she insists, shooing us away.

Jacob and I offer our goodbyes and head for the door. Cero follows us excitedly, thinking that he's going somewhere, too. I crouch down and scratch behind his ears. "Sorry, buddy," I tell him, feeling guilty. "Not this time." I really need to take him with me soon. It's been too long since he's been out on the trails, and he enjoys it as much as I do. I slip on my shoes and grab my backpack before following Jacob outside.

"Where to?" he asks.

"You'll see," I echo his response from earlier. I'm hoping he'll enjoy our destination as much as I do. We'll end up at one of my favorite places. "There's something I'd like to show you."

He opens the passenger door for me and I step inside. "Sounds interesting."

"Okay, turn left here," I direct Jacob to the road leading to the trailhead. "There's a parking lot right up there," I advise, pointing to the barren lot. Not many people hiking on a weekday, I suppose.

"Is there somewhere to get a map?" Jacob asks as we grab our packs from the back seat.

I shoot him a confident smile. He has no idea how many times I've hiked this trail. I could hike it backward. With my eyes closed. "We don't need a map. I know this place like the back of my hand."

"Well, I guess I'd better follow you, then." He holds his hand out, gesturing for me to take the lead. After a moment, he sidles up next to me, matching my stride.

"How long of a hike were you planning on taking today?" I ask him.

"Didn't really have a plan. I was just going to hike until Luke started whining and wanted to go back."

I stop abruptly, feeling guilty that I've taken him away from his friend. I know they took this trip together with the intention of hanging out and doing guy stuff. I hope he doesn't think I'm trying to keep him all to myself. Although, that doesn't sound like such a bad idea. "I'm sorry." He turns and looks at me quizzically. "I didn't mean to impose on your plans with Luke. I didn't realize this was something you guys had planned to do together."

He takes a few steps back to where I'm standing and brushes my jaw with his fingertips. "You're not imposing on anything. Luke made his decision when he chose to stay in bed with Tiffany. Besides, I asked you to come. I want you here with me. So don't feel bad about Luke's absence. He and I will have plenty of time to hang out."

His assurances fill me with a sense of relief. "Okay."

"Let's keep going." He grabs my hand and we walk side by side. We continue in silence for a few minutes, just taking in the sounds of nature. Leaves rustling, birds singing, the dull thud of our shoes hitting the dirt. But the sounds are nothing compared to the smells. Clean air and the scent of pine needles pervade our senses.

"How long have you lived with your grandmother?" Jacob asks.

"About six years, but my brother and I stayed with her a lot even before that."

His brow furrows with a look of contemplation. It's obvious he wants to know more, wants to dig a little deeper. I hope he doesn't. I don't want to get into all the ugliness and pain.

"If you don't mind me asking, what happened to your mother?"

I wince at his inquiry. Even though I knew it was coming, I still wasn't prepared for it. He knows my father died in a coal mining accident and that I haven't seen my mother in a long time, but he doesn't know why. I've been dreading this conversation and trying to avoid it since we met. I hate talking about this. I'm embarrassed and ashamed at what my mother has become, but more than that, it hurts. It hurts like hell knowing she chose a life of drugs - and the man who keeps her high - over her children.

I know it's not fair to *not* share my past with him, especially since he told me so much about his family. Telling me about his sister must have been incredibly painful for him, but he did it anyway. He wanted me to know him, really, truly know him. I owe him the same.

"My mother is a drug addict and an alcoholic," I confess, unable to look him in the eyes. "She took off years ago and left my brother and me in my grandmother's care."

"Abby..." Jacob begins, dumbfounded. I don't think he was expecting that revelation.

I sigh, knowing I should continue, but not wanting to reveal all the gory details. He deserves to know the truth, though, considering all that he's told me.

"My dad's death was really hard on my family, my mom especially. He was the love of her life. They'd been together since they were teenagers. They were high school sweethearts." I smile to myself, imagining my parents young and in love. "After the accident, she started drinking. She drank more and more to numb the pain, but eventually, the booze wasn't enough so she moved on to pills. Oxy's, Xanax, whatever she could get her hands on. Sometimes she did both, washing her pills down with a fifth of vodka. Or Jack. She wasn't really picky by that point." We stop walking and Jacob squeezes my hand reassuringly, encouraging me to continue. I try to be brave. I want to be brave for him like he was for me. So, I push through the ache in my chest and the lump in my throat.

"At some point, I don't even remember when, she started shooting up. She'd long since lost her job and had burned through most of the settlement from Dad's accident. She was starting to get desperate. She begged my grandmother for money, but she wouldn't feed into Mom's habit. Ethan and I were practically living with my grandmother by then, but she wouldn't let Mom stay there because of the drugs. We tried several times to get her into rehab, but she refused to go. My grandmother threatened to call the cops on her and rat her out for the drugs if she didn't at least give up custody of my brother and me. She was afraid of what would happen to us in that house, especially to me." I'm sickened at the thought of what she feared my mother would subject me to just to pay for her next hit. Addicts can be desperate, malicious people sometimes.

"The straw that finally broke the camel's back was the day she hit me. She'd been verbally abusive for a long time, but had never done more than push me around." I tremble as I remember the moment it all changed. Jacob turns my body so I'm facing him and takes my free hand in his. I take another deep breath and continue, unable to meet his gaze.

"She was screaming horrible things, things about me, things about my dad. I started yelling back. I'd never done that before. I'd always been too afraid of her to fight back, but I couldn't keep it all bottled up any longer. I called her a crack whore and she slapped me. She slapped me so hard, it busted my lip and rattled my teeth."

I pause a moment, not looking forward to revealing the worst part. "I hit her back. I balled up my fist and hit her as hard as I could. I wanted to keep hitting her. I wanted to hurt her as badly as she'd hurt me, but that wasn't possible."

My breathing is fast and labored, tears burning the backs of my eyes, threatening to spill over. I feel panic rising like bile in the back of my throat. "The pain she inflicted on me went way deeper than anything I could possibly do to her." My words come out weak and low, barely above a whisper. I squeeze my eyes shut, trying to stem the flow of tears pooling in the corners of my eyes. I inhale deeply through my nose to calm my breathing so I can go on.

"Before she had a chance to get back up and come after me, I grabbed my brother and took off to my grandma's house, running as fast as our legs would carry us. We made it almost two miles before a neighbor saw us and picked us up. Thankfully, Mom was too high or drunk to find her keys.

"We didn't see her much after that. She gave up custody and took off with some low-life dealer named Mickey. Last I heard, they were running drugs between Detroit and some small river town in Ohio to fund their habit. She calls me once every couple of years asking for money, but other than that, I don't hear from her. I don't even know if she's still alive."

I continue to stare at the ground after I finish. I'm mortified, and I can't look at Jacob. I can't stand to see the pity and disgust I'm sure is written in his face. He's quiet for a moment and then he wraps his arms around me and tucks my head under his chin.

"Dear God, Abby. I'm so sorry," he whispers into my hair. "How old were you when that happened?"

"Fifteen." Jacob's warm arms squeeze me tighter, and I know I've never felt safer in my life.

He pulls back and places his hands on each side of my face, tilting it up to look at him. "I'm sorry you had to go through that. No one deserves to be treated that way."

Feeling brave enough to lift my eyes, I look into his and see no disgust there. Not even pity. Yes, he hates that I had to go through something so horrible, but he doesn't feel sorry for me. Relief washes over me like a weight has been lifted from my shoulders. There's no judgment on his part and no need to feel ashamed on mine. A peacefulness settles into my soul, and for the first time since that day, I feel free of this burden.

"Tell me more about your brother," Jacob inquires after we begin to walk again.

Eager to move on to a happier topic, I begin, "Ethan is younger than me by about a year and a half. He's a musician and a singer, and he fronts a local band." My baby brother is insanely talented. He's been the lead singer of his band since he was seventeen. I love to see how much he's accomplished.

"Does he live with you and your grandma?"

"Not anymore. He and his bandmates all live together." I giggle at the thought of their living arrangement. Four grown men packed into a single wide trailer. "He insisted on moving out when he graduated high school. He works at a garage during the week and plays music on the weekends."

"Is his band any good?"

"They're amazing. I look for them to take their gig to Nashville soon." I know I'm beaming with pride, but I can't help it. I just know he'll be a big star one day.

"I'd like to hear them play."

"Well, you'll get the chance this Saturday if you come to The Barn with us," I tell him, hoping he'll say yes.

"Is that another bar in town?"

"No," I answer with a wry chuckle. "It's kind of out in the sticks." He seems skeptical, so I explain The Barn to him. "Sam Jameson owns a two-hundred-acre farm a few miles outside of town. There was a big, red barn on the property that his granddaddy built, but it was dilapidated and not much use to his livestock. His wife wanted him to tear it down, but he had a better idea. He fixed it up, ran electricity and plumbing to it, and added a stage and a bar. He even built onto it, adding a bathroom and small kitchenette. He basically turned it into a night club." I bet old man Jameson never expected *that* when he built it.

"He rents it out for wedding receptions, family reunions, proms, things like that. He has parties there, and there's almost always live music on Saturday nights during the warm months. My brother's band plays there a lot." Tiff and I have been to many a party at The Barn. Jameson lets pretty much anybody in. He even lets younger kids in as long as they have a parent present. They just have to leave by ten o'clock. That's when things start to get rowdy.

"So, everybody just calls it, 'The Barn?'"

"Yep."

"Okay. Count me in."

I smile to myself. I can't wait to introduce him to my brother and spend the evening dancing with him. I feel lighter, having bared my deepest, darkest secrets to him. Even Tiff doesn't know the full extent of the story. Ethan was in his bedroom that day, so he doesn't know that Mom and I got into a physical fight. Only my grandmother knows what really happened, and now Jacob knows as well.

A sharp bend in the trail looms ahead of us, a heavily shaded area just beyond. As we approach, Jacob excuses himself and steps away, disappearing into the dense thicket. I continue up the trail a little further to give him some privacy to relieve himself. As I pass a familiar giant oak, I rub my hands over the bark, my fingertips skimming over the rough, bumpy ridges. I remember a trick I once played on my brother, and it gives me an idea.

I slide in behind the enormous tree trunk, my body fully concealed, and press my shoulder against it, listening for Jacob to approach. A moment later, I hear his voice call out to me.

"Abby?" He sounds a good twenty yards away. "Where'd you go?" I keep quiet and listen for the crunch of twigs under his feet, waiting for him to close in on my hiding spot.

When I hear him draw near, I hold my breath and wait until he's about to step into my field of view. Just as he passes by the tree, I jump out and startle him, yelling, "Boo!"

He jumps back and nearly falls on his ass. "Shit!" he yells, clutching his chest. "You scared the hell out of me." He's trying to catch his breath, but a smile slowly spreads over his face. I laugh at him openly and unabashedly. "You got me good," he admits with a teasing glimmer in his eyes.

"Yes, I did," I respond proudly. I love to play around and scare people, especially Tiff, even though she gets super mad when I do it to her. My grandfather used to scare the snot out of us on a regular basis when we were little, often jumping out from behind a door or the couch to grab us. Once our racing hearts slowed down, we would squeal with laughter as he tickled our bellies. That's one of the things I miss most about him since he passed. It's why I try to keep his spirit alive by using his antics on my friends.

"Oh, so you think you're funny, huh?" he asks as I continue to howl with laughter. Suddenly, his face changes from humored to stern and my smile fades away. *Uh oh, is he mad?* He didn't seem mad just a second ago.

Jacob steps up to me, an unreadable expression on his face as he slides the straps of my backpack down my shoulders. He presses me up against the trunk of the tree, never breaking eye contact. The rough bark digs into my back, and I nearly lose my footing on the over-sized roots jutting up from the ground. His eyes flare with desire before he covers my mouth with his. He coaxes my lips open with his tongue and I eagerly allow him entrance. His kiss swallows my moans and he presses his body into mine, the proof of his arousal growing against my belly. I gently sink my teeth into his lower lip as he pushes his hands into my hair.

His scent and the taste of his mouth consume me, overwhelming my senses, smelling like fresh rain and bergamot. I trail kisses down his jaw, onto his neck, and inhale deeply, savoring him. I lick and suckle my way from the base of his throat to the skin covering his Adam's apple. When he swallows hard and groans, I feel him twitch against my stomach, inciting my desire. "Abby," he exhales my name. I don't know where this sensual confidence is coming from. I've never been this brazen with a man before, but Jacob coaxes the vixen out of me.

I slide my hands down the hard ridges of his stomach and grip his belt, unbuckling it with trembling hands. I pop the button at the top of his shorts free and slide the zipper down slowly. He grabs my wrists, stopping me before I can push them down over his hips, and presses his lips to mine roughly.

"If you don't stop now, I can't promise I'll be able to stop before things go too far," he growls against my mouth.

"I don't want you to stop," I whisper against his lips.

He groans and presses me harder against the tree. "I want you. I want you more than I've ever wanted anyone before." He's practically panting from excitement. "But I'm not gonna take you here, out in the open, where anybody can see us." He kisses me once more before leaning his head back and closing his eyes tightly. "I would lose my mind if anybody else saw your perfect, naked body. I'd end up in jail."

I shudder at his possessiveness, even more turned on than before. "Then take me away from the trail," I whisper enticingly into his ear. I feel him smile against my cheek.

"Damn it, how am I supposed to have any fucking self-control when you talk to me like that?"

It's my turn to smile. I don't want him to have any self-control right now. I want him to lose himself to me, but he's holding back because we're out in the open. He kisses me one last time and steps back, refastening his pants. He picks our backpacks off the ground and hands mine over. Even though I know he's only being sensible, I'm disappointed that he stopped things from going any further. I was ready to do things to him that I've never had any desire to do to a man; things I've only done to please a boyfriend, never because I desperately wanted to. But I want to with Jacob. I want to taste him and drive him mad with pleasure. Too bad that will have to wait.

"Cheer up, babe. I'll give you whatever you want once we leave here," Jacob tells me with a wink and a smirk. He must have noticed the defeated look on my face.

We continue on the trail, making small talk about our families. He tells me about his brother, Logan, who is going to be a sophomore in high school. Logan is already a varsity football player with a 4.0 GPA. He's destined to go places with his talent and smarts.

I tell him about my Aunt Roselyn and my dad's parents who live in Charleston. Roselyn may be my employer, but she's more like a second mother to me. When my brother and I weren't at our grandmother's, we were with Ros and her husband Phillip. Their son, Waylon, is two years younger than Ethan and, much to his mother's distress is determined to join the Marines.

When we hear rushing water, I know we've finally made it to our destination. We step into a clearing and Jacob lets out an appreciative whistle when he sees where I've been leading him. The rushing water of Dunloup Creek flows over the falls, crashing into a crystalline pool below. I can't imagine a more perfect place to spend the day with Jacob.

Chapter Fourteen

Abby

"THIS PLACE IS INCREDIBLE!" JACOB announces, taking in the view. "I can see why you like it here." He grabs my hand and leads me to the edge of the water, setting his pack on the ground. I drop my bag next to his and plop down on a flat, moss-covered rock.

"Are you hungry?" I ask. I'd decided to take the long way around, so we've been hiking for a while already.

"Starving," he replies.

"I've got some trail mix, beef jerky, granola bars, and apples." My go-to snacks when I'm on the trails.

"You don't know how good that sounds right now," he groans, patting his stomach.

While I set out our snacks, he pulls two bottles of water from his pack. I grab a couple of hand sanitizing wipes and hand one to him.

One eyebrow shoots up and he looks at me with amusement. "I'm kind of a germaphobe," I confess with a shrug, tearing open the individually wrapped wipe. "And I don't have time to get sick." I can't take any risks when it comes to my health. If I can't work, I don't get paid and if I don't get paid, I can't afford school.

"I guess I'd better take care of you, then. We can't have you getting sick," he replies with a wink.

My heart flutters at the mention of him taking care of me. It's not that I want to depend on a man to supply my needs, but the thought of a man who wants to take care of his woman is a sentiment I can appreciate.

I grab an apple and sink my teeth into the shiny, green skin. The tart flavor bursts on my tongue and I bring a napkin up to my chin to keep the juices from dripping into my lap. Jacob swipes a thumb over my bottom lip where some of the sticky liquid has escaped, and my breath hitches momentarily when he sticks that thumb in his mouth and sucks the juices off it. The simple, yet intimate act conjures images in my mind of his mouth on my body. I glance away from him quickly, sipping my water to cool my rapidly rising temperature, thankful he's too focused on our makeshift meal to notice the blush staining my cheeks.

"Have you ever encountered any wild animals out here while hiking?" Jacob asks before tearing into a strip of jerky.

"Sure I have. I see squirrels and birds and rabbits all the time. I even see deer out here sometimes." I finish my apple and toss the core into the woods. Perhaps we'll see one today if it finds my leftovers.

"No, I mean dangerous animals, like a bobcat or a bear. Something that could potentially be lethal."

"I've never encountered anything dangerous like that, no. I've come across a few poisonous snakes, but as long as you don't bother them, they usually won't bother you," I assure him. "But I'm always prepared just in case I do come across something I can't outrun."

He looks at me inquisitively. "What do you mean?" He chews his beef jerky before swallowing it, studying me with genuine curiosity.

"I just make sure I have this on me," I say, reaching into my bag and wrapping my fingers around the cool metal. Jacob's eyes go wide when I retract my hand. "I trust my .38 to keep me safe out here." I hike solo a lot, and a girl has to protect herself from predators, both the human *and* animal varieties.

"Damn. Remind me never to piss you off," he jokes, laughing and eyeing my gun. "Do you even know how to use that thing, little lady?"

I scowl at him and he laughs, amused by my chagrin. "Just because I'm carrying a revolver doesn't mean you get to talk like we're in a Western."

"I'm sorry," he apologizes, trying to suppress his mirth. "I just can't imagine you shooting something, especially with that big hunk of metal. But I definitely feel safer with you now." His smile grows exponentially, crinkling the corners of his eyes and making my heart dip down into my stomach. This man's smile does crazy things to my insides.

With our hunger momentarily sated, Jacob and I sit in silence for a while, gazing out over the water. The sound of the waterfall crashing into the creek below is enough to lull me to sleep, was I not acutely aware of Jacob's proximity. He leans back on his elbows, taking in the scenery surrounding us. I long to crawl into his lap, my thighs straddling his hips, and run my hands down the ridges of his muscular torso. My heart rate picks up at the thought of feeling every inch of his hardness pressed firmly against me.

"Can you swim in this creek?" Jacob asks after studying the water for a moment.

"Sure can. People do it all the time."

"Well, then let's get in," Jacob proposes, standing up and toeing off his shoes.

"Wait. What? Now?" I ask in confusion.

"Yes, now," he answers with a grin. When he reaches down, I accept his outstretched hand and he pulls me to my feet in one swift movement.

"But I don't have a bathing suit," I argue.

Jacob eyes my chest. "Are you wearing a bra?"

"Yes," I answer slowly with suspicion in my voice, instinctively crossing my arms over my chest.

His eyes dip lower. "Are you wearing panties?" he asks in a playfully seductive tone. My thighs clench together when the word "panties" crosses his lips.

I blush and avert my gaze. "Yes."

"Then we're all set."

"But–"

"Come on, it'll be fun."

How could I possibly say no to that roguish smile and those blue eyes alight with mischief?

I follow his lead and slip off my shoes and socks, and then loosen my hair from its braid, twisting it into a bun on top of my head to keep it dry. I start to pull off my pants but stop abruptly, a vague memory of choosing my undergarments this morning popping into my mind. *Shit.* I didn't think this through very well. The white sports bra and matching panties aren't going to conceal much once they're wet.

Jacob turns to me, all clothes but his shorts removed and piled haphazardly at his feet. His hands hover at his fly as he eyes me with concern. "Everything alright?"

"Yes. It's just... I um..." I stammer. He steps closer to me and I tilt my chin up to maintain eye contact with him. I give him a sheepish grin. "All of my undergarments are white."

He looks me over, not understanding my dilemma, but the moment it clicks for him, he bursts into laughter. I, however, am not the least bit amused. I might as well go naked with everything he'll be able to see.

"Ah, it's okay," he assures me between guffaws. "I won't look when you get out of the water." His laughter dies down and he eyes me with a look of red-hot lust. "Unless you want me to, of course."

The heat of his gaze and his devious grin send a wave of desire through my center. "Okay," is all I can manage to mutter. He places a quick kiss on the tip of my nose and steps back while undoing his zipper. He drops his shorts but leaves on his boxer briefs. That's a damn shame. I slip off my pants and tank top as fast as possible and cross my arms over my chest. Jacob's amused expression unnerves me. I want to slap him and kiss him at the same time. It's kind of infuriating, but also arousing.

He reaches out to me and brushes his fingers over my arm. "Come on," he says with excitement. I unfold my arms and place my hand in his. He leads me to the edge of the water and I dip my toes in. It's still a bit chilly this time of year, but nothing I can't handle. We sink down into the water until we're hip deep.

"You doing okay?" he asks. I nod my head and let him lead me into deeper waters. He pulls us further until the water covers our shoulders and our heads are all that's visible. "There. Now we'll be used to the cold."

We wade deeper, closer to the waterfall, and he wraps his arms around my waist. His warm flesh feels wonderful against my cool skin. It keeps the chill of the creek water out of my bones. I wrap my legs around him and he cups his hands under my bottom for support, pressing my lower half into his. I bite my bottom lip to stifle my moan and he hisses in a breath when his hardened length meets my center. His eyes flare with heated desire as he removes one hand from my ass and brings it up to my face, pulling at my chin with his thumb and releasing my lip from between my teeth. Cupping the back of my head, he kisses me slowly, temptation mounting between us. He squeezes my ass and rolls his hips, grinding his erection into me.

A low rumble vibrates through his chest and a quiet growl escapes his lips. I hear the waterfall approaching behind me, and I turn to see how close we are, stiffening when I realize we're only a few feet away. The water is pouring down at a moderate pace. It's not crashing violently into the creek below, but it's enough that the mist from it dampens our skin as we draw near.

"Do you trust me?" he asks, reaching for my hair tie.

"Yes," I reply breathlessly, relaxing as I stare into the icy blue depths of his eyes.

He releases my hair and it falls down my back, its ends swirling into the cool water. He continues forward, bringing my back closer to the fall until I feel the spray from it on my shoulders. He shoves his hands in my hair and crushes his lips to mine, his tongue slipping into my mouth, exploring, tasting. Breaking our kiss, he tilts my head back gently and I close my eyes.

Cold water pours over my scalp and down my neck, sending shivers down my spine. His lips brush the base of my throat and I gasp as his warm tongue glides over the sensitive skin of my neck. He nips and licks at me while stroking me deliciously with his own arousal. The chilling sensation of cool water rolling down my neck, mixed with the heat of his mouth on my throat is intoxicating. All thoughts of keeping my hair dry are long gone, replaced with pure ecstasy from Jacob's touch.

He finally backs us away from the waterfall and pulls my lips down to meet his, shifting my body so that I'm no longer flush against him. I let out a disappointed sigh and he chuckles.

"Don't worry," he whispers in my ear. "This only gets better." He slowly brushes his fingers down my stomach, stopping at the waistband of my panties and teasing the edge with a gentle tug. "I want to touch you," he growls.

I'm panting, white-hot desire coursing through my veins. "Please, Jacob."

I feel him smile against my neck. "Please, what?" he teases as he hooks two fingers inside the elastic.

"Touch me."

As soon as the words leave my lips, his hand dips inside the material, parting me. His fingers slide up and down my slick heat, coating me with my own arousal. He presses the pad of his finger against my sensitive nub and I cry out. His lips crash against mine, muffling the sound. He rubs with gentle circles until I'm ready to explode. Right before my body is wracked by an earth-shattering orgasm, he stops.

I want to scream in frustration, but he thrusts two fingers deep inside me, causing me to gasp. He curls them forward, rubbing me in just the right way. Releasing my mouth, he moves to my ear and grips its lobe between his teeth. His fingers continue to move in and out of me in a delicious rhythm.

"You don't know how bad I want to taste you right now," he growls into my ear, his voice gruff and strained with carnal need.

I bet it's not any more than I want you to.

The moment he removes his fingers, I feel empty. I want him to fill me until there is no space between us. Just as quickly as he left, he returns his attention to my sensitive nub and resumes his euphoric assault. I'm so close at this point, I might die if he pulls his hand away before finishing this time. The pressure builds quickly and I know I'm about to shatter. His free arm tightens around my back, pressing my side into his torso, his hardened length digging into me.

"Let go, baby. I got you." His words are my undoing. I shudder my release and cry out. He lets me ride the waves of my orgasm for a moment before sliding his long, skillful fingers back inside. He strokes me, brushing his thumb over my sensitive bundle of nerves every now and then. I feel him, hot and hard against my hip, and I want him inside me. For one, lust-hazed minute, I consider ripping his boxers off and wrapping my legs around him until he sinks into me, but I'm too close to another orgasm. I climb higher and higher, moaning my appreciation for his talents. Then I'm falling, my whole body shaking as I come down from my high.

"Fuck." Jacob sucks in a shaky breath, pulling his hand out of my panties. "That is the sexiest thing I've ever seen." He kisses my temple and I feel him smile. "I almost got off just watching you."

My face heats and my cheeks redden, embarrassed that he's seen me in such an intimately vulnerable state. I bury my head in his chest, unable to look him in the eyes after coming completely undone in his hands.

"You're amazing." He brushes his lips over my temple again.

His sweet words and reassurance embolden me. I'm not usually very brazen when it comes to sex or men in general, but I want to make him feel as good as he just made me feel. With a shaky hand, I reach down and cup him through his boxers. He's long and hard, the cool water doing nothing to stem the heat between us. I slip my hand inside his waistband and grab his shaft. His head tilts back, eyes closed as a moan escapes his lips. I want nothing more than to wrap my lips around him, tasting him and driving him mad with pleasure. But with our current location, that's not an option. I guess we'll both have to settle for my hand. I tighten my grip on him and slide my hand up and down in a rhythmic motion.

"Abby," he breathes my name, his voice thick with desire. I could never tire of hearing him say my name in that sexy timbre.

I trail kisses up the side of his neck as I continue to stroke him under the water. He runs his hand up my side, over my ribs, and cups my breast. I push his boxer briefs down over his hips, freeing him and making it easier for me to pump up and down his length. His short, panting breaths let me know I'm doing this right.

He hooks his thumb into the top of my bra and pulls one side down, exposing my breast. I gasp when his warm, wet mouth clamps down on its hardened peak. He circles his tongue around my pebbled nipple before flicking it, sending a jolt of pleasure between my legs. I squeeze my thighs together to soothe the ache.

Soon, his fingers are tangled in my hair and his mouth devours mine. He kisses me and nips at my bottom lip, his tongue slipping into my mouth as he lets out a groan. I feel him jerk and tremble, and I know he's about to find his release. Warmth spreads over my hand as he lets go, his hand fisting in my hair. When he shudders one last time, completely spent, I release him and slip my arms around his neck. He's breathing hard, his head tilted back as he tries to catch his breath. He pulls me in tight and I press my head to his chest.

"That was...just...wow," he expresses, his breathing slowly returning to normal. "I don't think I've had a hand job since Senior Prom," he chuckles. Those crude words coming from anyone else would be a turn-off for me, but coming from Jacob's mouth, it's sensual and makes me feel like a sex goddess. "And I don't remember it *ever* feeling that good."

He smiles down at me and kisses my forehead before settling his gaze on my body. My chest is just above the water and he can see my dark, erect nipples through the white material clinging to my skin. Heat rises into my cheeks as he appraises me.

"I better get you out of this cold water. You're shivering." He rubs his hands up and down my goosebump-covered arms. I want to tell him it's not from the water, but I don't. My skin is getting all wrinkled and I'm ready to put my clothes back on. I want to finish our hike and get him somewhere private where we can really explore each other.

Part of me feels guilty for being so ready and willing with him when I've only known him a handful of days. Things have never progressed this quickly with any other guy before, but it's different with Jacob. Our connection runs deeper and the pace is heightened with the knowledge that our time is limited.

I try to push that thought to the back of my mind as we wade over to the edge of the creek where our clothes lay, warming in the sun. Jacob steps out of the water first, then turns and reaches for my hand. I grab it and am immediately pulled into his arms. He wraps them tightly around me and presses his lips to mine.

"You look so good in that wet underwear," he whispers against my lips. "I just want to lay you out right here and peel it off you. It leaves nothing to the imagination."

My cheeks flame and my stomach dips, heat pooling between my thighs again. How can his words turn me on and embarrass me at the same time?

He reaches into his backpack and pulls out a worn, navy blue blanket and wraps it around my shoulders. I clutch its edges together as he retrieves my clothes, trying to conceal as much of my nearly naked body as possible. He returns with my clothing and leans in, rubbing his hands over my back to warm me.

"If you need any help getting those wet panties off," he begins, his hot breath fanning over my cheek, "I'm your guy," he offers playfully. With that irresistible smile, I consider taking him up on it.

"Thanks, but I think I can manage," I reply unconvincingly even to my own ears.

"Suit yourself," he replies with a shrug. "I'll just hold this blanket up around you in case any other hikers come along."

"Thanks," I reply, slipping out of my undies. There's no way I can walk around in wet underwear. I'll just have to go commando in my yoga pants. "I hope there weren't any passing through while we were in the water. They would've gotten one hell of a show." Jacob's rich, deep laugh brings a smile to my face.

"All of our action was going on under the water. They never would've seen a thing," he assures me.

I finish changing, leaving my bra on because it will eventually dry and I don't dare go without one. I offer to hold the blanket up for Jacob so he can slip his wet boxers off.

"Nah, I don't care if anyone sees me," he reveals with a wink.

"*I* care!" I blurt out before I can stop myself. He raises one eyebrow at me in inquiry. "I mean, I don't want anyone else seeing your junk." *Real smooth, Abby.* I cringe at my idiocy.

He just shakes his head and chuckles. "Alright," he concedes. "My junk is all yours."

Once again, my face burns and I duck my head to hide my flushed cheeks.

He changes quickly back into his shorts and takes the blanket from me, rolling it up and shoving it back into his bag. His phone chimes from his pocket right as he finishes dressing. A scowl appears on his handsome face as his eyes scan the message. My fingers itch to smooth over his knitted brow but I refrain, his look of irritation stopping me in my tracks.

He shoves his phone back in his pocket with a grimace and picks his backpack up. "Guess who just rented a shit load of camping equipment and is insisting on meeting up with us later?" he queries humorlessly.

I let the disappointment wash over me, trying not to let it show on my face. *There goes my chance of exploring more of Jacob's delicious body.* I was really looking forward to getting him alone. Like, completely alone. Not a soul within miles of us. Now, our friends are butting in on our plans again.

"Oh," I reply. "That could be fun, I guess." I shrug and wring out my hair. It could be, I suppose. It's just not what I had in mind. I'm sure Jacob can sense I'm not thrilled by the idea.

"You don't understand," he asserts, a burning intensity in his icy blue eyes. "I have plans for you. Plans that don't involve our friends." He steps up to me and presses his body against mine, his arms encircling my waist. "I want you all to myself. I want you where I don't have to worry about anyone else hearing you scream my name. I want you where Luke and Tiff aren't even on our radar."

Well, at least we're on the same page. "I want that, too," I reply, my words barely above a whisper. He holds my gaze for a few seconds before capturing my mouth in a quick but passionate kiss.

He grabs my hand and leads me back to the trail. This time, I take him down the shorter route.

"If we're camping tonight, I need to get a change of clothes and tell my grandmother what's going on. Tiff has to work 'til six," I calculate, glancing at my watch. "So, we should have plenty of time."

He stops abruptly, causing me to bump into him. "Wait," he interjects, turning towards me. "You actually *want* to camp with those two?" he asks incredulously.

"It's not the worst idea in the world." I don't know who I'm trying to convince, me or him. "Besides, you said Luke already rented a bunch of camping gear."

"Knowing Luke, he probably rented a 2-person tent and a sleeping bag. Not exactly enough for the four of us."

"You're probably right," I respond with a giggle. "I can bring my stuff. I have plenty of gear."

"Well, alright. If that's what you want to do."

"Do you mind if I bring Cero? He loves camping, and I would feel better having him with us."

"I don't mind at all. I like that big furry beast," Jacob replies with a grin.

"Great! He's going to be so excited."

We make pretty good time getting back to Jacob's SUV. Heading towards home, I start to feel a bit of excitement at the prospect of being snuggled up in a tent with Jacob. We'll set up far away from Luke and Tiff so we can maintain at least a modicum of privacy.

It's thrilling being out in the wild, knowing all that nature has to offer is right outside the thin material of your tent. You can make love under the stars and swim naked with nothing but moonlight to guide you. Not that I've ever had the chance to do either, but I've dreamed of both. And then there's the fire. There's nothing like the sound of wood crackling and popping in a campfire, complete with roasted hot dogs and marshmallows and anything else you can fit on a stick. It makes the bug bites and squatting against a tree to pee totally worth it.

This camping idea is getting better by the minute. I may just have to thank Luke for butting in on our plans this time.

Chapter Fifteen

Jacob

On our way back to Abby's house, she insists on rolling the windows down and enjoying the warm breeze. She releases her still damp hair from its twist atop her head and I savor the scent of her windblown locks as the air carries it towards me, a subtle perfume of sweetness and wildflowers. She smells like spring and summer, renewal and fresh starts. Like warm, sunny days and honeysuckle vines. I've never smelled anything more enticing. I breathe her in, letting her scent imprint on my memory.

She leans against the door and crosses her arms over the window sill, resting her chin on her forearms. Her eyes flutter closed as she takes a deep breath, enjoying the rays of the late afternoon sun on her face. She seems content. I hope I have something to do with that.

After a few minutes, she straightens and rolls her window back up. "I wonder if Tiff even knows what Luke's planning for tonight. She's not really the outdoorsy type."

"I don't know," I answer, glancing over at her. It's nearly impossible to keep my eyes on the road when she's sitting next to me. "But she seems to go along with whatever he wants to do."

She looks at me with hesitation, contemplating her next words. "You know he's going to get his heart broken, right?"

Her eyes widen in surprise at my howl of laughter. That's a novel idea. Luke getting *his* heart broken. I don't think he's in any danger of that happening. When I glance back over at Abby, her eyebrows knitted together in a scowl, my laughter fades. She's not joking.

"Luke would need to *have* a heart for it to get broken."

"I see the way he looks at her," she shakes her head and sighs, "but she doesn't do relationships, and she will crush him." I think she almost feels bad for the guy. Not that Luke is at risk for getting hurt, but the bastard would kind of deserve it. He's broken enough hearts in his day. Fortunately for him, he never gets attached, and Tiff is no different. They'll have their fun and go their separate ways when it's over. No harm done.

What about Abby and me, though? What will we do when it's time for me to leave? Will we stay in touch? Am I going to drive down here every chance I get to spend time with her? Will she come to Arlington to see me?

Why am I even thinking like that? I don't know what this is or what we're doing. I've known her for what, four days? This could just be a summer fling. I really need to get it together. She may not even want anything to do with me once I'm gone. I shake myself from my thoughts. They're not doing me any good right now.

"Don't worry about Luke," I reassure her. "He's a big boy. He can handle himself." She turns back to face the road, dragging in a deep breath and letting it out slowly in another sigh. I don't think she believes me, but I know my friend. This trip will barely be a footnote in his long history of hookups.

When we pull into her driveway, I park next to her beat-up truck, realizing how rundown it looks in the light of day with its rusty fender, crooked bumper, and dented passenger door. I know it's all she can afford, but I hope that thing is at least safe to drive. Surely her brother wouldn't let her drive around in that bucket of rust if it wasn't. I hope he's keeping up with its maintenance since he works in a garage.

A feeling of guilt settles in the pit of my stomach like a ball of lead. Knowing my parents dropped at least eighty grand for my vehicle makes me feel like a spoiled prick. I don't like to receive anything I don't feel like I've worked for, but they gifted the Range Rover to me when I completed my Bachelor's degree. They said I earned it. The thought was always in the back of my mind that they did it more for themselves than for me. You know, keeping up appearances and all.

I hop out and grab her backpack, slinging it over my shoulder. I eye her truck, looking for any visible problems, but see nothing that causes alarm. Part of me wonders what she would do if I just bought her a new car, but I quickly push that thought out of my mind. She would never go for it. There are plenty of girls back home who would, rich girls who expect extravagant gifts like that. But not Abby. She's different.

Cero greets us as soon as we walk through the front door. We both stop and pet him a moment before continuing deeper into the house. "Enisi?" Abby calls out. "Are you home?" No answer. "Hmm, I wonder where she went?" Abby disappears into the hallway and comes back holding her cell phone to her ear, listening to her voicemail. "Guess she went into town with one of her friends," she discloses, pulling the phone away and hitting the end button. "She must not have realized my phone was sitting on my bed."

I hope Abby's grandma doesn't get mad if she comes home and I'm alone with her granddaughter. I would never want to show her any disrespect. Abby seems at ease, though, so I keep my reservations to myself. She's a grown woman, after all.

"I need another shower after swimming in that creek," Abby announces with her nose wrinkled up in disgust. I don't know what she finds unpleasant, because I think she looks beautiful and smells like Heaven. "Give me ten minutes?" she asks.

"Take your time," I tell her, feigning a cool, calm demeanor. In reality, the thought of her a few feet away, naked and wet is enough for me to contemplate pouring a pitcher of ice water down my pants to keep from following her into the bathroom.

I take a seat on the couch in the living room with the intention of waiting on her while she's in the shower. I sit on the edge of my seat, elbows on my knees, and clasp my hands together. I'm itching to touch her again, but I can't risk it. Her grandmother could walk through the door at any moment.

I sit as long as I can, only a few minutes before I begin to pace. Images of Abby's luscious body, soap suds sliding down her skin, invade my every thought. I wander mindlessly with no destination until I end up in what I can safely assume is her bedroom. Oh, shit. This is probably worse.

I lean down, resting my palms on the edge of her dresser, and take a deep breath to calm myself. I notice she has four framed photos, her sweet face smiling back at me from each one. The large photo in the middle is with her parents and brother. She has her mother's complexion and facial features, but those green eyes are definitely her father's.

She looks so young and carefree in the picture with Tiff. She can't be more than twelve or thirteen. There's a picture with her grandma, standing side by side in front of the house we're in now, the love between them evident in their embrace. The last photo is of Abby with her father. It must have been taken shortly before he died, for she appears to be about ten years old. Her hair is braided down each side of her head, not the single braid she wears now. She has skinned knees and is holding a fishing pole. Her father proudly displays the day's catch with a huge grin splitting his face. Abby also beams with pride. It must have been her catch. I can't help but smile, thinking about how happy she must have been at that moment.

I set the framed photo back down and catch movement out of the corner of my eye. Seeing the photos that Abby cherished had distracted me from my near painful arousal, but now, seeing her wrapped in nothing but a towel instantly reignites my desire. She stands in the doorway of her bedroom, clutching the fluffy pink towel to her chest, her hair piled on top of her head with a few loose tendrils snaking down around her neck. Her skin glistens with moisture and I want to lick every bead of water from her body. She's surprised to see me standing in her bedroom. She doesn't seem upset, though – more like she's...excited.

"What are you doing?" she asks in that sexy, breathy voice to which I've become accustomed.

I stalk over to her and cup her cheek with my hand. "I couldn't sit around and think about you in the shower, so I started pacing and ended up in here. Your pictures gave me the distraction I needed to keep from joining you."

"Why didn't you?" she asks, all breathy again. "Join me, I mean," she clarifies.

"For the same reason I don't lay you down on that bed right now and lick every delicious inch of your body." She gasps as I pull her towards me. "I have no idea when your grandma will be home, and I don't want us to get caught in a compromising position." It's one thing to have Luke and Tiff catch us fondling each other, but things won't go over so well if her grandma catches us in the act. I can just picture it now, the small, elderly woman chasing me out of her house with a shotgun.

I reach down and grasp her hands, pulling them away from her chest. She releases her towel and it slides to the floor. I just need to see her. I don't plan on doing anything, I just want to feast my eyes on her exquisite form. At least that's what I tell myself. The curve of her full breasts and the flare of her hips are enough to drive a man insane. I reach up and cup her breast, stroking her nipple with my thumb. Her eyes close and her head falls back as a moan escapes her lips. That's all it takes for me to lose all of my control.

"Fuck it," I growl and pick her up, kicking the door shut. I am insane with lust. To hell with the consequences. She wraps her legs around my hips as my tongue dives into her mouth. I carry her to the bed and set her down gently.

"Jacob," she breathes my name. As much as I want to thrust deep inside her and lose myself to her tight warmth, it's too risky. It's best if only one of us needs to get dressed in a hurry. Besides, when the time comes, I want to take my time with her, savor every moment, every sigh, every touch. I don't want to worry about having to rush or getting caught.

A sense of guilt washes over me at that thought, but it fades away quickly when I see the look of lustful need in those emerald eyes. I kiss my way down her neck before lavishing her breasts with my mouth. I gently suck one stiff peak and twirl my tongue around it, eliciting a sexy-as-hell moan from her. Her quiet little gasps and moans are the sexiest sounds to ever grace my ears. Don't get me wrong, I can appreciate a woman screaming my name, but the subtle noises I evoke from Abby are even hotter.

I run my hand down her abdomen and around her hip, gripping her full buttock tightly. My fingers dig into the juicy flesh as I kiss my way down her stomach. Her breathing becomes more rapid as I smooth my other hand up the inside of her thigh. She gasps when I skim my fingers over her silky heat, spreading her moisture around. I rub slow, gentle circles over her clit, causing her to writhe beneath my touch. She squirms, flexing and relaxing each leg and rubbing her heels against the bedspread as if the sensation is almost too much for her to handle.

She whimpers when I pull my fingers away, gasping when I replace them with my tongue and flick it against her sensitive flesh. The erotic sound fuels my need to make her come. I slide two fingers inside her and bring my mouth back down on her, licking and sucking. I breathe in her sweet scent, trying to ignore the pulsing need growing in my groin. Her hand instinctively snakes into my hair and I pin her wrist to the bed. If I let her touch me like that, I'll cave to my own desires.

I work her over with my tongue, her whimpers and gasps guiding me, letting me know exactly what she likes. My fingers thrust in and out of her tight center, finding that spot I know will make her explode with pleasure. She grows more restless and begins to writhe with her impending release, her back arching off the bed. I continue to stroke her, both inside and out. I know she's close. I feel her muscles tightening. She cries out as she finds her release and I help her ride out the waves. I crawl up her body and gaze down at her in the afterglow of her orgasm. Her eyes are closed and she's panting, her hands clenched, fisting the blanket at her sides.

I graze her jaw with my fingers and press my lips to hers. She groans and opens her mouth to me. I lick inside, letting her taste herself on my tongue, a soft smile forming on her lips when I pull away. Lacing my fingers through hers, I lie down beside her and pull her to her side, facing me. She nestles into my neck and sighs contentedly.

"That was amazing," she whispers. I grin and stifle my laughter.

"Why are you whispering?"

She giggles quietly. "I don't know," she answers and burrows deeper into my embrace. "Something that beautiful and perfect deserves quiet reverence, I suppose."

The shrill ringing of Abby's phone startles us both and we jump out of her bed.

"Shit!" she barks out, clutching her chest. Then she realizes she's still naked and attempts to cover her exposed flesh. I grin at her bashful nature and toss her towel to her. She has nothing to be shy about after what we just did.

She wraps her towel back around her and answers the call. "Enisi, where are you?" she says into the phone, her voice laced with nervous energy. I wince, hoping her grandmother doesn't notice how jumpy she sounds. "Oh, um, no. I don't think there's anything I need right now. Thank you, though," she adds, visibly relaxing. She talks to her grandmother for a few minutes, letting her know she'll be camping tonight before hanging up. She plops down on the edge of the bed and looks up at me, sighing with relief. "She's at the store. We have at least ten minutes before she gets back."

I sidle up to her and press a chaste kiss to her pouty lips. "You better get dressed, then. Before I rip that towel off you and lay you back down on that bed." I shoot her a wink and walk out of her bedroom. I need to walk away from her before I do something stupid and get caught.

I'm too restless to sit down, so I lean against the kitchen counter and check my voicemail. Mom's left me her usual daily message. It's so long, my phone cuts her off. She can be so overbearing sometimes, but I know it's just because she loves me. Sometimes I think she's making up for lost time because of the way she just mentally checked out after Peyton died. It was like Logan and I didn't even exist. She finally snapped out of it and realized she was still needed as a mother. Even though she drives me crazy most of the time, I'm glad she came back to us.

Abby steps into the kitchen a few minutes later, dressed in plum-colored, cropped gym pants with yellow stripes down the sides of her legs. Her matching yellow racerback tank accentuates her ample cleavage and the sun-kissed glow of her skin. "My camping gear is in the garage," she starts.

"I'll help you load it up," I suggest quickly, pushing off the counter. If I spend any more time perusing her curves, we'll never make it out of here.

We load our supplies into the Range Rover and grab some food for Cero. The over-sized dog hops in the back seat like he belongs there. He sits in the center, eyes trained forward like he knows where we're going.

"Hey, watch the leather, man," I deliver before thinking, doing my best imitation of Matthew McConaughey. Abby looks at me with wide eyes, seemingly caught off guard by my lame impression. I instantly grow nervous, thinking I've said something really stupid. Not everybody appreciates random movie quotes. *She probably thinks I'm an idiot now.* She surprises me when she bursts into laughter, clutching her stomach as she guffaws.

"Oh, my gosh," she manages, gasping for air. "I love that movie!"

I laugh with her, relieved that she doesn't think I'm a jackass. "Alright, alright, alright," I add as I shift into drive, a triumphant grin plastered across my face.

"Should we pick up some food or drinks? We can swing by the mini-mart down the road," Abby offers.

"Nah, Luke texted me earlier all the stuff he got. It sounds like there will be plenty."

"Yeah, plenty of beer, probably," she murmurs to herself.

I chuckle and she looks at me sheepishly. She's so cute and she doesn't even know it. I reach over and grab her hand, entwining my fingers with hers.

"Hey, do you care if I stop at the cabin so I can shower and change? I'll be quick," I promise. I prefer to be fresh and clean when I slip into a sleeping bag with her later.

"No, not at all. We've got time."

Abby and Cero stay on the porch while I clean up. I try to get her to bring him inside, but she insists that the owner wouldn't want her one-hundred and ten-pound mass of fur wreaking havoc on the place. They hang around outside, Abby rocking on the porch swing with Cero at her feet.

I hold Abby's hand on the drive to the campsite where we've agreed to meet our friends. I just can't resist the need to touch her, even if it's just her hand. When we pull in, I see Luke standing beside a pristine black Toyota Tundra. *What the...?* "Really?" I pronounce incredulously to myself. Hitched to the back of the truck is what appears to be a brand-new camper. I open my door and get out, heading for Luke.

"Hey J, look what I rented for our little camping trip," Luke announces as he cracks open a can of beer. Tiff is filling a small cooler with ice a few feet away from him, adding brown glass bottles and aluminum cans periodically.

"What the hell, man?" I bark out, unable to hide my irritation.

"What?" he asks, completely unaware that this is not at all what Abby expects out of camping. She does tents and sleeping bags, not campers with pillowtop mattresses and plumbing. Before I have time to respond, Luke's eyes bulge with fear and he gapes at something behind me. I turn around to see what has caught his eye, and notice Abby holding the rear door of the Rover open. Cero barrels past her and heads straight towards Luke and Tiff. Luke stumbles back, nearly losing his footing and busting his ass, but he grips the side of the rented truck and regains his balance.

"Holy fucking hell! What is that?" Luke exclaims, scrambling to put as much space between himself and Abby's imposing dog as possible.

"Cero!" Tiff crows and the dog nearly bowls her over as she crouches down to wrap her arms around him. He nuzzles her neck and licks her face, throwing her into a fit of giggles.

"That," I reveal, pointing to Cero, "is Abby's dog."

"That IS NOT a fucking dog!" Luke cries, pointing an accusatory finger at him. "That's a wild animal!"

"He's a wolf hybrid," Abby explains, sidling up next to me. "And he's completely harmless," she reassures him. I smirk at Luke, noticing the amused look on Abby's face. She's enjoying his discomfort just as much as I am.

"I didn't know you were afraid of dogs," I taunt.

"I'm not," he huffs. "And *that's* not a dog," he repeats, cautiously eyeing Cero. Tiff stands back up and I stifle my laughter when she rolls her eyes at him. Abby covers her mouth with her hand to conceal her amusement.

"It's okay, baby," Tiff coos. "Cero won't hurt you. He's the most well-behaved dog ever."

"Just slip him a hot dog and he'll be your best friend," I add, winking at Abby.

By the time we set up our tent and build a fire, Luke has grown more comfortable around Cero. He has yet to get within three feet of him, but he's no longer cowering in the animal's presence. The sun is starting to set, casting a brilliant glow that reflects in Abby's emerald eyes. The gold flecks surrounding her pupils shimmer like a long-buried treasure.

"I still don't know why you guys won't just stay in the camper with us," Luke probes, handing me another beer. "There's plenty of room, and it'll be much more comfortable."

I twist the top off my bottle and take a swig. "We didn't come out here to sleep in feather beds and air conditioning like a bunch of pansies," I reply, goading him. "We came out here to do some real camping." His mouth flattens into a straight line, an unimpressed look crossing his face. I take another drink and make sure the girls aren't within earshot. "Besides, the last thing I want to hear is the sound of you railing Tiff in the next bed over." And that's exactly what would happen. Those two can't keep their hands off each other, and they're not the least bit discreet about it.

His lips morph, turning up in a devious smile. "Well, in that case, I guess we won't have to try and be quiet now. Thanks, pal." He slaps me on the back and makes his way over to Tiff. She's bent over the cooler, reaching for a cold drink. He grabs her by the hips and she squeals. I look away, not wanting to witness him groping her.

Abby walks over to me, stepping over a log. "We have the food ready for roasting. Hungry?" Her excited smile is contagious. I drape my arm over her shoulders and lead her back to the fire.

"Starving," I reply.

"Weenies first," Tiff announces with a giggle as we approach. She hands us everything we need for our hot dogs.

"Thanks." I take a seat in front of the fire and place my hot dog over it to roast.

"Want some chips?" Luke asks, tossing a bag to me.

"You know what's missing?" Abby asks, looking to Tiff.

"What?" Tiff asks, popping a chip into her mouth.

"Ethan," she replies. Tiff barks out a cough, choking on her food. Cero scrambles to his feet and rushes to her side, whining and nudging her thigh with his nose. That dog is smart *and* protective. Luke pats her on the back and she takes a drink to clear her throat.

"Why would you want your brother here?" Tiff asks incredulously, stroking Cero's head to assure him she's okay. I'm thinking the exact same thing. I thought she wanted to come out here to be alone with me. Having her little brother around would definitely put a damper on things.

"To play music," Abby answers as if Tiff should already know. "Don't you remember how we all used to sit around a bonfire and listen to him play? Everybody would sing along. We had a blast."

"Yeah, we had a good time," Tiff shrugs. She doesn't seem to have the same nostalgic connection to these experiences as Abby does. "I have my iPod if you wanna listen to music," she offers.

Abby's shoulders slump and a dejected look crosses her face. "I guess that'll do."

Tiff retrieves her iPod from the truck and returns with it, playing some older country music. We listen to it for a while, sipping our beers and watching the fire.

"Have you heard Tiff sing yet?" Abby asks, turning to Luke. Tiff scowls at her best friend as though she's just betrayed her.

"No," Luke replies, peering at Tiff with intrigue. "I have not."

"Well, she has a beautiful voice."

"Is that so?" he asks, interest glinting in his eyes.

"It is," Abby replies.

"She's exaggerating." Tiff shoots her a dirty look, but Abby just brushes her off.

"She won all the talent shows in school, and always got the lead in our choir programs." Tiff rolls her eyes, earning a laugh from Abby.

"If I remember correctly, *you* were always the one I was competing with for those leads," Tiff replies with a smirk. "And you beat me more than once."

"Hey, don't turn this around on me," Abby responds with a light-hearted chuckle.

"I knew you had mad rapping skills, but I didn't know you could sing, too," I tell her. "Why don't you two sing something for us?"

"No way!" they both exclaim at the same time.

"Aw, come on. It'll be fun," Luke encourages.

"Sorry babe, not gonna happen," Tiff answers.

Oh, how wrong she is. Because it does happen. Later in the night, once she and Abby have a few more beers, Luke convinces them to sing for us. They whisper conspiratorially amongst themselves, deciding what to sing. Finally, after much debate and a lot of tittering, they settle on a song.

"We're gonna sing, "Hell On Heels" by the Pistol Annies," Tiff announces, placing her beer bottle on the ground. The more she drinks, the thicker her country accent gets.

"Okay, here we go," Abby instructs, and they both giggle.

"Okay, okay," Tiff adds. "Be serious," she deadpans, grasping Abby's shoulders and looking her directly in the face. I try diligently to suppress my laughter at her somber expression.

They both finally get it together and count to three before singing the opening chorus in perfect harmony. I'm instantly enraptured and mesmerized. It's obvious by the way their voices blend seamlessly that they've sung together for a long time. The first verse belongs to Abby. Her sultry voice slides over the words like warm honey. It's sweet and sexy, a combination that is perfectly Abby. Her hips sway to the music in her head, and I'm entranced with the motion. Her eyes smolder, boring into mine with a promise of love and lust. I want to reach out and touch her, pull her into my lap and kiss her until she's breathless.

She begins the second verse, but Tiff takes over half-way through. Her voice is completely different from Abby's. It's not nearly as sultry, but she has a greater range. It's ethereal and graceful, alluring as a Siren's call. She sings the third verse and they finish the song, their voices blending perfectly.

"Whoo!" Luke hollers loudly when it's over and we both begin to clap. Even Cero howls his approval. Luke stands up from his chair and sweeps Tiff into his arms. "Wow, babe. That was fucking amazing!" She giggles her thanks and wraps her legs around his waist.

I pull Abby into my lap, sliding my arms around her waist and brush her lips with mine. "That was incredible," I tell her and nuzzle my face into her neck. Her sweet scent overtakes my senses and I'm lost to the inviting warmth of her body. She flattens her palm against my chest as I kiss her jaw. Her hand fists my shirt and my fingers dig into her hip when the sound of someone dramatically clearing their throat startles us.

Chapter Sixteen

Abby

"**Y**ou guys ready to make s'mores?" Tiff asks, looking down on us with a knowing smirk.

"Yeah, sure," I reply and slide off of Jacob's lap. I instantly miss the feel of his warm body. The night has become somewhat chilly, and I lament the absence of his arms around me.

"Reese's cups or Hershey's?" I ask Jacob as I gather the ingredients.

"Reese's cups, definitely," he replies with one of his devastating smiles.

"Ah, a man after my own heart," I sigh. He chuckles and helps me prepare the marshmallows for roasting.

We spend the rest of the night eating s'mores and talking about music and movies and, unfortunately, a detailed description of how Luke lost his virginity. Jacob just shakes his head and grins, his shoulders vibrating with quiet laughter. When the conversation finally comes back to TV shows, I realize we all have something in common.

"Who do you think will end up on the Iron Throne?" Jacob asks Luke.

We've been deep in a discussion about one of our favorite shows for the last twenty minutes.

"I don't know, man. I hope it's the hot blonde chick with the dragons," Luke replies. "If not, she should at least have a lot more nude scenes. That might make up for it." I just roll my eyes. He's such a guy.

"What do you think?" Jacob asks, turning towards me.

"Nobody," I answer simply.

"What?" he responds, confused.

"I don't think anybody will sit on it. Everybody will be dead. Or turned into ice zombies." Makes sense, considering how things have gone thus far.

My simple answer stuns them into silence.

"Okay," Luke drawls, stretching out the last syllable. "Thanks for the input, Debbie Downer." The three of us burst into laughter at his snarky comment. We've had a bit too much to drink, and it's making us giddy.

"Don't take any offense to Luke. He takes that show very seriously," Jacob offers with a wink.

"Who wants another beer?" Tiff asks, rising from her chair. She stumbles, nearly crashing into the fire. Luke grabs her by the waist to keep her from plummeting into the flames.

"Maybe you should let me get the next round," Luke offers. He takes her by the shoulders and steers her back into her chair. She complies and sits patiently as Luke grabs us all drinks. She pouts when he hands her a bottle of water instead of another low carb beer.

"Are you excited to go to The Barn Saturday?" I ask, distracting her from her disappointment.

Tiff stiffens at my question, and a look of discomfort crosses her face. She recovers quickly, but her reaction unnerves me. Maybe it's all the alcohol in her system.

She hesitates for a moment, chewing on her cuticles. She only does that when she's anxious. I have no idea what she could possibly be anxious about. "I think I'm gonna sit this one out. I've gotta work all day Saturday and open on Sunday."

"I know. I'm working with you, remember?" She's being weirdly evasive and I don't like it. Something is up with her, but I can't quite put my finger on it.

"Yeah, I remember. I was just so exhausted last Sunday after staying out so late." She was exhausted because she was hungover. If she takes it easy on the booze, she might not feel so bad the next day.

"We can just stay for a couple hours and call it a night," I plead. "Ethan's band is playing, and I'm really looking forward to seeing them. I haven't heard them play live in a while."

All eyes are on Tiff now, and her look of apprehension worries me. Her arms are hugged in close to her body and she's progressed to biting her thumbnail, a sure sign of her growing unease. I wonder if there's something she's not telling me. Is she getting tired of Luke and doesn't want him to go? Maybe I shouldn't have asked in front of him. But Jacob already knows, so Luke would find out eventually anyway.

Finally, she sighs and answers, "Okay, I'll go. But can we leave by midnight?"

"Twelve-thirty?" I negotiate. She gives in, shrugging her acceptance.

"What's the barn?" Luke asks, and I tell him about the Jameson's place. He seems pretty excited by the time I finish. "Sounds like fun." He smiles at Tiff and takes a long gulp from his beer. She's a little more relaxed but still seems pensive. I need to get to the bottom of whatever is bothering her.

The night bleeds into the early morning as we sit around the campfire shootin' the bull. It's just after one a.m. when I decide to call it a night since I have to be at work at nine. I stand and stretch my arms high above my head, an involuntary yawn escaping. Jacob stands and brushes my hair from my face.

"Getting tired?" he asks.

"Yeah, I think I'm going to get ready for bed."

"I'm pretty worn out, too."

"You can use the bathroom in the camper to wash up if you want," Tiff offers. "It's better than trying to brush your teeth with a bottle of water."

"Yeah, and there's toilet paper," Luke adds.

"I think we might just take you up on that offer," I tell them. Jacob and I grab our things and head for the camper, and then take turns using the small restroom and brushing our teeth.

Luke and Tiff are entering the camper when I step out of the bathroom with my travel bag, clad only in my sleep shorts and cami. I cross my arms over my chest, feeling self-conscious in my skimpy top, but I hadn't planned on Luke seeing me in it. Fortunately, he's too busy pawing at Tiff to pay me any attention.

"Good night. Sleep tight," I say, hugging my best friend.

"Don't let the bed bugs bite," she replies, giving me a gentle squeeze. This is something my dad always said to us at night when Tiff would sleep over. After he passed away, she continued the tradition. It's one of the many reasons I love her so much.

Jacob exits the camper, and as I follow behind him, I hear Luke asking Tiff, "Are bed bugs a real thing?"

Before the door closes behind me, I catch her response. "No, I think it's some kind of old wives' tale." I giggle to myself at her naiveté.

"What's so funny?" Jacob asks with a sexy grin.

"Oh, nothing. Our friends were definitely cut from the same cloth."

Suddenly, he scoops me up in his arms and I let out a surprised yelp. Cero is instantly at Jacob's feet, whimpering in concern and pawing at his leg. I spend the next few moments reassuring him that I'm fine before he relents and curls back up by the fire. I'm surprised he even moved. He's been overfed and lethargic, sleeping for the past hour or so.

Jacob carries me over to a large log laying close to the fire and places me on my feet. We drop our bags to the ground and he sits, reaching for both my hands. He pulls me on to his lap facing him, and I straddle his thighs.

"I've been waiting all night for this." His husky voice and minty breath warm my face. He cups the back of my head and pulls me close, my lips brushing against his. I feel his erection grow, pressed against my core as he kisses me. He grabs my hips, pulling me down harder onto his arousal, and I moan my approval against his mouth.

He pulls back briefly and releases my hair from its loose bun, allowing it to cascade around my shoulders. Spearing his hand into the hair at the base of my skull, he pulls me back to him, kissing my lips roughly. His other hand presses into my lower back and my hips involuntarily start to move. He groans and deepens our kiss, his tongue thrusting against mine, tasting me, devouring me.

He suddenly breaks the contact and pulls his shirt off, tossing it haphazardly on the ground. He crashes his lips back down on mine, and I feel his warm skin against the tops of my breasts. The sensation is wonderful and I want to feel even more of him against me. This time, I break the kiss to discard my top just as he did his. His reverent gaze falls over my breasts, and I blush as his eyes rake over my bare flesh. I don't even notice the chill in the air anymore. The heat of his eyes and hard body are enough to keep me warm.

One hand comes up to cup my breast, and his thumb grazes over my nipple. My hips jump once more of their own volition, and he tightens his grip on me. His head dips down as he takes the tight peak into his mouth, sucking gently. I gasp and clench my thighs. He releases my nipple and I slide my arms around his neck, pressing my chest against his.

"Fuck, you're perfect," he growls into my ear before biting down on its lobe. He kisses his way along my jaw and back to my mouth. "I think it's time we take this to the tent." I couldn't agree more.

"Okay," is all I can manage to breathe out.

Never releasing his hold on me, he stands back up, grabbing our bags and clothes, and carries me to the tent. Setting me back on my feet, he hurriedly unzips the opening. Once we're inside and the flap is closed back up, he turns on the little battery powered lantern I brought with us. With just a little bit of light, I make my move and practically tackle him to the ground. I sit astride him and resume what we started by the fire. I slide my fingers inside the waistband of his shorts and start to pull them down, but he stops me.

"You first," he insists with a wicked grin. Before I know it, he's flipped me onto my back and I'm staring up at him from atop our sleeping bags. He moves down my body, kissing his way between my breasts and past my navel. He kisses my lower belly as he hooks his fingers into the waistband of my shorts, sliding them down. I lift my hips so he can get them past my ample bottom, grinning triumphantly at the surprised, yet pleased look on his face when he sees I'm not wearing any underwear.

"You are so beautiful." He moves back up my body, scorching me with his slow, sensual kisses. "I want you so bad," he breathes into my neck. "But I'm not going to take you. Not yet."

Why not?! I want to ask, but I can't find the words. My head falls back and my eyes close as he slides his fingers down my slick center.

"Because when I take you," he continues, answering my unasked question, "it's not going to be in a tent with our friends a few feet away." He slips two fingers inside of me and curls them forward. I moan and arch my back, savoring the feeling of his hardened length digging into my hip. "It's going to be somewhere we can be alone, where you can moan and scream and let go completely." He strokes his thumb over my sensitive nub as he thrusts his fingers in and out of me. My knees begin to shake with my impending release. "I'm going to worship your body and make you feel things you've never felt before. I'm going to make you come until you shatter into a million pieces, until your body is spent and your legs shake when you try to stand." His words nearly send me over the edge, but he removes his thumb and slows the fingers inside me before I can climax.

The moment his warm body leaves my side, I want to protest and beg him to come back. But before I can say a word, his mouth is on me, his tongue stroking the spot his thumb just abandoned. I gasp at the euphoric sensation. His fingers resume their speed, working in and out of me until I'm ready to explode. Finally, I let go, my release shaking my entire body. I cover my mouth with my hand so nobody hears me cry out.

Jacob works his way back up my body and pulls me in for a kiss. I can still feel his hardness against my belly. I peer down and see him straining painfully against his shorts.

"Lay back," I whisper in his ear, hoping he won't stop me this time.

He complies and lays on his back with one hand draped over his chest and the other gently stroking my arm. I remain naked, not only for his benefit, but for mine as well. I know he enjoys seeing my body, and it makes me feel sexy and empowered knowing I have this effect on him.

I make quick work of removing his shorts, and then his boxers. When he springs free, my mouth begins to water. I've never wanted to do this so badly before. No man has ever made me feel the way Jacob does. Maybe that's why I'm so eager to please him. He gives before he ever takes. He doesn't expect me to return the favor. He has pleasured me multiple times today, but never once asked for anything in return, and I want to give him everything because of it.

I kiss him passionately one last time before sliding my body down his. Taking him in my hand, I stroke him a few times before sliding my lips over his swollen tip. He groans and begins to breathe faster. I keep my hand wrapped firmly around him, stroking him at the base as I swirl my tongue around his throbbing head. Finally, I sink down onto him, taking him to the back of my throat. I pull back and pump my fist around his hardened length as I glide my mouth up and down. His hands fist into the material of the sleeping bag beneath him.

I can't believe how good he tastes and how turned on I am just from doing this to him. Part of me wants to climb on top of him and sink down onto his arousal. That would guarantee pleasure for both of us, but right now, this is about him. And I don't think he'd let things go that far yet anyway. I think he knows I'm not typically that kind of girl, but for him, I could be. I want to be.

Soon his body starts to stiffen, and I know he's close. I speed up the motion with my hand and alternate sucking him deep into my mouth and swirling my tongue around the tip. He hardens even further and I can tell he's about to come. Suddenly, he yanks me back up his body and captures my mouth in a bruising kiss. He wraps his hand around mine, guiding my strokes until he releases onto his stomach. His grip on me loosens, his whole body relaxing.

I look for something to clean him off with while he catches his breath, but I find nothing. I put my shorts back on and search for my top. "I'll be right back," I say slipping it over my head. Stepping out of the tent, I tiptoe my way towards the camper and find some of our supplies still sitting out. Grabbing a handful of napkins, I return to Jacob and help him clean up.

"Come here," he commands, opening his arms to me. I comply and lay down next to him. I wonder why he pulled me away before his release but say nothing. He hooks his finger under my chin, lifting my face to his. His lips brush mine in a sweet and gentle kiss.

"I wanted to kiss you," he hints, studying my face. Oh. *Oh, that makes sense.* He dips his head and kisses me again, this time probing his tongue between my lips. I open up and let him in, savoring the taste of him. He pulls back and kisses my forehead, remaining quiet for a few moments before speaking again. "I've never wanted to do that before, ya know," he starts. "Kiss a girl afterward." He takes a deep breath and lets it out slowly. "You're different, though. There's something special about you." His words warm my heart and those butterflies take flight in my stomach again. I nuzzle into his chest and take in the masculine scent of his skin.

We lay there in silence for a while, Jacob gently stroking my back with his fingers. "What's your schedule like tomorrow?" he asks.

"I'm working all day."

"What time do you get off?"

"Ten."

"You're working thirteen hours tomorrow? That's insane!" he announces, his voice laced with worry.

"Well, technically, I'm only working twelve. Ziplines from nine to five, then Rosie's from six to ten," I elaborate. Not that the hour break makes much of a difference.

"Still, that makes for a long day. Do you always work like that?"

"Only during the summer. I don't have much time to work during school. That's why I'm working like I am now. I have to save up."

"You're amazing, you know that?" he proclaims reverently, kissing my forehead. "Most people couldn't do what you do. Hell, I know I couldn't do it."

"Sure you could," I assure him. "People do what they have to. It may be hard right now, but it will pay off in the end."

"Okay, what are you doing the day after?"

The fact that he's trying to plan a way to spend more time with me makes my heart flutter and my insides tingle with anticipation. I want to sigh and melt into this sleeping bag, but I try to control my excitement. "I work at Rosie's from four to ten, but I have to do yard work before I go in," I reveal with a pout. The yard work really should've been done today, but I wanted to spend time with Jacob. These are the things Ethan used to help out with when he lived at home. Now it's all up to me.

"How long will that take?"

"A few hours," I reply.

"A few hours?" he asks, surprised. "Why on earth would it take that long?"

"Well, between mowing and raking and weed eating, there's a lot to be done." I doubt he's ever done any of those things, and probably has no idea what all it entails.

"What if I help you? Will that make things go faster?" Somehow, this man continues to surprise me. He's always willing to help with whatever I need.

"Well, sure it would, but I can't ask you to do that."

"You didn't ask," he replies with a genuine smile. "I offered. And I insist." *How can I say no to that?* "Let me help you. Then we can do something fun before you have to work."

"Okay, I'll let you help me. But on one condition," I add with a sly smile.

"Name it."

"You have to let me make you dinner Friday night." Dinner is the perfect way to show him my appreciation, and I've always heard that the way to a man's heart is through his stomach. Plus, I have ulterior motives. Promising him a home-cooked meal ensures that I'll get to spend more time with him.

"Done," he replies without hesitation. "I'm looking forward to it." He tugs me in closer and kisses me one last time before we fall asleep.

THE NEXT MORNING, the alarm on my phone goes off way too early. I groan and silence it, hitting snooze. Jacob stirs beside me but doesn't wake. I take this opportunity to study his beautiful, yet masculine face and sculpted planes of his upper body. At some point in the night, he must have covered us with a blanket. I'm warm and toasty snuggled up next to him. We never got into our sleeping bags, instead, using them to lie on. I start to drift off again, but my alarm screeches in protest.

I silence it again as Jacob yawns and stretches next to me. "Better get up," he admonishes sleepily. "Don't want you to be late for work." He wraps his arms around me and pulls me into his chest.

"How can I possibly get up with you lying next to me?" The words are out of my mouth before I can stop them, and a huge grin splits Jacob's face.

Quicker than I would've thought possible, he moves on top of me and stares into my eyes. "I could stay here with you like this all day." He leans down and presses a sweet kiss to my lips. He doesn't know how good that sounds.

My alarm chooses that moment to blare again and I groan my frustration. Jacob and I dress quickly and I start to pack everything up again.

"Don't worry about that," Jacob offers, placing his hand on my arm. "I'm going to take you to breakfast before work, then I'll come back and take care of all of this."

Part of me wants to protest. It's not fair for him to have to pack my gear up by himself. But I can tell by the look in his eyes, there's no arguing with him. And breakfast sounds fantastic right about now.

"Are you sure?" I ask, not wanting to take advantage of his kind nature.

"One hundred percent," he answers with that dazzling smile of his.

I change into my usual uniform of white shorts and blue t-shirt, brush my teeth with a bottle of water, and braid my hair before leaving the campsite. Jacob texts Luke to let him know not to leave before he gets back so nothing happens to my gear. I'm not too worried about that happening though since our friends will probably sleep until noon.

We drop Cero off back home before heading to breakfast. Sitting in a corner booth of the little roadside diner, we crack open our menus. "What's good here?" Jacob asks, scanning the laminated pages.

"Everything," I reply. "Don't let the looks of this place fool you. It may be a hole in the wall, but the food is phenomenal. Especially after a long night at the bar," I add with a wink. He chuckles and sets his menu down.

"How would you know? You just turned twenty-one," he points out with a smirk.

"That doesn't mean anything around here. It's not hard to get into bars in this town when you're underage. Besides, I had a fake ID."

"You little rebel," he grins teasingly at me.

"Y'all ready to order?" the waitress asks as she approaches our table. Her name tag reads "Millie." She looks to be about forty with a mass of unruly, dyed red curls piled on top of her head and secured with a pencil. Her lips are painted the same crimson shade as her hair and she has a sweet, motherly smile.

"Yeah, we're ready," Jacob answers and motions for me to go first.

"So, what was it like growing up around here?" Jacob asks once we've placed our orders.

"I suppose it's just like growing up anywhere else," I answer with a shrug, sipping my orange juice.

My response amuses him. "I doubt that," he replies with a laugh. "It must've been a lot different than growing up in Arlington. Here, you're surrounded by beauty and nature. I was surrounded by politicians and lobbyists."

Hmm, surrounded by liars, I think to myself. Politicians aren't exactly known for their honesty. They tell the people what they wanna hear, pretending to care about them, while in reality, most of them just want to stay in power and pad their bank accounts with the taxpayers' hard-earned money. I keep that thought to myself, though. I don't want to offend Jacob by insinuating his dad is dishonest. He may be a perfectly nice guy, for all I know. One of the good ones.

Throughout breakfast, we discuss our childhoods and how different it was growing up in our respective hometowns. I mostly talk about the time before my father passed away. Those were happy times. There's too much anger and hurt in the years that followed to discuss over breakfast. Besides, Jacob already knows about my mom's drug problem and what she put Ethan and me through as kids.

Jacob tells me about growing up in the public eye and how dedicated his parents are to making a difference. That must be where he gets his passion for helping others. I can tell he has tremendous respect for his father just by the way he talks about him. I'm starting to like this guy, despite his occupation.

We finish our breakfast and although I insist on splitting the check, Jacob lays down two twenty dollar bills on our table. That's nearly double what our meal costs. As a waitress myself, I truly appreciate a generous tipper. I shouldn't be surprised, though, because Jacob is generous in everything he does. It just makes me love him even more.

Whoa! Where did that thought just come from? Do I love him already? Is that even possible? My head is still reeling from my inward revelation when he takes my hand and leads me out the door. I'm quiet as he helps me into his car and slides in next to me, my thoughts consumed with the possibility that I may be in love with this man after knowing him less than a week.

This is ridiculous. You can't fall in love with someone that fast! Love takes time to build and grow. It must be nurtured. I just have a tremendous amount of respect for him. And I like him. A lot. He's a wonderful, giving, selfless person who gives me really good orgasms.

"Hey," Jacob interrupts my racing thoughts. "Are you okay?"

"Yeah, I'm fine." I try to act cool when inside I'm coming unraveled.

I. Love. Him.

This epiphany hits me like a ton of bricks. And it scares me to death. What if he doesn't love me back? It will crush me. Then again, what if he does? He's leaving soon. What happens then?

"Abby, you're shaking." Jacob grasps my hand and I look up to see his face etched with concern. "Do you feel alright? Did that food make you sick?"

"No, no. It's nothing. I'm okay. Must be a sugar rush from the pancakes and orange juice." He eyes me skeptically, sensing that something is off. "Really." I smile and try to reassure him. "I'm fine." I can't tell him what I'm actually thinking. He'll think I'm a lunatic.

He laces his fingers through mine and brings our entwined hands to his lips, placing a gentle kiss on the back of my hand. "Okay, but if you start feeling bad, call me. I'll come pick you up early." He already plans to pick me up when I get off work so I don't have to catch a ride home with one of my co-workers. I'm extremely grateful for that since I know Caleb would be the first to volunteer to take me home. No effin' way. I would *never* get in a vehicle with him.

When we pull up to the entrance of New River Adventures, I thank Jacob for bringing me to work and hop out of the car. He gets out and swiftly comes around to my side, surprising me when he pulls me into his arms.

"I'm going to miss you while you're gone," he admits, cupping each side of my face, dipping his head and pressing his lips to mine. His tongue barely grazes my bottom lip, but it's enough to send searing heat down between my legs. I grip his biceps to keep my knees from buckling beneath me. His kiss is all too brief. "See you at five." With that, he gets back in his car and leaves me standing there like a love-struck idiot.

Once my legs no longer feel like Jell-O, I turn to walk into work. Avery is standing there, mouth agape like she just witnessed something shocking.

"Holy mother of all hot guys!" she exclaims. "Who was *that?*"

I feel the flush of embarrassment creeping up my neck and flooding my cheeks as I duck my head. I hadn't realized anyone was standing there to witness our PDA, though I have a feeling Jacob knew and was claiming me as his.

"That's Jacob," I answer hastily and scurry past her before she can ask any more questions.

Chapter Seventeen

Jacob

DROPPING ABBY OFF AT WORK IS HARDER than I thought it would be. I'm not ready to give her up after the night we shared. She was so sexy with her lips wrapped around me, her hair cascading over my groin and tickling the tops of my thighs. Her beautiful, naked form was nearly my undoing. I wanted to lay her on her back and spread her wide open so I could bury myself deep inside her, and I know she would have let me. I could see it in her eyes. She wanted me too, but I couldn't do that.

Our first time is going to be epic. Unforgettable. Earth-shattering. I'm going to make it perfect for her. It will be like nothing she's ever experienced before.

Her tan legs poking out of those little white shorts are enough to make me reconsider letting her out of the car, but I do. She tries to slip out without giving me a kiss goodbye, but I'm not letting her off that easy. I get out and round the hood, reaching her before she can get very far. Holding her soft face in my hands, I claim her mouth with mine. I don't care that one of her coworkers is standing there gaping at us. Actually, I kind of like the fact that someone is watching. Now they'll *know* she's mine.

Reluctantly, I let her go and hop back into my car. I need to leave before I change my mind, throw her over my shoulder like a Neanderthal, and take her back to my cabin to ravage her.

I drive back to the campsite so I can start packing it up. It looks as though Luke and Tiff have yet to join the land of the living. They were probably up all night breaking in the mattress. I'm sure Luke will want to tell me all about it later. He likes to recount his conquests to me in great detail as if I care about where his dick has been.

I finish loading Abby's gear and start cleaning up. I didn't realize how much of a mess we made last night. It's nearly eleven o'clock when Luke emerges from the camper, squinting his eyes and shielding them from the bright morning sun with his hand.

"What the hell are you doing, J? You're being loud as shit," he complains, obviously annoyed at being woken up before noon. I can't help but laugh at his appearance. He's noticeably hungover and looks like cousin Eddie standing in the camper's doorway.

"What the fuck's so funny, asshole?" he asks irritably.

"You, dick breath," I chuckle. "You look like you belong in a trailer park." He's shirtless, with bare feet and only a pair of mesh shorts hanging low on his hips. It doesn't help that he's scratching his balls. All he needs now is a cigarette dangling from the corner of his mouth and a trucker hat to complete the look. I grab the bag of leftover hot dog buns and toss them to him. "Help me clean this place up. It looks like a frat house exploded out here." There are beer bottles and red plastic cups littered on the ground and folding lawn chairs surrounding the remnants of our campfire. Thankfully, the girls put most of the food away so it wouldn't attract unwanted visitors in the middle of the night.

Luke grumbles something unintelligible and retreats back inside. He returns a few minutes later wearing a t-shirt and flip flops, still looking douchey as hell.

"You're more annoying than an itchy ball sack, ya know?" he grumbles as he snatches a trash bag from my hands. Luke's digs are more amusing than they are insulting, especially considering how he was scratching his own sack only moments earlier.

"Cleaning up your shit is the only way to relieve the itch," I quip. He just glares at me and flips me off. He's so cranky in the morning.

Luke continues to grouse as we clean up around the campsite. I ignore his contemptible protests and work until everything is cleared out.

The sound of Tiff exiting the camper draws our attention her way. "Hey, gorgeous," Luke greets, wrapping his arms around her waist and pulling her in close. I avert my gaze when he kisses her, practically shoving his tongue down her throat. He's such an animal.

Tiff finally pulls away from his sloppy kiss and looks up at him. "Could you take me home now? I've gotta work later and I have a ton of stuff to do beforehand."

"Sure, baby. Let me just finish up here and we'll head out." He slaps her ass as she turns to leave, eliciting a squeal and giggle from her. "It's a shame we aren't going to be here for long," Luke divulges, turning back to me. "I could have a lot of fun with her."

"Isn't that what you're doing now?"

"Well, yeah, but we could have even *more* fun if we didn't have to leave so soon."

This is weird. He's never wanted to spend more time with one of his fuck buddies before. Maybe Abby was right. Perhaps Luke *is* developing feelings for Tiff.

I leave Luke to attend to his girl and head back to my home away from home. He and I plan on fishing for a few hours today, so I stop to get some bait on the way. I load up our fishing rods and tackle box and wait for him to return, although I'm starting to get impatient since I need to be back in time to get Abby. He's obviously not in any hurry to get back and has never given two shits about wasting anybody else's time. Plus, he knows it annoys the piss out of me.

Finally, around twelve-thirty, he comes strolling in with a shit-eating grin on his face and a spring in his step. I don't even want to know what that's all about, but he tells me anyway.

"Sorry I'm late," he gloats. "Had to give my girl a little something to keep her satisfied for the rest of the day." *Man, he's a pig.* "Mmm, *mmm*, that girl is insatiable." He licks his lips and grabs his junk like I'm supposed to be impressed. "You are a shame to the male species."

"Oh, come on. Don't act like you aren't doing the same exact thing," he scoffs incredulously. "And I'm not judging you for tapping that." Luke must read the apprehension on my face. Technically I'm not "tapping" anything, but he doesn't need to know that. He doesn't need to know what I do or don't do with her. That's between me and Abby and I'd like to keep it that way.

"Wait a second." His eyes narrow with suspicion. "You haven't fucked her yet, have you?"

I shoot him a warning look, but it doesn't stop him. "Oh my God, you haven't!" he exclaims and bursts into laughter.

"Luke," I warn. I will kick his ass if he says one cross word about her.

"What the hell are you waiting for, you big pussy? She one of those goody-two-shoes who won't put out? Or is she just surfing the crimson wave and you're riding it out until you can get some?" he bellows with amusement.

"Not another word, fucker," I bite out through gritted teeth. This is his final warning.

Luke sobers when he sees the dangerous look on my face and notices my fists balled at my sides. This wouldn't be the first time Luke and I have rolled, but I know he doesn't want to go there with me. He knows I'll wear him out.

"Jeez, dude. Chill. I'm just busting your balls." He holds his hands up in surrender. Or to block the punch he knows is coming if he doesn't shut his trap.

"Come on, bro. Let's just relax and do some fishing." Luke throws his arm around my shoulders to lead me outside. He's trying to lighten the mood so I don't wreck his face. I elbow his side and shove him through the door.

"I don't know if I'd call what you do 'fishing,'" I taunt.

AFTER ONLY THREE and a half hours on the water, Luke and I come away with four trout and one catfish. I can't rag on him too much since he did catch two of the trout. I plan on grilling some of them for dinner one night when we have Abby and Tiff over.

I'm thankful for the time my father spent teaching me how to clean and cook fish. Our little weekend fishing trips are some of the fondest memories I have of my childhood. As busy as he was, and still is, he always made time for his family. We got at least two or three of these long weekends a year with him.

Lately, mine and Logan's schedules haven't permitted these trips, and I feel guilty about that. Dad always made time for us; we should make time for him. Maybe we can come back before the end of summer and I can introduce him to Abby. That is if she wants to continue this thing we're doing once I leave. I find myself hoping more and more that she does. This can't be over when I go home. I'm not sure I'll be ready to give her up.

I'm not sure I'll ever want to give her up.

I'm running a little late to pick up Abby, so I leave the fish in the cooler, checking to make sure there's plenty of ice to keep them from spoiling while I'm gone. Once I drop Luke off with the day's catch, I head to New River Adventures. I enjoyed my fishing trip and spending time relaxing with Luke, but I've thought about Abby all day and can't wait to see her. Even while Luke was rambling on about Tiff and her "huge rack" and "tight little ass"- his words, not mine - I was thinking of ways to show Abby what she means to me. Our time is so limited, it'll have to be something we can do in a few short hours. Plus, she's not like most girls. A dozen roses and a fancy dinner won't impress her. She's more interested in the experience, something more visceral. I have something special in mind for her, but I'm gonna have to make a few phone calls first to see if I can pull it off.

I pull into the parking lot at ten past five. I don't see her anywhere, so I decide to get out and lean against the passenger side door. I want to be the first thing she sees when she walks through those gates. After a few more minutes with no sign of her, I start to get worried, wondering if she got tired of waiting on me and caught a ride home with someone else. Surely, she would've called to let me know. Besides, I was only ten minutes late.

Finally, I see her small frame scurry around the edge of the gate and I'm filled with relief. Until I see the guy trailing closely behind her, following her out. He's average-sized, with an average build and short brown hair. Nothing special, nothing impressive. It's Abby's expression that alarms me. She looks upset, but there's another emotion playing on her face. She seems uncomfortable and maybe even a little bit scared. The way this douche is leering at her pisses me off. He must have done something to upset her.

The more I scrutinize him, the more I realize there's something familiar about his face. I know I've seen him before. Then I remember... He's the asshole from my first day here, the one who was eye-fucking Abby right in front of me, and the one who I was worried wouldn't secure my harness properly because he was mad Abby was checking me out instead of him. I wanted to deck him *then*; now, I want to make him choke on his teeth.

What did he do to my girl?

I push off the side of my car and start towards him, seething with rage. When Abby lifts her gaze to meet mine, she holds her hands up, begging me with her eyes not to go after him. She can tell that I know something's up, and she rushes towards me, flattening her palms on my chest.

"Please, Jacob. Let's just go," she pleads.

"What the fuck did he do to you?" I scan my eyes over her body and settle on her face, searching for any physical signs that she's hurt, praying I don't find any. When I look back up, that piece of shit has the nerve to smirk at me as he gets into his car and fires up the engine.

"He didn't do anything to me. He's just a creep." She grips my biceps, forcibly trying to keep me in place. He peels out of the parking lot, sending gravel flying out behind him. The tail lights of his candy apple red Mustang taunt me like a matador luring an angry bull to his demise.

"Abby," I start, trying to calm myself down and slow my rapid breathing. "I'm going after him right now unless you tell me what happened. Did he hurt you? Did he touch you?" *I'll kill him with my bare hands if he did.*

"No." She shakes her head. "Well, yes. He touched me. But not like that," she adds hurriedly. "He grabbed my arm." Anger burns inside of me and my nostrils flare as I try to pull in air. "I'm not hurt, though. I'm okay."

She sure didn't look okay walking out here with him stalking behind her. I pull out of her grasp and get in the driver's seat. "Get in the car," I instruct through the rolled-down window, staring straight ahead with my jaw clenched so tight, it might snap in half. She complies and climbs in as I punch the ignition button to start the engine. When I grab the gear shift to put the car in reverse, she covers my hand with hers to stop me from backing out of the parking lot and following him.

"Look at me."

I can't look at her. I'm about to blow my lid, and I'm afraid for her to see me lose control.

"Jacob," she whispers, and I feel her soft hand cup my cheek. She coaxes my face towards hers, forcing me to look into her eyes. "He's not worth it. I'm okay. He didn't hurt me," she reassures me. "Please calm down. If you go after him and something happens, *that* will hurt me. I don't want to see you hauled off to jail."

I know she's right, but all I can think about is bashing in that little fucker's brains. I've worked really hard to keep my anger under control, and I'll be damned if I let this little cocksucker negate all the progress I've made.

Being with Abby brings out emotions I've never felt before, and my instinctual need to protect her makes me a little crazy at times. I truly care about her, and can't stand the thought of someone hurting her. Just thinking about him putting his hands on her makes my blood boil and my instincts kick into high gear. I will protect what's mine at any cost. But Abby's soft eyes and gentle touch are enough to pull me back from the brink. I could never do anything to hurt her, and seeing me arrested for assault would do just that. I try to clear my head and just focus on her.

"You promise you're okay? He didn't hurt you?" I ask, lowering my forehead to press against hers. I close my eyes tightly and wait for her reply.

"I promise." She presses her lips gently to mine and offers a sweet kiss. I open my eyes and gaze into the emerald pools staring back at me. Something electric crackles in the air between us and I capture her mouth, kissing her more deeply this time.

My adrenaline is still rushing and my heart is pounding from the anticipation of a fight, but all that energy is redirected when she slips her tongue between my lips. I kiss her back fiercely and revel in the sound of her lustful moan. I reach down, gripping the lever that adjusts my seat and push it all the way back. In one smooth motion, I pull her into my lap to straddle me and press my erection into her, wishing there were no boundaries between us.

I need her. I want her. And if I don't have her soon, I might just explode. She digs her fingernails into my shoulders and grinds her hips against me. I wrap my arms around her waist and pull her closer to my body, not caring one bit that we're sitting in the parking lot where she works. My hands slide up her back in search of the clasp on her bra, but before I have a chance to unhook it, my phone blares from my pocket, startling us both.

Abby pulls back, panting, and looks around as if she just realized where we are for the first time and climbs off my lap. "You better get that. It might be important," she asserts, smoothing her clothes.

Reluctantly, I pull my phone out and swipe my finger across the screen. "Hello," I bite out in irritation.

"Jacob," the familiar voice greets hastily. "Is Abby with you? I can't get ahold of her."

"Yeah, she's right here," I reply, handing my phone to Abby. "It's Tiff."

"Hey, Tiff." Abby greets her friend and then listens for a moment. "My phone died and I haven't had time to charge it." She pauses briefly, and I hear Tiff's frantic voice through the phone, warning her of the time. "Oh, shit! I didn't realize it was that late." Abby's panicked now and gives me the sign that we need to leave so I pull out of the parking lot. "I'll be there as soon as possible." She hangs up the phone and hands it back to me. "Shit," she exclaims again. "I should've picked Tiff up already. She's freaking out because I'm never late, and wasn't answering her calls." Abby worries her lip between her teeth, and although I think it's hot as hell, I hate to see her in distress.

I pull her hand into my lap and lace my fingers between hers. "I'll just pick her up and drop you two off at work. I'm sure Luke won't mind grabbing a late dinner and a few beers, and then we can take you both home."

The hopeful look on Abby's face makes me glad I thought of this solution. "You'd do that? I don't want to put you out."

"You're not putting me out. I'm happy to do it."

Her tense shoulders visibly relax and she takes a deep breath. "Thank you so much. You're about to save me from my Aunt Roselyn's wrath. Trust me, I do *not* want to get on her bad side."

Abby asks to borrow my phone again so she can text Tiff and let her know we're on our way. "She still probably won't be ready," she adds with an eye roll, handing my phone back. She seems to have forgotten all about whatever happened earlier at work. I hate to bring it up again, but I need to know exactly what transpired.

"Before we get to Tiff's, I need you to tell me what happened earlier with that guy. What's his name, anyway?"

She lets out a defeated sigh. "Caleb."

That's all she offers, forcing me to probe further. "What did Caleb do to you?" I try to keep my voice even and calm. Losing my cool again will just upset her.

"I came out to meet you, but you weren't there." I know she doesn't mean anything by it, but her remark stings. I already feel guilty about being late, and her comment just makes me feel worse. "My phone died as I was trying to call you, so I went back inside to find another phone. I was going to call Tiff and have her get your number from Luke because I couldn't remember it, but Caleb found me in the office and cornered me."

It takes everything I have to keep my body language neutral and remain calm, but I feel my grip on the steering wheel tighten, causing my knuckles to turn white. He cornered her. She must have been scared, and it's all that asshole's fault.

"He asked me out and when I refused him, he got upset. He asked me why and wanted an explanation for not wanting to date him. I told him I wasn't interested and that I was seeing someone. When I tried to leave, he grabbed my arm. I have no idea what he would've done to me had someone not come into the office just then."

Guilt and anger consume me. If I had just been there on time, this wouldn't have happened. "I'm so sorry, Abby. I should've been there."

"It's not your fault," she tries to assure me. "Caleb is a creep, and he's always made me feel uneasy. Until now, he's never been that aggressive towards me. I'm going to talk to my boss about it. Avery's the one who walked in on us, so I have a witness."

"Why would you need a witness? Is your word not good enough?"

She hesitates. "He's related to the owners of the company, and I'm afraid they'll take his side if I don't have someone to back up my story."

They better not dismiss this incident! I glance at her, noticing a fresh bruise forming on her arm from his assault. I swear, I'll hire the best damn legal team money can buy to bring that place down if justice is not served for her.

"They won't take his side. I'm sure Avery will back you up." The conversation ends as we pull into Tiff's driveway.

She hops in with a big smile on her face. "*Now* I see why you were running late," she teases, oblivious to the tension in the air. "I bet it's a nice change, *having* a chauffeur instead of *being* one, for once." She tosses a folded up green t-shirt into Abby's lap. "Here. I figured you'd need this."

"Thanks, Tiff," Abby conveys, visibly relieved. "I hadn't even thought about it."

"Any time, sugar," Tiff replies in a faux southern accent, adding a wink for emphasis.

The three of us make small talk until I pull into Rosie's parking lot with only a few minutes to spare.

"Thanks for the ride." Tiff smacks her glossy lips against my cheek before bouncing out of the back seat. Abby giggles as I attempt to wipe the glittery, sticky residue off my face.

"Thank you for driving me around all day." Abby reaches for the door, but I stop her, gently cupping her hand with mine. I pull her toward me and kiss her, stroking my thumb over her cheek. She's got to quit trying to leave without kissing me goodbye. I know she's a little hesitant to initiate physical contact, but she must know by now how much my body is drawn to hers. I'm addicted to the feeling of her lips on mine, her skin against my skin.

"We'll be in later for dinner." I brush a few rogue strands of hair from her face and gently press my lips to hers again, then to her forehead. "Goodbye, Abby."

"Bye, Jacob." Her breathy reply assures me that I still have the same effect on her that I did the first time we kissed. I leave her there, comforted by the fact that she'll be safe and I'll be back to get her soon.

A few hours later, I return with Luke. Being a Wednesday night, the restaurant isn't nearly as packed as the first time we came. The hostess beams at me when I ask to be seated in Abby's section. She has yet to notice us, so I silently observe her as she works. It's impossible for me to look elsewhere when her beautiful form sweeps past the bar and through the dining area. Watching her bring a tray full of drinks to a small group of teenagers, she balances it easily, moving with a lithe fluidity that must have taken months to master. Her genuine smile inspires my own and I grin like an enamored fool. That's the effect she has on people. You can't help but smile back at her. I find myself enjoying the moment, watching her without her knowing.

"Dude, stop creeping on her. You're practically stalking her with your eyes." Luke's ugly mug enters my field of vision, breaking my line of sight.

"Like you don't eye-fuck Tiff every time you see her."

"Yeah, maybe," he admits. "But I don't look at her like I wanna get married and have her babies," he teases.

Luke's comment stuns me. Is that really how it looks? That's certainly not what I have in mind. I'm twenty-three years old. Marriage and babies aren't even on my radar.

"You're insane," I mutter as Abby approaches our table. She greets us warmly and takes our order. Throughout our meal, she stops by our table every chance she gets, as drawn to me as I am to her. Every cell in my body wants to invite her to spend the night with me, but it's not the right time yet. I know what will happen the next time she crawls into my bed.

Thankfully, the last hour of her shift goes by quickly, and at ten o'clock I get to whisk her away. She rides shotgun and Luke and Tiff slide into the back seat, as usual. Everything feels so natural now, the four of us hanging out.

"What time do I need to be there tomorrow?" Since I'll be helping Abby with yard work, I want to make sure I show up on time.

"I need to go for a run in the morning, so I probably won't get started 'til about nine-thirty or ten."

"Would you like some company on your morning run?"

"Sure." A huge grin splits her face. "If you think you can keep up," she adds teasingly.

"Oh, I can keep up," I assure her with a cocky grin. Unfortunately, that cocky grin is wiped off my smug face the next day when Abby's morning run nearly kills me.

Chapter Eighteen

Abby

LOOK BACK OVER MY SHOULDER FOR the third time in as many minutes, just to make sure Jacob hasn't collapsed on the side of the road. He straightens and gives me an enthusiastic thumbs up as he struggles to climb this formidable hill. I try to keep a steady pace without leaving him behind. Only a mile or so left to go and this will all be over.

I slow my pace to a leisurely jog and allow him to catch up to me. "How ya doin'?" I ask, nearly out of breath myself.

"Great," he answers between gasps for air.

Typical guy. He doesn't want to show he's struggling or that he can't keep up.

"One. More. Mile," I tell him between breaths. Even I'm winded at this point. Keeping my sentences short and sweet is a necessity. "Almost there." He gives me another thumbs up but avoids talking.

We finally crest the top of the hill and start our descent. I see my house in the distance and know we're only a few minutes from our reprieve.

We coast into my gravel driveway on momentum alone, and I rest my arms on top of my head and try to calm my breathing. Jacob bends over with his hands on his knees, sucking in big gulps of air. He looks like he's on the verge of puking his guts out, so I look away. Nobody wants to be seen like that.

A few minutes pass before he stands upright and walks over to me. Silently, he takes the water bottle from my hands and drains it in one long gulp. He finished his off two miles back.

"Damn, woman." He's still trying to catch his breath but is no longer gasping for air. "Are you trying to kill me?" he teases, smiling as he shakes his head.

"Thought you said you could keep up?" I taunt playfully.

Jacob's face grows serious and he leans his body into mine, his lips only a hair's breadth away. "Oh, I can keep up." His tongue darts out to wet his lips and my eyes move involuntarily to his mouth. "When it really counts."

Oh, my. I think my whole body just melted into a pool of lust. Jacob wraps one arm around my waist and pulls me in tight, cupping my cheek with his free hand and just barely grazing my lips with his. The heat and moisture from his sweaty body melds with mine. I wish there were no clothes between us so our slick bodies could slide over each other freely. I'm tempted to lean up and lick the bead running down the side of his neck, the insatiable desire to taste the salty sweetness of his skin overwhelming my senses, but I refrain. We're standing in front of my grandmother's house, after all.

When he releases his hold on me, I step back and take a deep breath. I've got to get my head on straight or I won't get anything done today.

"We'd better get something to eat and rest for a few minutes before we get started," I announce once I catch my breath.

"I don't know how you do it," Jacob declares, wiping the sweat from his face with the bottom of his shirt. I'm momentarily struck speechless by his rock-hard abs, now on full display. My mouth waters in anticipation of running my tongue between each and every ridge. He finally pulls his shirt down and I snap my gaze back up to his face. If he caught me ogling him, he doesn't let on. "How can you have the energy to do yard work after that? I'm beat."

"Oh, well… um." I stumble over my words, feeling guilty for expecting him to help out after subjecting him to that long, grueling run. It's already above eighty degrees and the sun is blazing hot. It's going to be sweltering today. "You don't have to stay. I can take care of the yard. I'm used to it," I maintain with a shrug.

"Hell, no. I'm not leaving you here to do all this by yourself!" he proclaims. "I'm just amazed that you have the energy left to do *anything* after what we just did. You must have an insane amount of endurance." His praise causes me to blush. Thankfully my face is already flushed, so he doesn't notice.

"Okay, well, if you're staying, we need to get some food in us. Can't have you passing out on me." My needling earns me a cocky smile.

"Never," he promises before placing a quick peck on the corner of my mouth.

Jacob follows me into the house and I instruct him to sit at the table. He's so exhausted, he doesn't even argue with me. I hand him a knife and a large, shiny red apple to slice while I toast some whole grain bread and spread almond butter on it. Better keep it light. Full bellies, manual labor, and humid, Appalachian heat don't mix.

After breakfast and a short rest to let our food digest, I change out of my sweaty running clothes, swapping my compression shorts and tank for my usual lawn mowing attire: a pair of cut-off jean shorts and bikini top. Might as well kill two birds with one stone and work on my tan. Jacob's eyes widen when I step out of my bedroom, surprised to see me so scantily clad. I grin to myself, relishing my ability to cause such a reaction. "Ready to get started?" I ask as his eyes roam over my body.

"On what?" He raises one eyebrow suggestively. "You, or the lawn?"

I giggle, swatting his arm as I attempt to slip past him. He grabs me before I can get by and pulls me against his chest.

"You really are trying to torture me today, aren't you?" he whispers in my ear, pressing my body up against his. The fire in his eyes nearly consumes me, weakening my legs and my resolve not to pounce on him. He lowers his head and kisses me chastely before taking a step backward. "Two can play this game, you know."

He smirks and pulls his t-shirt over his head. I stand there, helplessly entranced, as he strides leisurely to the kitchen table and drapes it neatly over the back of a chair. My eyes drink him in, his muscles flexing with every movement. "Better get started." He grins and holds his hand out, motioning for me to lead the way. I command my brain to pick my chin off the floor and force my feet to move.

When my limbs begin to function on their own again, I lead Jacob out to our shed and unlock the weathered, wooden double doors. They creak in protest when I push them wide open, allowing sunlight to flood the interior so I can check for snakes. Copperheads love hiding in there, but luckily, there are usually enough black snakes around to keep the venomous bastards away.

Satisfied the rickety building is momentarily snake free, I pull the archaic push mower out, followed by the only slightly newer weed eater. I grab the rake and gas can before closing the old doors back into place.

"Ready?" I ask Jacob, handing him the weed eater. I'll let him start with that since I've already pushed him to his physical limits today.

"Yep. Where's your mower?"

I glance down at the rusted old hunk of junk in confusion. "It's right here," I point out, grabbing the handle.

He looks taken aback for a moment. "*That's* what you cut your grass with?" he asks incredulously. "You don't have one of those ride-on mowers?"

Oh, bless his heart.

"Nope, this is all I've got." Riding mowers are expensive and something I don't have the money for. It's a luxury we just can't afford. Besides, we've only got an acre and a half of non-wooded land on our property. It's not so bad to push mow.

I guess my earlier assumptions were right. He's never done this type of work before. I sometimes take for granted that his life is much different from mine. Most of the boys I grew up with could cut grass, clean a shotgun, and skin a deer before they hit puberty. But Jacob is looking at the old Cub Cadet like it's some kind of primitive relic.

"Have you ever cut grass before?"

He lets out a humorless laugh in response to my question. "Yeah. Once." A pained look flashes briefly across his face. "I got in a lot of trouble for it." He takes a deep breath before adding, "Damn near got someone fired, too."

"What?" I ask, perplexed.

"It was a long time ago," he explains. "My mom was still struggling with Peyton's death."

A sense of unease creeps into my mind and settles in my bones. I know how much his sister's death still affects him. There's so much pain in his voice when he says her name. I'm not sure I should ask him to elaborate, but judging by his tormented expression, this isn't something he's been able to share with anybody. Plus, I have a feeling his despair has been trying to claw its way out for a long time.

I place my hand gently on his arm, but he won't meet my gaze. "What happened?" I ask softly.

His pensive countenance tells me he's debating whether he should proceed with this story. He places his hands on his hips and lets his gaze roam over my backyard, squinting against the sunlight. Patiently, I wait for him to reveal what he's been holding in.

After a few beats of silence, he takes a deep breath and begins. "It was the first week of summer vacation and I was restless. I needed something to do to occupy my pre-pubescent mind." He smirks, briefly meeting my gaze. "Ray, the head of lawn maintenance and gardening for my family's estate, was there with his crew that day. Ray was a cool guy. He never treated me different because of my family name or because of my dad's position. He even taught me how to hit a curveball and sink a free throw every time." He smiles at the fond memory before continuing with his story.

"Anyway, one day I was bored out of my mind, so I asked Ray if I could help him cut the grass. He immediately shot me down, saying that if I did his job, then he wouldn't be needed anymore. He ruffled my hair and turned to walk away, but I just wouldn't leave it alone. I had this grand idea that learning to drive his monstrosity of a mower would be like driving a car, and what twelve-year-old boy doesn't want to drive a car?"

His eyes finally meet mine and my heart breaks at the sadness swimming in them. His jaw clenches and he looks away before continuing. "I begged him to let me at least make one pass on it. Just one. I promised him I would be careful and wouldn't go too fast. He finally caved but swore me to secrecy. I couldn't tell my mother. That should've been my first clue. He was apprehensive, and I should've known better.

"I climbed up into that seat like I was climbing into an Indy race car." A small smile touches his lips before he forges ahead. "Ray showed me all the controls and explained how everything worked. I was way more excited over the prospect of mowing the lawn than I should have been, but I'd been sheltered my whole life, never allowed to do anything that could get me hurt or ruin our image. No menial work for Senator Daniels' sons," he mocks. "I didn't even know how to wash my own clothes when I went off to college. How pathetic is that?" he scoffs, shaking his head and looking down at his feet.

I can tell he's ashamed, but it's not his fault. It's just how he was brought up.

"Getting up on that lawn mower was freedom to me. And maybe a little rebellion. I knew my mother wouldn't like it, and that made me want to do it even more. I'd only made a few passes when I heard her screams of fury." He winces as he recalls the incident. "She came barreling down the yard in her tailored pantsuit, her high heels sticking in the soft ground. I'll never forget the look of fear on Ray's face when he pulled the keys out of the ignition and helped me down." He pauses and takes another deep breath, and I know the next part is going to be bad. The far-off look in his eyes tells me he's reliving this memory, seeing it over again.

"She was inches from Ray's face, screaming at him. 'How dare you let my child cut the grass when you're the one I'm paying to do it?' 'How dare you put him in danger like that!' I was crying because I was afraid of what she was going to do to him. What she was going to do to *me*. I truly thought I'd done something wrong, something that put my life at risk. I felt so guilty.

"It wasn't until I was a little older that I realized what the real issue was that day. To her, that kind of work was beneath her, and by extension, beneath me. We were better than that. God forbid somebody saw me doing such a demeaning chore. It was all about appearances to her."

I can't help but feel anger towards his mother, a woman I've never met. Who treats their child that way? And for that matter, who treats someone the way she treated Ray? I grit my teeth to keep from letting my disgust show.

"Finally, hearing the commotion outside, Dad walked out of the house and trekked across the lawn towards us. At that point, she was threatening to fire Ray and promising he would never find work in that town again. It made me sick to see her throwing around her power like that. That's the day I realized what a bully she was. Even though he was a grown man, all Ray could do was sit there in shock and take her abuse.

"My father was finally able to calm her down and get her back into the house. When I looked back at Ray, his jaw was clenched in anger, his eyes staring daggers at the back of her head. But his features softened when he looked at me. I was quietly sobbing. A twelve-year-old boy. Sobbing," he winces, "and praying Ray wouldn't lose his job. I told him I was sorry for getting him in trouble, but he assured me none of it was my fault. For a minute, I thought Ray was going to cry right along with me. Instead, he became stoic as my father approached. He apologized vehemently, but Dad waved his hand dismissively and promised he would remain employed.

"Dad sent me back into the house, but I lingered, wanting to hear what he would say to Ray. I was afraid he would take Mom's side and fire him. He started talking about anger, depression, and grief, but I didn't understand any of it at the time. So, with my tear-stained face and snotty nose, I trudged back up to the house and locked myself in my room, leaving Ray to his fate.

"I was ecstatic to see him back the next week, but I didn't dare go near him for fear of getting him in trouble again. I avoided him for years after that. I didn't talk to him, not even a "hello" in passing. I felt bad because I liked Ray, but I couldn't risk doing something to make him lose his job. It wasn't until I got my first car that I had the balls to face him again. He helped me check the oil and showed me how to change a tire. With my mother's permission, of course."

His obvious resentment towards his mother makes my heart hurt. I understand that feeling all too well.

"Anyway," he continues as if he hasn't just revealed something huge about his past and his family to me, "Ray and I are cool now, but I've never attempted to cut grass since. And I've certainly never used one of those," he adds, pointing to the push mower. His eyes crinkle at the corners with a genuine smile, and his playful tone eases some of the tension.

I'm glad he feels comfortable enough to share such an intimate, long-buried secret with me, but I wonder what he might still be holding back. I guess that will have to wait until later because by the way he's trying to start the weed eater, I fear for his safety.

AFTER TWO HOURS, we're nearly finished with the yard. It usually takes me much longer, but having Jacob here is a huge help. Once I showed him how to use the weed eater properly, he took to it like a pro. We're raking up the last of the grass clippings when my grandmother comes out with two large glasses of lemonade.

"You looked thirsty," she asserts, handing me a drink. I guzzle it as ice cubes clink against the side of the glass.

She hands Jacob a glass when he approaches us, but studiously averts her eyes. His sculpted, bare chest glistening with sweat is conveniently at eye level. Her tan cheeks flush deep red and I know she was checking him out. I can't blame her. She may be in her sixties, but she can still appreciate a good-looking man.

"Jacob, you've worked so hard helping Abigail," my grandmother praises. "You must let me pay you for a job well done." She turns towards the house, planning on retrieving her checkbook, no doubt. She has no idea how little Jacob needs her money.

Jacob puts his hands up. "That won't be necessary, ma'am. Abby is making me dinner tomorrow night. That's all the payment I need." He winks at me and smiles, revealing perfect, gleaming white teeth. His smile could give any leading man in Hollywood a run for his money.

"That sounds like a great idea. I'll make a homemade peach cobbler for the two of you."

"Peach cobbler sounds wonderful. I've never had it before."

"Well, you're in luck, because I make the best peach cobbler in all of West Virginia." With that, my grandmother pats Jacob's cheek and turns and walks back into the house. I think she might be falling for him just as hard as I am.

"I want one of those." I look at Jacob in time to see him gazing longingly at her retreating form.

"Huh?"

"Your grandma. I want a grandma like that," he discloses, pointing to where she just disappeared into the house.

"Yeah, she's pretty special." I smile warmly at the thought of my enisi.

"I don't remember my dad's mom. She died when I was little. Breast cancer, I think. My other grandmother is a lot like my mom, more concerned with appearances and fundraisers than baking for her grandkids."

My heart aches to think that he never had a grandmother to make him cobbler and cookies and apple pie. It makes me cherish mine even more.

"Well, I'm positive that if you flash that mega-watt smile enough, my grandmother will make you all the peach cobbler you want." I wrap my arms around his waist and smile up at him, resting my chin on his chest. He deserves to have someone fawn over him. "And if you play your cards right, she might even make a special blackberry cobbler, too. But you'll have to share that one with me," I add. "She doesn't make those very often, and they're my favorite."

"No way," he replies, shaking his head. "If I get a blackberry cobbler, I'm eating the whole damn thing," he taunts, squeezing me tight. "In one sitting," he adds playfully. He presses his lips lightly to mine before releasing me. As I start to walk away, he swats my butt and I yelp in surprise.

"You better hope she didn't see that," I warn playfully, pointing toward the house. He tosses his head back and laughs before throwing his arm around my shoulders and kissing the top of my head. Those are quickly becoming my favorite kind of kisses.

Chapter Nineteen

Jacob

CRACKING OPEN ONE EYELID TO A sliver of blinding light, I'm momentarily struck with a sense of confusion. Where am I, and what time is it? I slowly peel both eyes open and take in my surroundings. The late afternoon sun blazes through a two-inch gap in the curtains of my bedroom. I groan and roll over, burying my head in the crook of my arm. I must have passed out after my shower, exhausted from my morning with Abby. How she does that on a regular basis is beyond me.

After we finished raking all the grass clippings and pulling weeds in her flower beds, we ate a delicious lunch of homemade potato salad, fried okra, and ham sandwiches that her grandmother prepared for us. A guy could get used to that kind of cooking. After lunch, we treated ourselves to ice cream from the dairy bar down the road.

The rest of the afternoon was spent on Abby's front porch swing talking to her grandmother, or enisi, as she uses the Cherokee word to address her, and watching her weave a dream catcher. I was entranced by the beautiful art form and contemplated asking her to make one for me. She could take her time and I could use it as an excuse to come back.

I didn't leave until it was time for Abby to get ready for work. When I got back to the cabin, it was all I could do to wash the sweat and grass from my body before collapsing face-down on my bed.

I must have slept at least a couple hours judging by the feeling of cotton in my mouth and the pounding in my head. As I'm drifting back to sleep, my phone begins to chirp with my mother's ringtone. I'm not really in the mood to talk to her right now, but I've been avoiding her lately. If I don't answer, she'll just continue to call until I do. Might as well get this over with now.

"Hello?" My words come out as a croak through my sticky, dry throat.

"Jacob, honey, can you hear me?"

"Yeah, I can hear you."

"Well, I was just calling to check on you. Haven't heard from you in a few days." The subtle accusation doesn't go unnoticed. Though I've texted her every day, she hasn't technically *heard* my voice. My mother is a master of the guilt trip. "Are you having a good time?"

I smile to myself, thinking of Abby. She's made this trip more fun than I could have imagined. "Yeah, it's been alright," I offer, downplaying how much I've enjoyed it here. I don't want to sound too excited or she'll catch on and start asking questions. I don't want her knowing about Abby. At least not yet.

"You don't sound very enthusiastic about it. Does that mean I can convince you to come home early?" Her voice is hopeful, but there's no way I'm cutting this trip short. If anything, I'd like to extend it.

"Nah, Luke and I still have a lot we want to do. We may even stay a few extra days. There's more to this place than I thought."

"Oh, no!" my mother gasps dramatically. *Here we go.* "You promised you'd be home in time for our Memorial Day party," she reminds me.

That was before I met Abby; now I can't even think about anything else. The thought of leaving her kills me, but if I'm not home for this party, I'll never hear the end of it.

Our annual Memorial Day party is a big deal to my mother. She rents a huge, white tent and has the pool opened, even though nobody would dare risk getting their hair wet or ruining their stick-up-the-ass reputation by getting in and actually enjoying themselves. She even has the event catered. Most people just grill hot dogs and hamburgers or roast a hog. Not my mother. No, we have hors-d'oeuvres and champagne. It's just a pretentious display of wealth disguised as a fundraiser. Don't get me wrong, she raises a shit load of money for multiple veterans' charities. Still, it's a bit over the top. Abby would hate it.

I pinch the bridge of my nose and squeeze my eyes shut. The building pressure in my skull is becoming too much, and if I don't say something to placate her now, she won't give me a moment's peace until I give in. "Of course, I'll be there. You know I wouldn't miss it." There's no use arguing with her, so I tell her exactly what she wants to hear.

"Yes, well, don't forget the Greysons are coming. They've made considerable contributions to your father's last two campaigns and are willing to go the distance with us should he set his sights on the White House."

She says this as if there was ever any doubt. She's been dreaming of the presidency since Dad's first term in the Senate.

"Be sure to pay special attention to their daughter, Maggie," she continues, undeterred by my lack of response. "I hear she was quite taken with you at last year's party."

I can just see the wheels turning and hear the hope in her voice. She has this grand idea in her head that I'll one day marry the Greyson's daughter and join our two families in wedded, politically advantageous bliss. Maggie Greyson may be a beautiful, intelligent young woman, but she's shallow and boring like the rest of the socialites that garner my parents' approval. A week ago, I wouldn't have cared. I would have entertained her, maybe even snuck her into the pool house after everybody left for some late-night fun, but that was before. Before Abby.

"Hey, Mom, I gotta go. Luke and I are heading out to dinner soon. I'll talk to you later." It's not exactly a lie. I'm sure we'll go to Rosie's in a little while. I need to end this call before she gets any more ideas in her head about me and Maggie.

"Okay, sweetie. I'll talk to you tomorrow. Love you," she coos.

"Love you too, Mom." And I do. I love my mom. She hasn't always been the best parent, but I've tried to look past her flaws and forgive her for what she put me and my brother through as children. Deep down, I know she loves us and would do anything for us. Not everybody has that. I know Abby doesn't. Her mother chose a life of drugs and a scumbag boyfriend over her family. I guess I'm lucky to have the overbearing, protective mother that I do.

After I dress and brush my teeth, I go looking for Luke. I find him sitting on the couch in the den playing Xbox.

"It's about damn time you rolled out of bed. Abby must've worn your ass out," he smirks, not moving his eyes from the screen.

"Yeah, well, it wasn't as much fun as you'd think. We went for an hour-long run, then did yard work. I thought I was going to pass out from heat exhaustion."

"That sucks. I thought you meant something different when you said you were gonna mow her lawn." He raises his eyebrows suggestively, quite amused with himself. He grunts when I blast him in the back of the head with a throw pillow.

"Easy man," he chuckles. "I'm just kidding."

I sink down beside him on the couch and grab the extra controller, joining in on the game. "So, what's the plan for tomorrow?" he asks.

"We're booked for a day of white-water rafting. Think you can handle that?" I taunt.

"I can handle it better than you handled ziplining." *Ouch.*

"I don't know. I'm guessing you'll blow chunks before the day's over," I challenge. Last time we were on a boat, he turned an unnatural shade of green and had to pop a couple Dramamine tabs to keep from losing his lunch. And that was on a luxury yacht sailing through the Chesapeake Bay.

"You wanna bet money on that?" Luke never passes up an opportunity to make a bet.

I ponder a moment, an idea forming, one that will rescue me from my mother's little matchmaking scheme. "No, I think we can make things a little more interesting."

Luke glances over at me and raises one eyebrow inquisitively. "What did you have in mind?"

"If you toss your cookies tomorrow, you have to entertain Maggie Greyson at my parents' Memorial Day party."

"Done," he smirks again. "Maggie Greyson is smokin' hot. Besides, I was already planning on going."

"And you have to get in the pool in a Speedo." His face falls at the addition, but he recovers quickly, his smug façade back in place.

"Whatever. I'm not gonna lose anyway. Now I have to think of something for you." A devious smile pulls up one side of his mouth. "Hmm, let's see," he says, rubbing his chin in contemplation with his thumb and forefinger. "I got it!" he announces, snapping his fingers. "When I win, you have to go skydiving with me."

Fuck. I wasn't expecting that. If I don't agree to this, he'll never let me live it down. But if he wins, I'll have to jump out of a fucking airplane. A perfectly good plane. There's no justification for that.

"Fine," I agree begrudgingly. *He better not win.* I'll have to make sure he drinks plenty tonight. Not that the notion will be much of a challenge. I've got to ensure the odds are in my favor come tomorrow morning.

I LOOK FORWARD to seeing Abby's sweet face as soon as I walk into Rosie's. I know I spent the entire morning and most of the afternoon with her, but I can't get enough. She's like a drug and I need another hit.

The restaurant is packed, and we end up having to wait a while to be seated. When the hostess leads us to our table, I figure out why it's so busy. There's a major baseball game tonight, and it's playing on every TV screen in the place.

"Here are your menus," the hostess announces, blonde curls bobbing in her ponytail. "Don't forget, it's half price draft and wing night. Your server will be with you shortly."

Tiff sidles up to our table and pulls out her pen and pad. "Hey, guys, what are y'all drinkin' tonight?"

"Couple Bud Lites, sweet cheeks," Luke answers, undressing her with his eyes.

"Bring us a couple shots of Cuervo too, Tiff."

"Ah, I like where this night is going," Luke declares, rubbing his hands together with anticipation and excitement.

"Be right back." Tiff leaves to get our drinks and I catch sight of Abby. She sees us and waves from a few tables away. She smiles, ducking her head and tucking a strand of hair behind her ear. Still so shy with me at times… and it's so damn sexy.

Tiff brings our drinks and Luke downs two shots of tequila, one right after the other. When we order our food, Luke orders another shot, smacking Tiff on the ass playfully when she leaves our table. If he's not careful, he'll end up getting us kicked out of here and probably banned.

"Hey, how you guys doing tonight?" Abby asks when she approaches our table. Her usual sweet smile lights up her face, but I can tell she's worn out.

"Hey Abby," Luke greets her.

"We're good," I answer. "How about you? You must be tired." I'm still exhausted, and I had a two-hour nap. I can't help but be concerned, but she just shrugs. "What time do you get off tonight?"

"Ten-thirty. Tiff and I have to close." When she frowns and scrunches up her nose, I just want to kiss it all away. She's adorable even when she's making that face.

"That's a shame," I reply, taking a sip of my beer, attempting to pique her interest.

"Why's that?" she asks, taking the bait.

"Because after all the hard work we did earlier, a nice, long soak in the hot tub would've been the perfect end to the day."

She blushes and I can tell she's remembering the last time we were in that hot tub together. Or more likely what happened before. Her in that little string bikini was like every man's fantasy come true.

"I agree. That *would* be nice."

I know it'll be late when she gets off work, but maybe I can convince her to come home with me for just a little while. She left that little bikini hanging on the shower rod to dry, and it's been taunting me ever since. I'd give anything to see her in it again. Or out of it.

I lean forward on my elbows, bringing myself close enough to notice the faint scent of honey on her skin. "Perhaps you could spare just a little bit of your time this evening to take advantage of a severely underutilized hot tub? I mean, we've been practically negligent."

A small smile curves the edges of her lips. "I think I could manage that. I don't have to be back here until eleven tomorrow. I'm sure I could spare an hour or two. My muscles *are* feeling kind of sore." She rolls her shoulders for emphasis.

"Well, if you play your cards right, you may just get a message for those sore muscles."

Her body shivers visibly and I can't hide my cocky grin.

I LOSE TRACK of how many shots Luke downs, but he's already slurring his words and cussing like a sailor. Loudly. I've gotta get him out of here before they *throw* us out. Tiff brings him a cup of coffee in the hopes of sobering him up, but he's too far gone for that.

"You coming over tonight? Abby's coming. We can all get in the hot tub again." Luke tries to entice Tiff to come home with us with his lopsided grin and typical panty-dropping charisma, but tonight it doesn't seem to be working.

"I don't think so, big guy." She leans in and bats her big blue eyes at him to soften the blow. "I think you've had a little too much to drink tonight, and I'm not sure I'm strong enough to rescue you if you pass out in the water."

He frowns and furrows his eyebrows. I half expect him to cross his arms over his chest and stomp his foot like a four-year-old, but he doesn't. Instead, he reaches out and grabs her around the waist, pulling her towards him.

"If I promise not to drink too much, will you come stay with me tomorrow night?" he asks, burying his face in her neck and inhaling deeply. This is completely abnormal behavior for him. He never gets this affectionate with women, even when he's hammered.

"Sure thing, sweetie." She caresses the side of his face gently before wiggling out of his grip. He reaches for her as she slips away, but lets his arms fall to his sides as he watches her retreating form.

I pay our bill and leave Tiff a substantial tip. She deserves it after having to put up with Luke's drunk ass all evening. Seeing that we're leaving, Abby stops by our table, balancing a tray full of tall draft beers.

"Y'all headin' out?" she asks, shifting the load from one hand to the other without spilling a drop.

"Yeah, I need to get home and put him to bed," I tell her, nodding towards Luke. He flips me off and scowls. "Do you remember how to get to the cabin? Are you okay with driving yourself, or do you want me to come back and get you?"

She shakes her head and smiles. "No, I remember. I've been navigating these parts for a long time. I'll be just fine," she assures me. I sometimes forget how independent she is. Knowing how little she needs me both drives me crazy and turns me on. I love the fact that she's self-reliant, but I also want to be her damn hero. Corny, I know.

"Okay, I'll see you in a little bit, then." I quickly brush her cheek with the backs of my fingers, fighting the temptation to use my lips instead. Luke stumbles halfway to the door, and I catch up with him just as he's about to topple a waitress with a tray full of food. He smiles down at her and winks, causing her to blush and giggle.

"Come on, Casanova, let's get you home."

The wait for Abby to get to the cabin isn't long but feels like an eternity. When I finally hear the timid knock, I jump to my feet and rush to open the door.

"Hey," she greets, smiling up at me. Her right arm is crossed over her body, her hand holding the opposite elbow. She looks like a shy school girl talking to her crush for the first time.

"Hey, come on in." I step aside to let her pass. She seems nervous, and I grin to myself. She's so different from the girls I'm used to back home, with their noses in the air and perfectly manicured nails they wouldn't dare to risk soiling by doing yard work. She's modest, sweet, and completely unaware of the effect she has on most guys.

"Do you want a drink?"

"Just a water would be fine," she answers, following me into the kitchen. I grab two bottles from the fridge and hand one to her.

"Your bathing suit is sitting on the vanity in my bathroom. You want to slip it on and meet me outside?" I nod towards the balcony. As much as I want to assist her, the wisest thing I can do right now is leave her alone to change.

"Sure."

She heads towards my bedroom and I step out onto the balcony, pulling my t-shirt over my head before easing down into the water in my board shorts. My achy muscles instantly relax in the hot water. I lean my head back and close my eyes, waiting on my bikini-clad angel. A few minutes later, she walks through the sliding glass doors with an over-sized beach towel wrapped around her petite frame. My eyes roam over her curves when she drops the towel and steps into the water, a pulsating need rushing into my groin. She sinks down across from me with a sigh, and I could swear the temperature rises when she does.

"Wow, this was a good idea." She closes her eyes and rests her head on the ledge behind her.

"What are you doing all the way over there? It feels *much* better on this side," I assure her. I want her close to me.

"Is that so?" Her flirtatious response turns me on even more.

"Come see for yourself."

She wades over and starts to sit down beside me, but I don't let her. Instead, I pull her onto my lap and rest my hands on her hips. "Better?" I inquire.

"Much."

I hate to bring this up, but there's something that's been nagging at me and I have to ask. "So, did you ever talk to your boss about what happened with Caleb?" She stiffens in my arms and I immediately regret asking. But she didn't mention anything about it today, so I was worried they either weren't taking her seriously, or she'd been afraid to say anything.

She sighs and drops her gaze to my chest. The defeated look on her face makes my heart ache and anger burn like acid in my gut.

"Yeah, I talked to them. They're going to change Caleb's schedule around so I won't have to work with him while they investigate the incident."

Investigate? What the hell does that mean? That little cocksucker cornered and harassed her. He put his hands on her! I don't say anything though, because I don't want to upset her. I just nod my head and change the subject.

We talk for a long time, all the while I'm kneading her tight muscles. I start with her shoulders and back and work my way down to her thighs. I know they must be sore from her run and pushing that archaic mower around her yard. I move her off my lap so I can reach her calves and feet. When I get down to her heels, she lets out a soft moan as her eyes close and her head falls back.

"That feels absolutely amazing. My feet hurt so bad after a shift at Rosie's."

"Glad I could be of service." She opens her eyes and lifts her head up to meet my gaze.

"I think your fingers might be magic," she sighs as I switch to her other foot.

"You have no idea, sweetheart."

"Oh, I think I have *some* idea," she responds playfully. Her green eyes glow with heat and need, and I can't take anymore. I release her foot and pull her back onto my lap.

"Perhaps I should show you the full range of what my fingers are capable of doing." I wrap my arms around her back, pulling her against my body and capturing her mouth with mine. "And my tongue." With that, I use my tongue to tease a trail down her throat to her collarbone. She moans and squeezes her thighs, locking me in their tight grip. I press my erection into her, eliciting another moan. Fuck! I'm going to lose it if she doesn't quit making that sound.

I slide my fingers down the edge of her bikini bottoms to the inside of her thigh. "Do you want me to use my fingers?"

"Yes," she breathes. I slip them inside her bottoms and graze her slick heat with my knuckles.

"Do you want me to use my tongue?" I continue to stroke her lightly.

"Yes," she sighs again, her hips thrusting against me. She gasps when I slide two fingers inside her. I kiss my way down her chest and pull one of the triangles covering her breasts to the side with my teeth. She cries out when I pull the dark, pink bud into my mouth.

"Shhh, baby. You're gonna have to be quieter out here." I don't want anybody else hearing her cries of pleasure, especially Luke. Voices tend to echo out here, and I'll be damned if I let the people in the other cabins hear her.

"Oh," she responds with a blush, her eyes downcast. "Sorry." She goes to move her top back into place, but I stop her. She misunderstood the meaning behind my warning.

"Hey." I place my finger under her chin and tilt her face up to mine. "I don't want anyone else hearing those sexy sounds you make. *I'm* the only one who gets to hear those, okay?" She nods her head in understanding. "Maybe we should take this inside." She agrees and climbs off my lap and out of the hot tub.

I lead her into the house and she shivers as the air conditioning blasts cold air through the vents. "It's freezing in here." She pulls her towel tighter as we hurry towards my bedroom.

"You can crawl under my blankets and try to get warmed up if you'd like."

"Actually, I'd love a shower, if you don't mind. I always smell like hamburger grease and stale beer when I get off work." She wrinkles up her nose in disgust and I can't help myself. I lean down and kiss it.

"I think you smell wonderful," I assure her. "But if you want a shower, then be my guest." I'm disappointed she isn't all over me now like she was in the hot tub, but I tell myself she just wants to be squeaky clean for all the things I plan on doing to her. I sure as hell hope that's the case, and it's not because she's having second thoughts.

"Thank you."

I tell her where to find the towels and washcloths, and tell myself not to follow her in there. She didn't invite me to join her, so I need to just have a seat and wait for her to finish.

Then my imagination starts running wild, my fingers itching to help her out of that bikini.

I hear the cabinet door open and close.

I want to rub soap onto every inch of her bronzed skin.

I hear the spray of the water turn on.

I want to feel her slick body pressed up against mine.

I hear the blood pounding in my ears.

Fuck it. I can't wait any longer! I don't want to waste another minute denying myself the chance to be with her. If she wants this as badly as I do, there should be nothing holding me back.

I enter the bathroom quietly to see her still in her bikini, testing the water temperature with her hand. She reaches back to untie her top but I stop her, grasping her fingers in mine. "Let me," I practically growl in her ear. She startles and gasps at my touch but lowers her hands, allowing me access.

I slowly untie the top strings and let them fall, exposing her breasts. As I release the ones behind her back, the bikini top hits the floor. Leaning down to brush her ear with my lips, I whisper gruffly, "Get in." She complies and steps into the warm spray. I follow her in and turn her body towards me.

"Abby." One word. Her name. It's all I can say. I want her so bad. She's breathing heavily and won't make eye contact, instead, staring at my chest.

She wants this too but is afraid to make the first move, so I get down on my knees in front of her. A wry smile spreads across my lips at her shocked expression. I kiss her lower belly just above where her bottoms rest, and with both hands, untie each set of strings. I pull the thin material from her body and toss it aside. I want her bare. I want to see all of her.

I grab some soap off the shelf and lather it in my hands. Starting at her feet, I gently wash from her toes to her hips, making sure every inch of her is clean. But I don't touch her *there*. Not yet. I gently knead her buttocks with my soapy hands before turning her back around, facing away from me. I wash her back and shoulders, messaging her muscles as I go. I rub her arms clean before grabbing the shampoo bottle and squirting some into my hands. She sighs with pleasure as my fingertips massage her scalp. Her long, dark hair clings to my chest as I work my way down.

After I rinse conditioner from her hair, I move on to the parts of her body I saved for last. Once more, I grab the soap and work up a lather. Her flat stomach is first as I rub gentle circles over it and work my way up to her breasts, gently caressing them as I go. Temptation gets the best of me and I roll and pull each of her nipples into tight peaks. Her head falls back on my chest and she moans. Finally, I slide my hands down to the fronts of her hips and start moving towards her center with slow, circular strokes. I slide my hand between her legs, parting her. I take my time, carefully cleansing her. Her breathing is fast and heavy and I know she's as turned on as I am. I can feel it on my fingertips.

She whimpers when I pull away to grab the hand-held showerhead. I sweep it over her before aiming it between her legs, taking my time rinsing her, ensuring no soap is left behind. She moans as water sprays against her sensitive flesh and she grips my wrist, her fingernails digging into my skin as she directs the spray where she needs it. I press my lips to her shoulder and smile against her neck. My efforts have had their desired effect, but I won't let my showerhead claim her orgasm. That's for me. So, after a moment, I pull it away and put it back in its holder.

I spin her around and lower myself back down in front of her again, lifting one of her legs and placing it over my shoulder. Pinning her hips against the tile wall, I press my face into her and take a long, slow lick. Her legs shake as I grip her tightly, my fingers digging into her thighs. My tongue darts out and starts making slow circles around her sensitive nub. I work her into a frenzy until she's writhing, her hands fisting in my hair as she calls out my name. Her whole body trembles with her release.

When I stand back up, I kiss her parted, panting lips and she throws her arms around my neck, kissing me back fiercely, passionately. Then her hands are on the waistband of my shorts. I forgot I still had them on. She frantically unties them and her urgency makes me impatient for her touch. Once she has them loose, she shoves them down my legs and I step out of them. She grabs the soap and goes right to my straining erection. As her hands slide up and down my shaft, I brace myself with one arm against the wall behind her. When I lean in, she kisses me, biting my lower lip.

I grab her wrists and pin her arms above her head. Eyes closed, my forehead pressed against hers, I try to calm my breathing. I'm about to lose control, and I'm not sure she's ready for that. I open my eyes and watch the suds slide down my thighs and escape down the drain. As I pull away, two emerald pools stare back at me, her gaze full of desire and pleading. Pleading for what, I'm not sure.

"Abby," I begin and take a deep breath, "If we don't stop now, I'm going to fuck you."

Her breath is coming in and out in pants. Her voice is light and breathy when she replies, "What are you waiting for?"

That's all the prompting I need. I crush my mouth to hers and press her against the wall. When I bend down and lift her up, she wraps her legs around my waist. I press myself against her and capture her breast in my mouth, sucking hard. She cries out, arching her back as I rub my length up and down her slick core, coating myself in her wetness. When I press my head against her opening, she whimpers.

"Please," she begs, and my control shatters. She gasps as I bury myself inside her and I still.

I've done it. There's no going back now. When she starts to rock her hips, I know she's okay with this. I rock with her, and soon, we have a steady rhythm going. When my feet start to slip and I can no longer keep up the same pace, I know it's time to take this to the bedroom.

"We need to get out of here before we fall." Pulling out of her is damn near painful, but I do it. I release her, setting her on her feet and turning off the water. We wrap towels around our bodies haphazardly, not even bothering to dry off before we head towards the bed. I've only got one thing on my mind, and that's getting this beautiful woman underneath me.

Chapter Twenty

Abby

WE STUMBLE TO THE BED IN A series of frantic kisses and hastened caresses before crashing onto the mattress. Jacob lands on top of me and presses his lips to mine, slipping his tongue inside. His kiss is urgent and demanding and I give in without hesitation, opening up to him. Together we slide to the middle of the bed, and he cups one hand beneath my bottom and pushes my hips towards him. He pulls back and looks into my eyes.

"Are you okay with this?" he asks, searching my face for any signs of doubt. He won't find any. I want this as much as he does.

"Yes," I breathe. He thrusts into me without breaking eye contact, and I bask in the sensation of him filling me. He braces himself with one hand beside my head and continues to press my hips into his with the other. He kisses me deeply, his tongue exploring and tasting. I can't get enough of him, so I wrap my legs around his hips, urging him deeper.

His responding groan excites me. I slide my hand into his hair and around to the back of his neck and nip at his lower lip with my teeth. He leans up and smiles down at me before burying his head in my neck, nibbling at my ear and jawline, sending chills down my body. My already tight nipples strain against his chest. The ache between my legs multiplies when he takes one stiff peak into his mouth, sucking hard. His rhythmic thrusts and hot tongue ignite a fire in my core only he can extinguish.

"Please," I beg him. I don't even know what I'm begging for, but I know he'll give it to me.

He leans back, changing the angle of his entry, and lifts my hips. His fingers dig into me as his grip tightens, and the change in position sends a mind-blowing sensation through my core. As my climax builds, I arch my back and moan, his name a whisper on my lips. The pressure builds and builds until it finally explodes as if something has burst inside of me, warmth spreading from my center outwards.

Once I come down from my high and my panting eases into near normal breathing, I notice he has stopped moving. For a moment I think he's done and has climaxed, but then he starts to rock in and out of me slowly, and I realize he's still hard. His stamina is surprising. And impressive. He kisses me passionately and I wrap my arms around his neck. No one has ever made me feel the things he makes me feel. Neither in bed nor out of it.

He releases my mouth and continues his slow, delicious thrusting. "Tell me what you want," he growls into my ear.

Everything! I want to shout. "You," I say instead, panting. "Just you."

"Roll over," he commands. I comply, rolling onto my stomach. He kneels between my legs and trails kisses from my lower back to my shoulder. His tongue slides along my skin, tasting me, teasing me. Cold chills cover my body when he pushes the hair off the back of my neck and presses his lips to the bare skin. Tender kisses sweep up my neck and the side of my face as he fists his hand into my hair, gently urging me to look over my shoulder so he can reach my mouth. The long, slow probe of his tongue matches his slow, deep thrust and I moan into his kiss. His lips graze my shoulder, his pace quickening as he nips at my skin. I throw my head back, moaning, another orgasm coiling deep inside me.

How does this man make me feel so alive? I never knew sex could be like this. This position feels surprisingly intimate. It's not something I usually like, but he makes it personal. He kisses my skin reverently and whispers into my ear. The heat of his words alone could send me over the edge.

I feel the pressure building once again and am overcome with the same euphoric sensation from before. I cry out, lost in the pleasure he elicits from my body. He lets out a deep, erogenous groan and I feel him grow inside me with his impending release. He stiffens as he fills me with his warmth before collapsing beside me. Kissing the side of my head, he pulls me close and tucks me into his chest.

"Wow. That was amazing," he mumbles into my hair. I would have to agree.

We lay there quietly for a moment catching our breath, our bodies entwined and hearts racing. A few minutes pass before he breaks the silence.

"Abby?" he begins, his tone serious, regretful almost. I tense, afraid he's going to ask me to leave. *Maybe he's done with me now that he's gotten what he wants.* "Can I ask you something?"

"Sure, anything," I respond. The tension in his voice makes me a little nervous, but I try to hide my mounting anxiety.

He doesn't speak right away, and I sense his trepidation. My unease grows with every second he remains silent.

"Are you on birth control?" he asks finally.

I breathe a sigh of relief. "Yes. Yeah, of course." I feel him relax behind me, his worry melting away with mine.

His fingers trail up and down the side of my arm, causing goosebumps to spread over my skin. "I've never done that before, you know, without protection. I want you to know that."

"Neither have I," I assure him. It's not like me to be irresponsible like that, but I was so lost in him; I couldn't think rationally with his lips on my skin and his hands in my hair. We'll have to be more careful next time.

Next time.

"I didn't even know it could feel that good. You're incredible." I blush and he urges me back towards him. He maneuvers my body so that I'm facing him and reaches down to brush his thumb over my cheek. "Could you be any more perfect?" His icy blue eyes stare into mine, and I squirm under his praise. I press the side of my face into his chest and neck and snuggle closer to him. He chuckles at my shyness, knowing that I'm avoiding his appreciative gaze. "And did I mention how adorable you are when you're being bashful?"

I turn completely into him, burying my face in his collarbone so he can't see me blush. His chuckle turns into full-on laughter, and I can't help but laugh with him. He kisses my forehead and I wrap my arm around his waist, resting my cheek on his chest. We talk for a little while, but soon, my eyelids become too heavy to stay awake. I drift off to sleep to the slow, rhythmic sound of his heart beating against my ear.

I wake sometime later with a dry mouth and a full bladder. I stumble my way to the bathroom, guided only by the glow of the bedside lamp. When I've finished using the restroom, I fill a cup of water and gulp it down in one drink. I catch my naked reflection in the mirror and my cheeks redden at the thought of everything that happened in this bathroom and in Jacob's bed. My hair is a tousled mess, further evidence of our intense lovemaking. My lips are swollen and pink from Jacob's demanding kisses, and my skin is flushed with that after-sex glow. My eyes soften with an unspoken affection for a man I hardly know.

I walk back into the bedroom and go in search of my clothes. I don't even remember what I did with them. It seems odd, walking around Jacob's bedroom naked in the middle of the night. I finally locate my clothing draped across the arm of one of the chairs in the sitting area and reach for my underwear.

"Don't." A deep voice startles me. "Leave them off. I'm enjoying the view." Jacob is awake and lying on his side watching me from his bed, a seductive smile gracing his lips. "Come here," he invites as he lifts the edge of the comforter, welcoming me back in.

Walking back towards him, I attempt to cover as much of my nakedness as I can, but it's useless. He's seen it all anyway. The man bathed me. There's really no need to be modest in front of him anymore.

I crawl back into bed beside him and he reaches over, turning off the lamp. His mouth is instantly on me as soon as the lights go out. His demanding kiss ignites my desire again, and I feel the need growing between my legs. He lies back and grabs my thighs, coaxing me to sit astride his lap. I straddle him and feel his hardness press into me. I lean down and taste his lips, licking and probing. He groans and pulls my hips down harder on his erection.

"You're in control now," he whispers in my ear. "What is it that you want?"

"You," I echo my earlier response. I moan as he rocks back and forth, rubbing against me in just the right spot.

"And what do you want from me?" He wants specifics.

"I want you inside me." As tame as my response is, it qualifies as talking dirty for me. His appreciative groan assures me that was the correct answer.

I lift my hips and he directs himself to my opening. My gasp fills the silence between us as I sink down onto him. These sensations are so new to me; the feel of him filling and stretching me, his bare skin against mine. I'll never get enough of him. I begin rocking back and forth, finding my own rhythm as he grasps my hips. I let my hands explore his arms and chest, feeling the muscles bunch and strain beneath my fingers.

He slides one hand down my front, his fingers finding the junction where our bodies meet. "Fuck," he groans, rubbing my wetness over the sensitive flesh. His words and the motion of his fingers bring me to the brink again.

He pulls away and I huff in frustration. *I was so close!* He chuckles, amused with my impatience. "Don't worry. I'll take care of that ache between your legs soon enough," he assures me.

I involuntarily tighten around him at his lascivious words and sexy voice. He thrusts deep into me and I gasp as my muscles grip him tightly. His hands slide up my torso to cup my breasts. It's hard to keep up the steady rhythm of my hips with the incredible sensations flooding my body.

"Lean back a little," he urges, directing me with his fingers pressing gently against my stomach. I do, and he slides his hand back down to the needy spot he abandoned earlier. I'm more open to him now, and the angle of his penetration is even more satisfying. He begins to rub his thumb over me again, and within moments, I explode, my body convulsing and legs shaking. He releases with me this time, extending my pleasure. Spent, I collapse onto his chest and he wraps me tightly in his arms. We take a moment to catch our breath before attempting to move or speak.

I finally slide off his body and lie next to him, hand pressed to my chest to calm my still racing heart. Jacob sits up and turns the bedside lamp back on before slipping out of bed.

"Don't go anywhere," he bids with a roguish grin before leaning over and pressing a quick kiss to my lips. I couldn't go anywhere right now if I wanted to with my body sated and muscles limp from post orgasmic endorphins. "I'll be right back." He returns a moment later, washcloth in hand, and climbs back onto the bed, pressing the warm cloth between my legs. I swallow thickly, emotion clogging my throat at the intimate and unexpected act. No other man has shown me such care and appreciation after sex. When he returns from discarding the washcloth in the bathroom, he climbs in beside me, pulling the covers over our chests as I nuzzle into his side. He gently pushes my hair from my face and kisses my forehead. The sweet gesture causes a tingle in my chest and a flutter in my stomach. I've fallen hopelessly and irrevocably in love with this man and I have no idea what to do with those feelings. They're so new to me, and I don't know how long this is going to last.

Living in the moment isn't something I've ever been good at. I've always been looking forward, working towards something, *planning*. But I don't know if there's any kind of future for Jacob and me. He'll be leaving in a little over a week, and I have no idea where things will go with us. If I want any part of him, I'll have to settle for what he can give me right now. I know he's worth it, but will I be able to let him go when the time comes? Will he be able to just walk away from me, from what we have?

Jacob snuggles me closer as if he can sense my worries. His fingers gently stroke my arm as he presses his lips to my hair. "I'd better let you get some sleep," he half-whispers. I feel him smile against my scalp. "Although, I could do that with you all night long."

"Me too," I confess. He sighs and hugs me tighter. We lie there, wrapped in each other's arms, and I let the sound of his rhythmic breathing lull me back to sleep.

I AWAKE ON my own the next morning when sunlight slithers its way through the cracks in the curtains. I peek over at Jacob asleep on his stomach, the side of his face pressed into the pillow and his arm draped over my ribs. Unable to resist the urge, I reach over and stroke his temple. He is so beautiful. I could wake up to his perfection every morning.

He begins to stir so I pull my hand back. I don't want him to think I'm some kind of creeper who likes to caress his face while he sleeps. Although, that's exactly what I'm doing.

He cracks one eye open and smiles. "Good morning, beautiful."

My heart flutters and I return his smile. "Mornin'."

"Come here," he says, rolling onto his side and pulling me in close. "What time is it?"

"I don't know. Must not be too late, since my alarm hasn't gone off yet."

He rolls over and pulls his phone off the nightstand. "Eight twenty-seven," he announces, glancing at the screen. "You want some breakfast?"

"Sure," I reply. I'm famished after last night's activities.

"How do you like your eggs?"

He's actually going to cook? I thought he was just going to bring me a Pop-Tart or something. "Scrambled." For some reason, the thought of him cooking for me makes me feel all warm and fuzzy inside. Stupid, I know. "Do you want some help?" I ask and start to get out of bed, but he holds his hands up to stop me.

"Nope. You just relax and I'll take care of everything."

I smile up at him, certain that my love for him is evident from the look on my face. I can't hide my feelings for him, and I don't want to. He leans down and kisses me passionately, but pulls away before things can get too heated.

"I'll come get you when it's ready."

He slides out of bed, giving me an unobstructed view of his sculpted backside. I blush, thinking about how my fingers must have dug into his flesh as he thrust in and out of me last night. He glances over his shoulder and winks at me. I've just been caught ogling him, and I'm so embarrassed. I pull the sheet up over my head to hide my reddened face. His resulting laughter does little to ease my shame.

"Look all you want," he laughs as he makes his way towards the door. I inch the sheet down my face so only my eyes are visible. His derrière is now covered by a pair of gym shorts, the waistband settled low on his hips. "It's all yours." He slips out the door and down the hallway, leaving my head spinning from his words and his exceptional glutes.

He's all mine.

After a moment of quiet reverie thinking about last night and Jacob's amazing body, I decide to take a quick shower. Needless to say, after our night of beautiful and intense lovemaking, I need one. I intend to just hop in the shower until I see that glorious bathtub again. I locate the complimentary bottle of bubble bath and turn on the water, skimming my hand over the surface as I watch the tub fill with lavender-scented suds.

Slipping into the tub soothes the delicious new ache between my legs, and the warmth and the jets relax my over-worked muscles as I sink down far enough for the water to graze my chin. I squirt body wash into a loofah and run it over my entire body at a leisurely pace. I'm in no hurry. This bathroom is currently my sanctuary, and I plan on staying here as long as possible.

I finish washing and lay my head back, resting it on the edge of the tub. I play with the bubbles, picking up a hand full and then blowing them away. Little white puffs float through the air for a second before landing back on the surface of the water. I close my eyes and relax, feeling like Julia Roberts in *Pretty Woman*. Except for the whole prostitute thing, of course.

My eyes drift open at the sound of the bathroom door opening, the hinges barely creaking. I'd left the door cracked only an inch or two, but wasn't anticipating any company.

"I should have known," Jacob offers ruefully, striding towards me. His tall, muscular frame moves gracefully, like a panther stalking its prey. He sits down on the side of the tub and turns his torso to face me. "This is the only reason you came back here, isn't it? It had nothing to do with me. I saw the way you looked at this tub." His teasing smile makes me giggle.

"You caught me," I admit jokingly.

His smile fades and a familiar fire burns in his eyes. "Now, how should I punish you for deceiving me?" His hand disappears under the water, shrouded by resilient bubbles that refuse to dissipate. My breath hitches as his fingers slide up the inside of my thigh.

"Jacob," I whisper. His fingers inch closer and closer to my center, but I resist the urge to grab his hand and guide it the rest of the way. I'll be patient and let him take his time. He knows what he's doing, after all.

Before he can make the contact I so desperately need, he stands up and pulls his shorts down, freeing himself from the confines of his clothing, evidence of his arousal staring me in the face. He sinks down into the tub across from me, his eyes never leaving mine. When he reaches for me, I move towards him, a magnet finding its polar opposite. He pulls me into his lap and I straddle him. His thumb, wet from my bath water, rubs across my lower lip. I press my hands to his bare chest and feel his heart thundering under my palms.

"I want to feel your mouth on me again."

I whimper at his request. Or maybe it's a demand. Hell if I know, but it's *hot!* I crash my lips against his and kiss him fervently. Water ripples all around us, splashing onto the floor as I rock against him.

"Fuck," he growls when I finally release his mouth. "I hope you're done with your bath." He stands abruptly, pulling me to my feet. His hand clasps around mine and my stomach clenches with excitement as he guides me back to the bed.

Chapter Twenty-One

Jacob

THE SCENT OF FRESH STRAWBERRIES and maple syrup invade my nose as I finish up breakfast. I fill two plates with fluffy pancakes and top them with fruit and homemade whipped cream. Abby still hasn't emerged, so I make my way to my bedroom, the sweet aroma of hot cakes and syrup wafting down the hall behind me. I hope she likes what I've prepared. I expect her to still be curled up in bed, perhaps having fallen back asleep, but when I open my bedroom door, she's nowhere to be found.

"Abby?" I call out, but there's no answer.

I freeze, momentarily panicked that I pushed her too far and she slipped out somehow without me knowing. When I notice the bathroom door is slightly ajar, I walk over to it hoping to find her in there. I raise my hand to knock but stop short at the sounds of water lapping against the sides of the tub. I exhale my relief that she didn't get spooked and take off and is only a few feet away, taking a bath. Once again, my mind is flooded with images of her naked and covered in suds. I close my eyes and let my head fall back between my shoulders, stifling a groan. I swallow hard and take a deep breath before pushing open the door. I might lose it all in my pants like a thirteen-year-old boy finding his dad's stash of Playboys.

The door swings wide and I stand at the threshold. All my expectations and fantasies are shattered. The real thing is so much better. I try to play it cool, tempting and teasing her, but it's no use. Before I know it, I'm in that tub with her and she's in my lap. The water is warm, but her body is damn near scalding, especially that slick little spot between her thighs. I may have spent most of the night there worshipping her, claiming her, my name a moan upon her lips, but I could never get enough. I need to feel every inch of her, and those luscious, pink lips are beckoning me.

"I want to feel your mouth on me again," I admit to her. It comes out a little harsher than I intend, but fuck, if this girl doesn't have me wound up tight. I don't think she minds, though. A little whimper escapes her lips just before she captures my mouth in a kiss filled with promises of seduction.

A moment later, we're in my bed tangled in the sheets and each other. I roll onto my back and pull her on top of me. She presses her lips to mine gently before raising up and resting her bottom on her heels, kneeling between my legs. I try to raise up with her, but she presses her palm against my chest and gives me a little shove. She doesn't utter a word, but her eyes say, "Lay back down." I do as I'm expected, my stomach clenching, anticipation lighting every nerve ending on fire.

She slides her hand down my torso, her fingertips gliding along my abs lower and lower until she reaches my erection. She palms me, wrapping her dainty fingers around the base, and her head descends slowly until her lips graze the tip. I pant as I watch her stroke me and take me to the back of her throat. She pulls back, her tongue brushing the tip, before sinking back down again. I don't want to take my eyes off her, but they close of their own volition. Can a man die from pleasure? If so, I've got one foot in the grave.

Her mouth and hands are a euphoric escape, and in this moment, I can think of nothing but her. I wish I could spend the whole day in this bed, wrapped in her arms and worshipping her body.

I need to be inside of her. I'm not going to last much longer, and I want to feel her body quake beneath me when I come. I sit up, pulling her up with me. Before she can protest, I flip her onto her back and cover her body with mine. When I pull her knees up and settle in between her legs, her sweet, slick heat is ready for me. She's as turned on as I am right now. I groan and bury my face in her neck, inhaling her scent, a scent that is purely Abby.

I can't hold back any longer. I plunge deep inside her, my kiss swallowing her gasp. Her tiny sounds turn into groans as I pin her arms above her head. Her legs snake around my hips, pulling me in deeper. I thrust in and out of her slowly, attempting to drag out as much pleasure as I can for her by delaying my own release, but she urges me to go faster. Her heels dig into my flanks, making me feel like a prized steed at the Derby. My girl is demanding. And insatiable. And I love it.

My girl. That's exactly how I think of her. *Mine.* She has consumed my thoughts and burrowed her way into my soul, and I know I couldn't stop this thing happening between us now if I wanted to. And I don't. It scares the shit out of me, opening myself up this way and letting someone in, but there's no way to un-feel what I'm feeling. It would be impossible to extract her from my heart at this point.

I gaze upon her beautiful face, this woman who now owns me body, mind, and soul. Her eyes are closed, lips parted slightly, dark tendrils of hair splayed across my pillow. My chest constricts, and in that moment, *I know.* I know with every fiber of my being that I love her. I'm in love with this woman, and I'll never be able to *un*-love her.

I pick up my pace, needing to feel her shudder with release and her legs quiver with pleasure. I don't have to wait long. Her body pulses around me and I join her in ecstasy.

"WHY THE FUCK are there cold eggs on the stove?" The skillet clatters as Luke tosses it haphazardly back onto the cooktop. His bare back faces us and his dark hair is sticking up in all directions. 'Hangover hair,' he calls it. It's after ten o'clock and Abby and I have finally emerged from my bedroom. We've been enjoying each other all morning, our breakfast long forgotten.

"I got...distracted." That's all I offer in explanation. I hear a muffled giggle coming from behind me and I turn towards Abby, one eyebrow raised suggestively, and give her a playful wink. She must've been thinking about our morning romp as well.

"Does that mean you finally got lai-" Luke begins, turning towards us. "Oh, hey, Abby," he says when she steps out from behind me. At least he had the decency *not* to finish that sentence.

"Just turn the burner back on low. They'll warm right up." I nod towards the discarded eggs, needing to change the subject. I don't want Abby to think I discuss our sex life with Luke. Unlike him, I don't kiss and tell.

"Whatever. I just need coffee." He grimaces and rubs his temples with both hands. *Good, maybe I'll win that bet we made.* He grabs his cup of black coffee and heads back to his room.

"I'm going to run into town and grab a few things when Abby leaves for work and then come back to pick you up," I call after him. "Be ready by eleven." He flips me off before disappearing up the stairs. His surly mood isn't unusual after a night of shooting tequila straight.

I reheat our breakfast as best I can. I scrape the strawberries off the pancakes, but the whipped cream had melted into them already. Hoping it will help the chewy pancakes, I throw a cup of maple syrup back in the microwave and nuke it again. All in all, our breakfast isn't half bad. We eat in companionable silence, a sign of our growing comfort with each other. When we finish, I grab my keys and head for the door.

"You ready, beautiful?" I slide my hand into the back of Abby's hair and pull her in for a quick kiss. She closes her eyes and leans her head against my chest, resting her hands on my shoulders. For some reason, this small gesture causes my heart to constrict.

"Not really," she sighs with disappointment. I'm not ready, either. I don't want to let her go. "But I don't guess I have much of a choice." She raises her head and looks back up at me, smiling sweetly even though I know she doesn't want to leave.

"Don't worry." I press my lips to her forehead. "We have a date tonight, and I can't wait to taste your cookin'." She smiles for real this time, and it's the most beautiful thing I've ever seen.

"So, you finally sealed the deal with Abby, eh?" Luke asks as we secure our life jackets. "Guess you're not as big a pussy as I thought you were." His laughter rings out over the water. I'm not as amused.

"Do you *want* me to throw you out of that raft?" I threaten, gripping the yellow paddle in my hand until my knuckles turn white.

"Chill, bro. I'm just messin' with you." He snaps the chin strap of his helmet, securing it to his head. "I've never seen you this protective over a girl before. What's so special about this one?"

I grit my teeth. I don't want to talk to Luke about this. He's never once cared about a girl. Admittedly, I've never felt anything like what I feel for Abby, but I'm not a detached and unapologetic man-whore like he is, either.

"Forget it. You wouldn't understand." Seriously, I'm not talking to him about my feelings. No fucking way.

"Try me," he challenges, all hint of teasing gone. The sincere look in his eyes stuns me and I cave.

"It's just-" I start, but don't really know what to say. "I care about her," I finally admit. "She's not just some hook-up. I want to keep seeing her. Even after we go back home." Luke nods as though he understands. For some reason, it makes me want to keep going. "I have something real with her. Something that could last. And I want it. I want her. I don't want anyone else to ever touch her again. To love her. Just me."

Luke seems surprised by my admission but quickly masks his shocked expression. "And how does she feel? Have you told her any of this?"

"No, but I think she feels the same way. The way she acts, the things she's shared with me. You don't do that with just anybody." I *know* Abby feels something. I don't know how deep it goes, but it's there. I hope she's fallen just as hard as I have.

Luke opens his mouth to respond, but our instructor's booming voice cuts him off.

"Okay, everybody, listen up!" I try to concentrate as he goes over all the risks and safety hazards, but my mind is fixed on Abby and what our future might hold. I've gone whitewater rafting a few times, but never on this river. I hope Luke is listening because he's never done this before.

Fifteen minutes later, we're floating down the river at a leisurely pace. We haven't hit any rough water yet, but I know it's coming. Soon, we're paddling like crazy, bright yellow oars slicing in and out of the water like the needle on a sewing machine. Arms pumping and pulse pounding, angry waves chopping at us trying to claim us for the watery depths below. Sweat drips from my brow and chills of excitement pebble my arms.

When I look at Luke, I see unbridled terror in his stormy grey eyes. *Please don't panic, Luke.* Panicking could be disastrous for all of us.

Luckily, he holds his shit together and we glide into smoother water again. Suddenly, his face contorts and I think he's in pain. I don't see any visible signs of injury, but he glances at me with his eyebrows furrowed and teeth gritted. Before I can ask what's wrong, he leans over the side of the raft and heaves violently into the river. Groans of disgust echo all around us from our raft mates as Luke purges himself of every last drop of acid in his stomach. He scowls at me as I bellow with laughter, triumph and relief fueling my mirth.

"Fuck you, J," he grumbles as he wipes the remainder of his bile on his wrist.

"Guess this means you'll be spending Memorial Day entertaining Miss Greyson," I taunt. "In a Speedo," I add, reminding him of the stipulations of our bet. Luke gives me the middle finger for the second time today.

As we're packing up, ready to head back to our cabin, Luke makes a confession of his own. His voice is so low, I barely catch it.

"I kind of like Tiff, too."

I nearly drop my keys when he utters those six words. Luke has never, in all the years that I've known him, admitted to actually *liking* a girl.

"She's different from the girls I usually sleep with," he continues. "There are no pretenses. She doesn't expect anything. She's content with just hanging out and hooking up. She's not trying to be my forever. I like that."

It's my turn to be surprised. This day is full of revelations for both of us. It's not an admission of love, but it's more than Luke has ever given anyone.

Maybe Abby has been right all along.

Chapter Twenty-two

Abby

THE LUNCHTIME RUSH IS ALWAYS BUSY, but today it's downright brutal. There's a crowd of people waiting in the small foyer for a table and we're down a server. An hour into my shift and I'm ready to throw in the towel.

Exhaustion aside, my muscles are deliciously sore from my night spent with Jacob. Just the thought of him brings a smile to my face and a blush to my cheeks.

"You are way too happy right now. I kind of wanna punch you in the face." Tiff sidles up beside me at the bar and throws her tray down. She's in a foul mood and it's barely past noon. "Seriously, why are you in such a good mood?" She studies my face for a moment before her eyes widen with understanding and she gasps. "You didn't!" she barks, a little too loud for my liking.

"Shhh," I try to quiet her, glancing around nervously. I don't want anyone else to hear this conversation.

"You little hussy. You finally did it, didn't you? You slept with Jacob." I give her a sheepish look, a dead giveaway that she guessed right, and her smile grows exponentially.

"It's about damn time," she huffs.

"Just don't say anything to anyone. I don't want everyone around here knowing my business, and word of that will spread like wildfire." News travels fast in a small town. Whether it's gossip or truth, people don't hesitate to spread it. And me hooking up with an out-of-town stranger is some serious fodder for the rumor mill.

"Don't worry. I'd never tell anybody." She winks at me as she grabs her tray and heads back to her tables.

Rosie's finally settles down after another hour or so. I make my rounds to my recently vacated tables to collect tips. As I'm stuffing the bills in the front of my apron, I feel the hairs on the back of my neck stand up and not in a good way. Not like when I sense Jacob's presence.

"Abby." I cringe at the familiar voice and turn slowly towards the person I dread seeing.

"Caleb," I reply curtly, crossing my arms over my chest. "What are you doing here?" Needless to say, I'm less than thrilled to see him. The smug look on his face infuriates me. He knows he's making me uncomfortable.

"I just wanted to clear the air between us. You know, because of the other day."

"I don't have time for this." I try to brush past him but he sidesteps my evasive maneuver, using his body and one of the tables to block me in. I don't like this. I feel like a cornered animal and I'm ready to strike.

"Look, I'm sorry about the misunderstanding at work."

Misunderstanding? Is he serious right now? What he did goes well beyond the boundaries of a simple 'misunderstanding.' I don't say anything, though; I just wait for him to finish so I can get this awkward encounter over with and get back to work.

"Sometimes my approach can be a little too..." he pauses for a moment, trying to find the right word, "forward," he finishes. He does his best to inject sincerity into his words, but I'm not falling for it.

"You see, when I want something, I go after it." It takes every bit of southern charm within me not to roll my eyes at him. "And I'm not used to being told no."

I bet you aren't, creep. He's still doing his best to woo me. He thinks his smile is debonair, but it's not. It's almost sinister, as though I can see all his darkest desires reflected in the black depths of his pupils.

My stony silence flusters him and his smile fades. "Anyway, I just came here to apologize and call a truce. I don't want what happened to interfere with our working relationship." He holds his hand out, waiting for me to take it for a shake.

I heave a deep breath and grit my teeth, doing my best to keep from telling him where to go and how to get there. This guy harasses me, puts his hands on me, and I'm just supposed to carry on like it never happened?

Maybe I'm being unreasonable here. Maybe I should give him the benefit of the doubt. Either way, he's not touching me again. I square my shoulders, put my hands on my hips, and look him straight in the eyes. His cocky smile falters and he drops his hand.

"Alright," I grit out with feigned courage. "We can call a truce." His lips twitch, arrogance marring his features once again. "But." I raise my hand, my index finger sticking up in the air. I lower my voice and he leans in to hear me. "If you ever put your hands on me again, I'll make sure that you're *never* able to have children."

His eyes widen almost imperceptibly before his cool façade slides back into place. He studies me for a beat, gauging whether I mean what I say, I suppose, and then his expression turns odd, his eyes darkening. It's almost as if he's... aroused? A shiver runs up my spine and I shrink back a little. *Is that what he's looking for? Someone who will put up a fight?* The cold fingers of unease wrap around me, feelings of dread settling in my gut. He just nods and smirks at me before turning away.

I watch as he heads for the exit, wanting to make sure he actually leaves. He stops and flirts with the hostess, flashing his artificially whitened smile at her. I can't ignore the sinking feeling in my gut. I know we made peace, but I can't help feeling like this isn't the last I'll be seeing of Caleb.

AT FOUR MINUTES past seven, my truck roars to life when I crank the ignition. I can't wait to see Jacob tonight, especially after my unnerving encounter with Caleb. I contemplate telling Jacob about him approaching me at work, but decide I really don't want to spoil our evening so I resolve to forget about it. It won't accomplish anything anyway. It'll just upset him.

My elation at spending the evening with Jacob leaves me distracted on my drive home. I'm still in my own little world when I pull into my driveway, and nearly side-swipe his Range Rover. I press the heel of my hand into the center of my chest to calm my racing pulse. I can't imagine how much it would cost to repair such a high-end vehicle. I can barely afford the insurance on my truck as it is.

Once my heart rate slows back down to normal and I can breathe again, I grab my purse and open my door, wondering all the while why Jacob is here already. Hope blooms in my chest. Maybe he's just as excited to see me as I am to see him and he simply couldn't wait any longer.

When I walk into the house, my step falters at what I see. Jacob and my grandmother are sitting at our kitchen table talking and laughing. The corners of her dark eyes crinkle with her broad smile. Her weathered hands are wrapped around her favorite coffee cup, the one I got her that says, "Wild and Wonderful" with an outline in the shape of West Virginia. Jacob's head is tossed back with a whole-hearted, gut-trembling belly laugh. My heart feels like it could burst right out of my chest. They look like... family. *My* family.

"Abigail." My grandmother's sweet voice shakes me from my thoughts. "I was just telling Jacob about your first junior high dance."

I remember that day like it was yesterday, and I know what's got them so tickled. We had just returned from the salon after getting our hair done and were trying to take some pictures at the river. Tiff, ever the fashionista in her four-inch heels, stumbled on the dock. She grabbed my arm to steady herself, but instead of stopping her descent, pulled me down with her. We crashed ungracefully into the water, ruining our fresh up-dos.

My grandmother motions for me to join them, so I pull out a chair and sit down at the small table. She turns back to Jacob and continues her story. "You should have seen the scowl on my Abigail's face, but the best part was Tiffany's theatrics. You would have thought she was drowning. She came up out of that water spittin' and asputterin' and gaspin' for air." All three of us are laughing now. Looking back, it really was a comical scene, though at the time I certainly didn't think so.

"Tiff stomped off, looking like a drowned rat and muttering curse words under her breath," I add.

"I can only imagine," Jacob replies, shaking his head in amusement. He knows just how prissy my best friend is.

My grandma glances at her watch and stands up. "I'd better head out now or I'll be late for Bingo." She winks at me and grabs her purse from the counter. I know Fridays aren't her usual Bingo night. She must be trying to give Jacob and me some privacy.

"Don't you wanna stay for dinner?"

"No, sweet girl, I've already eaten. But I made you two a peach cobbler. It needs to come out of the oven in half an hour."

I pull her in for a hug and kiss her cheek. "Thank you." Not just for the cobbler, but for giving Jacob and me this chance to spend some time together.

She cups my cheek with her hand and smiles softly. "You're welcome, sweetie." She lets go of me and turns toward Jacob. "You kids have fun. I'll be back in a little while." She gives me a pointed look to let me know that although she trusts me and respects my privacy, no funny business is allowed under her roof.

"I'll walk you out." Jacob laces his arm through hers.

"Oh, that's not necessary," she objects half-heartedly, but her smile tells me she loves that he offered.

"It's no problem," he assures her. "I insist." He flashes those pearly whites and my sixty-four-year old grandmother turns into a giggly teenager right before my eyes.

"Well, if you insist..." She grips his arm with her free hand and lets him lead her to her car.

I gather all the ingredients and supplies I'll need to prepare dinner while Jacob helps my grandmother outside. She really doesn't need the help. She's quite capable, but she enjoys his display of chivalry, something she hasn't had since my pappy passed away.

I'm standing over the sink, peeling a potato when I feel warm, strong arms wrap around my waist.

"Hey." Jacob's hot breath tickles my ear.

"Hey, yourself." I try to suppress the tremor that runs through me at the sound of his voice and the feel of his body pressed against my back.

"I've been warned to behave myself, so you better give me a job to do so I can keep my hands busy." I like just how busy his hands are right now. One hand presses against my bare belly, sliding higher and higher towards my breasts while the other anchors me to him, possessively gripping my hip. I let my head fall back and moan.

"Damn it," he growls against my neck. "You're making it really hard to follow her rules." His words break through the lusty fog that has overtaken my brain. My grandmother must've given him a talkin' to while they were outside.

"I'm gonna be honest with you," I begin in the sultriest voice I can muster.

"Mm-hmm," comes his distracted reply. His lips trail languorously up the side of my neck.

"I really hate peeling potatoes." I say the words slowly, wondering if they will even register.

His hands and lips freeze, and I try hard to suppress my humor. He steps back a little as I turn to face him. As much as I want his hands all over me, we've both been warned. My grandmother could come home at any time, so we have to be careful. I don't really *want* to deny him, so I'm trying to keep this light and fun.

I hand him the veggie peeler and nod my head towards the heap of unpeeled Idahos on the counter. He smirks at me as I scoot over, letting him take my place. He swats my behind and I yelp in surprise.

"That's for teasing me," he says, but eases the sting when he leans down and presses his lips gently to mine.

I smile as I grab a quart Mason jar of canned green beans and open them. "So, what are we making?" he asks.

"Fried chicken, green beans, mashed potatoes and gravy, and cornbread."

"Sounds delicious."

"It is," I assure him. "All my grandmother's recipes." I grab a container of bacon grease from the fridge and add some to the pot for the green beans.

Jacob scrunches his nose as he looks on with a worried expression. "What is *that*?"

"This?" I ask, holding up the container. He nods. "It's just bacon grease. Adds flavor to the beans." He looks at me like I have three heads. "I'm guessing you've never cooked with it before."

"Never," he confirms.

He turns back to his task and continues peeling potatoes. A moment later, he leans back and just looks at me, mischief glowing in the icy blue depths of his irises. He stares at me so long, I grow self-conscious under his scrutiny. Finally, he reaches out and lifts the edge of my shirt, glancing first at my back and then at my front. He looks unsatisfied with what he finds there, so he proceeds to bend down and lift the hem of my shorts. His warm fingers trail along my skin, leaving tingling paths wherever he touches me.

"What are you doing?" My curiosity finally gets the best of me.

"Where do you put it?"

"What?" I'm really confused right now. I don't know what he thinks I'm hiding.

"Where do you put it? The bacon grease, the cornbread, the tub of... whatever that greasy substance is over there." He motions towards the can of shortening.

"Crisco?"

"Yeah, that." His hands are on me again, exploring, analyzing, a smile playing on his lips. He begins poking his fingers into my sides, somehow finding the most ticklish spots on my body. "Tell me! I have to know!" he demands playfully. I double over and twist my torso to get out of his grasp, but it's no use. He's too strong and too determined. His hands make their way from my hips and up past my armpits, tickling them as he goes before finally zeroing in on my neck, all while I giggle and gasp for breath.

After a moment of torturing the sensitive area behind my ears and along my hairline, he releases me and I step back. His playful smirk makes it hard not to smile. "I hate being tickled," I inform him, trying my best to scowl, but doing a piss-poor job of it.

"Didn't look like you were hating it *too* much."

His wink and cocky grin do funny things to my stomach. I don't even realize I've begun to pant until he reaches for me and shoves his fingers into my hair. His lips crash down onto mine and his tongue sweeps into my mouth. I moan when he presses me against the counter.

"Your body is amazing." His low voice rumbles in my chest as he runs his hands over damn near every inch of my exposed skin. "I love every part of it." His whispered breath tickles my ear and I shiver. "I could never choose a favorite." I hear the smile in his voice.

"I love these soft, pouty lips." He kisses me gently, emphasizing his words, and then places his hands on my ribs, his thumbs rubbing the undersides of my breasts. "I love every curve and dip." His hands inch down my sides and settle on my lower back, where two little dimples appear on each side of my spine. "I really, really love this." He cups my backside with both hands and squeezes, pressing his groin into my belly. "Hmmm, I think I may have found my favorite."

I'm suddenly lifted into the air and then set back down on an empty section of the counter. His mouth is on mine, his arms crushing me to him, and I feel his length pressed against my center. He devours me, licking and tasting, consuming my thoughts and overwhelming my senses.

A strange gurgling sound begins to register in my distracted mind. Jacob releases me quickly and runs to the stove, pulling a pot off the burner.

"It was boiling over," he explains.

"Oops." I hop off the counter as a blush spreads over my cheeks. I turn the burner down and replace the pot. Cooking with Jacob might be a bit of a safety hazard. "We'd better focus on dinner before we burn down the house."

"Good idea." He gives me a quick peck and returns to helping me prepare our meal.

An hour later, our plates are full and silence reigns over the kitchen as we dig into the delicious food we prepared together. We work well as a team. Well, as long as we can focus and keep our hands to ourselves.

"This may be the best thing I've ever tasted." Jacob dips his fried chicken in his mashed potatoes and gravy before devouring it with enthusiasm. "Seriously, I don't know how you do it. If I had someone to cook like this for me all the time, I'd weigh four hundred pounds."

"Well, you can't eat like this every day. My grandma and I cook like this once a week. That's it. She has some health problems, so we try to eat right most of the time."

"I'm sorry to hear that. You'd never know by looking at her."

"She takes pretty good care of herself, although she likes to sneak and eat sugary snacks when I'm not looking. She knows she's not allowed to have them because of her diabetes, but she's got a rebellious streak a mile long. She'll do something just because you told her not to." I smile fondly as I think of her.

"I like her even more now," Jacob confesses before shoving a huge chunk of cornbread in his mouth. I love that he enjoys the food I cooked. I don't know what it is, but there's just something about feeding the ones you love.

There's that word again.

There's no use fighting it anymore. I love him. And I'm not ashamed of it. I just wish I had the guts to tell him. But if he doesn't feel the same, it will crush me. I'd rather enjoy what we have now than to know definitively if his feelings for me run as deeply as mine for him.

Once we finish eating, Jacob helps me clean up and put away the leftovers.

"Make sure you take some of this back with you. There's plenty here."

"Woman, you're gonna be the death of me. But I'll gladly take your home cookin' any time you want to give it to me."

He winks at me and I feel heat flood my cheeks as they redden. Why did that sound so naughty?

I make us each a plate of warm cobbler and add a scoop of vanilla ice cream on top. We take our bowls to the living room and sit on the old, worn down couch. It may not be the prettiest thing, but it's very comfy. I flip on the TV as we dig into our desserts. I glance at Jacob when I hear a soft moan coming from my left.

"Holy shit, *this* is the best thing I've ever eaten. Please tell me you know how to make this."

I laugh at his ardent appreciation. "Yes, I know how to make it," I assure him. "I don't think it ever turns out quite as good as hers, though."

When we're done with dessert, I take our dishes to the kitchen and place them in the sink. They can wait until morning. When I return, Jacob motions for me to sit next to him and I curl into his side, resting my head on his shoulder. His big, strong arms and warm muscular chest are so inviting. We talk for a while, his fingers combing through my hair. Before long, the darkness of sleep enfolds me and I slip into oblivion.

Chapter Twenty-Three

Jacob

Abby's breathing slows and evens out as I run my fingers over her scalp, and I realize she's fallen asleep. I kiss the top of her head and breathe in her sweet scent. The most expensive perfumes in the world could never compare to how good she smells. She moans and sighs in her sleep and I hold her tighter. When she becomes restless, squirming and wiggling until she's in my lap, I think she's going to wake up, but she doesn't. She curls up into a ball, still asleep, and rests her cheek against my collarbone. Her breathing evens back out and I wrap my arms around her small body.

I can't believe how much this woman means to me already. I want to tell her, but I don't want to scare her away. She's known a lot of pain from those who should have loved and protected her, so she's understandably reluctant to open up and let anyone in.

My eyes close and I start to drift off, but soon am startled awake by the sound of the front door closing, putting me on high alert until I hear keys hit the counter. I glance over my shoulder as Abby's grandmother rounds the kitchen table, heading towards the hallway.

She catches sight of me and I smile. "She's asleep," I whisper, nodding towards my shoulder where Abby's head is rested. I certainly don't want her to think we're up to no good.

She sighs, her brow knitted with concern. "She works way too hard. And too much. God love her." She shakes her head. "She must be exhausted. I don't know how she does it."

Me either. This girl never stops. "Would it be alright if I go lay her in her bed? I don't want to wake her."

She nods her head in agreement. "Her room is the second door on the right."

"Thank you." I don't let on that I already know which room is hers. That would be unwise on my part.

I gather Abby in my arms and lay her gently on her bed, pulling the blankets over top of her. I kiss her head one last time before turning and walking towards the door.

"Jacob, I..."

Her voice is low and scratchy with sleep, but I turn and wait for her to continue. Her face is shrouded in darkness, so I can't see whether her eyes are open or closed. Sleep must have overtaken her again because she doesn't say another word. I pull her door shut quietly and head towards the front door. I find her grandmother standing over the sink, washing what's left of our dishes from dinner.

"Did you two have a good time this evening?" she asks.

"We did. The food was wonderful. Thank you for the cobbler."

"You're very welcome." She gives me a plastic container and places her hands over mine. Peach cobbler to go. I feel like I've hit the jackpot, but when I look into her worried brown eyes, my smile falters. "You seem like a good man." She hesitates, choosing her next words carefully. "Please don't break her heart. She's been hurt enough already." Her pleading look causes a lump to form in my throat. I would never do anything to hurt Abby.

"I won't," I promise her. She studies my face for a moment before her expression relaxes as if she can sense the sincerity in my words. She pats my hands and leads me to the door.

IT'S BEEN NEARLY twenty-four hours since I last saw Abby. I went to sleep last night thinking of her. I woke up this morning thinking of her. All my muscles were stiff, especially a certain one that didn't get any attention last night, in spite of him practically screaming for it. He was sorely disappointed.

Not that I can't spend time with Abby without being inside her. I like being with her no matter what we're doing. But having her body wrapped tightly around mine is my new favorite pastime. Damn it. Now I'm going to have to take a *cold* shower because I can't quit thinking about her.

As I step out of the spray and begin to dry off, my nuts feeling like they're shriveled up like raisins from the cool water, my phone beeps with an incoming text. It's my dad.

> Would you please tell your mother what you plan
> on wearing to the party? She's driving me crazy

He punctuates his last sentence with a gun emoji pointing at a yellow face with x's for eyes. The fact that he even uses emojis cracks me up. I'm glad he's finally getting the hang of it now. He used to put really silly ones on his texts that made no sense at all, like a random animal on a text asking me how classes are going. I shoot a quick text back to him, promising to let her know today.

I wipe steam off the mirror and debate whether I should shave. It's been about five days since I shaved last, and the stubble has grown in nicely. Abby seems to like it, so I think I'll just keep it a while. Anything to make my girl happy.

I'm excited to see her tonight. It's Saturday, the night we plan to go to The Barn to see her brother's band play. She's been dropping hints all day about her outfit choice, teasing me with images in my mind of her smooth, tan skin revealed by something short and sexy. That's definitely a sight I'm looking forward to seeing.

It's been a long day, and I've spent the majority of it with Luke, so seeing Abby will be a welcome change. Luke and I spent the day kayaking and hiking, only taking a break long enough to eat and for me to finalize some plans I've been trying to work out. I have a surprise for Abby and I can't wait to show her what it is.

Once I'm dressed and ready, Luke and I head to Tiff's to pick up the girls. When Abby steps through the front door, my jaw drops. My eyes slide over her entire body from head to toe. Big, soft curls frame her face, cascading over her shoulders and down her back. Her lips are glossy and pink like a big, juicy slice of watermelon just waiting to be bitten into. Long, thick eyelashes blackened with mascara accentuate her bright green eyes. Her plaid shirt is tied in a knot at her narrow waist and frayed denim shorts rest on her hips, a small sliver of skin exposed in between. Grey cowgirl boots cover her feet, the pointed toe and low heel subtly sexy. There's a lot of leg showing, and I like it. I've never really been into the country girl thing, but dear God, I'm into it now.

Tiff follows Abby out of the house in a short, flowy, cream-colored dress and denim jacket. Her brown boots match the belt cinching her waist. Although I only have eyes for Abby, I can appreciate how beautiful Tiffany is. She may be a lot of fun and likes to have a good time, but I can see her brokenness. Behind those sapphire eyes and flirty smile hides a lot of pain. I don't know if Luke can see it, but it's a web he's going to get caught in.

Abby climbs into the passenger seat and I kiss her immediately, tangling my fingers in her hair. I hold her to me possessively and claim her mouth with more aggression than I mean to. I pull back and see her chest rise and fall rapidly, neither of us aware of the other two passengers in the car. I shift into gear and peel out of Tiff's driveway before I have a chance to do something that'll embarrass us both. From the corner of my eye, I see Abby smooth her hands over her mussed-up hair and pull a tube of lip gloss from her pocket. I smile to myself as she swipes the applicator over her lips, knowing my hasty kiss is the reason for her tousled appearance.

Abby guides us to The Barn and we arrive within twenty minutes. She wasn't kidding about this place. It's a big red barn hemmed in by cornfields about fifty yards to our left and open pastures to our right, with lights twinkling in the distance. A farmhouse, maybe? I hear a cow moo somewhere in the vicinity, but I'm confident there's a fence separating us from any livestock. Right?

The Barn's parking lot is nothing more than loose gravel, and there are cars and trucks parked everywhere. Already, music from inside echoes into the night. An antique gooseneck light illuminates the front where two large red doors with white trim are tightly shut. Instead of approaching them, Abby and Tiff head to a smaller side door. I hold it open as the rest of our group shuffles inside.

The large, open room is dimly lit with Mason jar light fixtures hanging from the rafters. To our right, the stage is tucked into a corner, the band already well into their set. I spot Abby's brother right away. His olive complexion is a bit lighter than hers and his hair is jet black. Even from this far away, I can tell his eyes are dark, probably a chocolate brown, not emerald like his sister's. Where Abby is short and curvy, Ethan is tall and lean.

The band is playing something I've never heard before, but I kind of like it. It's country with a little bit of a rock-and-roll edge to it. Abby's brother belts out the words to this country party anthem, followed by an impressive guitar solo. He catches sight of her and nods his head, smiling like he's happy to see her. My chest constricts a little. I know Peyton and I would've had that kind of relationship if she were still alive.

Although still smiling, his eyes narrow when he looks past Abby to see who she's with. From this distance, I can't tell if he's glaring at me or Luke, and I worry he'll automatically hate me for being with her. He may be her younger brother, but I can sense how protective they are of each other. Without their parents in the picture, they've had to look out for one another.

Once the song is over, he turns to his bandmates and says something none of us can hear, but they nod their heads in understanding. The music starts back up as we settle into a table and Luke heads to the bar to grab the first round of drinks. Ethan does a pretty good job of engaging the crowd, his eyes roving over his captive audience.

His gaze lands on our table frequently, lingering for a moment each time. He never seems to focus on Abby or me, but I notice him eyeing Tiff. I glance across the table at her the next time he looks her way and see her cringe, averting her eyes from his meaningful stare. It's as if she's the woman he's singing the song for, like he's telling her *she's* the one that ain't worth the whiskey. But maybe I'm imagining things or I missed something somewhere because Abby doesn't seem to notice the odd exchange.

I lean down and speak into her ear. "Did Tiff and Ethan ever date?"

"What?" she asks incredulously. Then she cackles loudly, amusement twinkling in her eyes. "No way. Those two can't stand each other. And they don't have anything in common." She pauses for a second, then adds, "Well, except for singing. They've sung together a couple of times, but Tiff hates it."

Well, that answers that. Maybe.

Luke finally returns with our drinks as the song comes to an end. "Okay, folks, we're gonna take a little break. We'll be back in ten," Ethan announces and jumps off the stage, heading straight towards us.

"Hey, sis." He gives Abby a brotherly side hug. "Tiffany," he greets stiffly, barely glancing in her direction. She just smiles weakly and goes back to sipping her drink. "Who're your friends?"

"Ethan, this is Jacob," Abby introduces us, and I reach out to shake his hand.

"Nice to meet you. Abby's told me a lot about you." He smiles wryly and glances at Abby as a blush slowly creeps up her cheeks. She obviously hasn't told him about me. That shouldn't sting nearly as much as it does.

"And this is Luke." Ethan reaches out and shakes Luke's hand, nodding curtly. He says nothing, keeping his jaw clenched tightly shut. Tiff mouths something to him, but I don't quite catch her words. "They're visiting from Arlington," Abby continues, unaware of the tense exchange.

"Arlington? You're a long way from home." He eyes us, his words tinged with suspicion.

"Yeah, just needed to get away, ya know?" Luke responds, although Ethan barely acknowledges him when he speaks.

"Well, you guys enjoy the show. I'm gonna grab a drink before I have to go back on. Maybe I can get Shelly to slip a little Jack in my Coke." He winks, smiling wryly at his sister. She smacks his arm and gives him a scolding look before he heads towards the bar, disappearing into the crowd.

After a short break, the band returns to the stage and plays a couple more fast-paced songs. "We're gonna slow things down a little bit for this next one," Ethan announces into the mic as he drags two stools out onto the stage. "But I'm gonna need help from someone in the audience who knows this song." Excited murmurs fill the space, everyone dying to know who he's going to pick as he looks out over the crowd like he's searching for someone. He's got a shit-eating grin stretched across his face, mischief gleaming in his eyes. "You guys are in luck because we have the two-time Fayette County Talent Show winner here with us tonight," he broadcasts excitedly, and the crowd begins to cheer and look around.

Abby turns to look at Tiff as all the color drains out of her face. Tiff's eyes bulge with shock. She looks back and forth between Abby and the stage, panic marring her features.

"Everybody, please join me in welcoming Miss Tiffany Caseman to the stage." Ethan leads the crowd in a round of applause. People begin to hoot and holler, beckoning Tiff to the stage.

"Come on, Tiff," Abby urges. "Everybody wants to hear you sing."

Tiff remains glued to her seat, her shocked expression unchanging. Finally, she breaks out of her haze and glances around. Seeing that everyone within eyesight is watching her and cheering her on, she smiles timidly and stands up. This sudden shyness is in stark contrast to the confident vixen I know her to be. The cheers grow louder as she walks to the stage and climbs the stairs leading up to the band. She and Ethan sit atop the two stools as a stagehand places a mic stand in front of each of them. She glances over at Ethan with a pleading look, but he just smirks at her and grabs his guitar.

Someone begins to play the piano as Ethan strums a few slow notes on his guitar. The medley itself sounds like pain and want and need, haunting and hopeful at the same time.

Abby turns to me, her eyes lighting up. "I love this song."

"What is it?" The opening cord is unfamiliar, a song I've never heard before.

"'Poison and Wine' by The Civil Wars."

Just then, Ethan's voice carries over the sound system. He only sings one line before Tiff comes in, her soft, sweet voice floating over the words like a butterfly's wings. They go back and forth, line for line, singing their parts to perfection. Together, they sing the chorus, harmonizing like lovers, two people who know every cadence and tone of each other's voice.

They glance at each other every now and then during the next verse, but when Ethan sings the last line, he looks directly into her eyes. A promise. A regret. Something they can't take back.

Simple. Arduous. Poignant.

At these words, she can't look away and neither can he. They repeat the chorus over and over, claiming not to love each other, but promising to always do so. When the song ends, a hush falls over the crowd and their gazes remain locked on each other. A few seconds pass without a sound before the room erupts, cheers and clapping drowning out all other sounds. Ethan and Tiff don't even flinch at the cacophony of their enraptured audience. It takes a moment for their hypnotic hold on each other to break.

"Wow, those two really know how to perform," Abby leans over and says to me above the roar of the crowd.

That didn't look like a performance to me. I can't say for sure, but my gut tells me there's more to their connection than just music. But I let it go.

"You were amazing." Abby pulls her friend in for a hug when Tiff returns to our table.

"Thanks," Tiff replies dispassionately.

Luke and I head to the bar to grab another round of drinks. "Man, Tiff's really got a set of pipes on her, huh?" Luke throws back a shot and orders another. "I mean, I already knew that," he says suggestively, playfully elbowing me in the side. "But seriously, it's a lot different hearing her sing on stage with music and everything."

I nod my agreement and head back to our table. After a few more rounds of drinks and a few more songs, the band decides to slow things down again.

"Alright fellas, I'm gonna help y'all out right now." Ethan's lopsided grin elicits cheers and whistles from the females in the crowd. "Grab your honies and head to the dance floor for some Florida Georgia Line." The audience erupts in excitement. *Must be a popular band.* "This one here is called 'Dirt.'"

I may not know this song, but I'm not about to miss out on an opportunity to slow dance with Abby. I grab her hand and lead her onto the dance floor, pulling her in close and listening to the words of the song. We're both silent as I soak in their meaning, realizing how close they are to how I feel about her. I can see myself settling down with her one day. I know it hasn't been long, but she's it for me. I place one hand on her back and grip her free hand with mine as she rests her cheek on my chest. I bask in the warmth of her body and her sweet scent.

When the song is over, we return to our table just as Tiff and Luke slide back into their chairs. I'm a little shocked that Luke slow danced with someone, but then again, he's surprised me a couple times this week.

Abby downs the rest of her drink and places the empty cup back on the table. "I'm gonna run to the ladies' room and get another drink. Anybody want anything?"

Tiff gives her an order, but Luke and I both have full beers so we decline. When she gets back, she hands Tiff her usual Long Island and sips on one of her own. We enjoy the music until the band takes another break and recorded music starts to play over the sound system. Classic rock is playing now, and a few of the older patrons trickle out onto the dance floor. I pull Abby to her feet when 'Ready for Love' begins to play.

"Where are we going?" She giggles tipsily, and I'm taken aback by how intoxicated she seems. I didn't think she'd had that much to drink, but then again, she's pretty small, so it wouldn't take much.

"They're finally playing something I know." We sway to the music and when the chorus begins, I sing to her.

Her whole body shakes with laughter at my off-key attempt to serenade her with Bad Company. I'm a terrible singer, but I mean what I'm saying. Or singing, rather. I *am* ready for love. For her love.

"Oh my gosh," she gasps. "How do you even know this song?"

I shrug. "Dad's a big fan. He has this record on vinyl."

"You continue to surprise me with your knowledge of good music. I'd pegged you as a Snow Patrol, Coldplay kind of guy," she titters, a giddy tinkling to her voice. I'm not sure how to take that. It almost sounded like an insult, but that's completely out of character for her. I brush the odd comment off and dance with her until the song ends.

Walking her back to our table, I notice that she's stumbling quite a bit. Luke and Tiff are gone who knows where. They probably found some dark broom closet to screw in.

Abby finishes what's left of her drink and stands up, swaying a little before gripping the chair for balance. "I'm going to the ladies' again."

"Are you alright? Want me to come with you?"

She just waves me off and I watch her disappear into the crowd, weaving. She heads for the back of the building towards the restrooms and out of my sight.

She's been gone for a little bit when I start to worry. I hope she hasn't passed out somewhere. There's still no sign of Luke and Tiff, so I go in search of Abby by myself. I check the bar first and then the restrooms. I can't find her anywhere and I start to panic.

I grab some random girl and ask, "Do you know Abby Harris?"

"Yeah," she answers, looking at me skeptically.

"Have you seen her?"

"Umm, yeah," she replies hesitantly like she doesn't want to tell me where she is.

"Where is she?" I want to shake her. I'm growing impatient and I just want her to tell me what she knows.

"She just left with some guy." My heart sinks until it lands in the pit of my stomach, and I feel the urge to puke. Either she decided to spend the night in someone else's bed, or some dickhead is taking advantage of the fact that she's too wasted to even walk straight.

"Are you sure it was Abby?"

"Yeah, it was definitely her. She was with some dark-haired guy. I think his name is Kevin or Caleb or something." Fear and panic morph into full-blown terror. She must sense my escalating desperation, because she points to a door leading out back and says, "They just went out that door a minute ago."

I release her and barrel towards the exit, knocking into people on the way. I don't even bother to apologize; my thoughts are focused on finding Abby. *If he leaves with her... I don't even want to think about what will happen.*

I burst through the back door and suck in a breath, filling my lungs with the balmy midnight air. I look around, searching for her, praying they're not gone yet. Finally, far to my right, past multiple rows of cars, I see them. Rage fills my chest when I see his arm wrapped around her waist, supporting her weight as he practically drags her towards his douche-mobile. The Mustang is parked near the back of the lot and they're quickly closing the gap. I need to reach her before *they* reach *it.*

I take off towards them. "Hey!" I yell so he'll stop.

He turns to look at me. He doesn't stop, but it slows him down.

"Stop! Let go of her!" I'm running, my arms pumping at my sides.

"Mind your own business, dickhead," he has the nerve to yell back at me. He's overly confident I won't reach them in time.

Big mistake, asshole.

"Motherfucker," I grunt in frustration.

"Jacob!" I hear someone calling my name from behind, Luke maybe, but I'm too focused to stop now. I'm almost there.

"Abby!" A scared female voice this time.

"Abby!" Another male voice.

Finally, I'm within ten steps of them. Caleb turns and releases Abby when he sees how close I am, and she falls bonelessly to the ground. I shove him as hard as I can and he lands on the hood of his car. He was so close to having her in his grasp, it makes me sick to think about it. I'm charging him, ready to pummel his face, when I feel long, strong arms wrap around me from behind, pinning my arms to my sides.

"WHAT THE FUCK!?" I roar, thrashing and fighting, bucking like a bull. I'm gonna hurt whoever is keeping me from killing this fucker. "LET GO OF ME!"

"It's not worth it, man," Luke urges. "You can NOT go to jail!"

I know he's the voice of reason, but in this moment, it doesn't matter. I can't see past the fire in my eyes to think of the consequences. All I can think about is hurting this piece of shit so he can *never* hurt Abby again.

Caleb relaxes for a moment, feeling escape within his reach, and a smug expression slides over his features. But his eyes widen with fear a second before Ethan's fist connects with his jaw with a resounding crack. His head snaps back violently. Ethan must have gotten a run at him. *Good.*

"You son of a bitch!" Ethan is on top of Caleb now, raining down blow after blow. He grabs the collar of Caleb's shirt, lifting him off the ground before slamming his head into the gravel.

"Ethan," Abby calls weakly from the ground. With that sound, all the rage drains out of me and relief floods my whole body. Luke releases his hold on me and I go to her, crouching down next to her and pulling her limp body into my arms.

"Ethan!" Tiff yells. "Stop!" But her plea doesn't even register in his rage-fueled brain. "Ethan, please," she cries, her voice growing hysterical.

Luke finally pulls him off Caleb, but Ethan gets one last kick in before Luke wedges himself between them. Ethan shoves him, but Luke remains calm.

"Easy, man." He holds up his hands in a non-threatening gesture.

Who knew Luke could be so rational?

"If you ever come near my sister again, I'll fucking kill you!" Ethan spits out. Caleb moans from the ground, blood pouring from his mouth and nose, both eyes already swelling shut. His face is unrecognizable.

People are starting to surround us, having been lured outside by all the commotion. "The police are on their way," somebody offers.

"Thank you, Mr. Jameson," Tiff thanks the man who owns The Barn, Luke's arms wound tightly around her body. "Ethan, your hand." She reaches for his bloody hands, but he pulls away from her.

"I'm fine," he replies stiffly and looks away.

"Ambulance is on its way, too," Mr. Jameson adds.

"Abby goes first," I command. Neither Abby's brother nor that piece of shit on the ground is going before her. I know that little fucker put something in her drink. I don't know when and I don't know how, but in my gut, I know he did it. It's the only possible explanation for him being able to drag her out here, and it would explain the condition she's in. "I think he roofied her." The owner nods his head in understanding, his jaw tight with anger. This is his place, and that little cocksucker just shit all over his hospitality.

I dig my keys out of my pocket and hand them to Luke. "I'm riding in the ambulance with her. Take my car. I'll call you when they release her." I scoop her into my arms, cradling her under her shoulders and knees, and stand up.

"No way," Tiff and Ethan say at the same time. They look at each other, their expressions laced with contempt.

Ethan argues, "I'm her brother. *I'm* going with her," at the same time Tiff adds, "We'll meet you at the hospital."

I look at Tiff, accepting her response. "That's fine."

I turn to her brother. "No offense, but I don't care who you are. I'm not letting her out of my sight again. Not after what just happened. I know you're her brother, but I love her and I'm not letting her go."

Three sets of wide eyes stare back at me. It takes me a moment to figure out why, then I realize what I just admitted out loud, the truth I've known for days.

I love Abby.

Ethan's jaw clenches in anger, but he nods. "Fine. I'll meet you guys there."

"You can't drive," Tiff responds, motioning to his mangled knuckles, concern etched across her face. "Come with us," she pleads.

"I'm fine," he repeats through gritted teeth.

We finally hear sirens in the distance, multiple sets, by the sound of it. The ambulance arrives and the EMTs try to take Abby from me, but I refuse to let them.

"Sir, we need to get her into the truck and assess her."

I don't respond; I just climb into the back with her in my arms and lay her on the gurney. She drifts in and out of consciousness but reaches for me when I lay her down.

"Sshh, I'm right here," I assure her.

"Are you family?" the EMT asks.

I look at him and lie without blinking. "Yes," I answer sternly, leaving no room for argument. If he can tell I'm lying, he lets it slide.

"We need to get a statement," someone interjects, and I notice an officer standing at the back entrance of the ambulance, talking to the other EMT.

"You'll have to get it at the hospital," the EMT answers shortly. "She's drifting in and out." At that, the back doors slam shut and we head towards the nearest emergency room.

Chapter Twenty-Four

Abby

Beep.
Beep.
Beep.

Where is that incessant beeping coming from, and how do I make it stop? Seriously, why won't anybody turn that damn thing off? And why does my bed feel weird? These aren't my sheets. My sheets are soft and worn. These are stiff and scratchy. And my bedroom doesn't smell like antiseptic.

Beep, beep, beep.

My eyes fly open and I sit straight up when it finally dawns on me that I'm not at home. I instantly regret it, though, when the artificial lighting pierces through my retinas straight into my brain. I shut my eyes against the offending light and press the heel of my hand to my forehead. *Damn, my head hurts. What the hell happened?*

"She's awake," a hushed voice announces, followed by the sound of shuffling feet.

"Abigail." I feel my grandmother place her hand softly on my back.

"Enisi, where am I?"

"You're in the hospital, sweetheart."

"Why? What happened?" I mentally catalogue every part of my body. Except for my head, everything feels fine. *Oh no, do I have a head injury? How long have I been asleep? Was I in a coma?* I start to panic until I hear my brother's voice.

"That son of a bitch Caleb roofied you."

"Ethan!" my grandmother scolds him for cussing. If she only knew the foul mouth that boy has on him.

"Where's Jacob?" I pray he's not in jail for killing Caleb. If I'm here, that means he must know what Caleb did to me, and I know he'd never let that go unanswered.

"He's out in the lobby, pacing the floor, about to lose his shit," Ethan answers. My grandma just sighs and shakes her head.

"Why isn't he in here?"

"Enisi made him take a break and let me come back to sit with you. Two visitor policy," he explains, mouth flattened in annoyance. "She practically had to pry his fingers off the bed rail." He chuckles and she scowls.

"I want to see him."

Ethan nods and walks out the door. Not even a minute passes before Jacob barrels into my room, chest heaving and eyes wide with worry.

"Abby." He rushes to my bedside and pulls me into his arms. I press my face into his chest and inhale his scent. Manly, woodsy, and warm. Perfect.

"I'm so glad you're not in jail," I blurt out.

His tense body relaxes and I feel his chest vibrate with laughter. "I'm right here, baby girl. I've been waiting on you to wake up." Warmth engulfs my insides at the affectionate moniker he uses to address me.

"Your impulsive brother is the one who will probably end up in jail," my grandmother interjects. I look to Jacob for an explanation.

"When you didn't come back to the table, I went looking for you. I found you out behind The Barn with Caleb." Jacob grits his teeth and my stomach sinks.

I was out back with Caleb? And I was roofied? What did that sick bastard do to me?

Jacob heaves a deep breath and continues. "He was practically dragging you to his car. You couldn't even stand up. I chased him down and shoved him away from you, but Luke grabbed me before I could do anything else. While I was trying to fight him off to get to Caleb, your brother came out of nowhere and took matters into his own hands. Caleb was unconscious by the time the ambulance got there." His jaw clenches angrily and I can see that he wishes he was the one to put Caleb in the hospital.

Oh, God. The hospital.

"Please tell me he's not here. He doesn't know where I am, does he?" I start to panic. The thought of him finding me and trying to finish what he started terrifies me.

"No, he isn't here. Thankfully, they took him somewhere else."

"Is Ethan in trouble?"

My grandmother takes my hands in hers. "We don't know yet. The police questioned him, but he hasn't been arrested, so that's a good sign. But he could still be charged with assault." Her eyes fill with worry and her chin quivers. One grandchild in the hospital and the other potentially facing jail time. My grandmother doesn't deserve this kind of heartache.

"Caleb will most likely be charged with possession of a controlled substance, at the very least. We've heard that he still had the drugs on him. That alone should put him away for a while," Jacob assures me. "But he could be charged with attempted kidnapping, too." His forearms flex, the muscles straining as his grip on my bedrail tightens. I fear he's going to snap the metal rod in half, his barely contained anger rolling off him in waves.

"Hopefully the courts will take into account what Caleb did to you, and that Ethan was trying to defend you," my grandmother adds.

Jacob and my grandmother share a look, and I worry that they're keeping something from me. "What?" I demand. "Is there something else I should know?"

"We found out something else last night," Jacob relents. "This isn't the first time Caleb has done something like this. He's been accused of sexual assault before, and there was even suspicion that he had drugged the girl."

I gasp, my blood draining from my face.

"The rumor is that his family paid the girl off and convinced her to drop the charges," my grandmother adds. "She'd waited to come forward, and by the time she told her parents what happened, they had little evidence to go on, so they let him walk."

My stomach churns at the thought of Caleb putting his hands on me. "He didn't..." I hesitate, unable to speak the words. I take a deep breath and try again. "He didn't *touch* me, did he?" Jacob sees the pleading in my eyes, knowing that I'm begging for confirmation that he didn't.

His jaw ticks with anger. "That son of a bitch would be in the morgue if he had."

"Oh, thank God!" I dissolve into a mess of relief and tears as Jacob holds me. He lets me fall apart in his arms, doing his best to hold me together.

A man in green scrubs walks in as I'm wiping moisture from my eyes. "Ms. Harris," he confirms, glancing at the chart in his hands. "I'm Dr. Benson. I have your test results back, and I'd like to go over them with you." I nod my head, urging him to continue. "If you would prefer to do this in private..." He lets the suggestion hang in the air.

"No, it's okay." I just want to get this over with.

"We did some routine lab work," he begins, consulting my chart again. "Blood counts were good. Electrolytes and kidney function are right where they need to be. Your X-rays looked fine. Pregnancy test," he pauses, flipping to the next page. I hold my breath, my stomach in knots as I wait for the result. It can't happen that fast can it? "Was negative," he finishes finally and I exhale my pent-up breath, hoping my grandmother is too preoccupied with the doctor to notice my relief. "You were unconscious when you came to us, but your family assured us that no assault had taken place, so we did not perform a rape kit." I cringe at his harsh, straight-forward words. He pauses for a moment, ready to deliver the bad news. "Unfortunately, your tox screen came back positive for Rohypnol." I feel my eyes widen as Jacob cusses under his breath. I look at my grandmother, who covers her gaping mouth with her hand. The heartbroken look on her face kills me.

It's not like I didn't know what happened, what Caleb did to me. But to have the doctor confirm that he slipped me a date rape drug with the intentions of doing God-only-knows what, makes me want to vomit. I clench my stomach with my hands to keep its contents where they belong.

"So, what happens now?" I just want to get out of here and go home. I feel uncomfortable and just *icky*. Knowing that pervert was a minute away from having me alone makes me want to scrub my body in scalding hot water until my skin is raw. I can't imagine how I would feel if he had actually *done* something to me.

"There's an officer waiting to speak with you. They need to get your statement. Then the nurse will go over your discharge instructions and you can go home. You won't be able to drive for the next twelve hours because of the drugs in your system, so someone will have to drive you home."

"Will I be able to work today?" I can't afford to miss a shift at Rosie's, but I don't know if my head or my heart could handle it.

"I wouldn't recommend it. You need to go home and rest."

"Don't worry, I'll make sure she takes it easy the rest of the day," Jacob assures him, threading his fingers through mine.

"Well, if you don't have any other questions, I'll send in the officer."

"Thanks, Doctor."

Moments later, a uniformed officer walks through the door to my hospital room with a clipboard and a set of papers. My life has already changed irrevocably, but now it will be in writing. I'm a victim. That's how everyone will see me now, and I hate it.

"Ms. Harris, I'm Officer Richardson. I just need to get your statement regarding what happened with Mr.-" he glances at his clipboard, "Caleb Carlisle."

Just the sound of his name makes me cringe. He asks me to recount the evening and I do, to the best of my ability. I don't remember much after dancing with Jacob and him singing to me, and even that memory is incredibly fuzzy. I do remember seeing Caleb on my first trip to the restroom, but I tried to avoid him at all costs. I hadn't told Jacob I saw him because things were going so well and I didn't want his presence to ruin our evening. Now I wish I would have.

At some point I just blacked out, and there's a big, blank space where there shouldn't be. I have no recollection of leaving The Barn, of Jacob finding me, or of Ethan beating Caleb to a pulp. That's probably a good thing. Even though there's a vengeful side of me, a very human side, that hopes my brother broke every bone in Caleb's face, seeing him do so would've been too traumatic for me to handle.

Once Officer Richardson leaves, I close my eyes and rest back on the pillow, my head throbbing. The constant sensation of feeling like I'm going to throw up will not go away. Jacob grabs my hand and squeezes.

"Are you okay?" I know he's not asking about my headache or my nausea. I can deal with that. He wants to know where my head's at.

"I will be." He leans in and kisses me on my hairline just as a nurse walks in to discharge me. When she's finished removing my IV and going over my instructions, I turn to Jacob and tell him, "Take me home." He nods and hands me a stack of clothing.

"Tiff brought these for you. She didn't think you'd want to wear what you had on last night."

She's right. I might burn those clothes.

"Thank you." I walk to the restroom on shaky legs and change from the hospital gown into the t-shirt and running shorts Tiff brought me. I catch a glimpse of myself in the mirror, wincing at my matted hair and the fresh bruise blossoming on the side of my face. My scalp is sore, like I've been dragged around by my hair. *What did that asshole do to me?* By the looks of things, I must have fought back at some point. If I didn't feel so defeated, I might actually be proud of myself for that.

I try to walk out, but the nurse insists on taking me out in a wheelchair per hospital policy. She's young, maybe close to my age, and I assume she's new to her job. She gapes at Jacob's Range Rover when he pulls up to the ER entrance. I stand up and turn around to thank her, but her eyes are focused on the shiny vehicle behind me, though they follow Jacob hungrily as he jogs over to me to help me into the car. "Take care," she mumbles, still watching Jacob. The spike of jealousy from the nurse ogling him quickly dissipates when he places a sweet kiss to my temple and opens the door for me.

The sun is just starting to break over the horizon and I wonder how long I was unconscious. The ride home is quiet, neither of us knowing what to say, and I feel the tension rolling off him. I know he's fighting to control the rage burning deep inside, but that's not what this is about. Something else is bothering him.

When we pull up to my house, Jacob shuts the car off but makes no move to get out. He gazes out the windshield, refusing to meet my eye. After a few beats of silence, he finally speaks.

"I'm so sorry," he pleads mournfully, eyes downcast.

I just stare at him, stunned, confused by his apology. "What on earth do you have to be sorry for? You *saved* me. I don't even want to think about what that monster would have done if you hadn't gotten to me when you did."

He shakes his head and grips the top of the steering wheel with both hands, his knuckles blanching. "I shouldn't have let you out of my sight. You were gone for too long, and I waited longer than I should have to come looking for you." His jaw is so tight, it might crumble under the pressure. His shoulders are tense, his arms flexed and veins popping out on the surface of his skin.

I place my hand on his straining bicep, but he won't meet my gaze. He just continues staring a hole through his windshield. "This is not your fault," I assert with resolve. "There's nothing you could have done to prevent this. People like him are predators." I refuse to say his name. He doesn't deserve to be acknowledged as a human being. "They watch and wait, and when they find their opening, they strike. If it hadn't been last night, it would have been some other time. I thank God you were there." I swallow back the emotion clogging my throat, and fresh tears sting my eyes. "If you hadn't been there, he would have succeeded."

His eyes widen and flash to my face, and I see he hadn't considered that scenario. If Caleb had waited to do this a week from now, Jacob would already be gone. He wouldn't have been there to save me. A thousand emotions pass between us, expressed with nothing but our eyes. Suddenly he grabs both sides of my face and presses his lips to mine. I suppress a wince at the painful sensation spreading over my left cheek and temple. I don't want to draw attention to my battered face.

Jacob releases my lips and presses his forehead to mine, his eyes shut tightly. "I don't know what I would have done if something had happened to you." I can feel his hands shaking. "You have no idea how much you mean to me."

My lips and heart both tremble at his admission. I close my eyes and let him cover my face in kisses. I can't even speak. I want to tell him that I *do* know, because I feel the same way, but I'm too overcome with emotion.

Jacob releases me and helps me out of the car. He holds on to me as I make my way towards the front door, as if I might not be strong enough to bear my own weight. My grandmother opens the door and ushers us inside.

"Do you want something to eat? I can make you some breakfast," she offers. I'd sent her home before giving my statement, not wanting her to hear all the gory details as Jacob filled in the blanks. She was reluctant to leave me, but with Jacob's assurances that he would bring me straight home, she finally gave in. Now she's hovering, waiting within reach in case I fall apart.

I shake my head. I can't even think about food right now. "I just want a glass of water."

"Go lie down and I'll bring it to you."

Jacob follows me to my room, never releasing his hold on me. I sit on the edge of the bed and he crouches in front of me, sliding off my shoes. I can't help myself. I reach out and stroke his hair. He's so sweet and caring. The pain in his eyes makes me frown.

"Tell me what you need, Abby," he pleads. "I'm lost here. I don't know what to do to make this better."

A sad smile spreads over my lips. "There's not much you can do. Just be here."

"I'm right here. I'm not going anywhere," he promises.

My grandmother brings me a glass of water and some pain relievers, watching as I swallow the two white tablets and gulp down the whole glass. She stands next to Jacob, wringing her hands, her worn face etched with worry.

"I'd really like a shower before I crawl into bed." Neither of them act like they want to let me out of their sight, but they don't protest.

I spend a good forty-five minutes in the shower. I'm perfectly clean after the first ten, but I keep feeling like I need to wash him off me. I scrub until my skin is raw, and then I sit on the floor of the shower and cry. Scrub, then cry. Scrub, then cry. Over and over until the water runs cold. I dry off and slip on a pair of yoga pants and a sweatshirt. Even though it's at least eighty degrees outside, I'm shivering, a bone chilling coldness settling deep inside me.

I'm surprised to see Jacob sitting on my bed with his back against the headboard and his legs crossed at the ankles. I can't believe my grandmother is allowing this. She must realize how damaged I am and how much I need his comfort.

"Hey," he greets me and sits up straighter in the bed. "Feel better?"

"Yeah," I answer honestly. I actually do. I let the towel wrapped around my head fall and pull my damp hair into a bun.

"Come here," Jacob beckons. I crawl into my bed and lay on top of the covers with him, and he wraps his arms around me, pulling me in close. I nuzzle him and throw my arm over his abdomen. "I'm all yours today. I'm not going anywhere. Anything you need, just let me know."

"I need you to hold me." And so, he does. He holds me tight until sleep overcomes me and I drift into darkness.

MY BREATH IS coming hard and fast. I'm sweating. I can't move. He's on top of me and has his hand over my mouth.

"If you scream, I'll cut your fucking throat." I can't make out his face shrouded in darkness, but I know that voice.

I whimper as something cold pierces my skin and a trickle of warmth runs down my neck. His knife trails down my throat and to my chest, slicing the buttons off my shirt one by one. Sliding his blade underneath my bra, he severs the material in the center that holds the cups together. I sob as the cool air hits my fully exposed torso and he runs the blade down my stomach, circling my belly button with the sharp tip.

"Take off your shorts," Caleb demands, releasing one of my hands from its restraint. He slides down my body and removes a manacle from my right ankle, and I realize my legs have been spread wide and shackled. I try to close them, but he quickly wedges his knee between my thighs. My wrists burn from the constant friction of my efforts to escape. The evil glint of excitement in his eyes sends a terrifying chill down my spine.

"Please," I beg, tears running down the sides of my face, soaking the hair at my temples.

"Mmm, I like it when they beg."

This is some kind of sick game to him. He wants me to comply, to do as he says out of fear. I sob, terror gripping my insides. *Why is this happening to me?*

"Abby," he groans lustfully, his knife popping the button at the top of my shorts.

"Abby." His voice is becoming more forceful, more desperate. He'll have to kill me. I won't make this easy for him. I buck against my restraints and my captor, boldly defying him.

He's so mad at me for not doing what he says, he starts shaking me and screaming in my face.

"ABBY!"

I open my eyes and see Jacob's worried face mere inches from mine. His hands are on my shoulders and we're both panting. My clothes and brow are drenched with sweat.

"Oh, God," I cry out. It was just a dream. A horrible nightmare.

Jacob enfolds me in his embrace. "You were crying and whimpering, begging for it to stop. You scared the hell out of me."

"Caleb had me. I was strapped down and he was cutting my clothes off." Another sob breaks loose and he tucks me in tighter. "He had me," I repeat, my voice hoarse and strained. He holds me as big, violent sobs wrack my body and I let out all my fear and anger and sadness.

I don't know how much time passes. A few minutes, an hour maybe, but I finally calm down and my eyes are dry. Jacob brushes the hair off my damp forehead.

"What time is it?"

"It's almost two in the afternoon."

I stretch my arms over my head and yawn. "I've slept the whole day away." I never sleep this late. I don't have time to sleep this late.

"I think we can overlook it just this once," he assures me with a smile. I hope he was able to get some rest, too. I doubt he slept at all last night.

"Okay."

"You should probably call Tiff now that you're up. She's been blowing up your phone."

I immediately grab my phone and call her. I'm sure she's freaking out right now. Even though she's at work, she picks up on the second ring.

"Abby! Oh my God, are you okay? They wouldn't let us back to see you because we weren't family, and then your grandma sent us home." Her frantic greeting doesn't surprise me.

"I'm okay. Just a little shaken up." That's a lie. I'm a *lot* shaken up, but I don't want to worry her more than she already is.

"I can't believe that sick bastard drugged you! And then he *took* you!" I hear the muffled sound of her crying through my phone. Tears pool in my eyes, threatening to spill over. I blink them away rapidly.

"It's okay. I'm fine. He didn't get far with me." I look Jacob pointedly in the eyes. He's the only reason I'm here right now, safe and sound.

"I'm so glad you're okay. I've been worried sick about you." She sniffles before continuing, "I'm coming over when I get off work. I have to see you with my own eyes and make sure you're really okay."

I smile at her resolve. "Okay." There's no point arguing. Once Tiff makes up her mind about something, there's no stopping her. I hang up the phone and turn towards Jacob. "Tiff is coming over when she gets off work."

"What do you want to do until then?" My stomach rumbles and I realize I haven't eaten since yesterday afternoon.

"I need something to eat. I'm starving."

"What sounds good to you? I can run out and pick something up," he offers, slipping out of my bed.

"You know what I'd really like?"

"What's that, baby girl?"

There it is again. I'm starting to love it when he calls me that. My stomach flutters and I smile for the first time since waking up in that hospital bed.

"I'd like to pack a lunch and go for a little hike. I really need to get out of the house, and I know the perfect place where we can get away and nobody will bother us." There's a place not far from here, just a short hike, that has become my favorite spot on earth. There's a stream in the woods behind our house with a babbling brook and a big, flat boulder overlooking the water. The place is enchanting, magical almost, like a scene out of a fairytale. It's where I go when I'm troubled or just need to get away from everything.

"That sounds perfect."

Jacob helps me pack some sandwiches, fruit, and water for our impromptu picnic. I let my grandmother know where we're going so she doesn't worry any more than she already is. She seems reluctant to let me out of the house, but doesn't try to stop me. She knows what I need right now.

Jacob follows me out to the tree line and we stop. I whistle and wait a moment to see if Cero will come. I don't have to wait long. His big furry body runs towards me and nearly bowls me over.

"Hey, big guy. You wanna go to the creek?" I rub the soft fur on top of his head and he wags his tail excitedly as if he knows what I'm saying. He licks

Jacob's hand and nuzzles it, wanting his attention. Jacob crouches down and scratches Cero behind his ears for a moment before we continue through the woods.

It takes less than ten minutes for us to get where we're going. Once we arrive, I plop down in my favorite spot and watch as Cero splashes in the water. Jacob sits next to me and I set out the contents of our lunch. Neither of us has eaten today, so it doesn't take long to finish it off. The tall oak trees surrounding us provide plenty of shade, and the light breeze keeps the heat at bay.

"So, this is where you come to unwind?" Jacob and I are both leaning back, our weight resting on our elbows.

"Yep. This is my spot." His easy smile and soft eyes make me want to open up to him just a little more. "I used to come here with my dad a lot." I pause, thinking about him and how much I miss the moments we shared together here. "Whenever we'd come to visit my grandma, he would always slip out while she and my mom were cooking or talking and come down to the creek. When I was about seven or eight, I started sneaking out when I thought nobody was looking so I could follow him, thinking he wouldn't notice. But he did, of course." I shake my head and smile, remembering how stealthy I thought I was being. "One day, he hollered at me and told me to come on out, saying that he knew I was there. He'd known the whole time I was following him. I hung my head and revealed myself, thinkin' I was gonna be in big trouble." I still remember his somber expression and how it worried me. "He waved me over to him and we sat down together right here." I pat the ground beside me and pick up a couple of rocks, rolling them between my fingers.

"He told me this was where he came to think." What troubled him, I never did know. Our lives were perfect until we lost him. "He placed a tiny pebble in my hand and picked up a much bigger stone for himself. I thought he was just gonna start skippin' rocks, but he didn't. He closed his hand around it, clenching it tightly in his palm. Then he told me, 'Whenever something is bothering you, just tell it to a rock.' He brought it up to his mouth and whispered something only he could hear, then he said, 'After you do that, throw it in the water and let the creek wash it away.' He chucked his rock into the creek, and I watched as the strain of whatever was bothering him melted away. He told me to try it, so I whispered something to my rock, I don't even remember what it was now, and tossed it into the water. Once I did, I felt, I don't know... lighter, somehow. Maybe it was just speaking the words out loud that made me feel better, but it worked. So, I kept doing it. Since that day, I've thrown my troubles into this creek and let it wash them away."

I'm not sure it'll work this time around, but I'm willing to try anything. I take the handful of rocks I'm holding and throw them all into the water, as hard and as far as I can. I have a lot of troubles right now, so I try to give them all a head start. I want them as far away from me as possible.

"Sounds like he knew what he was talking about." Jacob gazes out over the water thoughtfully, and I wonder what troubles he needs to toss in there.

Tentatively, I hold out a handful of small stones and wait for him to take them. He peers down at my hand, hesitating a moment before taking them from me. He rolls them around in his hand, studying them. Finally, he tosses them into the water and rests his forearms on his knees, then takes a deep breath and exhales slowly. I'm not sure if it worked and he's more relaxed now, or if he's still holding on to whatever is bothering him, but after a long pause he glances at me and offers a weak smile. I slip my arm through his and rest my head on his shoulder. His warm, strong hand covers mine and I close my eyes, relishing the feeling.

We stay out by the water for a long time watching Cero splash and play. The afternoon humidity dampens my skin, the cool breeze long gone. I yearn to dip my feet into the cool stream. "Wanna get in?" I ask Jacob. "Just up to our knees?"

"That sounds like a good idea." We slip off our shoes and wade in the shallow edge of the clear water. "It's beautiful here."

"It is," I agree. When I gaze up at him, his eyes are trained on me. He moves in closer, turning my body to face him. Wrapping his arms around me, he leans in hesitantly for a kiss and pauses, unsure of how much physical contact I'm okay with right now. I close my eyes and tilt my head back, silently giving him permission. I melt into him, warmth spreading out from my chest and into my limbs, feeling safe in his arms.

Every inch of my body tingles in response to his touch and I grip the back of his neck with both hands, pulling him closer. I moan and deepen our kiss, a familiar spark coming to life. I'm not ready to do much more than this right now, but it feels so good to be in his embrace. He groans against my lips and I feel his arousal growing against my belly.

He breaks contact and pulls away, concern is etched in his face as his eyes searching mine. "Abby," he begins, but I know what he's thinking. He's worried about pushing me too far.

"We should probably head back." I save us from the awkward conversation that's about to happen.

We take our time walking home, neither of us in a hurry to get back. I find a large stick to play fetch with Cero, but once he realizes Jacob can throw it much farther than I can, he won't bring it to me anymore. Jacob runs and plays and wrestles with him, making me giggle, their mutual fondness of each other solidifying my trust in Jacob. I know I can count on Cero's instincts, even if my judgment is clouded by piercing blue eyes and a million-dollar smile.

A couple hours after returning home, there's a thunderous pounding on the door. I check the clock, realizing it's about time for Tiff to be showing up. It can't be her though, because she never knocks. She just breezes right in like she lives here, which at one time, she practically did. I open the door to find my friend, red-faced, huffing and puffing, her arms loaded down with goodies, foot raised in preparation of kicking my door again.

"Hey!" she greets me breathlessly. "I brought pizza and movies." She looks like she's about to drop everything in her arms. I take the bag of chips, cookies, and movies from her and open the door wide so she can fit through with the over-sized pizza box.

"Wow, Tiff, how many people were you expecting?" I ask jokingly. She huffs as she sets the pizza on the table and removes the plastic bag holding two two-liters of pop from around her arm, leaving red, angry lines carved into her forearm. I barely have time to take the bags from her and place them on the table before she pulls me in close and squeezes me tightly, her breath stuttering and coming in spurts as she tries to suppress her tears. After a long embrace, she lets go of me and greets Jacob.

"I should probably get out of here," he offers, pressing his lips against my temple. "I don't want to feel like the third wheel." Despite his playful smile, I can see that he's worried about me. And I'm really not ready for him to leave.

"Why don't we call Luke and see if he wants to join us? There's enough food here for ten people." I love Tiff, but I *need* Jacob. I want him to stay, but I don't want him to be uncomfortable and outnumbered by us girls.

"Sure, why not?" Tiff shrugs. Her indifference at the prospect of seeing him makes me wonder if she's losing interest already.

Jacob pulls his phone out of his pocket and dials Luke, inviting him to our little get together. Twenty minutes later, an unfamiliar car pulls into the driveway and Luke hops out of the back seat. I'm stunned when I open the front door and Luke wraps his arms around me, hugging me tightly.

"Hey girl. You alright?" he asks.

"I'm okay." I blink back tears and swallow the lump in my throat. Luke's unexpected affection catches me off guard and my strong façade begins to crack. After a moment, he releases me and goes straight to Tiff, picking her up and swinging her around. She throws her head back and laughs, and seems genuinely happy to see him. Maybe I misread her earlier.

"Hey beautiful." He smiles at her warmly and presses his lips to hers. "Did you miss me while you were at work?" His growing affection for her is sweet and endearing.

"Of course," she croons. I'm relieved that she's back to her usual self.

My grandmother returns from Sunday night church services as we're loading our plates with pizza and chips. Jacob invites her to join us, but she declines, having already eaten dinner with her ladies' Bible study group. She gives me a hug and bids me goodnight before retiring to her bedroom at the end of the hall. We spend the evening eating pizza and watching funny movies, laughing and joking in hushed tones to keep from disturbing my grandmother. It's like we haven't a care in the world, and that's exactly what I need.

Chapter Twenty-Five

Jacob

I wake up Monday morning to an empty bed and even emptier arms. I left Abby's house late last night and crawled into this king-sized bed alone. It was hard to do, but I knew I couldn't stay there all night.

The four of us had a really good time just hanging out at her house. Having us all together, spending time doing normal things, seemed to relax Abby tremendously. She laughed a lot and ate pizza and cookies and drank more Mountain Dew than I've ever seen anyone drink before.

She insisted on going back to work today, but I'm worried about her. I'm sure word of what happened Saturday has gotten around by now, but I hope nobody says anything to her about it. That would just upset her, and I hate to see her in pain.

I decide to grab a late lunch at Rosie's so I can check on her and make sure she's okay. Luke and I got up early to go kayaking and haven't eaten since breakfast.

"Feel like stopping by and seeing the girls?" I glance at Luke in the passenger seat. He's gazing distractedly out the window.

"Huh? Oh, yeah. That sounds good. I'm starving."

Rosie's is the slowest I've ever seen it. We missed the lunch rush and the dinner crowd hasn't started trickling in yet. Tiff finds us instantly and comes over to our table to take our order.

"Hey, gorgeous." Luke's eyes light up when he greets her. "How's it goin'?"

"Good, now that you're here." When she throws a flirtatious smile his way, his face splits into a grin so wide, his damn cheeks must hurt.

"Where's Abby? Is she doing alright?" I ask Tiff, hoping that nobody has upset her.

"She's on break, but she'll be back in a minute. It's been really busy up 'til now, so she really hasn't had time to think about anything."

"Anybody say anything to her about Saturday?"

"No, not since this morning when Ros took her into the office to talk to her. She was worried, ya know." Abby's aunt has always looked out for her. Of course, she'd want to talk to Abby and make sure she's okay.

"Where's she at? I need to see her."

Tiff turns and waves for me to follow, leading me down the hallway, past the restrooms, and through the back exit. Abby is sitting at a picnic table with a salad that looks like it's barely been touched sitting in front of her. Her eyes find mine when she hears the door spring open.

"Jacob." She gets up and runs to me, jumping into my arms. "I didn't know you were coming." Warmth engulfs my chest at how excited she is to see me.

"I had to see you." As if on cue, my stomach growls loudly. "And I was hungry." I smile down at her beautiful face. She looks tired but happy. I can live with that. "I want you to stay with me tonight." I don't mean to just blurt that out, but there it is, hanging in the air between us.

"Okay," she agrees easily. I need to hold her in my arms tonight and know that she's safe. It damn near killed me to be without her last night.

"Are you off tomorrow?"

"I was, but I picked up a shift here to make up for the hours I lost Sunday." She winces at the thought of lost wages. I hate that she has to live like that.

"What time?"

"Two to ten."

"Good, that gives us plenty of time."

"Time for what?"

"I'm taking you to lunch." For some reason I'm nervous, hoping she doesn't refuse. "I promised you we'd go back to Wolf's Den Lodge during the day, and I always keep my promises."

She grins and tucks herself into my chest. "Thank you," she whispers.

AT SIX FORTY-FIVE, there is a much-anticipated knock on the door and I spring out of my chair to answer it. Abby stands on the other side with a large duffle bag slung over her shoulder, her athletic body clad in running shoes, shorts, and a tank top.

"Hey," I greet her and take the bag from her arms.

"Hey. I need to go for a run."

"Let me change and I'll go with you."

I really should have known better than to agree to run with Abby again. You'd think I would have learned my lesson from the last time, but I didn't. This time is exceptionally brutal. The late evening heat and peak humidity make it hard to breathe, and it seems my companion is trying to outrun something. The pain, the fear, the helplessness. It's as if she can't run fast enough to get away from Saturday night. I do my best to keep up with her, letting her know I'm here. Whatever she needs, I'm right here beside her.

When we finally get back to the cabin, I collapse onto my bed and Abby heads for the shower, bag in tow. I want to join her, but aside from being exhausted, I'm afraid to push things too far right now. I'm just going to follow her lead. When she's ready, she'll let me know.

I do my best not to think of her for the twenty minutes she occupies my bathroom. When I start imagining her slick, naked body surrounded by steam, I jump out of bed and head to the bathroom down the hall. I'll just take my shower in there. Another cold one.

I return to my bedroom just as Abby steps through the bathroom door, towel-drying her hair. Her hand pauses and her step falters as she takes in my bare chest and the towel wrapped snugly around my hips. I stride over to where she stands and cup the back of her head. Her quick intake of breath just before my lips meet hers doesn't go unnoticed. Too bad she's already fully clothed. I move my lips and tongue softly against hers, pulling away before things get too heated. The room is thick with palpable tension. Our bodies need each other, but our hearts need to take things slow.

I walk to my dresser and pull out some clothes, placing them on the bed and turning my back to her. My towel falls to the floor and I feel her eyes on me as I slip on my briefs, followed by the rest of my clothing. I turn to catch her staring at me wide-eyed, her lip trapped between her teeth. I smirk, knowing I've had the desired effect on her.

"You hungry?"

She blinks, raising her gaze to my face and releasing her lip. I lift one eyebrow, waiting on her to respond.

"Uh, yeah. Sure," she answers finally.

I leave her to finish drying her hair and whatever else girls do after taking a shower, and head towards the kitchen. I slice up strips of steak and dice peppers and onions and season them before throwing them into an oiled skillet.

"Mmmm, something smells really good." I look over my shoulder and find Abby watching me from the other side of the island.

"You like fajitas?"

"I love fajitas."

I slide her a plate full of ingredients and a mixing bowl. "You want to get started on the guacamole?"

"Sure. What do I do?"

"Just mash the avocados and mix everything together. It's already been measured out. Then just test it and see if it needs anything else."

"Where did you learn to cook like this?"

"Dated a culinary student my junior year." I stir the meat and veggies and place tortillas in the oven to warm. "Took me four months to realize she was bat-shit crazy, but by then, she'd taught me quite a bit," I admit honestly. "The rest I learned from The Food Network."

"Wow, I could eat like this every night," Abby groans, pushing her empty plate away.

Funny, I thought the same thing when she cooked for me. I smile to myself at the thought of us cooking for each other every day, sharing a kitchen and a home.

After dinner, Abby and I curl up on the couch and search through the movie collection left by the cabin's owners. We both reach for *Dazed and Confused* at the same time, our hands bumping each other.

"Guess we don't have to argue over which movie to watch," I joke.

"Guess not," she giggles.

I have no idea where Luke is, but I'm glad Abby and I have the cabin to ourselves. Her sweet, contagious laughter is refreshing. We both quote all of Matthew McConaughey's most memorable lines right along with him. Abby does such a good job imitating him, I almost pull a muscle from laughing so hard. This girl is a whole lot of fun and a whole lot of sweet wrapped up in one tiny, beautiful package. I'm falling more and more in love with her every day.

As soon as the credits roll, I turn off the TV and stand up, reaching down to pull Abby to her feet. "Ready for bed?"

"Yeah," she answers, stifling a yawn.

We brush our teeth, our eyes meeting in the mirror. Hers are filled with trepidation, mine with worry. I hope she knows that I'd never pressure her to do anything. If cuddling is all she's up for, then that's what we'll do. I never thought I'd be the kind of guy who likes that sort of thing, but I could hold Abby in my arms for hours. The next time our eyes meet in the mirror, I wink at her in hopes of dissolving some of the tension. It seems to work, her shoulders visibly relaxing.

I remove my shirt, slip under the covers, and wait for her to join me. She pulls her hair up into a messy bun and climbs in beside me. She has no idea how beautiful she is with her hair pulled back away from her face. I wrap my arm around her waist and pull her in close to my body, placing a kiss on her forehead.

She reaches one shaky hand up to my face and cups my cheek. Her lips part with an inhale, ready to speak. She searches my face, uncertainty creasing her brow. I wait for her to say something, anything, but she remains silent. After a moment, she just sighs, afraid to say whatever is on her mind. I place my finger under her chin and lift her mouth to mine and kiss her slowly, lovingly, hoping to comfort her. She kisses me back with the same slow, languorous tempo and we keep on that way for a long time.

She pulls back, panting, our kiss having become more urgent. I swipe my thumb over her full bottom lip, collecting its moisture on my skin. Suddenly, she wraps her arms around me and kisses me more furiously than before, pressing her body to mine. We make out for a long time, her fingers clawing at me like she's trying to burrow her way under my skin, pouring all her fear and desperation from the last few days into our kiss.

After a long moment, she breaks away, chest heaving with her rapid inspirations. "Jacob," she whispers my name, her voice laced with tension and want and need. And maybe a little apprehension. Her cheek presses against my chest as her arms encircle my waist. I hold her as she clings to me, the safety of my embrace a much-needed comfort in her vulnerable state.

I hold her for a long time, rubbing my fingers up and down her back until she starts to relax. "Goodnight, baby girl." I press my lips gently to hers one last time and tuck her into my chest, my chin resting on the crown of her head. I do my best to avoid pressing my raging hard-on into her body, but it's difficult when that's exactly what I want to do. After all she's been through, I'm not sure she's ready for that, and I don't want to push her too far.

When her frame goes limp and her breathing evens out, I know she's asleep. I lie awake, thinking about the last nine days and how they've changed me, how Abby has changed me.

I know I'll never be the same.

Chapter Twenty-Six

Abby

WANTED MORE FROM JACOB LAST NIGHT. I wanted to let him touch me and kiss me all over. But I was afraid. I was afraid that once he started removing my clothes, I'd be back in the basement from my nightmare, back on that hard slab with my wrists and ankles shackled, a knee jammed between my thighs, forcing them open and a hand covering my mouth to muffle my screams.

It's amazing and terrifying what your mind will conjure when you have no recollection of what really happened to you. Caleb never got the chance to carry out his plans, but I think somehow my subconscious knows what he would have done. Maybe not the specific details, but it knows he would have hurt me. A man doesn't drug you and try to sneak you out the back door because he wants to have a nice quiet chat. He wanted something I wasn't willing to give and he was going to take it by force. Thank God, he never got the chance. Thank God, Jacob was there to stop him.

I close my eyes and take a deep breath, doing my best to clear my mind.

Today is going to be a good day Jacob and I are having lunch at Wolf's Den Lodge, and we'll hopefully get to eat outside on the deck overlooking the river.

I brought my favorite sundress with me. I guess you can say it's vintage; it was my mother's when she was a teenager. Pale yellow with little lilacs on it, the simple, cotton dress with its sweetheart neckline, inch-wide straps, cinched waist, and flowy skirt was more than likely bought at a second-hand store, but I love it. It's one of the few things of hers that I still cherish.

I'm in Jacob's bathroom getting ready when I hear voices coming down the hall. I peek my head out into the bedroom, surprised to see Tiff walk through the door.

"Hiya, toots," she says playfully, waving at me.

"Hey, Tiff. What are you doing here?"

"Well," she begins with a wicked grin. "I came home with Luke last night and saw your car here. You guys must have already been in bed, though." She gives me a playful wink and my cheeks flush. "When I came downstairs this morning, Jacob told me where you guys are going and I thought I'd offer my cosmetic services." She removes the clip holding my hair in a twist atop my head, letting it fall down my back. "What are you wearing?" she asks, shaking out my long, dark tresses.

"Mama's yellow sundress."

"Ooohh, nice choice."

"Thanks."

"You bring your flat iron?"

"I think so. I threw just about everything from my bathroom into that bag." I point to where it's sitting on the sink.

"Good," she nods, rifling through my things. "I think you should wear your hair down and straight with that dress."

"Okay." I trust Tiff's opinion on all things hair, makeup, and fashion.

Forty-five minutes later, my hair lays in a glossy sheet down my back, perfectly smooth, straight, and parted down the center. My makeup is done in warm neutrals, my eyelashes coated in black mascara. She managed to cover the bruising on the side of my face, which makes me both happy and sad at the same time. I tuck my melancholy into the back of my mind and let my excitement slide to the very front. I slip into my dress with a pair of white wedge sandals and some dainty silver earrings with a matching bracelet.

"I do believe you're ready, sister."

I can't take my eyes off my reflection in the mirror. "Thanks, Tiff." My hair looks beautiful. I've never seen it so shiny and straight. My makeup is impeccable. Even my eyebrows look better. I don't know what she did to them, but I like it.

Tiff regards me thoughtfully, one arm crossing her chest, the opposite hand cradling her chin.

"What?" I ask, looking myself over, wondering if there's something wrong with my outfit.

"Nothing," she answers innocently. "I was just thinking I should have recorded this and used it as a tutorial for my YouTube channel."

"You have a YouTube channel?"

Tiff scowls and drops her arms to her sides. "Really?" she asks incredulously. "I've had it for like, six months. I told you about it at Christmas."

"Sorry," I offer with a wince, feeling like a shitty friend for not remembering. It's obviously important to her.

"If you had Instagram, you'd know this. I post all my videos on there." I roll my eyes and chuckle at her persistence. She never gives up. Once she's done pouting, I thank her again for helping me get ready and shoo her out of the bathroom.

Jacob greets me with a pleased grin when I walk into the kitchen. "You look beautiful." He slides his arm behind my back and pulls me in close, grazing his lips over mine. "Ready?" I nod and return his smile.

We pull into the Lodge promptly at eleven-thirty, where Jacob hands his keys to the valet and escorts me inside. Never in my life did I think I'd be eating lunch somewhere that has valet service.

Jacob asks to be seated at one of the outdoor tables. He smiles down at me and squeezes my hand as she leads us towards through the restaurant. It's sweet gestures like this that make me fall even more in love with him.

Jacob taps the hostess on the shoulder, leaning down to speak to her in a hushed tone. I can't hear what he's saying. I only see her glance down and nod, quietly replying with a "Yes, sir." She shoves one hand deep into her pocket as the other opens a door for us, holding it as we pass through.

"Where would you like to sit?" she asks when we reach the deck.

Jacob turns to me and holds out his hand, silently encouraging me to choose our seats. I lead him to a small table closest to the railing. He pulls my chair out and waits until I'm seated comfortably before sliding into the chair across from me.

The hostess hands us our menus. "Your server will be with you shortly. Otherwise, you won't be disturbed," she assures us. I glance around, noticing we're completely alone on the deck, and I wonder if we're the only people who want to be seated out here. I thought this view would be much more popular.

I gaze out over the water, the late morning sun warming my skin. I close my eyes and tilt my face upwards, embracing the bright, life-giving rays. I can appreciate why some ancient cultures worshipped the sun.

When I open my eyes, Jacob is watching me, a lopsided grin pulling up one side of his delicious mouth. I blush, having lost myself to the beauty of the nature surrounding us for a moment. I open my lunch menu as the waiter approaches our table to take our drink orders. He tells us all about their brunch cocktails, but I'm not the least bit interested in drinking. It may be a while before I'm comfortable drinking in public again.

Once we've ordered our food and drinks, I motion to the deck rails. "Do you mind?" I ask.

"Not at all."

I stand up and take the few steps separating our table from the solid wood and wrought iron railing. I place my hands on the smooth surface and breathe in the fresh air. The sound of gently flowing water is incomparably peaceful. I hear the legs on Jacob's chair scrape against the floor as he stands. A moment later, his arms are wrapped firmly around my waist, his chest pressed against my back.

"It's beautiful up here." His lips move against my hair.

"It's absolutely stunning." I turn towards him and look up into his eyes, even more captivating in the bright sunlight. "Thank you for bringing me back. The view is amazing. You just don't get this anywhere else."

"You're welcome." He holds me tighter and presses his lips to my forehead. "I wonder what all of this looks like from the sky."

"I can't even imagine. I'm sure it's breathtaking." He smiles and kisses me one last time before leading me back to our table.

We enjoy our lunch at a leisurely pace. I don't have to be at work until two, so there's no rush. Jacob tells me more about his schooling and what he plans to do when he finishes. I tell him about how my love of nature led me to choose to study biology. It's just so easy being with him. He's everything I could ever want in a man. He's strong but kind. He's generous and driven. He's so easy to fall in love with. I never really stood a chance.

When we finish dessert, Jacob lays down his fork and studies me for a moment, contemplation etched across his face. Finally, he leans forward, placing his elbows on the table and resting his chin on his knuckles.

"How do you feel about staying with me the rest of the week?"

I do my best to hide my shocked expression, but I don't think I'm doing a very good job. Jacob winces at my reaction, his confidence faltering. He's basically asking me to live with him until he leaves. For good. I want more than anything to say yes, but I don't know if I should. It will just make his leaving that much harder. But I told myself I was going to go all in, that I wasn't going to worry about the future. Just live for today and enjoy what we have now. He opens his mouth and I fear he's going to retract his offer.

"Yes," I blurt out hastily, and probably a little louder than necessary. His eyes shimmer with delight as his smile grows.

"Great. We'll swing by your house and you can pack whatever you need for the next few days, and then we can take it back to the cabin."

I'm excited to spend the next few days with him. I'm not thrilled about the idea of telling my grandmother that I'll be gone until Saturday, but I'm a grown woman and she's never stopped me from making my own decisions. Or even my own mistakes. I just hope staying with Jacob isn't one of them.

On the way to my house, my excitement dies down a bit when I think of Jacob's best friend. "What about Luke?"

"What *about* Luke?" Jacob asks, confusion furrowing his brow. He glances at me nervously from the driver's seat.

"Didn't you guys come here to do stuff? Together, I mean? I feel like Tiff and I have kept you guys from... I don't know." I search for the right words. "Extreme... sport... outdoorsy stuff." Not exactly the best word choice, but it's the best I can come up with.

He chuckles and grabs my hand, lacing his fingers through mine. "Luke and I have had plenty of time doing extreme sport outdoorsy stuff." He kisses the inside of my wrist, and I'm certain he can feel my pulse race against his lips. "What do you think we do when you and Tiff are at work? Besides, if I had to spend *all* my time with Luke, I'd lose my damn mind."

I giggle, knowing exactly what he means. I like Luke okay, but only in small doses.

THAT EVENING, JACOB and Luke come to Rosie's for dinner during my shift. Tiff is their server until six when she gets off work, and then I take over. When I set Jacob's refill down, he pulls me into the booth next to him. I notice he hasn't drunk any alcohol since Saturday. I don't know if it's because he doesn't want to, or if he's afraid it will upset me. Either way, I'm glad since he always drives and Luke never turns down a drink.

Jacob nudges my ear with his nose, moving my hair aside. "Are you coming straight to the cabin when you get off?" He speaks low enough that no one else can hear, not even Luke. His deep voice sends shivers down my spine.

"Yes," I answer, a little breathless. The grasp of his hand clenching my waist and the hot breath on my ear do funny things to my insides.

"Good." He kisses my jaw just below my ear lobe and releases his hold on me.

"I'd better go check on my other tables." I reluctantly slip out of his grasp and return to work. I can't wait to get out of here and soak in that luxurious tub. My feet will be aching viciously by the time my shift is over.

When I get to the cabin, I find the guys in the den playing video games. Tiff is on the adjacent couch typing away furiously on her phone with her feet propped on the coffee table, foam toe dividers keeping her freshly painted toenails from touching.

"Hey sis, you want a pedicure?" She's the first to notice me, and then two additional sets of eyes turn to find me standing behind the couch. Jacob jumps up and wraps his arms around me, pulling me in for a quick kiss.

I make my way over to Tiff and sink down on the couch beside her. "Trust me, you don't want to go anywhere near my feet right now."

She giggles and nods toward Luke. "Can't be any worse than Luke's farts."

Eww.

"Whatever. You love the manly aroma of my flatulence," Luke responds, never looking away from the TV screen. Tiff rolls her eyes, a smile tugging up one side of her mouth as she swipes a finger over her nail to make sure the polish is dry before removing the dividers. "Ahh, you killed me! You bastard!" Luke tosses his controller down with feigned anger. "Since I can't conquer this kingdom, I'll just have to conquer my woman."

Tiff shrieks when he picks her up and throws her over his shoulder. "Put me down!" She pounds on his back, laughing all the while.

"I can't, Milady, I must protect your virtue," he belts out in a horrible English accent.

Tiff snorts. "I think it's a little late for that." Her voice echoes down the stairs as he carries her to his room. Jacob and I both laugh at their antics.

"Are you hungry?" Jacob asks, standing and reaching for my hand.

"No, I just want a bath." I slip my hand into his and let him lead me down the hall.

He turns the water on for me and pours the purple-tinged liquid into the tub, lavender-scented bubbles forming immediately. "I'd offer to join you, but I've already had my shower," he teases with a wink.

"Well, that's a shame," I tease back. "Too bad you aren't a little dirtier."

"Oh, I'm sure I could find a way to get dirty again," he offers, a heated look in his gaze.

"That's okay," I assure him and place my hands on each side of his face. As good as that sounds, I don't know if I'm quite ready for that yet. I kiss him gently, breathing in his clean, masculine scent. "I won't be long."

He leaves me to bathe, and I soak in the luxurious scented water. When I emerge from the bathroom, squeaky clean, the scent of flowers on my skin, he insists on rubbing my feet and I graciously accept his offer. It's exactly what I need. Being on your feet for eight solid hours is tough, but Jacob's hands feel heavenly.

We get into bed and face each other just as we did last night. We kiss and touch, our breath mixing in pants and moans. This is how things go for the next couple of nights. Little by little, we go further than we did the night before, both of us growing more comfortable with increasing physical contact. Jacob's hands and lips remain hesitant until I initiate a new form of contact, then he dives in with gusto. We still don't make love, but attaining the same comfort level as before will take time.

And time is something we don't have.

Chapter Twenty-Seven

Jacob

THURSDAY. ONLY TWO MORE DAYS before I say goodbye to Abby. I promised her I'd help her with yard work again today. She hasn't been home since Tuesday, having stayed with me the past couple nights. Having her here has been incredible. We cook and eat our meals together, and when she climbs into my bed at night, I get to kiss her and feel her body. Each night, we push things a little farther. I just follow her lead, going as far as she's comfortable.

Tonight, I have something special planned for her, something I've been working on for days. I had to pull a few strings to get it worked out on such short notice, but everything is falling into place.

After we finish up at her grandma's house and eat a quick lunch, we head back to the cabin to get cleaned up. We shower separately, much to my disappointment. It takes all my willpower not to join her, but I know if I do, I won't be able to help myself. I'll want to be inside her. But that has to wait. Hopefully, tonight she'll see how much she means to me. Tonight will be the perfect time for us to reunite with our hearts *and* our bodies.

"I need to run out for a bit. Can you be ready by four?" I have a few last minute details to take care of before we head out, and I also need to call my mother. She's been blowing up my cell phone and driving me crazy, and I've been studiously avoiding her calls.

"Sure. What are we doing tonight?"

"That, my dear, is a surprise." I cup each side of her face and brush her lips with mine.

"What should I wear?" she asks, trying to suppress her grin. She must like surprises.

I shrug, not wanting to give anything away. "Something kinda casual. Jeans. Nothing too fancy." I turn to walk away but stop, needing to give her one important piece of information. "No heels. Make sure you wear flats." High heels aren't really practical for everything I have planned.

She smiles and clasps her hands together in front of her chest. "Okay!" I kiss her one last time before leaving, savoring the sweetness of her lips.

When I return home just after four, Abby is sitting at the kitchen island waiting for me, her big, bright smile lighting up the entire room. Her hair is pulled back, a ponytail of loose curls cascading down her back. Her lips are painted red, the same color as the thin belt on her dark wash jeans. She's wearing a flowy, white, short-sleeved blouse with black polka dots, and her feet are clad in a pair of black ballet flats. She looks perfect.

"You are so beautiful," I praise, pulling her into my arms. Her face flushes at my compliment. It's true, though. She's the most beautiful thing I've ever seen. "Let me change my clothes and then we'll go." She nods and I kiss her forehead before disappearing into my room.

I throw on a pair of dark jeans and a pale blue button-up, rolling the sleeves up a couple turns. I catch my reflection in the mirror and scrub my hand over my newly acquired stubble. I've never had a beard before, but I kind of like it. I know Abby does, and that makes me want to keep it.

Our drive takes longer than I anticipated. I'm antsy to get to our destination, for Abby to see everything I have in store for her this evening.

"Where are we going?" Abby's bright green eyes look at me expectantly.

"If I told you, it wouldn't be a surprise." I give her a teasing smile.

"Can you at least give me a hint?" she prods.

"Hmmm," I ponder for a moment, enjoying the sight of her squirming in the seat next to me. It's the same way she squirms when she wants me to touch her, to make her come.

I clear my throat and shift in my seat a little. I can't think like that right now or we'll never make it to the airport. I try to think of the vaguest hint I can supply without giving anything away.

"Blue," I answer finally. Blue. The color of the sky, which is exactly where we're going to be in a half hour.

"Blue..." she repeats, concentration knitting her brows. "Blue could mean water. Are we doing something on the river?" She tries to hide her excitement, but I see it brimming just below the surface.

"Maybe. Who knows? It's a surprise." I grin at her flustered expression. She'll find out soon enough. We're almost there.

We pull up to the gate and the security guard lets us in after checking his itinerary and my ID. The airport is small, privately owned, and about an hour's drive from the cabin. When I learned about this place, I just knew I needed to do this. For Abby. I'm not a big fan of flying, but I'd do anything for her.

Abby's eyes widen as she glances back and forth between hangers. I stop the car and reach for her hand. Her big green eyes search mine and I give her a reassuring squeeze.

"Ready?"

"Yes!" she replies excitedly. I can't wait to see her face when she takes in the view of her beloved hometown from the sky.

She clenches my hand tightly as we approach the small aircraft. The closer we get, the tighter her grip becomes.

A middle-aged man in a pilot's uniform approaches us and reaches for my hand. "Mr. Daniels?" he asks. I nod and shake his hand. "I'm Freddie. We spoke on the phone. I'll be your pilot this evening. She's all gassed up and ready to go."

"Thank you."

I peer down at Abby as she takes it all in. Her eyes bulge as she assesses the Cessna we're about to board. "I've never flown before," she admits, looking up at me, her eyes wide with excitement and trepidation. "Aren't you afraid of heights?"

She must be thinking back to the first time we saw each other when she recognized my unease at the ziplines. "I'm not afraid of heights; I'm just not particularly fond of them," I assure her with a smile. I've flown before. Many times, actually. Once I'm in the air I'm okay. It's just getting to that point that's a little rocky.

Once we're secured in our seats with headsets in place so we can communicate, Freddie starts up the engine. We take off down the runway, gaining speed, and soon lift off the ground. Our ascent is surprisingly smooth, and I'm way more relaxed than I expected to be. Maybe it's because I have Abby beside me, holding my hand. She peers out the window, taking in the scenery, but all I see is her.

Finally, she turns to me and asks, "Where are we going?"

"You'll see."

She returns my smile and cups my cheek. "You're like a real-life Christian Grey, aren't you?"

"A Who?"

She giggles at my perplexed expression and shakes her head. "Never mind."

We soar through the sky, passing over grassy hills, pine trees, and breathtaking mountains. It really is beautiful from way up here.

"If you look up ahead, you'll see the New River Gorge Bridge," our pilot's voice crackles over the headset.

Abby's eyes dart to mine in sudden realization and she mouths a silent "Thank you." She's plastered to her window for the rest of the ride, and I take the opportunity to enjoy the view as well. We follow along the river for a long time, revealing lush, green foliage and the enchanting, crystal blue sparkle of water. I knew this place was special, but the aerial view takes things to a whole new level. It's absolutely stunning.

Our aerial tour is over much too soon. When we land, I help Abby down and thank Freddie, then we head back to my SUV. I climb into the driver's seat, but before I can start the engine, she pounces on me. Her hands, her lips, her scent. She consumes me with her kiss, her fingers raking over my scalp. When she finally pulls back, her breath rushes in and out in a pant.

"If you keep looking at me like that, we'll never make it to our next stop," I warn. I'm not above throwing her in the back seat and finishing what she started.

"There's more?" she asks, stunned.

"Oh, baby girl, there's a lot more."

Her pupils dilate and I lean in for one last kiss before starting the car and taking off.

"So, what's next?" she asks after we pass back through the security gate.

"Are you hungry?"

"Starving." For more than just food, judging by the look in her eyes.

We pull into the Shady Brook Vineyard shortly after. A young woman dressed in a crisp white shirt and black dress pants meets us at the door.

"Mr. Daniels, Ms. Harris," she greets, nodding to each of us with a warm smile. "Your private tour will begin shortly. Your guide, Martin, is on his way." She leads us inside and motions for us to sit at a small round table. "Would you like a glass of wine while you wait?"

Abby tenses beside me, her grip tightening on my hand. My eyes find hers, looking to her for an answer. I don't want her to feel uncomfortable, so I wait for her to respond.

She traps her bottom lip between her teeth and glances at me. I nod, letting her know that whatever she chooses is fine. After everything she's been through, she's reluctant to drink, and understandably so.

"Sure," she answers finally, relaxing and sinking down into her chair.

"And for you, sir?"

"I'll have a glass as well." We listen as she recites the wine list from memory and make our selections.

"I can't believe we're getting a private tour. How did you pull that off?" Abby smiles around her glass as she sips the sweet red liquid.

"I have my ways." My evasive answer satisfies her and she prods no further. I don't want to tell her that I paid them what they would bring in over a weekend to close this place for a private tour and dinner. On a Thursday.

A man in khakis and a blue polo with the winery's insignia approaches our table and introduces himself as our guide, Martin. He begins the tour by walking us through the building, showing us the wine press and cellar. Abby runs her fingers over the bottles, studying their labels while Martin explains the winemaking process. As we move deeper into the lower level, we see endless rows of casks lined against the old stone walls, the damp, musty smell nearly concealed by the fragrant sweetness of wine. Martin recites the history of the one hundred-twenty-year old building to us, explaining how his family turned the surrounding landscape into a vineyard.

When we reach a large oak barrel with a tap already in place, he pours us each a glass of Pinot Noir to sample. We sip on it slowly as we finish up the indoor portion of the tour.

Once we exit the building, Martin leads us out towards the vineyard. I hold Abby's hand, our fingers entwined, and watch her face light up as she takes in her surroundings. The view of the rolling hills lined with row after row of grape vines rivals that of our aerial excursion.

"This is amazing," she proclaims, her eyes scanning the horizon.

"You like it? You're really having a good time?" I was a little nervous bringing her here, but seeing the excitement shining in her eyes eases my worry.

"I love it. Thank you for doing this. It's beyond amazing."

"You're welcome, but this isn't over yet. Things are about to get a whole lot more fun." She opens her mouth to respond, her lips forming an "O", but I tug her hand before she has a chance to speak. "Come on," I say, pulling her along as we follow Martin. If I know Abby as well as I think I do, she's going to enjoy my next surprise.

We stop at the edge of the vineyard where two large wooden barrels await. Abby leans over and peeks into one, assessing its contents. She looks at me curiously, wonderment alight in her eyes, a smile tugging at her lips.

Martin instructs us to remove our socks and shoes and roll up our pants legs. After cleaning our feet, I help Abby into her barrel and step into mine. She scrunches up her face when she feels the fruit squishing between her toes, but her smile never falters.

We begin slowly, lifting our feet and smashing the fruit gently. Once we acclimate to the sensation of stepping on them, we pick up speed. We stomp the grapes, both of us trying to outdo each other, smiles splitting our faces in two. We move faster and faster until Abby loses her footing, her body toppling sideways. I reach out and grab her, steadying her by the elbows. Tears spring from her eyes, her whole body shaking with uncontrollable laughter. I love seeing her like this. Happy and laughing, young and carefree like she should be.

We laugh together as she grips my forearms and tries to regain her balance. I had no idea this would be so much fun. I almost turned them down when the winery offered to let us do this, but I'm glad I didn't. The elation on Abby's face and her uninhibited mirth make everything worth it.

I climb out of my barrel and help her out of hers. As soon as her feet hit steady ground, I pull her in for a kiss.

"That was fun," she breathes against my lips, her palms flattened against my chest.

"I'm glad you enjoyed it." I remind myself that Martin is standing nearby, waiting for us. I want to dive headlong into another kiss, one that will curl her toes and make her moan, but not here. Not with an audience.

We wipe the juice from our skin and slip back into our shoes. I take her by the hand and we follow Martin into the vineyard. We walk through rows and rows of grapes, stopping every now and then to sample the ripe ones. He explains how each species of grape is made into different kinds of wine, and how to pair them with food.

I lace my fingers through Abby's and try to memorize her face as the sun sinks lower in the sky. It's nearly set when we reach the end of the last row. She gasps and covers her mouth with her hand when she sees what's waiting for us.

"Jacob," she whispers softly.

There's a small, candle-lit table covered in a white linen tablecloth about ten yards away. The young woman from earlier is standing off to the side with a white towel draped over her forearm, waiting for us to take our seats. I lead Abby to the table, tugging gently on her hand. I pull out her chair and motion for her to sit down. Instead, she throws her arms around my neck and kisses me deeply. When she finally releases me and takes her seat, I ease into the chair across from her and smile. Candlelight dances across her face, her eyes reflecting its warm, yellow glow.

"May I offer you a glass of Chardonnay?" The woman asks lifting a bottle from a silver bucket full of ice, and we reluctantly pull our gazes from each other.

"Yes, please," Abby replies and I nod. She pours us each a glass before placing a serving tray full of cheese, olives, bread, and various spreads and oils in front of us.

"Thank you," I tell her before she slips away. We sip from our glasses and snack on our appetizer platter as we wait for our food. I had a special meal prepared for us.

Our salads come first and we devour them within minutes. If we weren't so hungry for food, our hunger for each other would overwhelm us and I'd have to clear this table to make room for our bodies.

My mouth begins to water as the smell of roast lamb wafts through the air. By the time our waitress places our plates in front of us, I'm ready to dig in.

"Enjoy," she offers with a smile. "If you need anything, just ring the bell." She picks up a small silver bell resting on our table and gives it a little shake. I didn't even notice it sitting there. I've been too busy thinking of all the ways I could make love to my dinner companion on top of this table.

"What is this?" Abby asks, cutting into the meat on her plate.

"It's lamb. Have you ever tried it?"

"No. Never."

"It's excellent." I bite into mine and chew, savoring the delicious mix of flavors. Rosemary and garlic, maybe a little thyme.

Abby brings her fork to her mouth hesitantly and takes a small bite. "Mmmm, this is really good!" she exclaims between chews.

The fiery sunset makes way for the light of a million stars to twinkle in the night sky above us. We finish our dinner, and I pour her another glass of wine as our waitress returns with dessert. One plate holds a slice of tiramisu, and the other a large piece of red velvet cheesecake. I dig my fork into the first dessert and hold it out, offering her the first bite. Gently wrapping her lips over the prongs, she slides the decadent piece of tiramisu off my fork and moans. I squeeze my eyes shut at the heady sound. I made it through dinner without pulling her from her chair and sampling her own sweetness. Surely, I can make it through dessert.

"That is delicious." I lift a bite of cheesecake to her lips next and let her sample it before I try the desserts myself. Watching her enjoy the rich, sweet cakes and lick her lips between each bite is driving me crazy. How can watching a woman eat be so damn sexy?

"I don't think I can eat another bite," Abby announces as she sets down her fork and swipes the cloth napkin over her lips.

Good, I'm ready to get out of here and get her home. I give the bell a ring and the waitress returns to our table.

"Martin will return shortly to take you to your car," she informs us when we tell her we're ready to leave.

A few minutes later, Martin pulls up in a golf cart to escort us back to the parking lot. "I hope you two enjoyed your evening. Please, come back and see us again." We hop off the cart and I thank him, shaking his hand with gratitude. This evening was perfect. I can't thank them enough for helping me pull this off.

Abby walks to the passenger side and waits for me to unlock the doors, but I don't. I stalk up to her and place my arms on each side of her body, caging her between me and my car. I watch as her chest rises and falls rapidly, anticipation glinting in her eyes. When I can no longer stand the torture, I bend down and crush my mouth to hers, devouring her sweet taste and consuming her moans. I press my body to hers, the proof of my desire digging into her belly.

"Jacob," she whispers in that low, panting breath to which I've grown accustomed.

"Get in the car," I command, releasing my hold on her. We need to get back to the cabin. Now. I open her door and wait for her to climb inside before shutting her in and taking my seat beside her. I drive as fast as I possibly can without endangering ourselves or other motorists, the need to be inside her fueling my impatience. I just hope she's as eager as I am. I throw the car in park and jump out as soon as we get home.

Home.

That's exactly what this feels like. Anywhere Abby is feels like home to me. I shove the key in the lock and push through the front door. It doesn't look like anyone else is here. Good.

I grab Abby's hand and lead her towards the hallway. I can't wait another second to touch her and feel her tremble against my fingertips. Stopping and pressing her against the wall, I swallow her gasp with my kiss. She responds immediately, wrapping her arms around my neck and snaking one hand up the back of my head, holding my mouth to hers. I pick her up and she instinctively wraps her legs around my waist. Our tongues intertwine as I grind my hips, pressing myself against her core. She's hot and needy, and I can't wait to bury myself inside her.

"I need you," I confess, my voice hoarse with desire.

"You have me."

I search her eyes for meaning, hoping she's saying what I think she is. She holds my gaze, her deliberate stare telling me not to hold back. That's all I need. Pulling her away from the wall and continuing towards my bedroom, her lips never straying from my waiting mouth, I place her gently on the bed and cover her body with mine. Her soft moans and quiet sighs make it hard for me not to simply start ripping off her clothes.

Reaching between us, I loosen her belt and unbutton her jeans. Two soft, warm hands slide beneath my shirt and rub up my back. I pull away just long enough to unroll my sleeves and begin loosening the buttons. Abby's eyes burn with desire as she watches my fingers. With shaky hands, she reaches up and starts unbuttoning my shirt from the bottom. When it finally falls open, she slides her palms over my shoulders and I shrug out of it.

She helps me pull her top over her head before discarding it on the floor. I finish undoing her jeans and slide them down over her hips, noticing how her thighs quake, the anticipation affecting her just as much as it affects me. I hook my fingers inside the tops of her panties and wait for her to lift her hips before pulling them off. I kiss my way up her leg from her knee to the junction of her thighs. She gasps when I slide two fingers inside her and press my lips to her lower belly. I continue to kiss her, lower and lower until I reach her clit. My tongue darts out and I taste her, swirling it over and around as my fingers work inside her. She moans and gasps and squirms until her body shakes with her release.

"Jacob, please," she begs. I know what she wants, what she needs, and I'm prepared to give her everything.

I lean up and she hastily unzips my jeans. My erection springs free when I slip out of my pants and boxers. She swallows hard as she drinks me in, her eyes trailing slowly up my body until they meet mine. She sits up on her knees and pulls my body towards her, cupping the back of my neck. My arms crush her to me as my lips crash into hers.

Before I know it, I'm sprawled on top of her, her heels digging into the backs of my thighs. I rub myself against her slick, inviting warmth, and she moans as my shaft strokes her core. Finally, with one long, hard thrust, I'm buried deep inside her. I pause for a moment, letting her body adjust to me. She clenches her muscles, soundlessly encouraging me to continue, so I do. I make love to her, making her come and moan my name, and then I slow down and kiss her, letting her know she's mine and that she's all I'll ever want.

I hold off as long as I can, but finally release when she climaxes for the last time. I kiss her face and push her hair back once she comes down from her high. She looks a little sad when I pull out of her, almost as though she feels empty without me. But I know I've marked her. There's no way she'll ever forget me now.

Chapter Twenty-Eight

Abby

'M READY TO GO HOME. I'M READY TO crawl back into Jacob's bed and spend the next twelve hours wrapped up in his arms. Last night was amazing. I'd missed him. I'd missed the way his bare skin felt sliding over mine, the fullness of him inside me, and his fingers wrapped in my hair, gently tugging my head back, his lips exploring every dip and curve of my neck. Thinking about him makes me long for his touch, his kiss, and the feeling of his body pressed against mine.

These last two weeks went by so fast. A man I didn't even know fourteen days ago has somehow become the most important person in my life. He stole my heart, and I pray he never gives it back. It's his. Forever.

I've been stuck at work all day while Jacob and Luke spend their last full day here doing exactly what they came for. They're out exploring all the New River and its surrounding area has to offer, and I must admit, I'm a little envious. I sidle up next to Tiff at the bar and lean in to speak into her ear.

"I'm so ready to get out of here." My patience is growing thin. I'm ready for this day to be over so I can get back to Jacob, but at the same time, I don't want his departure to come any faster.

She nods in understanding. "Me, too."

"What do you think the guys have planned for us tonight?" I'm sure this being their last night in town, they'll have something special in store.

"I don't know about Jacob, but I'm pretty sure Luke's plans involve a can of whipped cream and a blindfold." She winks at me before sauntering off with her tray. She's probably right. I doubt we'll see much of each other once we get to the cabin. We'll both be, ahem, occupied.

On the ride home, I start to feel flutters in my stomach. For the first time in days, I'm nervous to see Jacob. I know our time is coming to an end. The hours are dwindling down, and I don't know when I'm going to see him after tomorrow. I hate the sinking feeling in my gut. The possibility of never seeing him again is becoming real to me.

What if this is it? What if, once he leaves, he moves on and has no desire to see me anymore?

I throw my old, beat-up truck in park when we pull up to the cabin, and I'm at their front door before Tiff even steps foot on the gravel. When I walk inside, Jacob is in the kitchen standing in front of the oven. He pulls a glass dish out and sets it on the counter, our eyes connecting from across the room.

"Hey, beautiful." His easy smile fades when he takes in the distressed look on my face. I feel like bursting into tears so I scurry to his room, the sound of his footsteps closing in behind me.

"What's wrong?" He places a hand gently on my shoulder, but I shrug him off, keeping my back to him. I can't face him just yet. I blink back the tears and take a few cleansing breaths. When I finally turn around and meet his eyes, they're filled with concern.

"Jacob," I whisper.

"Tell me what's wrong." The pleading look on his face nearly breaks me.

"What are we doing here?"

"What do you mean?"

"I mean *this*," I say, motioning back and forth between us. "Us." I pause and take a deep breath so I can continue without shattering. "What happens when you leave? This can't go on forever."

He steps towards me, leaving almost no space between us, resolve etched on his handsome face as he peers down at me. He looks fierce, almost intimidating. "Yes, it can." He snakes one hand into my hair, cupping the back of my head. "And it will." His mouth crashes against mine and he slips an arm behind my back, pulling me closer. I gasp when he tugs on my bottom lip with his teeth. He picks me up and places me on the bed, crawling over my body. I feel his hot breath against my skin as he kisses his way up my neck.

"You are *mine*." His icy blue eyes darken, and I believe him. "I'm not giving you up so easily." He cups my cheek and presses his lips to mine, telling me everything I need to know with a kiss. "We're going to make this work. We'll do whatever we have to do." His lips find a new place to kiss between every sentence. My cheek. My forehead. My nose. "What we have is too good to give up on."

I shiver. Knowing he's willing to try, willing to put in the effort of a long-distance relationship, fills me with hope. And a little fear. This won't be easy, but it will be worth it.

We make love for the first of many times tonight.

LUCKILY, THE FOOD is still warm when we emerge from the bedroom. Luke and Tiff are already seated at the table with their plates in front of them. I hadn't noticed the candlelight, bottle of wine, or the soft music playing in the background when I stormed in earlier. Heat floods my face, my cheeks flushing in embarrassment over my earlier behavior. I was on the brink of a full-blown panic attack. The thought of losing Jacob had me in knots, a firecracker ready to explode.

I slide into the vacant seat next to Tiff and give her a weak smile. She grasps my arm and pulls me close to her. In a low voice she asks, "Is everything okay?"

"It is now," I assure her. She studies me for a moment, and when she decides my answer is genuine, she releases me and returns to her meal.

Jacob pours me a glass of wine, our eyes meeting over the flicker of tiny flames. There's a new intensity in his gaze, a look of resolve that wasn't there before. He's determined. This means as much to him as it does to me, and he's willing to try. I bring my glass to my lips and drink, never taking my eyes off his, silently promising him the same.

I relax more and more as dinner goes on. Jacob and Luke entertain us with stories about their teenage years and all the trouble they got into. I haven't laughed this hard in a long time. Their tales of rebellion and bad boy ways are oddly endearing.

"How about a dip in the hot tub?" Jacob whispers in my ear as I place my dirty dishes in the sink. He grabs my hip and presses his lips to my temple.

"Okay." I smile to myself, savoring the feel of his warmth against my side. I slip into the bikini that I never did take home and meet him outside. The night air remains warm from the heat of the day, but the water still feels sublime. After a long day, my back and feet appreciate the relaxing effect the bubbling hot water has on them.

Jacob pulls me into his lap and rubs lazy circles over my arms, then he cups his hands in the water and pours it over my shoulders. I shiver when the cooling air hits my wet skin. Strong arms wrap around my middle, crushing me to a rock-hard chest. I sigh with contentment. Nothing feels better than being wrapped in his embrace.

His lips graze my jaw, feathering soft kisses from my chin to my ear. I arch into him when his palm presses into my lower back and breathe him in as he nuzzles my neck, feeling his desire growing against me. My body responds to his arousal, moisture pooling between my legs. I want him again.

Jacob practically growls when I swivel my hips, rubbing myself against his erection. Strong hands and deft fingers slide up my back and tangle in my hair. He sucks my bottom lip into his mouth before plunging his tongue inside and I taste the sweet, crisp flavor of wine on his lips.

Before I can register what's happening, I'm being lifted into the air, water dripping off my body and splashing into the pool below. Jacob sets me on my feet just outside the hot tub. He steps out and wraps a towel around my shoulders before pulling me into him.

"You're driving me crazy," he groans.

I could say the same about him. He drives me wild with desire. I've never wanted somebody so badly in all my life. No matter how much I have, I can't seem to get enough of him. My body and mind are overwhelmed with the most glorious sensations when he's near me.

He scoops me up and carries me into the house, his eyes never leaving mine until he sets me on my feet in front of the shower. Just like the first night we made love, he slowly rids me of my bathing suit, pulling the strings of my bottoms with agonizingly slow movements. The wet material slaps against the tile as he moves to liberate the strings behind my neck.

My breath catches when his lips skim my jawbone and his teeth nip at my ear lobe. Two triangles fall from my chest and my nipples tighten as cool air hits my damp skin. Jacob studies me for a moment before speaking.

"Turn around." His low growl makes my stomach clench in the most delicious way possible. Anticipation settles low in my groin, causing a flood of heat and need. I obey and turn my back to him, feeling the remaining strings loosen from my back, and my top falls to the floor.

His eyes rake over me when I turn to face him again. Emboldened by his obvious appreciation for my body, I reach out and slip my fingers into the waistband of his shorts. I tug them loose and slide my palms against his hips, never breaking eye contact. His arousal springs free as I push his shorts the rest of the way down his legs.

He turns on the water and we step into the spray, steam surrounding us and fogging the glass. All I can think about is making love to him, touching him, kissing him, licking and sucking, but Jacob has other things in mind. He squirts body wash into his hands and works it into a rich lather, his fingers working like magic over my tense muscles. He cups my breasts from behind, kneading them and stroking his thumbs over the sensitive buds. My head falls back against his chest and I moan. His hand slides up my neck and cups my face, turning me so I'm looking up at him.

"You are so beautiful." His thumb glides across my lower lip and I suck it into my mouth. A silent gasp parts his lips. His eyes flash with carnal need and he groans. I pull back slowly, letting his thumb pop free. "Shower's over," he growls.

Without another word, he hoists me into the air and carries me to the bed. We don't even bother drying off. We're both needy and impatient, and there's only one way for us to get our fix. His lips are on mine, urging me to open up to him. He settles himself between my legs and I rock my hips forward, needing him inside me, but he holds himself back. He teases me, rubbing his length against me but never entering.

Just as I'm about to scream in frustration, his head dips to my chest and he kisses his way to my navel. He glances up, a wolfish grin playing on his lips. I know what's coming and I know it will be earth-shattering, so I brace myself. The anticipation of his lips on my sensitive flesh has me struggling to catch my breath. When his warm tongue meets my skin, I buck against him, my back arching off the mattress. A low chuckle rumbles deep in his chest as he presses his hand flat against my lower abdomen, anchoring me to the bed. He slides two fingers inside me and I come apart quickly. He knows just what buttons to push and how to push them.

"I love the way you squirm against me when you're getting close," he whispers as he thrusts into me long and slow, giving me exactly what I want.

Our night is filled with moments like these; him whispering the sexiest words in my ear, me coming apart in his hands and his mouth, me exploring his body with equal enthusiasm and vigor. We take and give pleasure throughout the night until our bodies can't handle anymore, falling asleep in each other's arms sometime in the early morning hours. I savor every moment like it's our last, because for all I know, it very well could be.

Chapter Twenty-Nine

Jacob

I CAN TELL ABBY IS TRYING NOT TO cry, holding back her tears and trying to hide her distress from me, but I know her. I see it in the set of her jaw and rigid shoulders. My bags are packed and the car is loaded. All that's left now is to say goodbye.

Much like our last night together, this morning was filled with desperate lovemaking, savoring each touch and taking advantage of the dwindling seconds of our time together as we try to memorize every inch of each other's bodies. I've cataloged every bend and curve, her soft moans and euphoric sighs, every detail of her beautiful face. I couldn't forget her now if I tried. Her existence is forever etched into my soul.

I've waited as long as I can to start the drive back to Arlington. Luke and I vacated the cabin hours ago, and we've been at Abby's house since eleven a.m. Normally, she would be at work right now, but since the incident with Caleb, she's been on paid leave from New River Adventures while the owners "consult their legal team," which is code for "we fucked up and don't want to get sued." They're panicking because they knew he was a problem but didn't do shit about it because he's family. Anybody else would probably take them for everything they've got, but Abby won't do that. She's just not that kind of person. She wouldn't even talk to me about it. It takes everything I have not to contact a lawyer on her behalf, but I can't undermine her wishes like that. She'd never forgive me.

One rogue tear finally breaks loose and slides down her cheek. I watch as it hangs off her chin, pooling fat and full until it becomes too heavy and falls, splashing onto her shirt. I feel just like that little drop of salt water right now, holding onto her until I can't hold on any longer, my heart shattering into a million pieces at the hurt reflected in her eyes. If I had my way, I'd stay a little bit longer, long enough to solidify what we have. But I can't. I have other obligations and commitments, things that can't and won't be ignored.

I brush my thumb across her cheek, sweeping away any remnants of moisture. I've kissed her until our lips are bruised and tender. I've assured her that we'll talk every day and that I'll come back the first chance I get. But nothing I say seems to allay her fears. She kisses me like it's our last. I cling to her, unwilling to let go, but knowing if I don't leave now, I won't get home until after midnight. My mother is already suspicious, and I don't want to add fuel to the fire. I know she'll stay up, waiting for me to come home.

"I have to go," I whisper into Abby's ear and press my lips to her hair.

"I know." She sniffles and inhales a shuddering breath, the kind you take when your body has been wracked by sobs. "Please be careful," she pleads, her big green eyes wide with worry. "And let me know you've made it home safe. I don't care how late it is."

"I will, I promise." My mouth finds hers and I place one final kiss on her lips. I squeeze my eyes shut, willing them to stay dry. I release her mouth and press my forehead to hers, my eyes still closed tight. "Goodbye, Abby."

"Goodbye, Jacob."

I let her go and turn away, emotion constricting my throat as I walk to my car. I don't know why, but there's a terrible feeling clawing through my chest like this is the last time I'll see her. I pause for a moment beside my car, my face hidden from not only Abby but Luke as well. He's sitting in the passenger seat feigning indifference, but I know better. I heave a deep breath, forcing air into my lungs before opening my door. It's harder to breathe the further I get from her. How am I supposed to draw breath when I'm three hundred miles away? I'll suffocate without her.

I pull it together and regain my composure before climbing in next to Luke. Through the windshield, I see Abby watching me, her arms crossed protectively over her middle as though she's trying to hold herself together. I know the feeling. Reluctantly, I tear my eyes away from her so I can back out of the driveway.

When my tires hit the blacktop, a sick feeling knots my stomach. I don't want to leave her and I don't want to lose her, but I feel like both are happening right before my eyes. I chance one last glance in her direction before driving off. She's crying in earnest now, tears streaming down her face. She turns her body into Tiff, who wraps her arms around Abby's shoulders and rubs her back. I clench my jaw to keep the emotion from leaking out and punch my foot down on the gas pedal.

A sense of melancholy fills the vehicle on the ride home, and not just from me. Luke stares blankly out the window, slouched in his seat, barely speaking the whole way back to Arlington. He doesn't even ask to stop and eat anywhere, which isn't like him at all. I never dreamed he'd get this attached to Tiffany, but he seems almost as downtrodden as me.

We pull up to Luke's house just after eleven that night, the brightly lit edifice betraying the cold, empty shell that awaits him. Luke's jet-setting parents are always away, off to some exotic paradise or foreign metropolis. Paris, Tahiti, Dubai. He used to go everywhere with them and has been all over the world, but when he was seventeen, it all changed. He wouldn't tell me why he stopped traveling with them, but I know something happened. His dad is a real prick, always has been, but he must have done something awful for Luke to give up his world travels.

"Later, man," I offer as he steps out. He just grunts and nods. No bantering, no smartass comments, no name-calling, nothing like the Luke I'm used to. He must really have it bad for Tiff.

Just as I suspect, my mother is awake and waiting for me when I get home. "Jacob," she croons when I enter the foyer. "You're back." She must have been pacing ever since she arrived from whatever charity event she attended because she hasn't even changed out of her gown. She wraps her arms around me and kisses my cheek. "How was your trip?"

I smile, thinking about Abby. "It was good."

She pulls me into the living room and down onto the love seat. "What is this?" she asks, stroking my cheek. "You've grown a beard." She smiles, but it doesn't reach her eyes. She doesn't say anything, but I can tell she hates it. She's always preferred the clean-shaven look.

I scrub my palm over my chin, remembering how much Abby liked when the stubble started coming in. "Yeah, I guess I did." I do my best not to smile like a love-sick fool, but I'm positive I'm failing at it.

"Well," she begins expectantly. "Tell me everything." She smiles up at me, beaming, actually.

Selfishly, I want to keep Abby all to myself. I won't tell my mom about her. Not yet, at least. "Luke and I had a lot of fun. We went whitewater rafting, rock climbing, kayaking, hiking, and zip lining." My smile grows as I remember the first glimpse I had of Abby. She looked like an angel in her powder blue top and bright, white shorts.

"That's wonderful!" Mom places her hand over her mouth, stifling a yawn. She's tired. So am I.

"I'd better get to bed. It was a long drive home." I haven't been away from Abby a whole day and it already feels like an eternity.

"Of course. We'll talk more tomorrow." She pats my hand and stands up, the lower half of her dress swishing as she climbs the stairs to her room.

After a quick shower, I slip into bed, my mind reeling from the past two weeks. How can two people from such different worlds find each other and be so perfect together? I've never been a big believer in fate, but there's no other way to explain it. Somehow, I found something I didn't even know I was looking for in the hills of West Virginia. I lie awake for a long time that night, thinking about Abby and planning how to make my way back to her.

The next morning, I awake late. Both my parents are already gone, finalizing plans for the big party, I'm sure, so I pour myself a cup of coffee and sort through my mail. It's mostly credit card offers and formal invitations to the usual summer events. One envelope catches my eye. It doesn't look like the rest, and I immediately know what it is.

I tear it open and skip over the letterhead and all the formalities that accompany a letter like this.

Dear Mr. Daniels,
Blah, blah, blah
We regret to inform you-

Wait! What? Not selected for this internship? My heart sinks. I almost forgot how badly I want this, how much this opportunity means to me. I've been rejected. I wasn't good enough to make the final cut. This is a devastating blow, a punch in the gut. I'm unaccustomed to these feelings—inadequacy, rejection, denial. This couldn't have come at a worse time. I pick the letter back up and continue where I left off.

You have been selected as an alternate
should any of the candidates be unable
to participate for any reason.

I check the postmark on the envelope, noting that it was sent out the day before I left. It's been sitting here almost two weeks. The internship starts in less than a month, and I can't imagine anybody dropping out at this point. This was a once in a lifetime chance and I blew it. All I can think about is how badly I want to talk to Abby right now. I wish she was here. I'd lose myself in those soulful eyes and the soft touch of her skin. Her soothing words would reassure me that I'm not a total failure.

I know I shouldn't be so hard on myself. This was a highly competitive internship, but I worked my ass off to make the grades and complete all the required volunteer hours. Apparently, my three-point-eight GPA and countless hours of community service weren't enough.

I try not to dwell too much on the sense of rejection and failure that plague my thoughts, focusing instead on the fact that I'll get a phone call this evening and will hear Abby's voice for the first time in over twenty-four hours. It was so late when I got home last night that I opted for a quick text instead of a phone call, just in case she was asleep already. She wasn't, of course. She texted me right back, and as much as it pained me to do so, I told her good night and set my phone on the nightstand, willing myself to leave it there. I wanted to spend all night on the phone with her like a love-sick teenager, but I wanted her to get some rest. My two weeks spent falling for her must have been exhausting on her part. All those hours she worked, trying to find time for me along with everything else. She needs a break and that's what I'll try to give her.

Four weeks later...

I'm in panic mode, trying to pack as quickly as I can and search for my damn phone at the same time. I haven't seen it since yesterday morning when I got the call that changed everything, which means I haven't spoken to Abby since then, either. We've talked almost every day since I left, and on the days we didn't get to talk, we texted. A lot. But I have no idea what her phone number is. I didn't bother to memorize it since I had it saved in my phone, the one I've been searching for since last night.

Son of a bitch!

I've looked everywhere. Under my bed, in my car, the fridge, the oven, every damn drawer in this house. I've questioned all the staff. *No, no one has seen it.* I even dug through my dirty clothes in case I left it in one of my pockets. Nothing. I've called it several times, even though I know by now the battery must be dead. It was my only link to her and now it's gone.

Luke is no help, either. He and Tiff aren't speaking. They had some kind of falling out and she stopped answering his calls. He erased her number and said he'd "never talk to that lying whore again!" So that option is off the table. I can't even find out what happened between her and my best friend because I don't have time to talk to him.

I've looked on social media, but I can't find Abby anywhere. I created a damn Instagram account out of desperation after Facebook and Twitter both left me empty-handed, but she's nowhere to be found. I understand she's busy, but damn, what twenty-one-year-old college student isn't online? I can't even find out if she received the gift I sent her, a new pair of hiking boots she desperately needed. I can't call to ask her how she liked them. I can't tweet her or write it on her wall because she doesn't. Fucking. Have. One.

I can't even tell her my good news. Great news, actually. Somebody withdrew from the internship at the last minute, so I'm boarding a plane to Africa in a couple of hours. I got the call yesterday morning, something about a medical emergency, but I didn't hear much else after they told me I was going. I hate to think someone else's misfortune is the only reason I'm getting this once in a lifetime opportunity, but I've dreamed of this since I learned about the program my freshman year. They asked if I could be packed and ready to go by Sunday night and I said, "Hell yes." Yelled it, actually. Scared the shit out of the housekeeper.

It was sometime between then and yesterday evening that my phone went missing. I'd love to share this news with her, but I can't find her. Short of driving to West Virginia and telling her in person, I have no way of letting her know I'm going to be overseas for the next six weeks.

When I arrive at the airport, it finally occurs to me that her boss would have her number. *Why the hell didn't I think of that before?* I ask to borrow my father's phone and frantically search Google for Rosie's phone number.

"Pick up, pick up," I plead as I make my way to the gate. I let it ring for what feels like an eternity, praying somebody will answer, but nobody does. I try again, desperate to reach someone. My flight is now boarding and I've run out of time. I check the search results again, just to make sure I'm calling the right number, and see a list of opening and closing times. Shit! It's Sunday. Rosie's closed over an hour ago. It's too late. I'm all out of options. Defeated, I hand back my father's phone, ignoring the questioning look in his eyes.

"Mr. Daniels." I lift my gaze to a middle-aged man with glasses and greying hair. "I'm Steven, the project manager. Looks like you made it just in time." He gives me a friendly smile, completely unaware of my inner turmoil. I take his proffered hand for a shake and try to return his gesture, but my smile comes out tight and strained. I need to focus on the path that lies ahead of me now, on this journey on which I'm about to embark. But all I can think about is Abby. When I get back, I'll find her. Nothing will stop me from finding her.

Chapter Thirty

Abby

MY EYES ARE RED AND PUFFY. My nose is raw from wiping it continuously for two days straight. I haven't eaten. I can hardly sleep, and I don't have the energy to run. The one thing that would probably make me feel better, I can't do, because I'm too weak to do anything but work and cry.

When Jacob calls, I try to keep the emotion out of my voice, but I know he hears it. He asks me all the time if I'm alright. I lie and tell him I'm fine, but I'm not. I'm a wreck. I have been since he left. I have this feeling deep in my gut that I'm never going to see him again. No matter how much he promises and how much he plans, the crippling sense of loss and dread won't leave me.

I finally regain a little bit of my appetite on the third day, and then I collapse onto my bed and fall fast asleep from sheer exhaustion and a full belly. I awake feeling refreshed and resume my routine of running and working. Jacob and I talk every single day for the first eleven days he's gone.

Not that I'm counting or anything. After that, we talk intermittently. Some days, just lots of texts. Some days only a few. We're both busy, but it hurts a little. I don't feel like he's making time for me. He doesn't work and he's not in school right now.

What could he possibly be doing during the few hours I'm not at work that he can't make time to call me?

He broke the news to me that he didn't get that internship he applied for via text. He tried to downplay it, but I know how important it was to him. He must be devastated that he didn't get chosen.

I've yet to tell him I love him. I'm afraid to. I'm afraid he won't say it back, but even more afraid he will. What would we do then? He's there and I'm here. We both have a year left of school and we're hundreds of miles away from each other. We've been trying to work out a time when he can come and visit, but I need some time off work if he's going to make the trip down here again. At least a three-day weekend, but I can't afford to lose the tips, and he has engagements through the next several weeks. Add to that the rapidly decreasing phone calls, and I'm in a serious slump.

God bless Tiff. She does her best to keep my spirits up. She does silly things to try to make me laugh, but all I can muster is a sad smile. She and Luke haven't been talking. Apparently, he confessed his undying love for her, and she completely shot him down. He tried to persuade her to rethink her decision, but she won't budge. She wasn't interested in anything serious while he was here, and he led her to believe the same. Now he's in love, and she's just ready to move on. I knew she would break his heart. As far as I know, Jacob isn't aware of this development, but I don't say anything. It's not my place to tell him.

It's been almost a month since Jacob went home, and things have settled down quite a bit. My emotions are still all over the place, but I'm coping better with his absence. I resigned from my job at New River Adventures. The owners didn't even try to persuade me not to leave. In truth, I think they were glad to be rid of me. Luckily, one of the servers at Rosie's graduated from nursing school and got a new job at the hospital, so she increased my hours. With tips, I make more there anyway.

Caleb was sentenced to twenty-eight months in prison for what he did to me; not nearly long enough, if you ask me. I still have nightmares about that night. I probably will for a long time. It makes me sick thinking about what he could have done to me. My stomach churns at the thought of him getting me alone and doing whatever unspeakable acts he had planned. Bile rises in my throat just thinking about it, the bitter taste hitting the back of my tongue, but I manage to swallow it down. I drink a glass of ice water to wash the taste out of my mouth and the sensation calms.

I get ready for work and head to Tiff's house to pick her up. She hops into the car with her usual enthusiasm and pulls out her lip gloss. I want to tell her not to overdo it like she obviously did on her perfume this morning, but I keep that comment to myself. She may be in a good mood right now, but it's easy to piss her off, and I have to work with her all day.

As soon as we walk through the back door of the restaurant, the smell hits me. Burning grease and fried chicken. Yuck! How have I never noticed that stench before? My stomach does a little flip again and I cover my nose with my shirt to keep from gagging. Luckily, I make it through the rest of the day without feeling that way again.

Tiff asks if I want to come in when we pull up to her house after work. I feel the exhaustion that I've gotten used to sinking in, but I say yes anyway. We end up painting each other's nails and giving each other facials, something we haven't done in a long time.

"How are you doing?" she asks as she swipes coral polish over the nail of my big toe. She doesn't raise her eyes, but I know she's gauging my reaction with her peripheral vision.

"I'm okay."

She sighs and screws the lid back onto the bottle of nail polish. "Really," she admonishes with a stern softness only she can project. "How are you doing?"

Tears well up in my eyes and spill down my cheeks. "I miss him," I confess. "I miss him so much it hurts." I sniffle. I'm not going to ugly-cry in front of her like I've done alone in my bed every night. "And he hardly talks to me lately. We text back and forth every day, but I've only spoken to him a few times this past week." Tears continue to roll down my face. "I'm afraid he's lost interest. Now that he's gone, the allure of me is gone, too."

"Oh, honey. I'm sorry you feel that way, but I'm sure that isn't the case. I saw the way he looked at you," she tries to assure me. "That man is crazy about you, but he leads a very busy life, just like you do. His dad is a senator, for crying out loud! I can't imagine the pressure he's under. He must be pulled in a hundred different directions on a daily basis." She wipes my tears away and pats my hands. "Cut him a little slack." She gives me a crooked smile. "Even though he's damn near perfect, he's still a guy." This makes me giggle, and it feels good to laugh.

Tiff stands abruptly and holds out her hand. "Come on. There's a whole pint of Rocky Road in the freezer." I take her outstretched hand and let her pull me to my feet. "And you and I are gonna demolish that sucker."

UGH, LATE NIGHT ice cream was a bad choice. Especially coupled with early morning running. I slow my pace to a jog, and then to a brisk walk. When that doesn't do the trick, I stop and bend over, trying to catch my breath. If I just breathe through it, it'll go away. The only problem is it doesn't. The Rocky Road is about to make a reappearance. My stomach clenches and I press my palms to it, willing it to calm. It doesn't work. I heave and spew last night's indulgence and this morning's sports drink all over the pavement. It splatters up onto my shoes and shins, which makes me heave again.

Once everything is expelled from my stomach, I dry heave for what seems like an eternity. My face is flushed and tears prickle my eyes. I splash cold water from my bottle all over my face and wipe it with the bottom of my shirt, then I pour some in my mouth and swish it around before spitting it out. I'm afraid to drink any of it, so I don't swallow a drop.

When it feels safe to move again, I turn towards home and jog back slowly. I hadn't made it halfway through my run before getting sick, so I'm back long before I have to get ready for work. I sit in the air conditioning for a while and sip ice water before running a bath and soaking my tired muscles in it.

Feeling immensely better, I realize a long, relaxing bath must have been what I needed. I dry off, get dressed, and tentatively nibble on a piece of toast. My stomach doesn't protest so I eat a banana on my way to Tiff's. When she gets in the door, she turns to me with a look of concern.

"Are you okay? You're looking a little pale." She studies my face for a moment. She knows I must feel bad if I've lost some of the color on my tan face.

"I'm fine now. That ice cream did me in, though."

"Ugh, for real. I woke up hella bloated this morning. You should've stopped me after that first bowl."

"Yeah, same here."

The rest of the day is uneventful, albeit busy, and my body is worn out when I pull into my driveway after work. I sit at the table with my grandmother and eat supper in silence.

"Abigail, I'm worried about you. You hardly eat, and I know you're not sleeping well. I can tell by the dark circles under your eyes. Plus, you look like you're losing weight."

She's right, I've lost nearly seven pounds since Jacob left. That's a lot on my small frame. "I'm okay," I tell her, though I'm not sure if it's the truth or a lie. I'm doing better, but I'm not doing well. I just don't want her to worry. I force myself to eat most of my dinner, hoping that will ease some of her distress.

I fall into bed early that evening, not even bothering to take a shower. I just don't have the energy. I'll get up early tomorrow morning and strip my sheets and wash the restaurant grime away.

But I don't wake up early. I snooze my alarm a million times. I don't get up until the increasingly familiar sensation overtakes me and I leap out of bed, barely making it to the toilet in time before vomiting violently into the bowl. I retch until my stomach is empty and my throat burns, a nasty film of bile covering my tongue. I must have overdone it last night at dinner after eating so little for so long. I flush the toilet, brush my teeth, and turn on the shower. I step into a stream of tepid water and let it cool my overheated skin. I feel feverish. I must be getting sick, probably a stomach virus. I've only felt this way one other time and I ended up having the flu.

I take some Pepto and pop a couple Tylenol when I get out of the shower. I'm shivering not only from the cool water but also from low blood sugar, no doubt. I can't stomach the thought of eating anything right now, so I sip some orange juice and grab a granola bar for the road.

I perk up around twelve-thirty, just in time for Tiff to show up for work. I need the extra money, so I volunteered to come in early to fill a gap in the schedule. She strolls up to me at the counter and we wait for our orders to come up.

"Hey, you wanna head to The Red Stallion tonight? It's Ladies Night, so half price drinks." She sings the last three words in a lilting soprano in an attempt to entice me.

"I don't know, Tiff. I'm not really feeling it." Not to mention the thought of alcohol makes me want to barf, and drinking in public scares me since the incident with Caleb.

"Oh, come on. It'll be fun."

I know she's only trying to get me out of my funk. We haven't been out in weeks, not since Jacob and Luke left. I just haven't felt up to it. I guess she feels like my mourning period is over. She pleads with me, using those big, blue, baby doll eyes, folding her hands together like a begging child. She mouths, "Please" and I lose my resolve. Manipulative hussy.

"Oh, alright," I acquiesce. "We can go."

"Yay!" She hops up and down, clapping her hands, and I roll my eyes.

I'm DETERMINED NOT to drink much tonight. I'll just have one when we get there because if I don't, Tiff will pester the hell out of me. We're all done up, of course, wearing short shorts and lots of makeup. We're both sporting ponytails with loose curls, hers high with all her hair pulled back from her face, mine low and to one side, a French braid along my hairline.

Tiff and I grab a drink, a Long Island for her, a Jack and Coke for me, and find an empty table. I've just finished mine off and Tiff is starting on her third when I come face to face with *him*.

"You ladies all alone tonight?" His voice is menacing, despite his smile.

"Fuck off, Grant," Tiff replies calmly before taking another sip of her drink.

"Go eat a dick. I wasn't talking to you," he snarls.

"Kinda seemed like you were. You did say 'ladies,' as in plural," Tiff points out. "But then again, you *did* fail freshman English, so maybe you didn't know that." His face flames with rage and embarrassment at her snarky response.

"You're a dumb cunt and nobody likes you."

Tiff gasps and presses her hand to her chest in mock anguish. "I'm wounded," she says dramatically. "I care so much about what everybody in this shit hole town thinks about me." She rolls her eyes and takes another sip through her straw.

Grant angles his body towards me, effectively cutting Tiff out of the conversation. "So, where's your boy toy? Haven't seen him around lately."

I do my best to keep my face impassive, even though his words sting. "What do you want?"

"You wanna dance, Abs?" I know he's drunk, but he must be high, too, if he thinks I'd ever let him put his hands on my body again.

"No thanks."

"What's wrong? You too good to dance with me now that you've been some rich asshole's side piece?" He sneers at me as if I disgust him. "I don't see him here now, so I guess you're back down to our level then, huh?"

I'm furious. My heart pounds and I see black creeping in on the sides of my vision. I ball my hands into fists and before I know it, I'm standing toe-to-toe with six feet and two hundred twenty pounds of drunk redneck. I hear wooden chair legs scrape against the floor as Tiff scrambles out of her seat.

"You know what, Grant? I will *never* be down to your level, and you'll never be up to my standards." He narrows his eyes, opening his mouth to say something, but I cut him off. "You wanna know why I never slept with you?" That shuts him up real quick. I sense a crowd gathering around us, anxious to hear the dirt. "I was afraid of what you'd give me. How many rounds of penicillin have you had, anyway? If you'd keep your dick out of trailer trash, that shit would probably clear up." I hear hooting and clapping, but the stunned look on Tiff's face says it all. Nobody expected me to stand up to him like that. Nobody expected those words to come out of my mouth. I feel good, elated even. For a moment.

Grant mutters under his breath, "Fucking bitch," and storms off, knocking people out of his way as he pushes through the sea of bodies surrounding us.

My elation is short-lived, and I'm instantly remorseful over the venomous words I spat at him. Tears well in my eyes and Tiff grabs my shoulders. "Do *not* feel bad about that. That lying, cheating bastard deserved it. Maybe now he'll leave you alone." This does little to make me feel better. "Here, drink this." She shoves her half-full glass under my nose and heads towards the bar. I do as she says, and she returns with two more drinks.

Two hours later, I'm dragging a seriously inebriated Tiff to my truck. Despite her best efforts, I managed to stay sober. She begs me to let her stay at my house because her parents have been giving her a hard time about coming home drunk. I let her, of course. She would do the same for me.

When my eyes pop open the next morning, a wave of nausea propels me to my feet. Once again, I'm running to the bathroom and emptying my stomach into the toilet. My violent heaving is loud enough to wake Tiff. She stands bleary-eyed in the doorway with a look of concern and confusion.

"Damn, if I'd known you were that wasted last night, I wouldn't have let you drive us home." She must think I'm hungover, that I drank way more than I did.

"I wasn't." I stand up and move to the sink where I splash cold water on my face and brush my teeth. "I think I have the stomach flu. I've been vomiting for days, and I've been really tired."

"I'm sorry. I didn't know you'd been sick. Have you had a fever?" She presses the back of her hand to my forehead, checking for a temperature.

"I don't know. I can't find the thermometer, but I was shivering when I got out of the shower yesterday. And after I throw up once, I'm fine. I don't get sick the rest of the day."

"Wait a minute. You only vomit in the morning?"

"Yes."

"And you're really tired?"

"Yeah, that's what I said."

She ponders for a moment, biting the nail on her pinky. "Abby, when was your last period?"

This question catches me off guard. I have to think on it a moment. "I don't know. Maybe around the first or second week of May. They're so intermittent, I don't really keep track." My periods are a little wacky from being a runner and having a history of ovarian cysts. My doctor prescribed birth control, hoping that would help, and it has, but my cycle isn't entirely regulated yet.

"Is there any chance you could be pregnant?"

"What? No!" I look at her incredulously. "Of course not," I say with less conviction this time. I begin rolling the possibility around in my mind. "There's no way. I'm on birth control." I sound less and less convincing, even to myself. I don't mention the pregnancy test at the hospital because even though I let myself believe the results were legit, I knew deep down there was no way to tell that soon.

A cold sweat breaks out over my brow. I hadn't considered this possibility. It's never even *been* a possibility before. I've always been careful. At least, until Jacob. He broke down my defenses and clouded my judgment. All rational thought left me the instant I felt his hands on my body.

My hands start to shake and I feel sick all over again. I drop down in front of the toilet, my knees banging against the floor, and dry heave for a good two minutes, but there's nothing left. I start to cry and collapse against the bathtub, my shoulders shaking. *There's no way. This can't be happening. How could I have been so reckless?*

"It's okay." Tiff wraps her arms around my shoulders and talks to me in a soothing voice. "Calm down." She pushes the hair out of my face and forces me to look at her. "We don't know anything for sure yet. You need to take a test." Her voice is calming, the voice of reason. I nod my head and dry my eyes. She helps me to my feet and leads me back to my bedroom. "I'm going to run to the drug store and buy you one. You haven't peed yet, have you?" I shake my head no. "Good, first thing in the morning is the best time to test." How on earth she knows this, I have no idea. Maybe she's had to do this before. I don't know. If she has, she never told me.

I'm waiting on pins and needles for her to return. When she does, I rip the plastic bag out of her hand and lock myself in the bathroom. I open the box with shaky fingers and pull a little white stick out and place it on the sink. I stare at it a good ten minutes, even though my bladder feels like it's about to rupture. I read through the directions. Twice. I finally pull my pants down and sit on the toilet. After a few deep breaths, I manage to relax enough to pee on the stick.

When I'm done, I replace the cap and place it next to the sink. Then I wait. I check my phone a hundred times in three minutes. I don't look at the test, not even a peek. A knock on the door startles me and I jump.

"Abby." It's Tiff. I breathe a sigh of relief. I feared it was my grandmother. "Are you alright in there?" I swing the door open. She takes in my disheveled appearance and the wild look in my eyes.

"I can't look."

"Sweetie, you have to."

"You look for me. I can't do it."

"I'm not going to do that," she answers calmly, rubbing her hands up and down my arms to soothe me. "This may be one of the most important moments of your life. It has to be you."

That makes sense. She's right. She's totally right. Her logic doesn't make this any easier, though.

I take in several deep, cleansing breaths and try to steel my nerves. My stomach is in knots. I can't believe I'm about to do this. The next few seconds could completely change the course of my life.

Finally, I force my eyes to the vanity top, and it takes my brain a moment to process what I'm seeing. Tiff catches me as I crumble to the floor. My legs are swept right out from under me by two little blue lines.

The-End

Epilogue

Jacob

OUR CARAVAN HAS BEEN TRAVELING this dusty road for hours. I watch as Steven wipes his damp forehead for the millionth time today. My own perspiration rolls down between my shoulder blades, soaking into my white cotton shirt. The sad excuse for air conditioning is no match for the stifling heat of the Saharan Desert. We flew into Khartoum this morning after two connecting flights and one long ass layover in Cairo. Getting to Northern Sudan was more complicated than I anticipated.

Our vehicle rolls to a stop and I peer out the window, waiting for the dust to settle around us. My hands grip the headrest in front of me, nervous energy vibrating my entire body.

"Looks like we're here," Steven announces, opening his door. He appears unfazed by our unfamiliar surroundings, but he's done this three times before. He's led projects in Rwanda, Sierra Leone, and one in Sudan already. It's unnerving being in a foreign country with foreign customs and a language I don't understand.

We are greeted by local leaders as soon as we step out of the SUV. After brief introductions aided by our interpreter, we're guided to our living quarters and reality begins to set in. There are few creature comforts to be found here. It's going to be hard adjusting to living like this, but I'm up for the challenge. This is the opportunity I've been waiting for. It's time to put my money where my mouth is.

The other interns and I meet with Steven and the rest of his team before dinner. He hands us each a binder and opens one for himself.

"This is your itinerary for this project. I've also included some helpful information regarding the community and local customs." He dabs his brow with a cloth napkin and pushes his glasses back up his nose before continuing. "If you flip to the last page, you'll find a copy of the contract you signed when you agreed to participate in the internship. I strongly urge you to review the rules you will be expected to follow while you are with us."

He peers at us from over the rim of his glasses, looking pointedly at each of us and letting his words sink in. I know what he's trying to say. Rule number one states that we are not to engage in any behavior that disrupts the lives of community members, including romantic and/or sexual relationships, etc. I.E., Don't bang the locals. I can't speak for the others, but I have no interest in starting anything while we're here. My mind is still consumed with Abby.

We go to bed at sunset, but I'm too restless to sleep. I hate that I'm halfway around the world and have no way of contacting her. She's going to be frantic when she's unable to reach me for the next six weeks. I just wish there was some way to get a message to her and let her know what's going on. And that I love her.

WE RISE EARLY the next morning before the sun has the chance to break over the horizon. Most of our work must be completed before mid-day when the heat becomes unbearable. When we finally break for the day, I'm drenched in sweat and we haven't even started any of the labor-intensive work yet, just the planning and designing.

I walk through the village, observing my surroundings and the people who live here. They live a hard life, many of them laboring in the scorching hot sun all day. Most of the villagers live in huts that don't look like they are even structurally sound. We're housed in one of only a few stone buildings within the community. The inhabitants must walk for miles just to bring water back to their homes, and often, the water they retrieve isn't suitable for human consumption.

My heart breaks at the reality of what these people endure every day, but my resolve is strengthened knowing I made the right choice in coming here. Now I know that something I do in my life will truly make a difference. However, my brightening mood shatters when I see them.

A group of children trudges towards me with jugs full of murky water on their heads. None of them can be older than six or seven, their slender limbs and hollow cheeks evidence of their malnutrition. I take in a deep breath and squeeze my eyes shut to suppress the emotion clogging my throat. Of all the hardships I've witnessed in my short time here, it's the kids that get to me the most. They go to bed with empty stomachs because this is their life. They wake up hungry because it's the reality they can't escape. I can't imagine the heartbreak of not being able to feed my child, or even give him clean water to drink.

I return to my room and sit on the edge of my bed, images of hungry children with sunken cheeks and bellies flashing in my head. I haven't cried a day in my adult life. Not when thoughts of Peyton invade my mind, breaking my heart all over again. Not when I thought I blew my shot at this internship. Not even when I had to leave Abby sobbing in her driveway. But today, as I think about how these young, innocent little ones suffer every day, I hang my head as sobs wrack my body and hot tears fall from my eyes, soaking into the dirt floor beneath my feet.

Though my soul is filled with anguish, my resolve is strengthened. I won't let them down. I *can't* let them down. I'm going to work my ass off while

I'm here to make sure this project is a success. And when I get home, I'll do everything I can to raise awareness for this cause. With my connections and my father's political clout, I have no doubt we can make a monumental impact.

In the meantime, I'll find Abby and finally tell her what I've known all along, that I love her and there's no one else I'll ever want to be with. I realized something in the short time I've been here… life is fragile and the future isn't guaranteed. When you know what you want, what you can't live without, go after it. And I want Abby. I want to wake up to her smile every morning and kiss her senseless. I want to make love to her every night and hear her say she loves me. I want to put a ring on her finger one day and watch as her belly grows round with child. *My child*. When I get back, we'll start on our happily ever after.

Playlist

"Regulate" by Warren G ft. Nate Dogg
"I'll Make Love To You" by Boyz II Men
"Hell On Heels" by The Pistol Annies
"My Kinda Party" by Jason Aldean
"Poison & Wine" by The Civil Wars
"Ready For Love" by Bad Company
"Dirt" by Florida Georgia Line

Acknowledgements

There are so many people I want to thank for helping me bring this book to life and I hope I don't forget anyone. To my husband, thank you for supporting this dream and for picking up the slack when I was glued to my keyboard. Me and our boys are lucky to have you.

Bobbie Jo and Tricia, you guys have been with me every step of the way. You've been my beta readers, my cheerleaders, and biggest supporters. You encouraged me to keep going even when it looked like I'd never finish the first draft, let alone the last. Thank you. For everything.

To Casey L. Bond, you've been not only an inspiration and a mentor, but also a friend. Thank you for taking the time to beta read this book and for always being willing to answer my questions. Your feedback and guidance have been invaluable.

Stacy Sanford, editor extraordinaire, you are brilliant! Thank you for polishing this book, shining a light right through my plot holes, and challenging me to fix them. Working with you has made me a better writer.

To my incredibly talented cover designer and formatter Cassy Roop, thank you for putting the beautiful finishing touches on this book. You brought my vision to life with this cover. Scratch that. You gave me something even better than I had imagined.

Thank you, Meaghan Royce for proofreading this book and being that final set of eyes I needed to make sure everything was in tip-top shape.

Thank you, Kiki Chatfield for all your guidance and for sharing your knowledge of this industry with me. I could not have made it this far in my writing journey without you.

To my readers, I can never thank you enough for picking up this book and taking a chance on a new author! There are so, so many books out there and you chose to read mine. I appreciate that more than you know and hope you loved what I wrote.

To my family and friends, thank you for your love, support, and encouragement throughout this journey.

Lastly, and most importantly, I thank God for the many blessings in my life.

About the Author

Ashley is an author and book lover living in Ohio with her husband and two sons. She's loved reading since childhood and has always enjoyed creating characters and stories. She finds inspiration everywhere: a song on the radio, a person she passes on the street, a place she's visited on vacation. She lets her imagination run wild and her fingers do the typing.

Connect with Ashley

Facebook - facebook.com/authorashleycade
Reader Group - facebook.com/groups/556822931488863
The Wild Hearts Series Discussion Group - facebook.com/
groups/2295958054010860
Twitter - /AuthorAshCade
Instagram - /authorashleycade
Goodreads - goodreads.com/author/show/18600951.Ashley_Cade
Bookbub - bookbub.com/authors/ashley-cade
Pinterest - pinterest.com/authorashleycade
Website - http://www.authorashleycade.com/
Newsletter - eepurl.com/gdWc9H